Jenna started at the sound of footsteps outside her bedroom door. She was dressed only in her diaphanous nightgown, and she reached for her green velvet robe. But the person outside the door did not ask to be admitted—he simply threw open the door and strode into the room.

Jenna's full lips parted in surprise as she quickly turned about. Blaise towered above her.

He was not dressed as she had known him, in his rough woodman's garb. Tonight he was wearing an elegant dark blue suit, a white ruffled shirt, and a blue brocade vest. Even in this finery, he exuded a raw masculinity and rugged persona.

His facial expression was unreadable as he looked down at her. Only his dark eyes spoke to her as they roamed her body, betraying his lust.

"I've come for what belongs to me," he said huskily.

His lips fastened on hers and his hands moved across her back. In an instant, he had lifted her and carried her to the fur rug in front of the fireplace. He held her fast, kissing her hard and caressing her as he tore away her nightdress. Jenna groaned as he became more intent, as he touched her in more intimate places. His lips were everywhere, and her flesh was aglow once again with his sweet torments.

Then Jenna moaned, unable to restrain her own reactions—her memories of him—her own wantonness, her deep love.

Her arms encircled his neck as her resistance melted into surrender.

JOYCE CARLOW

Timeswept

PINNACLE BOOKS
WINDSOR PUBLISHING CORP.

PINNACLE BOOKS are published by

Windsor Publishing Corp.
850 Third Ave
New York, NY 10022

First Pinnacle Printing: September, 1994

Printed in the United States of America

Chapter One

February 29, 1988

Jenna Stevens walked quickly across the hard frozen earth. The grass beneath her feet was brown, and the earth was no longer snow covered, although there were still patches of snow and shallow pools of ice here and there. Most of the snow had melted in the traditional January thaw, but the dark gray clouds swirling in the sky above seemed to forecast a fresh snowfall, a certain return to winter.

Aunt Hester's house was just down the street from historic Deerfield's Visitors' Center. Jenna thought her aunt's house was one of the nicest of the old homes that comprised the historic section of Deerfield.

Located in the northwest corner of Massachusetts, Deerfield was steeped in its own history, while at the same time, its present inhabitants earned their livings in the ultra modern, high-tech world of computers and electronic design. Raytheon, Digital, and IBM—all had offices within commuting distance. As a result, Deerfield retained its rural characteristics while at the same time supporting a well educated, well paid younger genera-tion of modern pioneers. Where once brave settlers had tilled the rich soil of the Deerfield River's flood plain and defended themselves against the French who had settled along the Saint Lawrence in Canada, today's pioneers were challenging the outer limits of mathematical and scientific progress. Yet much of the rich farmland, located in the meadows surrounding the town, was still being ploughed and planted, thus giving Deerfield an historic continuity that few places enjoyed.

This easy mix of old and new made Jenna feel proud, because it was here that she had her roots. And it was here she always came to find and renew herself when life in busy Boston overtook her.

Jenna paused before the white picket fence that surrounded her aunt's house, a house that had once belonged to her grandparents and to their grandparents before them. It was simply a huge house made of traditional white clapboard and featured neatly painted green window shutters on the dormered windows of the second and third floors. In the New England tradition, a covered corridor led from the back of the house to a large barn. In the front, a huge maple tree stood bare and rigid, its brittle branches shuddering in the cold February wind.

But Aunt Hester's house was not really what it seemed. Once it had housed Jenna's ancestors, but now it housed only Hester. Time and the changing economy had conspired to transform the house as well. Hester had never wanted to sell the house—not even to the historical society—so she borrowed money from the bank, and installed extra bathrooms and remodeled the barn and the covered corridor that led to it. Now, the barn housed a large recreation room and craft shop, while the covered corridor was lined with plants and paintings by local artists. The house itself functioned as an inn, and in the summer it was filled with tourists. Hester herself occupied no more than a small two room apartment in what once had been the toolshed. But it was winter now and the tourists were sparse. At this time of year, Hester prepared for the onslaught of spring visitors who annually flocked to the expensive resorts in the nearby Berkshires, and who stopped here for a romantic night, having "discovered" this historic old inn on a previous trip or heard of it from a friend.

As Jenna approached the house, the front door opened and Hester stood framed in the doorway. She was a tall slender woman with wiry gray hair, twinkling brown eyes, and an angular face. Her speech was like rapid fire and clipped like that of all native upstate New Englanders. It was also quite proper and lacked the slang common to Bostonians' speech.

"You're going to catch your death of cold out there!" she called out. "That wind is vicious! And just you look at those clouds! It's going to snow, Jenna."

Jenna quickened her pace and hurried in the front door. Hester closed it behind her. "Where on earth did you disappear to?"

"I just took a quick walk around the block to where the old Catlin house once stood, then back past the Stebbins' house and the church."

"Well, you should have put on a hat and scarf."

"I wasn't cold."

"No matter. There's a dampness in the air. Yes, there is, you mark my word, it's going to storm something awful. You know, it's just plain foolish of you to try to drive back to Boston tonight."

Jenna smiled and touched her aunt's arm affectionately. "You know I would have left this morning if I hadn't been trying to wring one more day of my vacation. I *have* to be at work tomorrow morning, Aunt Hester. It's only a two-and-half-hour drive, and once

I'm on Highway Two, it will be just fine. They do plough the roads, you know."

"And you know that sometimes it snows so hard they can't keep up." Hester walked briskly toward the huge kitchen at the back of the house. It was a real old-fashioned country-sized kitchen although Hester had modernized it. In the summer when the house was full of guests, she hired a cook to prepare the meals but now only one lonely pot simmered on the stove, its contents filling the room with a wonderful aroma.

"I remember the blizzard of forty-three," Hester reminisced as she lifted the top off the pot and stirred its contents with a huge spoon. "Of course I was only a girl then. But I remember. We couldn't open the front door for three days. The snow drifted eight feet high in some places."

Jenna smiled and sat down at the big kitchen table. "I'm sure I'll get home before the weather turns really bad. It hasn't even started yet."

"This time of year those gray clouds mean something. No, there's going to be a storm. I can tell by the feel of the wind."

Jenna didn't answer. She glanced at her watch—it was just three o'clock. She wondered if she should leave now, perhaps her aunt was right about the severity of the impending storm.

"I'm going to have dinner ready by four-thirty instead of five," Hester said flatly, almost as if she had known what Jenna had been thinking. "That way you can get started a little earlier."

Jenna inhaled deeply the aroma of simmering vegetables coming from the cooking pot. "I certainly wouldn't want to leave here without one last dinner."

"Well, I'm making one of your mother's favorites. I

know you like it too. It's New England boiled dinner, with apple pie for dessert."

"I can smell it," Jenna replied. Her Aunt Hester always spoke of her mother as if she were still alive, as if the accident that had killed her parents five years ago hadn't happened.

Jenna reached across the table and poured herself a cup of coffee from the percolator. She sipped it slowly, watching as Hester puttered about. "Are you sure I can't help?" Jenna offered.

"Absolutely not. Too many chefs spoil the broth. Besides, it's not work at all. It's just you and that old couple in two-o-one, the ones from Canada."

Jenna nodded. Offering to help was a formality. Her aunt considered the kitchen sacrosanct. It was "her" kitchen. She was used to doing things for herself, and even though Jenna was family, she refused all help save that of the "hired help" in the summer.

Jenna looked around and tried to picture this kitchen as it must have been long ago. The great stone fireplace wasn't used much anymore, and its walk-in side oven had been converted into storage cupboards. A large modern stove stood flat against the wall adjacent to the fireplace, but for atmosphere the hearth was set, and the mantel above it held jars of beans, grains, and spices.

Both Hester and Jenna's mother, Frances Corse, had been born in this house. Hester had remained in Deerfield, although she had spent four years in central Massachusetts when attending college at Smith. Her mother, Frances, had gone to college in Boston, and there had met Mark Stevens, Jenna's father.

Jenna was an only child. Her parents had been killed in a plane crash when she was nineteen and in her first year at Boston University.

That summer, the summer after her parents' death,

Jenna had spent the entire two months of her summer vacation in Deerfield with her Aunt Hester. That period, like this past week, had been a time of renewal, a time to take stock, to feel the spirit and history of this place while coming to terms with her parents' deaths. Jenna found that here, in Deerfield, she understood the time continuum. It was as if she gathered strength from her ancestors, as if there were something very special about this peaceful village that had once, long ago, been the very center of excitement—the frontier of the movement west with all the conflict that movement generated. Then later, it had been a hotbed of revolutionary activity. It was from Deerfield and nearby Concord, Greenfield, and Springfield that the famed minutemen had come.

Perhaps, Jenna pondered, she felt as she did about this place because her mother had read to her so much about it. She could not even pass the sign for the Concord turnoff on Highway 2 without thinking of the poem she had been made to memorize as a child.

"By the rude bridge that arched the flood, their flag to April's breeze unfurled, Here once the embattled farmers stood and fired the shot heard round the world."

"I trust you realize that you'll miss the service," Hester said matter-of-factly.

Hester's comment jolted Jenna out of her mental ramblings, "Service?" she questioned.

"The Anniversary Service. It's February twenty-ninth. It's at the church at midnight."

"You are right! I did forget. I'd have arranged things differently if I'd remembered the date," Jenna admitted.

Hester half laughed. "Well, it does come only every four years."

Jenna smiled back. She supposed she could be forgiven for not remembering that this was a leap year. It was on February 29, 1704, two-hundred-and-eighty-four years ago that Deerfield had been attacked by the French Canadians and their Abnaki Indian allies. Over one-hundred-and-eleven pioneers had been kidnapped. Some, including one of her ancestors, Elizabeth Corse, were never seen again. Indeed, the family would have died out if Elizabeth's brother, James, had not escaped and returned to Deerfield. He lived to sire a huge family, the family from which Jenna was descended. Tonight, as there was every four years on February 29, a memorial service was held in the local church. Following the service, the head of the local historical society delivered a lecture on the history of Deerfield and its role during the War of the Spanish Succession which began in 1703 and ended in 1709. And, she thought, I've no excuse for not remembering since I'm right in the middle of a book on the subject. Still, it was too late. She did have to get back to work.

"Odd that we have French Canadian guests tonight," Jenna said, thinking of Mr. and Mrs. LaBelle in Room 201.

"I think it's a good omen. Anyway, we buried the hatchet a long time ago. I'm going to invite them to the service. If you stayed one more night, you could come too."

Jenna shook her head. "No, I would if I could, honestly."

Hester wiped her hands on her apron. "Stubborn, stubborn, stubborn," she muttered. Then smiling, "I wonder where you got that trait?"

"I wonder," Jenna replied, a mischievous smile crossing her lips. Certainly, her Aunt Hester was one of the stubbornest people alive.

Jenna drained her coffee cup. "I think I'll go to the li-

brary and finish that one book on Deerfield I was reading."

"The children's book?"

"Today, it's called young adult fiction. Yes, that one."

"I'll call you when supper's ready."

Jenna unfolded herself from the chair and walked
through the main dining room with its warm maple furniture, into the center hall.

The library was typical of a proper old New England
home. It had a stone fireplace with old black wrought
iron tools. Near the fireplace, against the wall, was a
roughly hewn wood box with a brass latch.

The floor of the library was covered with a handmade
braided, multicolored rug. The big sofa and the two
overstuffed chairs were modern, but designed in the Colonial style. The coffee table was a real antique. Originally, it had been a blacksmith's table, and the scars of
its previous life were clearly visible in its highly polished
wood. The desk, which was over in one corner, was also
an antique. In fact, it was the oldest thing in the house.
Most of historic Deerfield's homes dated from the
American Revolution or slightly before. All the houses
that had previously existed, those built between 1669
and 1704, had been burned during the raid. But many
of their furnishings had survived, and these were in
those houses owned by the historical society and in private homes of historic significance. The old desk was
made of bird's-eye maple and had a large rolltop that
had fascinated Jenna since she was a child . . . that and
the possibility that the old desk might have, as many
did, a secret compartment. But she had prodded and
poked to no avail. If there was a secret compartment,
she had not found it either as a child or as a young
adult.

Jenna turned on the hurricane-style light on the small

table by the big comfortable wing chair and sat down. Her book was on the table just where she had left it. It was a small book of historic fiction about one of the young men captured that winter's night in 1704. In spite of being young adult fiction, she found it interesting, although it failed to tell both sides of the conflict.

In the kitchen, Hester Corse turned down the flame under her New England boiled dinner. It needed to simmer so the flavors of its varied ingredients could become one, resulting in a succulent rich broth heavy with turnips, cabbage, onions, and corned beef.

Hester walked away from the stove and sat down at the table; her thoughts were on her beautiful niece, Jenna Stevens.

Jenna was taller than her mother, nearly five feet six inches. Yet Jenna's figure was as well rounded as her mother's had been. Jenna had a tiny waist, full high breasts, a flat stomach, and rounded hips. Her skin was extraordinarily fair like all the members of the Corse family, and she also possessed the unusual green eyes that ran in the family. But her hair came from her father's side of the family. It was red-gold, a perfect strawberry blond in the summer when bleached by the sun and copper colored in winter. Jenna's features were sculpted, and her long neck gave her a kind of regal bearing. But her smile was warm and friendly, and she was no empty-headed beauty either, Hester thought with pride. She had graduated from Boston University with good marks, and she had a fine job as a market researcher at Goodman, Brache and Nelson, a well known Boston advertising firm.

Yes, at twenty-four, Jenna seemed to have everything going for her. As she thought about it, a frown of concern crossed Hester's face. "Seemed to have" was the key phrase. There was something wrong, something troubling Jenna, of that she was certain. Jenna usually visited Deerfield each year, and when her parents were alive, they had brought her to Deerfield every year for at least two weeks and often for the whole summer, if it wasn't one of the years they were traveling to some exotic destination together. Hester felt she knew her niece, and as surely as New England boiled dinner was bubbling on the stove, Jenna was trying to work through some difficulty.

Jenna had been quiet and withdrawn when her parents had been killed, but then Hester had understood the reason for her niece's reticence. Jenna had come to Deerfield and walked the quiet streets, ambled in the woods, trod the banks of the Connecticut and Deerfield rivers, and read in the library. She seemed to be taking strength from the past as she carefully contemplated the present and the future. We're alike, Hester admitted. We mourned together, yet separately.

But what troubled Jenna now? It was a question Hester found herself returning to over and over again. The only answer forthcoming from Hester's self-questioning was that Jenna must be troubled by a man . . . although an unhappy relationship on its own was probably not sufficient to make Jenna so self-searching, Hester decided. For a few minutes, Hester thought of going to the library and confronting Jenna. But she did not. If Jenna wanted or needed advice Jenna herself would come to her. If she just wanted to straighten her own rudder, as the saying went, she would simply think things through, and in the end, she would know the answer.

Hester stood up and began the trek to the second floor up the narrow back staircase. She had to tell the

LaBelles dinner would be a little early so her niece could get started back to Boston before it was too late.

In the library, Jenna continued reading, although she felt her eyelids growing heavy. She had walked nearly a mile in the brisk cold, and now the fresh air, exercise, and warmth of this room combined to make her sleepy. She didn't fight the heavy feeling of her eyelids. A short catnap before dinner would make her drive back to Boston easier. She half smiled as she dozed off, it was only four o'clock, and it was already dark outside. February was truly a month of short days.

Mr. LaBelle was a short stocky man with a thick salt and pepper mustache, heavy arched eyebrows, and a fringe of hair around his balding head. Mrs. LaBelle was small, almost completely round, and smiling. Both LaBelles were in their late sixties and both spoke English with a heavy Quebecios French accent. This, Jenna learned, was not their first visit to her aunt's inn. Hester Corse had studied French in college, and although she spoke a cultured Parisian French, the LaBelles liked it here because knowing the innkeeper spoke their language made them feel more at home in what they considered a foreign land.

Jenna, too, spoke a little French. She had studied it in both high school and college. But she was shy and hesitated to attempt conversation even when Mrs. LaBelle, who spoke English less fluently than her husband, lapsed into her native tongue.

"So, you work in Boston, eh?" Mr. LaBelle smiled at Jenna as he stirred his coffee. "And do you like it?" he added, not waiting for her to answer his first question.

"Yes, I like it. Sometimes it's a bit hectic."

"Like Montreal. Cars and people everywhere. We like Quebec better, but in the summer it's all cars and people too."

Like many of those from Quebec, he called Quebec City simply Quebec.

"We're from outside Quebec. We have a little restaurant. We can only vacation in the winter when the tourists are gone. Then we close up and come here for two weeks and then go on to Florida till the end of March. Your aunt, she never takes a vacation."

Jenna glanced at her Aunt Hester. "I tried to talk her into it once."

"Traveling is too much trouble," Hester muttered under her breath. "I saw the world when it was worth seeing. Now, it's all topsy-turvy."

"You don't want to go to a warmer climate in the winter?" Mr. LaBelle queried, looking at Jenna.

"Sometimes," she answered even as she thought of last year when she had spent most of her holiday in Aruba with Carlton Havers. Hester knew she had gone to the Caribbean, but she knew nothing of Carlton Havers. Only weeks ago, the memory of that trip would have been pleasant, now it was tainted by the quandary of her present dilemma, a dilemma she hadn't yet resolved in her own mind in spite of her two weeks here, and in spite of her constant attempts to address her own present and future.

As soon as Mr. LaBelle mentioned the Caribbean, Jenna had thought of the beautiful white sand beaches of Aruba at sunset. She and Carlton had walked for what seemed like miles along those beaches in the pink-gold glow of the evening. They had danced in one another's arms under the stars till dawn, and promises, now broken, had been exchanged in loving whispers.

The happiness and excitement of the first image was immediately chased away by the reality of the second image—her all too recent conversation with Carlton, the one that had sent her here filled with unhappiness, with regrets, and even with nagging self-doubts.

"Is something the matter, Jenna?"

Hester's concerned tone broke through Jenna's mental flight, and she looked up. "No, no. I was just thinking about the Caribbean."

"Oh, that's right. You went there last year, didn't you?"

"Yes, to Aruba." Jenna hoped no one would ask for details.

"Sometimes, we go to Martinique," Mrs. LaBelle said softly. "They speak French there."

"And it's very nice," Jenna said as she finished her coffee. She set the cup down in the saucer carefully and looked across at her aunt. "I really should be going," she announced. "I've got all my things in the car."

"I still wish I could stop you from leaving tonight," Hester said, a fretful expression filling her face. "There really is going to be a storm."

"I'm sure I'll be fine."

"Will you promise me if the driving gets too bad you'll pull off the road someplace and wait it out?"

Jenna smiled warmly. "I promise."

She pushed her chair back from the table and glanced at the LaBelles. "I'm glad to have met you. Have a nice holiday."

Mr. LaBelle stood and bowed from the waist. *"Bonne chance!*—good luck," he announced in French.

"Excuse me." Hester moved swiftly around the table and followed Jenna to the door. Jenna pulled on her shoes and then put on her three-quarter-length, brown

suede car coat and paisley scarf while Hester stood
nearby.

"You should have a warmer coat," Hester muttered.

"I'd be too warm. The heater in the car is very effi-
cient."

"Now you drive carefully, you hear. And remember
your promise. You're so stubborn."

Jenna smiled and hugged her aunt goodbye. "It's not
even snowing yet. I'll probably be back in Boston when
it starts."

"I certainly hope so." Hester looked down and then
up again, seeking Jenna's eyes. "If you want to talk, well,
I'm always here," she said.

Jenna nodded. "I know, and thank you." Her eyes almost filled with tears as she looked at Hester. She had
wanted to talk with her, but the time didn't seem right.
Maybe later. Maybe when she had thought it all
through for herself, when there was more time between
the event and her own hurt.

"I'll call you soon."

"And you come anytime. This place is as much yours
as mine, Jenna."

Jenna kissed her aunt on the cheek and hurried out
the front door and toward her white Toyota Tercel that
was parked in the driveway.

Chapter Two

Jenna slipped into the driver's seat and started the car, backing cautiously out of Aunt Hester's driveway. Then, just before turning the car to drive away from the house, she waved once again at her aunt who stood in the doorway mouthing the words, "Drive carefully."

She took one long look as she passed the old red-brick church, and then she turned the car once again at the end of the street. In a moment, she was on Highway 5, a narrow two lane highway that runs parallel to the larger, north-south Highway 91. Highway 5 crosses the Connecticut River before Greenfield.

It was a weekday, and it was just the time of day people would be leaving work in Greenfield. By taking this somewhat convoluted route, Jenna could travel to Montague, then on a less traveled local road, bypassing Greenfield's Town Center and its congested traffic. She could then cut east to Highway 2 without going west to Greenfield. This route cut about fifteen miles off the trip—fifteen miles and a lot of traffic. Massachusetts is highly populated and highly developed, but the state has done a good job of disguising its industrialization for the motorist. Wide greenbelts run along the highways, and thus, as soon as one is traveling between communities, one has the feeling of being deep in the woods.

It was that feeling that flooded over Jenna now as she headed down Highway 5 into the early darkness. There were seemingly no lights anywhere, and she was aware only of the tall peaceful thick pine trees on one side of the highway and the rock-strewn riverbank on the other.

Jenna turned on the radio and hummed along as her favorite Boston station played assorted Motown classics. She had driven only a mile or two when she was compelled to slow for the detour signs.

"Damn!" she muttered under her breath. "If I'd known there was construction on this road I would have taken the main highway even if it was further." But then she remembered the five o'clock traffic and decided to continue onward.

The flickering highway lights that marked the detour were of the sort that lit up only when the car's headlights hit them. "Well, too late now," Jenna said. "I hope it's not a long detour."

Jenna slowed down as the pavement disappeared, and the car bumped onto a hard-packed gravel road. "Detours," she murmured. The radio crackled with static, and she leaned down and tried to tune it out. "Probably the electrical power station." There was one nearby, and as the radio wouldn't perform without interference, she turned it off, continuing on in silence.

The car bumped along the rough road. Yes, somehow the detour sign and what it had led to seemed all too symbolic of recent events, and Jenna began to think again about the personal problem that had brought her home to Deerfield.

That's what Carlton Havers was in her life—a detour leading down an unacceptably rough road. She pressed her lips together, and then, for the first time in two weeks, tears began to fill her eyes and run down her cheeks. They were tears caused by mixed emotions—she felt hurt at what he had done to her, she was angry at herself because she had been so stupid, and she was experiencing a kind of total insecurity. The latter was a feeling she had never known before.

Carlton Havers was in his late thirties, a tall, slim, handsome man with deep blue eyes and dark hair. He was also ambitious. He was the youngest vice president of Goodman, Brache and Nelson, and it was an open secret that next year he would be taken into the partnership of the respected firm. Then the firm would become Goodman, Brache, Nelson and Havers.

Carlton was also wealthy. His father had been a U.S. senator, his grandfather a governor of the state. The Havers were old money, Back Bay Boston old money, people of financial and social influence. Carlton had graduated from Harvard, traveled widely in Europe, and studied in England for a time. He had a biting wit, a sophisticated charm, and a devastating smile.

Carlton belonged to the yacht club and owned a sailboat. Not just any sailboat, but a slick racer which had placed second in the Boston to Provincetown races last year. He was tanned, athletic, and, in every way, cultured.

Jenna pressed her lips together, she supposed that Carlton Havers was the man of whom every woman dreamt. He was darkly attractive, monied, powerful . . . Were those the qualities that had attracted her? She wasn't sure, she didn't trust herself anymore.

Still, Jenna felt forced to consider what had attracted her to Carlton. She thought back. She had just been hired by Goodman, Brache and Nelson when she had met Carlton. As a trainee, she was one of four newly acquired employees to be assigned to Carlton's team. The other three were Bess Armstrong, Jack Wilson, and Pete Simmons. But from the beginning she had received the accolades. Now, as she looked back, she wondered if she had really been praised for her good work, or if Carlton had favored her because he was desirous of her. That thought plagued her, and continued to plague her. To make a bad decision where a personal relationship was concerned was bad enough, but now she found herself questioning her success, and it affected her confidence even more than the broken affair.

She shook her head as she thought about it. She had considered Carlton off limits from the beginning. He was married, and she had no intention of taking up with a married man. She had worked with Carlton for nearly a month before he asked her out. Not that the first time was really a date, she wouldn't have gone if it had been. They had been working late, and he asked her to have a bite with him.

Much to her surprise, he had taken her to a secluded candlelit Italian restaurant off Beacon Street. She remembered thinking she wasn't dressed for the restaurant's elegance. She felt terribly uncomfortable, even afraid that she would run into someone she knew and that they would misunderstand the situation. He had laughed at her hesitation to go there, as well as at her fear of being seen. He waved away her fears of being too casually dressed. He had joked about it.

"Some restaurants keep ties for men who show up without them, perhaps they should have diamond jewelry on hand to dress up the women." Then he had added, thoughtfully, "Perhaps I'll suggest that to the maître d'—it could *make* a restaurant. After all, the clientele of any establishment is all important to its reputation." He laughed. "I only come here because Ted Kennedy comes here."

Was I impressed? Jenna asked herself. Her family wasn't poor but they certainly weren't members of the jet set either. When she was growing up, her parents often traveled with her. When she was ten, they'd taken her to India. But her parents didn't travel for social reasons. They were both academics, and they traveled to learn and sometimes to attend conferences. Carlton's life had clearly been different. He moved in the same circles with important powerful people. "Power attracts." Wasn't that a truism? Jenna wondered if that had been a factor in her own bad judgment.

At first, she and Carlton had talked only about business, and then she had made a casual remark about the long hours he worked in the office.

He had looked up at her, his eyes flickering with emotion and quietly confessed, "It's because I have nothing to go home to . . ."

Jenna remembered the whole conversation—it was the conversation that had opened all the wrong doors. It was the first "detour" sign, and she should have heeded it. She should have turned around and gone in the other direction.

"I thought you were happily married," she answered, knowing it was a somewhat silly reply. But his confession had taken her aback because they had never before discussed anything personal. And if his marriage wasn't happy, he had certainly kept it a secret.

Jenna was certain he was the subject of the daydreams of many a female employee, but there was no office gossip about him or about his marriage.

"Perhaps I fell for you because I genuinely felt you were confiding in me . . . perhaps that's what made me behave so stupidly," Jenna asked herself in the silence of the car.

Jenna forced herself to remember the rest of the conversation. "My wife left me a few months ago," he had told her as he looked down at his plate. Then, his eyes filled with pain. "God, I miss my children."

She had immediately felt terrible for him, and she had tried to express her concern.

"I had no idea . . . of course you miss them. Don't you see them at all?"

"When Tina deems it fit. But being a weekend parent doesn't satisfy me."

No, she had thought at the time. He wasn't the kind to be satisfied with that kind of parenting. He always seemed to be the kind of person who gave of himself, and she assumed that attitude had carried over into his home life.

"But don't you have regular visiting rights?" she had asked. "Can't you have them over longer periods?"

"We haven't sought a legal separation yet. It's hard on the children . . . you know, they have to talk to lawyers and social workers. We're trying to work out something that will be easier for them, at least that's my hope."

Jenna had asked what his wife hoped for. He seemed to indicate that she had other ideas, or was, in some way, more self-centered. But he wouldn't say much about her, and Jenna had thought this admirable at the time.

As she thought back over the beginning of their relationship, Jenna realized he had never actually said that his wife was more self-centered. Indeed, whatever ideas she had about Tina Havers were ideas that had been alluded to, ideas he had subtly planted. They were, she now admitted, ideas that had grown in the fertile soil of her own desire for him, her desire to see everything the way he saw it, her desire to believe everything he told her was true.

After he told her about his faltering marriage, he apologized to her. "Forgive me, Jenna. Forgive me for burdening you with my personal problems. I certainly haven't told anyone else."

"There's no office gossip about you," she said, trying to reassure him. "And really, I don't mind your having told me. I promise, I would never tell anyone."

"I know you won't."

He had reached across the table then and covered her hand with his. "I just had the urge to talk with you . . . because I knew I could trust you."

She remembered what happened after that all too vividly. His blue eyes seemed to penetrate her very being. They bore through her, and she felt a sudden discomfort, an embarrassment as his hand squeezed hers meaningfully. It was as if he were thinking very seductive thoughts and that somehow he had silently conveyed those thoughts to her.

"I'm terribly lonely, Jenna . . ."

She remembered thinking she ought to move her hand, but she didn't.

"Have dinner with me on the weekend," he asked, still holding her with his eyes.

"You're still married," she had ventured.

"We're separated, Jenna. It's all over between Tina and me. You didn't cause it, you weren't in any way involved. Just let me take you out, talk to you, be with you . . . Jenna, I admit I was attracted to you from the moment I met you. Is that so wrong?"

Again his eyes had held her. She shook her head slowly.

"So will you see me on the weekend?"

She had nodded even though all her instincts were warning her not to get involved with this man.

* * *

Dinner had once again taken place in a small intimate restaurant. There were additional confessions—he told her more about his unhappy marriage and about his wife's affair with a prominent Boston banker, Myron Debbs.

How could a woman leave a man like Carlton? Jenna had wondered.

Other dinners had followed, then he had taken her to the small apartment on Charles Street where he told her he had lived since moving out of his house. "No one at the office knows," he told her. "I still use the house as my mailing address, and I use my cellular phone exclusively. Tina doesn't tell anyone either. We just want to keep things quiet till we work out the details of our divorce."

They had dinner at his apartment that night, and that night he had taken her in his arms and kissed her, again confessing his attraction to her.

His kisses were magical. His fingers in her hair, his lips on her neck, his breath in her ear . . .

She had been wearing a black dress with thin little spaghetti straps. He slipped the slender straps down over her shoulders during a passionate kiss. She had thought of pulling away, but then she felt his warm hands on her flesh, and she glowed beneath his gentle erotic touch. But, on that occasion, she had been strong, although when she left him she was warm and flustered. Home, alone in her own bed, she had thought of him, and she had tossed most the night as she relived the feel of his hands on her bare skin.

She had wanted him. Gradually, slowly, he wore her down. They drove down to Gloucester for a fish dinner, and once home, she'd asked him up for coffee. They didn't have the coffee till the next morning.

Shortly after they entered the house, he had kissed her with such passion that she had been unable to object or even think. His hands had moved swiftly to caress her with such intimacy and such urgency that she had all but melted into his arms. He had carried her to the bedroom and made ardent love to her, and she had responded to him, heading blindly off on her own personal detour.

In the meantime, she did well at work, and soon she advanced in the company. Weekends were spent with Carlton—she never thought of it at the time, but she was, in essence, his mistress.

That past summer she had gone to Aruba with him, and they had spent nearly two weeks on the sun drenched isle dancing, making love, talking under the stars.

Now, it had all unraveled. "How could I have been so stupid?" she said aloud.

It was such a common story. What Carlton Havers had done to her, millions of other men had done to millions of other women. His tale of woe wasn't even original; he had used every line in the book. Affairs like the one she had with Carlton were the subject of a thousand novels ... "How was it I thought this was different? How was it that I had thought he was different?" she asked herself angrily.

"Stupidity plus desire," she admitted.

And the end was awful. He had gradually stopped seeing her as often as he had been. Then Jenna began noticing him a great deal with Margo Whitehead, a new girl in accounting, a tall shapely Kathleen Turner look-alike.

In a scene she felt she would never forget, he confessed that he had never left his wife, never even considered it. He told her he kept the apartment in the city only for convenience sake, and he told her she was one in a long line of women he had wooed, successfully seduced, and then left. "You value your career," he had told her meanly, "so you'll either leave the firm, or say nothing."

And what was unsaid was the most painful of all.

Jenna wondered if she had really been good at her job or if she had been promoted only because she had slept with Carlton Havers. It was bad enough to feel stupid, to feel duped and taken in by a man you had been deeply attracted to, but to also feel incompetent in your career was disastrous. In a sense, it meant that she had failed the first test in all areas of her life.

Jenna wiped the tears off her cheek. Only a month ago, she had felt confident, happy, and fulfilled. Now, she felt insecure, unhappy, and above all, lonely.

She shook her head to dispel her thoughts and peered out the window into the darkness. It seemed this detour, like the one she had taken in her life, would never end.

"Great," she muttered as the first wet snow began to fall. They were big snowflakes, and in the darkness in front of her headlights, they seemed almost hypnotic. It was as if she were trapped in one of those cheap little snow-filled paperweights.

The road again became paved, and Jenna breathed a sigh of relief. The turn onto the main highway could not be far. She speeded up a little even though the visibility was terrible.

She passed another sign, and then again, the pavement ceased. Jenna muttered. What was supposed to be a short cut was turning into the long way home. But she had come too far to turn back, so she continued on. Then, strangely, the road grew even more narrow, and she saw before her a covered bridge.

"I didn't know there was one of those around here," she said aloud. There weren't many of the old covered bridges left and most of those that still stood were not used. Rather, they were monuments. She entered it and drove slowly through it, over its one lane till she emerged again into the snow filled night. The road was still running parallel to the river, but now she was driving on the other side.

It was unseemly dark and silent. Jenna smiled, thinking again of the fact that this was the anniversary of the famous raid on Deerfield. "It must have been a night like this," she said, taking comfort from the sound of her own voice.

Suddenly, out of the dark shadows on the left side of the road, a full-antlered deer sprang in front of her. As she slammed on her brakes to avoid hitting the large buck, it flashed across her mind that it was not the season for deer to be running about.

The car suddenly skidded, and Jenna grasped the steering wheel and watched in a frozen panic as her car spun in a circle on the icy road. It didn't spin just once. It turned again and again. Jenna grasped the wheel tightly. It was as if she were caught in a maelstrom, and then the car seemed to leave the road altogether. She felt a horrible falling sensation as the car plunged, down, down the rocky embankment toward the rushing river. Everything was bumps and blackness and spinning and crashing until finally Jenna lost consciousness as her world spun round and round. It was as if she were a figure imprisoned in a paperweight, and it were being shaken by some violent hand.

Chapter Three

Jenna opened her eyes, aware of the cold above all else. She shivered violently trying to remember what had happened.

"Oh, my God," she whispered as the vision of her spinning car came back to her. She forced herself to sit up, and the soft wet snow fell from her upper body. But it had stopped snowing now, and the woods and rocky riverbanks were bathed in moonlight. She stared down the embankment with horror. The black river was swirling over the rocks, and her car was just then being sucked under. She could barely make out its sinking hulk in the white light of the moon. It was as if it were being sucked under by some great force; it was as if it were caught in a whirlpool. It was almost supernatural, she thought with a shiver. After all, the dam was upstream. The river here was not usually so turbulent, nor had she thought it that deep.

Jenna shook her head and moved cautiously to her feet, testing herself as she stood. "Well, at least nothing is broken," she said aloud, comforted only slightly by the sound of her own voice in the silence of the night.

Again, she shivered. She was soaked, and her shoes were wet and caked with muck. Had she somehow crawled up the riverbank? The details of the accident, especially how she had climbed to the snow-covered grass above the rocky river basin, were a mystery. Perhaps, she reasoned, she had some sort of temporary amnesia.

"And if you don't move you're going to have permanent freezing to death," she said aloud, even as she hugged herself to ward off another shiver. Her jacket was heavy with cold icy water. "Better off without it" she said, slipping it off, even as she began walking rapidly toward the road. She carried it over her arm. "God, it's cold," she murmured as she quickened her pace.

Jenna paused for a moment when she reached the dirt road. She had seen nothing in the direction from whence she'd come along this road when she was driving—not even a distant light. And how far had she come? She vaguely remembered the covered bridge. But she'd been lost in thought. She could have traveled a mile or even five miles. She shrugged and decided to go forward rather than backward. She knew there were no houses where she had driven. It couldn't possibly be far to where there were some she told herself.

Jenna inhaled deeply and trudged off into the night, praying that it wouldn't get any colder before she found shelter. Each gust of wind caused another deep shiver. She wouldn't have to be out long in this weather, wearing wet clothes to develop hypothermia. She quickened her pace, breaking into a run in order to warm her body.

A mile! She must have come at least a mile! And the road still wasn't paved. Indeed, it seemed to have grown narrower, and it was rutted, as if traveled by wagons. Yes, it wasn't like a road anymore, it was like an old wagon trail.

Ahead, Jenna saw a sign, an old-fashioned wooden

sign. She hurried up to it, and she peered at it curiously. What was written was etched into the wood and visible in the moonlight. It read "Boston Post Road."

How did this broken down sign get here? The Boston Post Road was paved and all but lined with inns, hotels, restaurants, and antique shops. Everything really old had been restored and refurbished, everything new had been built in the Colonial style. But this sign was roughly hewn and all but falling down. In any case, this, Jenna thought, was certainly *not* the Boston Post Road, no matter what the sign said.

For a second, she ran her fingers over the sign, and then shrugging, she trudged on, again breaking into a run.

She was dressed in a plaid wool skirt and a plain green sweater. Her suede jacket was over her arm. Her skirt and her sweater smelled of wet wool, her jacket just smelled. Her good leather moccasins squeaked with water and could hardly be seen for the mud that covered their tops.

Why in heaven's name hadn't she come to a house? This part of Massachusetts, in spite of its wooded appearance, was, after all, heavily populated. It wasn't as if she'd been dropped from a helicopter into the middle of Maine's wilderness or even the heavily forested areas of the Berkshires.

Jenna could see her breath in front of her now. Damn! It was getting colder. She was going to freeze to death. Her clothes were already beginning to grow stiff with the cold.

Jenna rounded a bend in the dirt road and heaved a sigh of relief. Set off into the woods, and clearly visible in the moonlight, was a log cabin. It was small and it was dark. But still it was shelter. "Under the circumstances," she said aloud, "I'll be forgiven for breaking in." Then she added, "If only I *can* break in."

Jenna hurried to the door. She banged loudly. "Anyone home! "Help me!"

To her surprise, Jenna heard a noise inside the cabin. Then, after a minute, she heard a heavy bolt being lifted, and the cabin door swung open.

The girl framed in the doorway seemed young—perhaps only twelve or thirteen. She wore a long white gown with full ruffled sleeves and a little nightcap. She looked at Jenna fearfully.

"An apparition!" she almost shrieked as she started to close the door.

Jenna moved forward, blocking the door with her foot. "You have to let me in," she said firmly. "I'll freeze if you don't!"

The young girl's mouth opened in surprise, but she stepped aside and then whispered, "Don't hurt me. I'm here alone."

Jenna had to squint to see her in the dark cottage. The only light was that of the moon as it filtered in from the funny slit windows. "Of course I won't hurt you. Goodness, turn on the lights. It's pitch dark in here."

"Lights?" the girl repeated. "No, Father told me not to light any candles."

Jenna frowned. Perhaps the electricity had gone out in the storm. Probably the girl's father hadn't wanted to risk her starting a fire so he had told her not to light candles.

"Who art thou?" the girl stammered.

"My name is Jenna, Jenna Stevens. I had an automobile accident. . . . I'm soaked, my clothes are all wet."

"Auto . . . automo . . . mobile? Thou speakest a strange tongue, and thy manner of dress is foreign to me. Are thou sure thou are not an apparition or a witch?"

Jenna stared at this girl whose own clothes were

heavy and odd looking. Had this child been locked up
in a closet for three hundred years? Perhaps her family
was of some strange religion that believed in keeping her
from the modern world.

"I am not an apparition or a witch. I will not hurt
you. Look, I'm very cold. I know it's an imposition, but
I'll repay you, I promise. Can you loan me some warm
dry clothes? If it's not far I'll walk on to the next house
unless you have a phone."

The young girl had seemed to relax only slightly. Her
hair was flaxen and fell to her waist. It hung down below her tightly fitting nightcap and fell over her slim
shoulders. She looked as if she had stepped right out of
the early eighteenth century.

"Warm dry clothes I can provide, but I cannot provide thee with a phone for I know not what it is."

Jenna nodded. Perhaps they were some strict Amish
family. She had heard the Amish spoke the way this girl
spoke . . . But how could she not know what a phone
was?

"I shall pull the curtains and light thee a candle," the
girl said. "But thou must hurry. Indians roaming the
woods might see the light, of this my father hath warned
me."

"Indians?" Jenna almost laughed. Surely, there hadn't
been any Indians in these woods for at least two hundred years. There wasn't, at least to her knowledge,
even a reservation in the vicinity.

The girl had already turned away. "My sister's clothes
should fit thee. She is off in Boston town with my
mother and brother. My father went to my aunt's and
will return on the morrow."

Jenna watched in silence as the girl took a stool and
stood on it to pull dark curtains over the slits.

"Those windows don't let in much light," she commented.

"They be not windows. They be openings for us to poke through our rifles if need be ... if we are attacked."

Jenna found it difficult to keep her expression from betraying her thoughts. What was this strange little girl talking about? She resisted prodding her. Now that she had stopped running, she was too cold to be curious. While it was true that there was no wind inside, the cabin was far from warm.

The girl climbed down, and in a moment, she fetched a candle.

Jenna watched in fascination as the girl went to a glowing iron pot in the hearth, stuck in a twisted braid of grass and drew it out, burning. She used the flame to light the candle.

"I have a lighter in my pocket," Jenna said matter-of-factly. "But it's probably too wet to work just now."

"Thou jest. If thou had a light in thy pocket, thou would'st burn up."

The girl moved away from the candle, and for the first time Jenna could see the room in which she stood.

She looked around it in absolute amazement. There was a roughly made table and several obviously handmade chairs. There were two beds covered with quilts, and there were several big trunks. There were a few utensils and a huge fireplace, one of those fireplaces with a walk-in oven next to it like the one in her aunt's kitchen.

This place looked for all the world like one of the restored houses of Deerfield that the tourists so love. Except, she thought, it seemed to be restored to an earlier period rather than to the period of the Revolutionary War.

"Is this a place like Deerfield or Sturbridge?" Jenna asked. Sturbridge was one of several restored villages but it was located in central Massachusetts. In the summer the populace dressed in Colonial costumes and went about recreating life as it once had been. The same was done in Deerfield. "Does this house belong to the local historical society?"

"I know of no village called Sturbridge, madam. And this house and land belong to my father."

Either she's putting me on, or this is some odd family, Jenna concluded.

The girl had put the candle down on the table. She opened one of the chests and was rummaging through it. "Here ye be," she said, tossing assorted garments on the quilted bed.

Jenna stared at the garments. The underwear consisted of a white chemise and panniers—a hooped framework that gave width to the designs of eighteenth century gowns. The hoops were made of cane and were covered with muslin. Jenna recalled seeing such clothing in museums. This clothing, she noted, was also clearly handmade.

The young girl soon added more clothes to the pile. There was a brown ankle-length dress of heavy, heavy wool, and there were also a solid cloak, thick wool socks, and odd well made shoes with large brass buckles.

"Have you nothing beside these costumes?" Jenna asked.

"These are what we wear," the girl insisted. "I have never seen clothes such as those that cover your body. They are most impractical."

"Beggars can't be choosers," Jenna said, striping quickly and redressing just as quickly in the strange clothing provided.

The girl fingered her discarded clothing, her eyes

wide. She ran her fingers along the seam of Jenna's skirt, shaking her head. "A talented human hand sewed this seam, see how straight these tiny stitches are!"

No phone, no car—could it be this girl didn't know about sewing machines, either?

The young girl tossed Jenna a laced corset. "Put this on over your dress," she instructed.

Jenna took it and laced it up. It pinched in her waist and seemed to lift her breasts even though she wore no bra since that, too, had been wet, and thus discarded. The corset was low cut, and most of her breasts would have been exposed had not her thin chemise filled the space from underneath. Lastly, the girl handed her an apron.

"You look quite proper now."

Jenna shook out her hair. "For a costume party," she said softly.

"I have not given you Prudence's party dress. She has that with her in Boston town."

Prudence? Jenna hid her smile. Odd though all of this was, the poor girl was trying to help her, and she mustn't make fun of her. "And what is your name?" she asked.

"Charity—Charity Anne Benson."

Jenna smiled. "I'm pleased to meet you Charity Benson. Now tell me, how far is the next house?"

"There is no next house. But Fort Deerfield is down the road another two miles."

"Deerfield? How did I get so turned around?"

"From whence comest thou?"

"Deerfield," Jenna answered.

The girl frowned, and looking back toward Jenna's discarded clothes. "Fort Deerfield—and you were dressed thusly?"

"Yes, of course. I was visiting my aunt, Hester Corse."

"I know of Elizabeth and James, but I know of no Hester Corse."

Jenna stood stark still as she stared at Charity. Was this some sort of joke? Elizabeth and James were the names of two of her ancestors. And why had this girl called Deerfield Fort Deerfield? Why indeed had she spoken of Indians?

Perhaps this girl was not quite right in the head. But even Jenna had to admit she seemed calm and sure of herself. The only other possibility was that she herself was dreaming. No, it was all too real for a dream.

Well, there was no point staying here. Once back in Deerfield she would make inquiries about the cabin and its strange occupant. "Are you quite certain it is only two miles to Deerfield?"

"Oh, yes. But thou cannot goest there tonight. It is far too dangerous to walk at night."

"It's not really all that late. Look, you keep my clothes, and I'll get them when I return your sister's clothing."

"That's agreeable, but thou should spend the night, madam. I implore thou. We've had many a raid."

Jenna laughed lightly. "As long as there are no motor-cycle gangs in the vicinity."

The girl shook her head. "I know not of what ye speak."

"Well, don't worry about me. I'll be back tomorrow with your sister's clothes." Jenna swung on the heavy cloak. Her aunt or anyone else who saw her would surely have a laughing fit.

"Be careful," the girl again warned.

Jenna started to leave, then turned abruptly. "I forgot something," Jenna said, walking across the room. She took her lighter out of her jacket pocket and thrust it into the pocket of her skirt. It was wet now, but it would dry and still be workable. Silently she cursed the loss of her purse. It would take weeks to replace all of her identification.

"God be with thee," the girl said.

"And with you," Jenna responded, as she headed down the road.

It was now icy out, but the clothes she had been given were extremely warm. And the clouds had cleared away. If it were snowing elsewhere, it was certainly clear here. The moon was full and the stars incredibly bright. In fact, she thought as she walked along, she had never seen them this bright. Usually, the lights from nearby towns diminished them. Maybe there was a general blackout of some sort ... Maybe that's why there had been no lights coming from Deerfield even though she was certain it was not really late. She had left her aunt's around five and driven for no more than half an hour before the accident. Of course, she had no way of knowing how long she had been unconscious—but considering how wet she was, if she had been there long she would have frozen. No, it simply could not be after seven o'clock. Still, as she walked further, presumably coming closer to Deerfield, there were simply no lights and no houses, and she felt a chill of fear as strange questions filled her head. It was as if a part of Massachusetts had disappeared. "I'm being silly," she said aloud to comfort herself.

Again, Jenna saw a sign. Oddly, it was the same sort of old sign she had seen before. She went up to it and stared uncomprehendingly at its message. Etched into the wood were the words "Fort Deerfield."

For a long moment Jenna stood stark still in front of the sign. She would have known if there was a fort here. She knew these roads like the back of her hand. She had been to every historic site in this part of the state. What was going on?

Jenna bit her lip and shook her head. Then she began walking on. She turned down a bend in the road and sucked in her breath. Before her was a stockade . . . the sort of stockade she had seen in pictures. It was crudely built, and from one of its four towers, the British flag fluttered in the night breeze. But Deerfield had no standing stockade! It had been destroyed in the raid of 1704.

Jenna trembled in fright and leaned up against a tall pine to keep from fainting. Instinctively, she lifted her gloved hands to her face and tried desperately to place in some sort of order or perspective all of the strange things that had happened to her this night. Then, in a near dreamlike state, she moved cautiously toward the stockade aware only that if she stood still, she would freeze.

Jenna pounded on the wooden gate.

"Who's there?" a strong male voice replied.

"Jenna . . . Jenna Stevens."

Cautiously, the gate was opened a small crack. Then an irritated and raspy male voice, hissed, "Get in here, woman!"

Jenna slipped inside. She looked around and felt her throat tighten and her breath shorten. This was certainly not the Deerfield she had left a matter of hours ago. This Deerfield was a huddle of small buildings behind the stockade—a stockade guarded by several young soldiers in eighteenth century British uniforms and some volunteer townspeople from the looks of it.

"Miss! Who are you? Where have you come from?" the male voice demanded.

Jenna stared at him. His Colonial British army uniform did not have the fresh look of a costume; it was grubby and appeared to be quite real. Furthermore, he spoke with a British accent, and he held an old British musket. There was one in the museum just like it—a flintlock musket, that's what it was.

She opened her mouth and felt as if she could not speak. Her world was reeling before her, she felt unsteady. What *was* happening?

"Well, what are you doing here? Where did you come from?"

Habit forced her to answer, caution forced her to be vague, an odd combination of fright and stunned bewilderment caused her to speak softly. "From the cabin of Charity Benson . . . she took me in. My . . ." Jenna hesitated, "wagon broke down," she finished.

"You shouldn't be out at night. You know that! You know how dangerous it is!"

"I was lost," she protested. Lost did not cover it—she felt lost in time, hurtled somehow backward—no, it couldn't be. It just couldn't. But at the moment, she felt little choice but to pretend.

He scowled at her. "You're not the new school teacher that was sent for are you?"

Jenna inhaled and nodded. Perhaps it would all end soon. She would wake up and discover this was all an extremely vivid dream. Or, perhaps, there would be gales of laughter, and it would all be explained as a gigantic hoax. No, the latter was too far fetched. But the truth . . . the truth, she was beginning to suspect, was even more unbelievable. Again, Jenna shivered. But this time it was not the cold. It was this place; the way people spoke and how they looked. She felt frightened, yet somehow curious and excited.

"Well, come along then. 'Tis the Reverend Williams who hired you, but there's no extra room in his house. He rubbed his chin thoughtfully, "I'll take you to the Catlin house."

"The Catlin house?" Jenna repeated dumbly. Only a few hours ago she had walked that way and stood by the side of a field, looking at the plaque that noted the previous location of the Catlin House.

"It's not really a rooming house, but it's big. Elizabeth Corse lives there with her mother, Mrs. Catlin. Her husband, James Corse, is our scout. He's away so they should have room. Mrs. Corse has two children, young Elizabeth and young James. The Corse family is building their own house, but it's not ready yet."

"Aye," he added, as they walked in the darkness. "The Catlin house is real large. They've got lots of room. Anyway, Mrs. Corse is on the school committee. Aye, we'll straighten everything out in the morning, and Mrs. Corse will get you all settled."

Jenna followed him away from the stockade gate. Little of Deerfield had survived the raid. But she had seen drawings of how the town had been laid out. There was a farm now near where the Catlin house had been. But naturally, the Catlins had farmed too.

They approached a big rambling house. It was made of logs and had the same kind of slit windows as had the cabin occupied by Charity Benson. It was not as large as the house she had left a few hours ago—her aunt's house, but with a chill Jenna recognized the original facade from drawings she had seen of the Catlin house.

How odd it was! In her mind's eye, she could see the map in the flyleaf of the book she had been reading. Inside the stockade walls, on what eventually became the back street of historic Deerfield, the Catlin house stood next to a large barn, while the houses of John Sheldon, the Stebbins family, the Reverend Williams, John Hawks, Samuel Carter, Thomas French, and three others whose names eluded her were on the main street. The church was in the center of the stockade's enclosed area. Outside the walls, extending down the rutted wagon road, thirteen other houses clung to the edge of this frontier community.

Jenna drew in her breath. Tonight's reality, her dream or whatever it was, had taken her back to the Deerfield she had read so much about, the Deerfield of the early 1700s.

It was a short walk to the Catlin house.

The British soldier pounded on the door, and after a time, a woman answered. She was dressed much as the girl in the cabin had been, but she carried a lantern.

"You woke me out of a sound sleep," she said, somewhat irritably as she stared at the soldier and then at Jenna.

"This is the new school teacher. Wagon broke down, and she's arrived with nothing but the clothes on her back."

"And in the middle of the night!" the woman said. Then, shaking her head she beckoned Jenna inside. "Well, girl, don't stand out there all night. It's cold out, you know."

Jenna stepped into the lantern light, her eyes scanning the room. Then she saw the familiar desk, the desk with the rolltop. But now it looked new, in fact, it looked as if it had just been made.

Seeing her staring at it, the woman spoke, "It's my new desk. I sent all the way to Boston for that."

"It's beautiful," Jenna said softly. Could this be reality? Another time dimension?

"What an odd accent you have. Where are you from, lass?"

Jenna thought quickly—where could she be from? "I came up from Virginia," she replied.

"And what's your name?"

Jenna breathed a sigh of relief. They hadn't been expecting a specific person. "Jenna, Jenna Stevens."

"Jenna Stevens from Virginia. I'm Elizabeth Corse. I have a daughter named Elizabeth and a son named James. But you'll meet them in the morning. Well, come along, I'll take you up to your room."

Jenna followed wondering why the girl in the cabin had sounded even stranger than this woman. Perhaps, she reasoned, she had been partially right. Perhaps she was a Quaker.

They reached the second floor, and Jenna followed Mrs. Corse down the long corridor. They stopped at the last door, and Mrs. Corse opened it, revealing a small room. She bent over and lit a second lantern. "Be sure it's out when you crawl into bed. There's a nightgown in that drawer that ought to fit, and all in all you should be snug as a bug in a rug."

Jenna nodded, then suddenly, she remembered . . . "What's the date?" she asked. Heaven knew—if you lose three hundred years, you could also lose days, she presumed.

Mrs. Corse looked witheringly at her, "February 29, 1704, of course." She whirled around and closed the door. "Sleep tight," she added.

Jenna stood in the icy room. Outside the moonlight fell on the newly fallen snow. Her window was edged in frost, but she peered out on the seemingly peaceful landscape. Was this real? Would she go to sleep and wake up in some hospital bed? Had she died in the accident? She felt totally bewildered, and yet alert. This couldn't be a dream, it was too detailed. Was it possible? Were there other time dimensions? Was she actually in another time period?

Jenna shivered. If she was, she had been thrust into a dangerous time and into a dangerous place. There was violence—people behaved differently, or so she assumed from all she had read. She tried to reason, although nothing seemed reasonable. Perhaps if this were a different time dimension, events she knew from history did not occur. If on the other hand, she had actually been thrust back in time—a time she had studied well—it was going to be a terrible night, and she and the survivors of this place would be faced with an uncertain future. If I am a survivor, she thought momentarily. But no. If fate had intended her death, surely she wouldn't have been brought here first. She shook her head, trying to understand, trying to make sense out of it. But it was no use, she could only pray she would somehow be returned to her own time.

Chapter Four

Jenna continued to stare out of the window. What if it were possible that she had somehow been transported back in history? If tonight were really February 29, 1704, should she warn the family and the fort of the impending attack?

No, she decided. If somehow what was happening to her was real, any action she might take would change history, thus altering the present ... or the present as she knew it. But didn't just being here alter history? She puzzled over her own question, and then drew her cloak back on, deciding not to go to bed. Perhaps there was some reason she was here ... Perhaps it would all become obvious to her if she was just patient and waited to see what would happen next.

Jenna sat down on the edge of the all too soft bed. She ran her hand nervously over her heavy, brown wool skirt. It was a trifle itchy, but its warmth was welcome.

If only I knew what time it was, she thought. Then she decided not to wait. She took several blankets off the bed, emptied the candelabra on the dresser and stuffed as many candles as she could into her pocket, and carefully, quietly, edged out of the door into the blackness of the hall.

Jenna tiptoed in the darkness. Hardly daring to breathe, she retraced her steps back down the stairs. She moved silently through the house, finally finding the large kitchen. In the hearth, a fire still smoldered. Jenna laid out a dish cloth and wrapped what food she could find in it, then she edged open the back door, and ran across the lawn to the shed. She slid inside, leaving the door open just a tiny bit. Warmly wrapped in her blankets, Jenna settled down to watch . . . to watch and to wait.

At what point she dozed off, crouched by the door of the shed, she didn't know, but she awoke with a terrible start at the loud sound of Indian war cries and the silence-shattering shots of muskets. The smell of smoke and gunpowder filled the air.

"Oh, God," she thought, remembering everything that had passed before. She had slept, but she had not awakened in the present, in a hospital, or even in her own time. She had awakened during an Indian raid, and even from her vantage point, she knew she had awakened where she had gone to sleep, in the Deerfield of the past, the Deerfield of 1704.

"Fire! Fire!" Jenna heard the alarmed cries of men, and she peered out the crack of the door. The roof of the Catlin house was ablaze, and the house next door was totally aflame. Men were running everywhere, and there were other men on horseback and Indians! There were Indians and more Indians!

Jenna grasped the door and stared into the night. Suddenly, a young boy ran from the house. He sprinted across the snow toward the shed. Just as suddenly, an Indian warrior darted toward him, tomahawk held high.

Jenna screamed, and the boy turned, barely eluding the blow of the tomahawk. The Indian stood startled for a moment, then he grabbed the boy, and the boy, strong for his age, began to struggle. He kicked and fought with his fists. Again, the Indian, much larger, raised the deadly tomahawk. Jenna screamed again and emerged from her hiding place. She threw herself with all her strength on the Indian while the boy continued to fight.

As suddenly as the first had appeared, three other Indians came to join the melee, and then there was another girl. One of the Indians had her by the hair, and she was shrieking and crying. Still another Indian prodded Mrs. Corse along, his ungainly musket poking her in the back. "Leave my children alone!" she demanded.

Jenna, too, screamed but this time she screamed because again she saw the tomahawk poised above the young boy's head. And she was powerless because a strong Indian brave held her tightly.

"Arrête!" a husky male voice shouted. *"Arrête!"*

The man who emerged from the shadows was broad shouldered and powerfully built. In the firelight, Jenna could not make out the details of his features. But she saw his jaw was square, his skin fair, and his eyes dark. He wore buckskins and a coonskin hat. Not the kind of frontier hat she had seen in film or on television, but a handmade hat with fur over the ears. He was a tall man, and in the eerie light, he cast a long shadow.

At the sound of his voice, the Indians stopped dead in their tracks, and the tomahawk fell limply to the Indian's side. Jenna knew he had shouted "Stop!" in French.

The man spoke rapidly in French. "A dead hostage is a worthless hostage," he said, although it took Jenna a moment to translate.

Then he turned and looked at them. His eyes rested for a long moment on Jenna, then in English he shouted, "Do as I tell you if you value your lives. Stop struggling! You!" He pointed to Mrs. Corse. "You go over there." He gave some direction in French, and one of the Indians took Mrs. Corse away. He spoke some more, and the boy and girl whom Jenna assumed must be Elizabeth and James Corse were marched to a nearby sledge and bundled onto it. Meanwhile, the fire on the roof burned brightly, and in moments, the whole second floor was ablaze.

"Our house is burning!" Elizabeth cried from the sledge.

Jenna turned toward her and saw that she was crying and staring at the house in horror.

The house next door burned with intensity, and it grew even lighter outside as the walls of the stockade were torched.

"And you, you come with me," the big stranger ordered as he yanked Jenna none too gently.

"I have some things in the shed," Jenna said, "Let me get them!"

The man didn't answer her, but he shouted at one of the Indians who ran to the shed and returned carrying the blankets and holding her small hand-tied knapsack. He handed the knapsack to her.

"Give the blankets to them!" he ordered in French, as he pointed to Elizabeth and James.

"Do we go now, l'Écossais?" the Indian asked.

"We go now," the man they called l'Écossais replied in flawless French.

Then he turned to her. "Pull your cloak close, my girl," he whispered into her ear. "It's a cold night, and we've a long walk."

Jenna felt a chill, but it wasn't just the cold. It was a chill of frightened excitement, even of anticipation. But her feelings were also mixed with concern. Where had they taken Mrs. Corse and the other older women? She looked back at Elizabeth and James. The most important thing, she told herself, was that she not be separated from them.

Again, she looked at this man l'Écossais. Who was this man? What was he doing with the Indians? More important, what was going to happen to her, and how would she survive in this time period? They walked further away from the light of the flames. They entered a wooded area where many Indians were gathering their human hostages as well as piles of material possessions taken from the houses of Deerfield.

"L'Écossais! *Nous sommes victorieux!*—We are victorious!"

The words were spoken in French by another man. But he was a smaller man, a stout man with a dark mustache and a heavy Quebeçois accent.

"*Oui* Sieur de Rouville," l'Écossais answered.

What followed, Jenna had great difficulty understanding. It appeared that this Sieur de Rouville and his French soldiers and half of the Indians were taking a large group of hostages with them, and that this l'Écossais was taking another group in another direction. She knew the hostages had been divided up after a time. Did this mean that in reality they had been divided up more than once?

"Mother!" James called out from the nearby sledge.

Jenna turned in time to see Mrs. Corse being led away by a group of French soldiers and Indians.

The Sieur de Rouville and l'Écossais finished their conversation.

L'Écossais suddenly turned and took her arm, propelling her forward. "You're a beauty, my girl." he again whispered into her ear. "Far better booty than I expected."

Jenna stiffened. "I am not your girl," she replied icily.

He laughed at her and pushed her forward.

"It's cold," Jenna complained.

"Well, I can't stop to warm you now," the man laughed.

Jenna turned angrily. "You're vile," she hissed.

He laughed again. "And you, my sweet, appear to be both spirited and spoiled."

Jenna's face flushed, and she was glad he couldn't see her clearly in the shadows.

"I expect you'll learn a few lessons in the coming months," he whispered. "Very important lessons."

Herded like cattle, they were moved along till they were away from the burning stockade.

A large group of men and women had been gathered together. Mrs. Corse was nowhere to be seen nor was the Sieur de Rouville. Apparently, I understood correctly, Jenna thought.

"*Allez-y*—Let's go!" l'Écossais gave the order, and the captives were prodded forward into the night. The children were dragged on sledges, but everyone else walked.

Jenna tried desperately to take stock of her surroundings—to find landmarks she knew from her own time in order to determine where they were. They crossed a meadow, and then they crossed the river on a low footbridge. Below them, ice lined the riverbank, but the water at the center moved rapidly toward the falls downstream.

L'Écossais guided them up a steep embankment. It seemed to Jenna as if they had come about a mile, most of it spent climbing steadily upward. In the distance, an orange glow filled the sky from the fire that burned Fort Deerfield.

L'Écossais halted the party on a level clearing, well hidden in the pines but probably about a mile above the Deerfield settlement.

"We'll wait here," he said in English.

"Why have we stopped?" Jenna asked.

"This is where the packs and horses were left."

"And just how long do you intend to march people through the snow?" In point of fact, she had read several accounts of this march, but none was terribly detailed, and events that were quite different from what had been recorded had already occurred.

"We'll be traveling till morning," he replied.

"That's impossible! There are mountains ahead."

"There are many mountains between here and Canada. But we will retrieve our packs and horses here so some can ride."

Canada—so near by modern means of transportation, so far in this time period! How could her ancestors have endured it?

She pulled her cloak more tightly around her and stared ahead into the darkness. The other captives were silent, and even the children were quiet.

L'Écossais disappeared into the trees with the Frenchman and a group of Indians. They returned with horses.

She watched as the children were loaded onto sledges together with some of the women. Many of the men would be obliged to walk with those Indians who were also on foot.

"Ready?" l'Écossais asked.

"Ready," one of the Indians returned.

L'Écossais rode a huge black stallion. Suddenly, with one unexpected sweeping motion, Jenna was lifted off the ground as if she were a feather. He pulled her up and onto his horse. He was riding bareback with only a blanket between him and the horse. She was made to sit in front of him, held in place by the reins on either side, the reins and this stranger's strong muscular arms.

He turned the horse, and they headed off. She was close against the body of this powerful stranger, even as the wind whipped across her face, she could feel his warmth against her. In the light of the fires, she had seen his dark brooding eyes and sandy colored hair. She reminded herself of all the dangers, not the least of which was his obvious attitude toward women in general and perhaps toward her in particular. It was wise to be aloof; she decided to try to control her speech and her natural impulses. It would be a terrible struggle to act as people seemed to expect her to act. And there was this man! His maleness was overwhelming, compelling in some way. She felt drawn toward him and repulsed all at the same time.

She thought for a moment of Carlton Havers, and she reminded herself that regardless of whether this was the past, a dreamy present, or some strange future, she would never make the same mistake again.

L'Écossais spurred his horse on, heading deeper into the dark forest. She could hear, but not see the others. This was a terrifying feeling. Jenna found herself gripping the animal's mane to maintain her balance. And it was terribly cold. The wind blew up beneath her cloak and numbed her thighs in spite of her heavy underwear.

The others were far behind. They were alone in the wilderness. Jenna said nothing, but she was well aware that in this time period, women were considered property, and that she had been captured.

"You're a silent wench," he said after a few minutes.

"I have nothing to say," she replied curtly.

"Prideful," he muttered.

"Why am I so privileged to be riding when others are on sledges or walking?"

He laughed wickedly. "I shouldn't want to damage valuable merchandise."

"I would rather be with the others."

"I'll think about it."

In time, they slowed again, and then they stopped while the others caught up with them.

They had reached steeper, rougher ground. From this point on, they stayed together.

L'Écossais dismounted and then lifted Jenna down. He pushed her toward the huddle of villagers. "This one wants to be with the others," he said, laughing.

Jenna stumbled through the snow toward the others. It was right that she, too, walk; still, she immediately regretted her hasty decision.

L'Écossais remounted his stallion and gave the signal. They again began their trek. Some Indians rode, most walked with their prisoners, prodding them along.

I can do this, Jenna kept telling herself, although she knew that little in her primarily urban existence had ever prepared her for what was ahead. True, she had done a lot of mountain climbing. But that was with twentieth century equipment! With winterized sleeping bags and with tents made of special materials!

She looked about. There were other women—many of them older than she, and they all seemed to be managing. And young Elizabeth Corse and her brother James had been let off the sledge, and they, too, trod on proudly.

What rhyme or reason is there for this? Jenna asked herself.

Her eyes fastened on James Corse. Perhaps that was it. Perhaps she was here to protect him in some way. He has to survive, she thought. If he does not survive, the future would be changed in ways she couldn't even imagine. It seemed as good a reason as any, and so, her mind racing, she plodded on in silence like the others.

At the same time, she raked her memory for all she knew, for all the details of history she could remember. Surely, there were things she knew that could help her survive. But she knew with certainty she would have to be very careful. Already someone had almost taken her for a witch. And being taken for a witch was no small worry. If this were really 1704 then it had only been a short twelve years since the Salem witch trials when twelve women had been tortured and hung and many others persecuted. To be seen as different was to be regarded with suspicion, and most certainly a twentieth century woman in the eighteenth century was different in ways Jenna could not even imagine. Any number of things could give her away, she thought.

After what seemed at least another two hours, l'Écossais circled back. He ordered them to halt.

Jenna looked about. This place she recognized. It was Petty's Plain, a clearing at the base of the higher mountains.

"Rest!" she heard him shout. "Stay together, rest."

Almost in unison, the group began to sit down. Some spread blankets on the snow, others found logs and sat on those.

Jenna brushed off a tree stump and almost collapsed with weariness. All around her she heard the whispers of her fellow captives—"Perhaps the soldiers are on their way to rescue us."

But she alone knew better. She knew exactly how this march would end, and yet she knew she was no less a prisoner than the others. Her knowledge certainly did not liberate her.

Elizabeth Corse was sixteen. She had blond hair and blue eyes which she had inherited from the Catlin family. She studied Jenna from afar and wondered where she had come from. She was a beautiful woman with red-gold hair and a voluptuous figure. The leader—or rather the man who appeared to be the leader—seemed to covet her. But who could she be? She was certainly not from Deerfield, although she had been behind their house. To Elizabeth she appeared to be very brave. She had saved James.

Elizabeth moved closer to Jenna. "I do not know you," she said. "Why were you behind my house? And from where did you come?"

Jenna smiled at Elizabeth. She was such a pretty young girl, and her expression was open and honest. She seemed friendly. But certainly she couldn't be told the truth. "I'm the new school teacher. I was on my way to Deerfield and my wagon broke down. Charity Benson took me in, and I arrived late last night. I was staying upstairs in your house, I heard noises in the yard and went outside."

"I must have been asleep when you arrived. Do you understand French? Do you know what has become of my mother?"

Jenna didn't know what to say. The fate of Elizabeth's mother was unknown, and sadly it was assumed, she died in captivity or perhaps when trying to get home, although Jenna had no way of knowing if either explanation were true.

"I don't understand French very well. I think she is with another group. I'm sure they were taken off in another direction."

Elizabeth bit her lip and looked into Jenna's eyes. "I hardly know you, but I feel as if I know you well. I hope we can remain together."

"We must try," Jenna said.

"James!" Elizabeth called her ten-year-old brother. "This is—was to be—the new school teacher."

James looked up. "Thank you for saving me."

"I didn't do anything," Jenna said. James looked very

bright and curious. He was very polite too, and she immediately liked them both. But then, she thought smiling to herself, they were relatives of sorts.

"What's your name?" Elizabeth asked.

"Jenna—Jenna Stevens."

"You do speak strangely. You're not from Boston, are you?"

"No, I'm from the Virginia Colony."

"That explains everything!" James said.

Jenna almost laughed, not *everything* she thought.

James and Elizabeth spread out a blanket and sat down next to her. They covered themselves with the other blanket and lay down. "We should try to take a short nap," Elizabeth suggested.

"I'm worried about Mother," James said seriously.

Elizabeth hugged her brother; it was clear that she, too, was worried, although she said nothing.

Jenna reached over and put her arm around James's shoulders. "Your mother will be all right. She wouldn't want you to worry. She would want you to survive."

"I'll try not to worry," he promised.

Jenna forced a smile. "Your sister's right. We should try to sleep a little."

Perhaps she was inordinately tired because they had walked some five miles in the cold, or perhaps her desire to sleep resulted from the clear, unpolluted night air; but even sitting up on a tree stump, her back against a full grown tree, Jenna dozed off into deep dreamless slumber.

"Awaken!"

Jenna blinked open her eyes and nearly fell off the tree stump. Others, too, had apparently fallen into a merciful and much needed sleep.

She drew her cloak even closer. A wind blew across the clearing. It was the unmistakable wind that always blows across the land just as the sun rises. She looked off into the east where a thin golden line was drawn across the horizon just as if an artist had taken a brush and slashed across the canvas of the night sky.

She stood up and stretched, then she took a handful of snow and rubbed it into her face. Cold though it was, it was refreshing.

L'Écossais, apparently the only one in the raiding party to speak English, walked among them. "Take off your shoes," he commanded. "The Indians will give you moccasins. They're warmer and easier to walk in. Do as you're told, and there will be no trouble."

In silence, most began to unlace their shoes. The Indians passed among them, giving out moccasins.

Jenna studied the moccasins curiously. They were not the beaded variety sold in tourist shops. They were plain, flat soled, and ankle high. They laced up tightly, and they were lined with thick fur. And she noted, while they lacked beads, some were adorned with porcupine quills.

"You're a stranger among us," a woman said as she looked carefully at Jenna. Jenna took her to be about thirty.

"My wagon broke down, and I was taken in by Charity Benson. I arrived in Deerfield just a few hours before the raid."

"She was to be the new school teacher," Elizabeth Corse said, edging closer. "She says she's from the Virginia Colony."

"I'm Mrs. Belding," the woman said, studying Jenna in a way that made her feel as if she were a butterfly under glass.

"Where in the Virginia Colony?" Mrs. Belding asked.

Jenna frowned, trying to think—then she replied, "Williamsburg—yes, Williamsburg, the capital."

The woman looked dubious and lifted her brow. "Jamestown is the capital of the Virginia Colony."

Jenna didn't flinch. "News is slow to travel," Jenna replied. "When the statehouse burned down six years ago, they moved the capital to Williamsburg . . . it's not far from Jamestown."

Jenna had only told everyone she had come from the Virginia Colony to explain why she was different. But Williamsburg was a restored area, and she had visited there a few years ago. While there, she had bought a guidebook that had explained that the capital of the Colony had been moved when the statehouse in Jamestown burned down for the fourth time in 1698. She thanked heaven that she had an interest in Colonial history and that she had a good memory for dates. In her mind, she tried to remember everything she had read and seen in the elegant Colonial capital. At least having been there gave her an edge if there were more questions. Mrs. Belding still looked as if she were still skeptical.

"No matter to me," Mrs. Belding replied crisply. "Especially now."

Elizabeth Corse looked Mrs. Belding in the eye. "Never mind, it's a good thing to have a teacher with us. Who knows how long we'll be gone. The children will still need to learn."

Jenna didn't say anything, but apprehensively she wondered what these children studied. She supposed she could teach them a great deal, but now she realized she must be on constant guard not to give herself away or raise the suspicions of anyone unnecessarily. If she revealed herself in anyway, they might come to believe she was a witch. No, she would have to be very careful. And however much she knew from books, there were many things she didn't know, couldn't know. In fact, she wondered, even with all of her knowledge of future events and inventions, if she could survive in this century. But am I, in fact, really in the 1700s—she asked herself again. And if so, for how long? Somehow, in spite of everything, she was not yet quite willing to accept what seemed to be her present reality. Although, she admitted, there seemed little doubt that she was tramping through the woods on a cold night and that she was acutely aware of her discomfort.

At that moment, l'Écossais and the French commander were passing among the Indians apparently giving orders. But the language they spoke was neither French nor English. It was clearly some Algonquin language, because it was the same language the Indians spoke among themselves.

"I wish I could understand them," Elizabeth lamented.

"I wish I had a hot cup of tea," Mrs. Belding muttered. Then, with a tone of undisguised superiority, she added, "I really don't care what they're saying. It's all just gibberish."

A few moments later, l'Écossais rode up and drew his immense stallion to a halt by the huddle of women. Again, Jenna felt herself dwarfed by his physical presence. He seemed to be a giant atop his horse and indeed, was a big man, a strong man. Just looking at him, she could recall the feel of his muscular arms around her as they had galloped through the night. She shivered, repelled by his apparent arrogance, yet unable to take her eyes off him. In the same way the river had drawn in her car, his dark eyes seemed to be drawing her, pulling her toward him.

"We will be climbing that footpath—single file," he told them matter-of-factly.

"Up Shelburne's Mountain?" Mrs. Belding asked.

"Up Shelburne's Mountain," he answered. "And as you were instructed."

Again, Jenna could see in her mind's eye the map of the route they seemed to be following. No doubt, they would climb the mountains and follow the Connecticut River till they came to what was now called the Winoski River. Jenna wondered by what name the river was called in 1704. Nothing came to mind.

Still, no matter how well she knew the look of the route they would follow on the map, she had no real idea what the ground was like. Only now was she beginning to understand the difficulties. No cleared paths, no roads, no flashlights—nothing save the wooded wilderness and the deep snow.

At that moment, l'Écossais gave the signal and they wearily resumed their march.

"Stay together!" l'Écossais shouted.

"Here," take my arm," Jenna told Elizabeth. It was getting lighter out, and when they paused for a moment, Jenna searched backward along the endless line of Indians, soldiers, and captives for a glimpse of young James, Elizabeth's brother.

After a second, she spotted him as he trudged along. He seemed none the worse for wear.

"You seem sure of foot," Elizabeth declared.

Jenna smiled. "For a time mountaineering was my hobby."

"Mountaineering? Hobby? What strange words are these?"

Jenna turned her head slightly to hide the confusion she was certain was revealed in her expression. Mountaineering, maybe—but now that she was reminded, the word hobby was probably unknown in the early 1700s. It was, naturally, a word associated with leisure time, and surely, these people had little or no leisure time in the twentieth century meaning of the word.

"Mountaineering is a word for one who climbs mountains, and hobby . . . it's, it's a word used in the Virginia Colony," she lied. I wonder how much I can blame on the Virginia Colony, she asked herself silently. So far she had blamed her accent and now some of her vocabulary on being from the Virginia Colony. She reminded herself again to be careful.

"Then are you expert in climbing mountains as a woodsman is expert in the woods?"

"Yes, more or less."

"How unusual for a woman," Elizabeth observed.

Jenna let silence reign for a short time. It was tough sloughing as they neared what she thought must be the summit.

"This is the top," Elizabeth confirmed in a moment. They joined the others in a small clearing. One could see the valley below, the meandering river, and in the distance still more mountains.

"If we're really being taken to Canada, we have to climb those mountains," Elizabeth pointed off into the distance. "If we complain, perhaps they would let us ride."

Jenna pressed her lips together defiantly. "I would rather suffer in silence than let any of those arrogant men hear me complain."

"I am in awe of you," Elizabeth said. "I am afraid, but you seem unafraid."

Jenna could not answer that after what had happened to her—was happening to her—she could not be afraid. She had seemingly slipped from one time dimension into another. If this were possible, what was there to fear?

The captives all gathered in the clearing while l'Écossais rode around them, and the Indians encircled them. "We will make camp when we have walked another six miles," he told them. "Then we will eat, and you will be allowed to sleep."

Jenna had counted silently. There seemed to be about thirty in their group. That meant that most of the hostages were in the larger group taken by the Sieur de Rouville. Later, as she recalled, all the hostages were divided into groups of three and four.

There were Indians ahead and behind them as well as sledges loaded down with booty. Jenna glanced at James. He was surrounded by Indians who appeared to be led by one of the French soldiers. He dared not move, although he had signaled his sister with a slight wave.

Jenna continued to ponder the idea that she had somehow been sent back in time to protect James.

"Move out!" Again, l'Écossais gave the signal, and again, they began walking, this time downhill and toward the valley.

Chapter Five

The sun was high in the sky when again they were halted on a wooded knoll.

When they stopped this time, no effort was made to keep the male captives from the female. James immediately joined Jenna and Elizabeth.

"It's a pretty spot," Jenna said as she dropped to the ground, weary with exhaustion.

James had his gloved hands in his pockets as he surveyed the place they had stopped. "And defensible," he added to Jenna's comment. "There's a good clear brook right over there, but to our rear there's a swamp. This is a good spot to camp, but also an easy spot to defend."

"Have you been here before?" Jenna asked.

"Yes, my father brought me. He's a scout, you know."

"Yes, the soldier who took me to your house told me he was a scout."

"Here, you! You're able-bodied. Get to work!" L'Écossais was again there, but this time he had tethered his horse and stood before them. He was most certainly well over six foot three in height, but he did not have the lean build of a basketball player. He was extremely muscular and strong like a football player. His sandy hair had sun-bleached streaks evident now that it was daylight. And his eyes! His eyes were most extraordinary. They were dark pools that could flash with anger or linger tauntingly. When he spoke to the others, he always seemed to be looking at her. It was a bold look, a look that made her wary and yet it intrigued her in a way she couldn't define.

"Go help those Indians. You'll be glad for the warmth of a wigwam when you're inside, and the fire is roaring." He pulled James to his feet and sent him off to join the other men.

"We can work too," Jenna said, pulling herself up.

She had taken a step forward, but l'Écossais restrained her by placing his large gloved hand on her arm. "A woman's work is preparing meals, tending children, keeping her man warm. This is not work for you."

Keeping her man warm. . . . As he spoke the words, his eyes had seemed to burn right through her. It was as if he were silently seducing her with his penetrating desirous look. Each of his words seemed laden with a special meaning—a suggestive meaning.

Jenna lifted her chin and looked back at him. No matter how distracting she found him, she had to make herself clear. "Women can do whatever men can do," she proclaimed. And the moment she said it, she regretted it. Again, she forgot where she was.

His reaction was immediate. He threw back his head and roared with laughter. Then he looked at her, his lips twisting in a knowing smirk. "Decency prohibits my telling you in front of all these ladies just what I can do that you cannot. But I do admire your spirit, if not your good sense."

"You're abominable!" she spit.

He did not answer her, but simply turned and walked away, shaking his head.

"You should not irritate him," Elizabeth suggested.

"You might need his protection. The Indians can be dangerous."

Jenna sat back down. Her face was still flushed from her encounter with this—this—this eighteenth century male. Then she looked at the ground. Of course, that was exactly what he was. He was an eighteenth century male.

The Indians and their white male captives made camp quickly and efficiently. Each, she surmised, had considerable practice. Soon, camp fires at the center of each wigwam burned brightly, and the Indians began to undo their packs.

Jenna and Elizabeth were herded into one wigwam together with Mrs. Belding and James.

Jenna said nothing of the bread in her own pack, although if they weren't fed, she intended on sharing it with all.

Soon l'Écossais appeared. "Here," he said, tossing a small pack on the floor. "Eat while the food is plentiful."

Then he paused and handed Jenna a container. "This is a *mocook*—or so it is called in the Algonquin tongue. It is used to carry maple sugar or sometimes wild berries. It is now filled with maple sugar. You may need it."

Jenna took the container and turned it over in her fingers. It was made of birch bark and was hand painted with intricate designs. "I can't take this," she said handing it back.

His reply was gruff. "Take it! I order you to take it!"

"Take it, please, my sister," Elizabeth whispered urgently.

Jenna nodded. "Thank you," she said not looking up at him and making her voice flat.

"Take care of it," he ordered, then he turned on his heel and left.

"He's probably smitten with you," Mrs. Belding remarked.

"I only took it because Elizabeth said we might need his protection."

"And so we might," Mrs. Belding agreed. "But, more likely, we'll need the sugar for energy."

"He's not so bad," James observed. "He's not French. He's a Scot. He told me that l'Écossais is the French word for Scot."

Jenna nodded. She should have remembered that the French name for Scotland was *l'Écosse*. "Did he tell you anything else about himself?" Jenna asked, trying to sound casual.

"He's a scout, like my father."

"Do you find him handsome?" Elizabeth asked. Her eyes twinkled slightly for the first time since they had been taken captive. "Even if he does lead the Indians and French, he is very strong."

"Probably a criminal," Mrs. Belding muttered darkly.

"I'm not at all interested in him as a man. He's much too boorish. But," Jenna added trying to give reason to her questions, "it pays to know one's enemy."

"Then he is quite a handsome boor," Elizabeth said.

"His arrogance takes precedence over everything else," Jenna concluded.

James was putting some meat onto a long green stick. He thrust it into the fire. "Women," he whispered, half under his breath.

Elizabeth paid no attention to her brother's distaste for their discussion of l'Écossais' looks. "Well, did he tell you about himself?" she asked, repeating Jenna's question. "I mean besides the fact he is a scout."

"Only that he was born in Scotland."

"A traitor to the British Crown," Mrs. Belding said

with disgust. "And to his own people. No doubt the scoundrel is a Papist too!"

Jenna kept her silence as she divided the rest of the food while James cooked the meat. Jenna, Elizabeth, and Mrs. Belding ate some meat, and then they boiled water and cooked some rice.

They all ate, and then almost immediately, laid out their blankets and collapsed onto them.

Jenna tried to think before she slept, but it was no use. She had breathed in too much fresh air and had too much exercise. Her body, her whole being, craved sleep.

Jenna opened her eyes suddenly and looked around. Somehow, she still had hope that this was some all too vivid dream. But she did not awaken in her bed at Aunt Hester's or between white hospital sheets. For the third time, she awoke to the same world in which she had fallen asleep, the world of 1704.

"Hurry," someone shouted. "We're breaking camp!"

Jenna scrambled to her feet and quickly gathered her belongings.

"Did you sleep soundly?" Elizabeth asked.

"Yes. But I'd give anything for a hot cup of coffee and a hot shower."

"What say you? Coffee—hot shower?" Elizabeth shook her head. "Life in the Virginia Colony must be different indeed."

"We warm the water and let it flow over us," Jenna said, quickly trying to explain a hot shower. And good grief, this was New England. She was certain they also drank coffee as well as tea. In fact, she was sure there were coffee houses in Boston in 1704. "Don't you drink coffee?" Jenna asked.

"I have heard of it, but not tasted it."

"Hurry, wrap your pack before the Indians come and take it from you or make you leave it," James said urgently. "We must take everything we can—we may need it."

"Why are they in such a hurry?" Jenna asked.

"Because we're only a day from Deerfield. The Indians know there is still danger of pursuit. Perhaps large reinforcements have already reached Ford Deerfield from the settlements below the Connecticut River valley."

Jenna held her tongue. There were no reinforcements coming. It would be a long while before search parties were sent out.

This time it was not l'Écossais who appeared at the entrance of their wigwam. It was a tall powerfully built Indian. He herded them silently out of the wigwam, quickly tore it down, and trampled the still smoldering fire. Then he covered the fire with earth and loose stones. Finally, he swept the ground with a tree branch.

Then they were all gathered together and given snowshoes. Under the watchful eyes of their captors they were obliged to put on the ungainly looking snowshoes.

Again, they marched on, stopping every two or three hours to rest. By nightfall, they had reached some nine miles beyond the Picommegan River. There they camped, following the same routine as they had the day before.

Gradually, Jenna put names to the faces of her fellow captives as well as to some of the Indians.

Thomas French had been the town clerk, and Mr. Williams was the town clergyman. Mrs. Williams was dead, but several of his children accompanied him including his eldest son, Samuel. In addition, Esther, Eunice, and Thankful Stebbins, Ruth Catlin who was

Elizabeth's Corse's cousin, and Sarah Hoyt were also in the group. The only married women were Mrs. Frary and Mrs. Belding.

The Indian names were the hardest. One was called Oioteet, and he seemed quite fierce, and another was Thaouvenhosen who seemed more important than the others. One almost pleasant fellow was called Suckkee-coo, and the most pleasant was called Mummicott.

But there were many villagers whose names she did not yet know except for her reading. Eventually, she would match the names to the people, she told herself.

It had been a long day of walking in the snowshoes. Jenna's legs ached as if all her muscles were in great bunches. When they stopped that night, there was hardly any conversation. They ate, and then they slept.

As morning approached, Jenna awoke. A soft rain fell against the outside of the wigwam. It was March 2, 1704.

That night they reached the banks of the Great River, which the Indians called the Quinneticot. This location, Jenna realized, was in what she knew as Vernon, Vermont.

For the first time all day, l'Écossais appeared. He strode into the small wigwam that she shared with Mrs. Belding, Elizabeth, and James. He was accompanied by the tall powerful Indian whose name she had not yet heard.

"You," he motioned to Mrs. Belding, Elizabeth, and James. "All of you, outside," l'Écossais ordered.

Jenna opened her mouth and stared at him. He seemed rigid, on edge. Why was he ordering the others away?

James hesitated and was pushed roughly by the Indian who started to lead them off.

"It's all right," Jenna said. "Do as you're told." She tried to read l'Écossais' expression, to guess what he wanted of her. Did he intend to have his way with her? She wasn't at all sure if he would force himself on her or not. He was sure of himself and arrogant, but everything else about him was a mystery. His attitude, his code of ethics—if any—she was unsure of.

"You gave them good advice," he said as he sat down. "Is there hot water?"

Jenna nodded and handed him the container of steaming hot water that had been simmering on the fire.

He carefully unwrapped a small packet and put its contents into the water. Then he produced two crude metal cups. "Coffee," he said flatly.

"You ordered the others away so we could drink coffee?" She felt incredulous. And why on earth had he seemed so angry?.

"The boy told me you wanted coffee, and I, too, desire some. But no, I did not order the others away so we could drink coffee. I ordered them away in order to speak with you alone."

"Have we anything to say to one another?" Silently, she wondered if he always seemed angry because that was what the Indians expected. His moods seemed to change suddenly.

"I will talk, and for once you will listen. You are obviously a prideful woman. You are strong too. I'm sure your legs ache, but you've gone on."

"Everyone's legs are sore from walking in the snowshoes."

"It will pass. Walking on snowshoes is an art. Once mastered, once the muscles grow strong, it becomes much easier."

"But now it is raining, and soon there will be no snow, just ice."

"Quite true and tomorrow we won't need our snowshoes. We're headed to the camp of those we left behind."

"I see," Jenna said carefully. She still didn't know what he really wanted.

"Traveling after that will be easer because all the sledges are there. Less will have to be carried."

"I'm sure that will be a relief."

"Now, I must ask you to hold your tongue. As you may have noticed, I alone speak English well. There is only one Frenchman with us, and sometimes it is difficult to control the Indians."

"I don't understand," she answered.

"Prideful woman, you and the others are captives. The Indians we lead had been wantonly attacked by soldiers sent from Fort Deerfield. Homes all along the Saint Lawrence have been burned by the English and their Mohawk allies. We raided Deerfield in revenge, and the Indians will hold all the captives for ransom."

"And if the ransom is not paid?"

"Then they will be kept as slaves."

"That's barbaric!" Jenna stared at him. "You're a civilized man, how can you permit this?"

"I am stopping worse by being here. I just explained that the Indians are hard to control. Now, you do as you are told. Do not talk back to me or someone is liable to end up dead. Be obedient."

"You cannot order me to be obedient!" Jenna's eyes blazed with indignation.

Suddenly, he reached out and took her arm. pulling her toward him. His face was close to hers, so close she could feel his hot breath on her cheeks. "Listen to me!

If you value your life, the lives of your young friends, you will do as I say!"

His eyes blazed, and for a long moment, they stared hard at each other. Then he drew in his breath, and smiled. "You have the sweet aroma of a woman. He dropped her arm and stood up, although he continued to look down at her. "It is a scent I have missed."

Jenna felt her face grow hot as he continued to look at her. He was so intense, so close. It was as if he were undressing her, ravishing her with his eyes—she felt her mouth become dry, and unconsciously she wet her lips.

"Beware sitting too close to the fire, my beauty. Its heat is penetrating."

She looked up at him, and wondered if he could see she was blushing in this light. But this time when he finished speaking, his eyes did not dwell on her. Instead, he turned.

He paused for a moment by the flap of the wigwam and spoke without looking at her. "Do you still have the box I gave you?"

"Yes," Jenna answered.

"Take great care with it."

Jenna watched as he lifted the flap and ducked through it, disappearing into the night.

Elizabeth, James, and Mrs. Belding found themselves huddled in a small wigwam with Sarah Hoyt, Mrs. Frary, and Ruth Catlin.

Ruth was the same age as Elizabeth, but she did not possess the same good looks or delicate blond coloring. She had mousy brown hair, and although her features were not unpleasant, her dour facial expression rendered her less attractive. Sarah Hoyt, also sixteen, was tall and thin. Her hair was braided, and her eyes were filled with sadness. Mrs. Frary and Mrs. Belding were brittle women, both appearing older than they were.

"The school teacher is an odd woman," Mrs. Frary commented as she poked her meat into the fire, and turned the long green stick slowly.

"Yes, I wonder if the Reverend Williams would have kept her on," Mrs. Belding added.

"I think she's very nice," Elizabeth said curtly. "She saved my brother's life and risked her own in so doing."

"Really." Mrs. Frary looked up from the fire. "And how did she do that?"

Elizabeth quickly retold the story, and James added a few of the pertinent details.

"What was she doing in the shed if your mother had let her in and escorted her to a room?" Mrs. Belding's eyebrows had lifted.

"She said she heard noises outside."

"And she just happened to have two blankets, several loaves of bread, and all those candles with her? I mean I saw what she had in her pack. How convenient."

Elizabeth found herself feeling annoyed with their questions and innuendo. "I don't know at what you are hinting, but I do knew she is a stranger in our midst, captured accidentally. I believe she deserves our help and trust. Besides, everything she had, she shared with all of us."

James, too, felt put off. He was in any case annoyed because he had been put in the wigwam with all the women. "You should be helping her, not gossiping," he added.

"Watch your tongue young man!" Mrs. Belding scowled at him and shook her finger. "Just because your mother isn't here doesn't mean you can talk as you like. I'll have the Reverend Williams box your ears if you're not polite."

"As Mother is not here, I believe I am in charge of James," Elizabeth said, looking at Mrs. Belding.

Mrs. Belding only made the disdainful guttural sound of, "Humph."

But Elizabeth was not to be put off. "I think we must be very careful," she said. "I think it would be unwise for anyone to know Jenna is not one of us."

"Is that her name? What a peculiar name," Mrs. Frary said.

Elizabeth didn't answer. "I think James and I should tell the Scotsman and the Indians that she is our sister."

"That would be a lie," Mrs. Belding said, raising her brow.

"A lie that helps protect one is different than a lie that would hurt someone," Elizabeth argued.

"I'm sure it is," James put it. "I don't mind telling everyone she is my sister. A long lost sister who was in the Virginia Colony."

"Oh, for heavens sake," Mrs. Belding muttered.

Elizabeth looked at each of them. "I want you to promise not to tell any of our captors that she isn't our sister. Do you promise?"

They all nodded their agreement.

"And we must tell the others to promise too," James suggested.

Elizabeth agreed. "I'll talk to the Reverend Williams. And he can tell the others."

"Tell the others, what?" L'Écossais peered into the wigwam, then stepped inside.

"That we shouldn't have to walk so far everyday," Elizabeth quickly said. She met his eyes and looked into them unblinkingly.

"I'm afraid nothing can be done about that. Now, you mark my warning. Don't plan any escapes or cause trouble. The Indians are hard to control. These Indians are warriors, they have little patience with schemes and plans to escape."

"We aren't planning anything," James said looking up at the tall Scotsman.

"Good," l'Écossais concluded. Then he looked at Elizabeth. "You and your brother can return to the other wigwam."

"What about me?" Mrs. Belding asked.

"Stay here," he replied.

"Jenna?" Elizabeth opened the flap of the wigwam. "We were told to come back."

Jenna smiled as James and Elizabeth crawled inside.

"Jenna, we've spoken to the others. We've decided it would be a good idea if the Scotsman and the Indians believe you are our sister."

"But won't the others tell?"

"No, they promised not to tell." Elizabeth touched Jenna's arm. "If they think you are not one of us—that you have no family—they might sell you to another tribe. I don't really know what they might do, but I fear to let them know you are a stranger among us."

Jenna covered Elizabeth's hand with hers. She rather liked the idea of playing sister to James and Elizabeth. Moreover, she was akin to them in spite of the centuries that separated them.

"I'd be honored to play your sister," she said. "Although I was not worried about being a stranger."

"It's better this way," Elizabeth reiterated. "I will talk to the Reverend Williams. You are different; some of our own women were a little suspicious about you."

Jenna searched Elizabeth's eyes—yes, she had sensed the looks the other women and girls gave her. They did think her different, and being thought different in this situation was certainly not the best thing. This, she knew, was very much the age of conformity.

James stirred the fire. "Did you find out anything when you talked with the Scotsman?"

"Only that we are on our way to meet up with some Indians who were left behind."

"We must be taken to the great camp. One of the Indians told me that," James said.

"L'Écossais told me we would summer with the Indians," Jenna revealed.

"That surely means we will be divided. Some will go with one group of Indians and some with another," James concluded.

Jenna gathered both Elizabeth and James into her arms. "We must not be separated," she said. "We *will not* be separated."

They both hugged her back, then James pulled away. "One good thing," he said looking up optimistically. "If we summer with the Indians, I will learn about their ways. I will know as much as my father."

Jenna smiled at him. In this time or any other, a ten-year-old was a ten-year-old. James Corse was filled with a boyish sense of adventure. He seemed to have few doubts about his future, about getting home to Deerfield

Elizabeth stretched out. "Tomorrow will be another hard day. We had better sleep."

Jenna agreed, and soon the three of them were under blankets and furs.

L'Écossais lay in his own wigwam and watched as the coals from the fire glowed. The camp was absolutely silent now, and he could hear the night noises of the deep woods. "I'm more comfortable here than in any other place," he said to himself.

Yes, as a man he had divided his time between city and woods. But as a boy he had spent more time in the forests, traveling with the Indians, learning their ways and coming to know their enemies, both animal and human.

He rolled over in his bedroll and lay on his back, staring upward. His thoughts were filled with the woman. For a moment, he wondered if he should have given her the *mocook*. It was important to him. In fact, it was one of the most important and valued of his possessions. The *mocook* had belonged to one he had loved, and it was all he had left of a bittersweet past.

No, it was only a wooden box. Again, he reminded himself to put no store in possessions.

He tossed back on his side, wondering why he was so restless. It was the woman. He kept thinking about her, about her pride, about her attitude which he found both annoying and intriguing. "Dangerous," he muttered. Yet she was desirable, and he most certainly wanted her even though she seemed strange—alien to this time and place. And it wasn't just her body he desired, perfect as it was. He wanted to explore her mind, confide in her, have her confide in him.

He shook his head, as if to shake himself free of her. To have the kind of relationship he wanted with this woman, meant changing his whole life, perhaps giving up his quest, his responsibility. No, he couldn't do that. He had to keep looking, and there was no room for her, even though he wanted her.

No sooner had he forced her away than he thought of the girl Elizabeth and her brother, James. They, too, presented him with a difficulty. He liked young James; he recognized his talents, and he knew, as the boy matured into a man, James would learn well. He liked the girl too. She was shy, pretty, and kind. Her eyes, too, flickered with intelligence. Yet he couldn't look at them without thinking of their father who was responsible for the greatest tragedy of his life. He shouldn't like them, he should hate them. But he couldn't. Fate had delivered them into his hands, and he vowed to protect them even though James Corse had not protected his loved ones. It was hard, not hard to like to protect them, but hard to be reminded of James Corse day after day, hard to be reminded of what had happened.

Again, he thought of Jenna, and again, he forced her from his thoughts. Soon they would reach the larger village. There would be Indian captives there. He would have to talk to them, find out if they knew anything. Oh, how he wanted to forget it all! But he couldn't forget now. He couldn't desert his memories. He could only rest when it was finished, when he found out what had happened.

Chapter Six

The rain had ceased and though the ground was still icy where the trees prevented the sun from shining, they were able to take off their snowshoes at this lower altitude and walk with greater ease on the spongy ground in just their soft moccasins.

Was it March twelfth? Jenna tried to count the days. But they all blended into one because of their unvaried routine. Each day they rose early, broke camp, hiked, rested, hiked more, than finally made camp in the early evening. It seemed as if they had been marching forever. At first, Jenna had tried to keep track of where they were and in what direction they traveled. But their route seemed to take many turns and twists.

She searched the sky above the river valley. The tall pine trees still dripped water with every movement of their branches in the wind, but the sky was blue, and great puffy clouds moved off toward the east.

The sun had already begun to lower slightly in the sky—it must be nearly four o'clock, Jenna decided.

"Each day seems longer than the one before," Elizabeth said, as they trudged along.

Suddenly, a piercing scream shattered the silence. It was a long Indian cry followed by a chorus of whoops.

The first cry had come from the head of their own column. "Listen," Jenna said, slowing her pace. "Listen—there's an answering whoop from the north."

"I hear it," Elizabeth whispered.

Again, there were whoops and yells, again answers in the distance. Then they could hear the sound of barking dogs and more cries—cries of greeting.

"We must be coming to the large encampment l'Écossais told me about," Jenna told Elizabeth. "These must be the members of the tribe that the war party left behind."

"I'm frightened," Elizabeth admitted. "This is where they'll decide our fate."

Jenna stopped and turned to look at her. She was so young. "Don't be frightened. I know everything will be all right." Jenna tried to sound confident. In truth, she wasn't certain if she should be so confident. She knew what would happen to the rest of the hostages if events came to pass as they were written in the books she had read. But in those books, Elizabeth Corse never returned to Deerfield, and naturally, she herself was not mentioned at all.

She shivered. In order for there to be any history of this event, James and the others had to return safely. Somehow, she had to watch over him, she had to make sure things happened as they should. At the same time, she had grown fond of Elizabeth and felt a need to protect her too. More and more, she began to feel her fate was tied to Elizabeth's fate. James had to return, but neither of them would return to Deerfield of that she was certain.

They moved on, single file, and then, like those before them, they rounded a sharp bend in the narrow footpath and entered a clearing. There was a ring of wigwams with smoke curling from their centers. A large outdoor fire burned, and some skins were stretched nearby to dry.

"This must be some sort of permanent campsite," Elizabeth whispered.

"I don't recall seeing any of these Indians before," Jenna said, as she searched the faces of the strangers. "Yes, I'm sure these must be the Indians who were left behind."

The Indians who stood about definitely appeared to be strangers to the prisoners, although they were certainly not strangers to their captors.

As more of the prisoners entered the clearing, the Indian dogs barked wildly. They were unkempt dogs, wolflike with matted fur and yellow eyes. All that Jenna found comforting about them was the fact that they appeared reasonably well fed.

This clearing lay near a place where the Connecticut River met a smaller stream. Behind the wigwams, a rocky mountain jutted out of the primeval landscape, and a narrow trail rose to what appeared to be a series of lookouts. Another narrow trail followed the stream which flowed into the Connecticut from the north.

The prisoners were herded into a circle, and as was the usual custom, the men and boys were separated from the women. Jenna and Elizabeth were moved in a group with the other girls and women closer to the river. There, for the time being they were left to stand around and talk to one another if they wished.

Jenna found herself studying a giant rock at the mouth of the river. The Indians, as was their habit, had carved pictographs into the stone. The newest of the pictographs revealed Indians with prisoners returning, as indeed they were, in triumph.

Their captors must have sent runners ahead because they already knew their brothers had been victorious.

She looked again at the newest pictograph. Yes, they had been victorious. This was a joyous occasion for them, and they had recorded it for those who came after.

Jenna edged closer to the rock and then ran her fingers over the carvings. Years ago—when she was ten or twelve—she had been taken to a place like this. A place with rocks that had pictographs etched into their stone. She wondered, if indeed, it had been this place. It was long ago, and the memory of her visit had faded in her own mind. Moreover, the future had changed this place, if this were the place.

Then she remembered, the rocks she had visited were a historic monument, and the state had erected a bronze plaque, a historical marker. Yes, now she remembered clearly. She had been a Girl Scout, and her troop was on a field trip here. She remembered running her fingers over the etchings then—she remembered because she had climbed over the low fence to reach the monument, and her Scout leader was angry. "You come right back over that fence young lady! Don't you touch that rock!"

Well, there was no one here now to stop her. She was now a part of the history that she once only had visited. She ran her hand over the pictograph.

"You seem interested," l'Écossais' familiar male voice suddenly said.

Jenna turned around abruptly. He stood just behind her. Elizabeth had moved away and was talking with Mrs. Belding.

"The carvings are fascinating."

"Few white people take an interest in what the Indians do."

"I'm interested. I'd like to learn their language."

"Algonquin is a difficult tongue."

"Do you know it?"

"I speak and can understand most of the time."

"Do you know what the rock means—I mean what the carvings on the rock mean?"

"They tell the story of the last Yankee massacre along the Saint Lawrence and of the wiping out of an Abnaki village. Then they tell of the retribution taken out on Deerfield, of their triumph. Tonight someone will add the final chapter. They will carve in figures revealing the number of captives."

"This fighting should stop. The Indians are being used."

He looked at her oddly, and she knew she had said too much, perhaps revealed too much. Her words, her attitude were not what they should have been for this time and place.

"You are not only a prideful woman, but you have unusual thoughts," he said again, looking her up and down boldly.

Self-consciously, Jenna pulled her cloak around her. She was all too well aware of how the clothes she wore looked. They were dirty and tattered, but also revealing. The bodice of her dress was far too low cut, and her skirt was torn up one side. She felt truly horrible, unkempt, and in need of a bath. She was beginning to feel like a wild animal. Perhaps her condition would make a good change of conversation. "We need different clothes," she complained. "These are not warm enough."

"Now that we've rejoined the main group, all the captives will be dressed in Indian garments. They are much more practical and considerably warmer," he promised.

"And I suppose all the women will hand over their rings with their old clothes. I saw what was taken from Deerfield. Some of those Indians could hardly walk under the weight of what they stole. I suppose you're a thief too."

He actually laughed at her. "Oh, my girl! It's not thievery, it's the taking of booty—you're booty!"

"I'm nobody's booty!" Jenna turned abruptly away from him. Oddly, she had no trouble forgiving the Indians because she knew their history. But who was this man? He had no excuse for his behavior. She walked on, intending to end the conversation now because, in spite of how he sometimes acted, she was suspicious of him and of the way he looked at her.

Elizabeth and the others had been moved off and were being divided up and assigned wigwams. She had been talking with l'Écossais and had not been moved. Clearly, he was important. Not even his idle conversations were interrupted.

"Halt!" his voice boomed out.

Jenna took a step and felt his strong arm circle her waist. He pulled her back and whirled her around. "I told you not to disobey!" His voice was low and menacing. He was barely moving his lips. "The Indians quickly lose respect for a man who cannot control his hostages. Especially a woman! I will have to punish you or someone else if you persist in this stupidity!"

Was he bluffing? Jenna stood still for a moment. She felt confused and unsure of what to do. She was seething inside with anger, but cautious of expressing it. He might be telling her the truth. Sometimes he seemed kind, sometimes cruel. Who knew of what acts he might actually be capable? She wasn't afraid for herself, but she had Elizabeth and young James to consider.

She took a step toward him and stood in front of him with her head down. Under her breath, she said, "Is this sufficient, my Lord, or should I kneel before you?" She spoke the words in the most sarcastic tone she could muster.

"Go to your friend!" He pointed off toward Elizabeth

who stood in front of a wigwam. Elizabeth's expression was apprehensive, but as Jenna walked toward her, she seemed to relax slightly.

"What passed between you and the Scotsman? Is everything all right?" Elizabeth asked anxiously as she touched her arm.

"Quite all right. You mustn't worry."

"I just don't know what I'd do without you. You seem to know everything, and you're so calm. Please don't leave me."

Jenna patted the girl's hand, "I won't leave you. I promise.

"Oh, dear—" Elizabeth whispered. She tugged at Jenna who turned around. James was being marched across the compound by a large Indian.

He looked around and saw them by the wigwam door. He turned and said something to the Indian who marched him toward them and then shoved him roughly toward the wigwam.

"I'm to stay with you," he whispered. "I don't know why."

Jenna pushed back the flap of the wigwam and ducked inside. The heat was welcome since the sun had disappeared, and the temperature once again seemed to be dropping. Elizabeth and James followed.

Jenna leaned over a roughly hewn pot, stirring it now and again. It was a watery stew, but still it would be hot and hopefully filling.

"The Indians are having some sort of meeting," James said as he peered outside through the wigwam flap.

"How can you tell?" Elizabeth was unfolding their pack. It included Jenna's blankets and now two skins provided by the Indians. The skins were much more practical. They were warmer, and because of the way they were dried and prepared, more or less waterproof.

"All the men are sitting round the fire, and now that they've finished talking, they're passing the pipe. That means they're sealing an agreement."

Jenna bit her lip and continued to stir. She dared not turn around for fear that she would reveal her apprehension. Elizabeth was right. At some point—she wasn't sure when—she knew that the captives would be divided and separated. Each, or in some cases each group, had gone with a different group of Indians. All of the books she had read were vague on this point, and truth be known, she was as much in the dark as Elizabeth and James. But of one thing she was sure, the point at which the separation would take place could not be far off. While they were traveling in a group, the Indians believed they were vulnerable to liberation by troops sent out to search for them from the many forts in Massachusetts. Once broken into smaller units, they knew both they and the captives would be harder to find. Those who hoped to find them and return the captives to their families would have to follow not just one trail, but many.

"Someone is coming," James said, dropping the wigwam flap and scurrying across the tent toward his sister.

The flap of the wigwam was flung open and a powerfully built Indian brave bent over. He peered in. Like the other Abnaki braves, his hair was cut short on one side, but remained long on the other. He wore a heavy skin shirt, leggings, and moccasins decorated with a few beads and matching feathers.

Jenna's eyes went to his finely sculpted face. His skin was copper colored, his eyes dark and impassive. He took a stride toward her and then taking her arm, commanded, "Woman come! Kewatin need a woman to cook his meal and give comfort."

Give comfort! Jenna stared back at him and then shook her arm loose. "Let me go! I'm not coming with you."

"You come now!"

Jenna stared back at him, and suddenly, he reached for her long red hair. In one movement, he twisted it around his hand and yanked her to her feet. She screamed and with her fist doubled, hit him as hard as she could. He lifted her as if she weighed nothing and slung her over his shoulder as if she were dead. He strode out of the compound and walked toward a large wigwam. Jenna pounded his back and screamed in vain.

In a moment, he dumped her unceremoniously on a pile of skins inside his wigwam. "White woman cook!" he demanded. He pointed to the ingredients and the pot, and he glared at her, his eyes narrow.

Jenna didn't move. He grabbed her and pulled her to her feet. Then he drew her close, holding her wrist in a way that caused her great pain if she struggled. Jenna felt the tears welling in her eyes as he pressed himself roughly against her.

With his other hand he tugged at her dress, pulling it down over her shoulder. She herself was only too aware he had exposed the curve of her breast, and she struggled, even though it hurt her. Then she began screaming, even though she suspected her screams would come to nothing. His eyes were fixed on her bare flesh, his breath was close—

"Kewatin!"

The voice was strong and male and came from outside the wigwam.

"Wait!" Kewatin answered impatiently.

In what seemed only a second, Kewatin pulled her hands behind her back and lashed her wrists together with a length of leather. Then he pushed her roughly

down on the bed of branches covered with skins and left
her without a word.

Jenna lay there for what seemed an eternity. Hot tears
ran down her face. What did he intend to do to her?
Most certainly, he intended having her, perhaps she was
to be his personal slave. Damn this time and place!
Damn, she admitted she just didn't know what to do,
what to say, or how to prevent him from fulfilling his desires.

All around, she could hear others eating, and soon
there were drums and what seemed to be a celebration
of sorts. Still nothing. No one came for her, not even
Kewatin reappeared.

Then, by the firelight, Jenna saw two large male figures outside the wigwam. She struggled to sit up and finally succeeded just as Kewatin held back the flap of the
wigwam.

"There woman," he said, then he spat on the ground.
"Bad woman, l'Écossais. You make mistake."

Behind him was l'Écossais. He was an even bigger
man than Kewatin.

For a long moment both men stared at her. Then
l'Écossais spoke.

"Take her to my tent. Lash her to a pole, hands and
feet," he ordered. "This woman must be taught a les-
son."

"Bastard!" Jenna shrieked. Why for one moment had
she even felt attracted to him—he was the worst possible
kind of man!

"Take her!" l'Écossais shouted.

Immediately, two braves appeared. They lifted her off
the ground and roughly carried her like a pig right
through the compound. They stopped by the great fire
where many braves were gathered. They all laughed at
her, and then a long pole was brought. One of the In-

dians carried the pole, and the others took her. She was taken inside a large wigwam and shoved down onto a pile of skins. The pole was driven into the ground, and then attached in some way to the wigwam. When it was secure, they lifted her up. In spite of her struggles, her hands were fastened to the pole, and then her ankles were tied. Jenna was completely immobile.

She panted from struggling, but was not truly hurt. Admittedly, those bruises she had were the result of fighting. But what was to become of her? It seemed clear l'Écossais intended beating her, then forcing himself on her—and perhaps worse.

In a few minutes, an Indian woman came. She was plump and motherly looking. Her thick hair was plaited and hung in two braids. Her body was hidden beneath layers of clothing and blankets. She carried a huge pot of hot water. She looked at Jenna, shook her head, and left without so much as a single word.

Then l'Écossais entered.

He loomed over her, his expression serious as the shadows from the fire in the center of the wigwam played on his face. His dark eyes bore through her.

"What are you going to do with me?" Jenna asked, trying hard to muster her pride.

"Whatever I want," he replied as he moved closer to her. He reached out and touched her bared shoulder, running his hand over her skin. His hand was hot, and as he moved it slowly across her flesh, she felt her face flush.

"Your body is to my liking, but your behavior is in need of correction. You have caused much trouble."

He grasped the material of her dress in his fingers, and she thought he was going to pull it away, exposing her breasts fully. But he did not. He let go of it and simply looked at her.

"What do you want?" she asked, hoping her voice did not reveal her emotions. The feel of his hand on her had caused her to tremble violently. His presence was overpowering.

"I want you to scream. Loudly, as you screamed for Kewatin."

"What?" She was filled with confusion.

"I could give you back. Kewatin wants you for his wife. He needs a wife because his wife was killed by the English. He thinks you would make a fitting replacement."

"I don't understand—" Jenna stammered.

"The pipe was smoked. The hostages and bounty divided. You were given to Kewatin. I've purchased you from him—and I might add at great cost. You and your brother and sister—James and Elizabeth. I own you now."

Jenna's mouth was dry. It was monstrous! "Nobody owns me," she returned. But there was no question her apprehension was increasing. Men could do anything!

"Please, you'll make me laugh. Do as you're told. Scream."

"But why should I scream?"

He leaned over. "You seem bright enough, but you behave stupidly. They *must* think I am punishing you, woman. You fail to understand anything. We could both be killed if they lose respect for me. Scream or I shall get a birch switch and give you good cause to scream!"

"If you were so concerned why didn't you buy me before I was given to that—that Kewatin?"

"I had no way of knowing who would claim you. And don't flatter yourself. I am concerned with all the hostages." With that, he yanked on her hair. "I'm through discussing this. Scream or I shall get the switch!"

Jenna closed her eyes and screamed. Not once, but

several times. Even as she screamed, she felt confusion rushing through her. What did he want of her? Was he really trying to help her?

Then she felt his hand on her shoulder. "Good," he said as he began to untie her.

Jenna shook her wrists, and then waited until he unbound her ankles. "Most uncomfortable," she whispered.

"But very effective for immobilization."

"What am I to do now?"

"You are to stay here with me and act the part of my woman. That is most certainly what Kewatin expects of you. You will prepare my meals and remain with me at night. Your sister and brother will be all right. If you do not obey me and act your part, you risk everything."

"And we can stay together—James and Elizabeth and I?"

He nodded. "The boy said you were his sister, and you had only just returned to Fort Deerfield the night of the raid."

"Yes, that's right. Tell me what do you want me to do," Jenna asked. She still did not really trust this man, but she had been helpless, and he could have done as he wished.

"Take a bath. Get out of those clothes and wash yourself in that water. I cannot stand to spend the night in a wigwam with a woman that looks as you do now. I have fresh clothes for you."

He handed her a clean cloth and a bar of soap. "The fire is hot, you'll dry as you wash. Those are your clothes." He pointed to a neat pile of Indian buckskin clothes. "Much more practical for being in the forest."

Jenna looked apprehensively at the flapping door of the wigwam.

"I'll watch the door."

He turned his back, and Jenna waited for only a moment. Her clothes were in tatters, and she felt terrible. Her desire to feel the hot water on her body was incredibly strong, stronger than her modesty.

Carefully, she removed the lighter she had hidden in her clothing and slipped it into the pocket of the buckskin overblouse that was folded together with the rest of the clean clothing. Then slowly, she stripped away her clothes. Once naked, she set to washing herself with a vengeance. She even plunged her hair into the water. It felt delicious to wash, to feel the warm water as she sponged it over herself. She rinsed as best she could.

At that moment, l'Écossais turned around.

Her naked body was wet and glistened in the firelight. His eyes shown brightly, wickedly, as they moved from her face downward, then slowly back up. A smile twisted on his lips. "It's only fair for a man to see that for which he paid so much."

Jenna looked down. Her skin was hot and seemed to tingle all over. His eyes were devouring her hungrily. It was almost as if she could feel him touching her, pressing her to him. The atmosphere inside the wigwam seemed heavy, tense, and filled with some form of raw electricity. She felt as if all of her nerve endings were tingling at once. Still, he only stared at her, albeit with undisguised lust.

Jenna snatched at the rough buckskin undergarment he had put near her and quickly pulled it on. It fell to below her knees. "Satisfied?" she said, tossing her wet hair back.

He watched her damp curls as they tumbled down over her shoulders. Shoulders he now knew were as white as alabaster. His eyes had told him that her skin was delicious looking and her breasts perfectly formed with lovely pink nipples. Her hips were well rounded, and her legs were long and lovely. All that had been hidden had been revealed, and she was beautiful—more beautiful than any woman he had ever had or even seen. But she was as strange as she was desirable. Her eyes said one thing, her mouth another. He did not answer her question seriously, although, in fact, he was quite satisfied with his purchase. Or would be in time.

He laughed. "I suppose you were worth the money—at least your body is worth the money. Your tongue is far too sharp to make you any real bargain."

"You're disgusting."

"Just play your role. And don't worry. I have no need to force women to my will. When you want me, you'll come to my bed willingly."

"When hell freezes over," she said coldly.

"My, what a colorful phrase. Best you try to keep your tongue in check too. Some of these Indians speak English."

"What would you have me do now?"

"Get my dinner," he replied. "But finish dressing first."

"May I see Elizabeth and James?"

"Tomorrow," he replied. "You're being punished, remember?"

Jenna nodded, vowing to keep conversation with this man at a minimum.

Jenna, adorned in Indian clothing, padded toward the stream with a large pot. It was early, and the sun had not yet melted the frost that lightly covered the ground causing it to sparkle like a field of diamonds. Yet there was no mistaking the sights and smells of spring. Here and there birds sang, and here, in the valley, at this lower altitude, one could see the bumps on the tree branches, bumps that would soon burst forth with the first buds.

"Jenna!"

Jenna looked up. Elizabeth, also carrying a pot, hurried toward her. "Oh, Jenna! Are you all right? Were you badly hurt?"

Jenna stopped and bent over the stream. "Sh! Come, come closer."

"I've been so worried about you. Oh, please tell me you weren't beaten. But you were, weren't you? I heard you screaming—what a hateful man! I did not think he was that hateful!"

"It's all right. I wasn't hurt. I was just made to scream to impress the Indians."

A frown covered Elizabeth's face. "Are you certain— you wouldn't tell me a lie would you?"

"No. No, Elizabeth, I'm all right, really. He didn't hurt me."

"I don't understand," Elizabeth said.

"Nor do I fully. But I'll try to help you to understand. He said I must act the part of his woman or the Indians will lose respect for him, and we would all be in danger. So, for now do as l'Écossais tells you. I don't fully trust him, but we have little choice if we are to stay together."

"Would they separate us?" Elizabeth's eyes were wide with fright.

"Not now, but I think the others will be separated from us three."

"How do you know?"

Jenna could not tell the truth. She could not explain that she knew all the hostages were split up—she knew from her reading. "He told me—l'Écossais told me," she lied.

"What will become of them—of us?"

Jenna couldn't answer the question. She shook her

head, then looked at Elizabeth, seeking to change the subject, lest she reveal too much. "I see you were given new clothes too."

"And one of the women brought water for a bath. It felt wonderful."

"I know," Jenna said. In spite of her experience with l'Écossais, she had enjoyed bathing and could not help wondering when she would be given another opportunity.

"Were you treated well?" Jenna asked.

"Yes. James and I are to stay with an Indian couple in their wigwam."

"We must braid your hair, Elizabeth. It will be easier to care for and won't get tangled."

"I have to help prepare breakfast now," Elizabeth told her. "But later in the day we'll meet. I'll braid your hair, and you'll braid mine."

Jenna nodded. "Take care and be careful," she advised.

Jenna turned restlessly in her bedroll, then sleepily pulled up one of the furs closer around her neck in response to the drop in temperature.

Outside, there was a noisy serenade of birds calling to one another. Jenna shook her head, becoming more fully awake. It was probably around five in the morning.

She listened for a few minutes. On the far side of the wigwam, she could hear l'Écossais breathing.

She forced her eyes closed, reminding herself that in an hour she would have to rise, reminding herself that she needed the extra hour of sleep.

It was then that she heard an ungodly whoop, and she sat bolt upright as the birds were silenced by the sudden awakening of the whole camp. Warriors were running past their wigwam, and she heard angry shouts.

L'Écossais was also awake. She saw his huge silhouette as he jumped up. He pulled up his leggings and grabbed his rifle. He was through the flap of the wigwam in a flash.

Jenna felt her heart pounding. Were they being attacked? By the British? By other Indians? None of this was in any account of the hostages she had read about. She struggled out of her bedroll and pulled on her own clothes, fumbling in the darkness with the laces. She slipped into her moccasins and hurried outside, half expecting to see the little Indian village in flames.

But there were no flames. Instead, most of the Indians seemed to be at the river's edge. They were shouting, their angry cries emphasized by clenched fists.

It was just barely dawn, just light enough to see. Jenna ran toward the river, toward the crowd of enraged Indians. Then for a second she paused. L'Écossais' voice shouted from the crowd. He was speaking their language, and she couldn't understand. Someone—one of the warriors— responded loudly. They were arguing, of that she was sure. And the warrior's voice was filled with vitriol.

Jenna deemed it dangerous to break through the crowd of Indians so she circled around a bit, moving further down the riverbank so she could see what was going on.

Partially hidden by the trunk of a great pine, she looked at the scene and was so horrified she had to cover her mouth with her hand to stifle her own scream.

Up to their waists in the still icy water of the river were Samuel Williams, Thomas French, and James! Holding them tightly, menacingly, were several Indian braves. L'Écossais had waded out to them, and now he stood, legs apart in a warlike stance, arguing loudly with

Oioteet, a large, strong Indian warrior who had already shown himself to have a foul nature.

Jenna eased closer, moving from tree to tree. But no one was watching her, all eyes were glued on the confrontation. Jenna scanned the group close to the river. Elizabeth was there. Aweont, the wife of Mummicott, had her hand firmly on Elizabeth's shoulder while Mummicott stood knee deep in the river, near l'Écossais. James and Elizabeth shared the wigwam of Aweont and Mummicott, and so it seemed that Elizabeth and James might have something to do with the angry dispute.

Then, with clarity, Jenna heard James.

"I was not trying to escape!" he shouted. "I was trying to talk the others out of it!"

"So he was," Samuel Williams confirmed. "It was my idea. If anyone is to be punished, it should be me!"

L'Écossais pushed James roughly behind him, then he spoke to Oioteet and the other braves quickly, firmly.

Mummicott grasped James and pulled him from the water, prodding him toward the shore. As James stumbled ashore, Elizabeth broke free from Aweont's grasp and went to help her brother.

L'Écossais prodded the others toward shore. Oioteet strode by his side, his face as black as a thunder cloud. As soon as he reached shore, he roughly pushed Elizabeth aside and grasped James by the arm. He pulled him roughly along with Samuel Williams and Thomas French.

Jenna hurried toward them, unable now to stay away. "What's happening?" she shouted. "Where is James being taken?"

For a moment, Oioteet stopped and stared at her. Then he flattened his hand and struck her hard across the face. The blow so startled her that she fell, managing to roll out of his way just before he kicked her.

Again, she heard l'Écossais shout angrily. Then he glared at her. "Take Elizabeth and go to the wigwam! Stay there!"

"James!" Jenna reached out, but l'Écossais struck her arm, "Do as you're told!"

Jenna sensed the angry eyes of Oioteet and Kewatin. L'Écossais's word about losing control and respect returned to her. Whatever had happened, she had to trust him at this moment. She moved away, taking Elizabeth's hand and pulling her toward the wigwam.

"They'll kill him," Elizabeth murmured. She was deathly pale and shaking.

Jenna pushed her inside the wigwam. "Tell me what happened?"

Elizabeth collapsed on the pile of furs, tears running down her face. "James heard them planning their escape. He sneaked away this morning to try to stop them, but while he was arguing with them, the sentries caught them all." Elizabeth wiped her face with her arm. "He wasn't trying to escape. He knew if Thomas and Samuel escaped the Indians would be angry, and we'd all be punished!"

Jenna put her arms around Elizabeth and held her. Elizabeth was frightened, so she tried to hide her own fear. Nothing was written about this! Perhaps things would not go as she had read. Perhaps, in this time dimension, everything was mixed up, different.

"What can we do?" Elizabeth sobbed.

Jenna just held her more tightly. "Just wait."

Blaise strode toward the wigwam of the chief. Something about the boy's story rang true. He was the son of a scout. He must know how volatile the Indians could be, and he seemed very aware of the fact that the escape of one or two would bring punishment down on the heads of all of the hostages.

For a second, he thought of the woman, sprawled on the ground. It was a wonder that Oioteet had not beaten her, or worse. And, at that moment, there was nothing he could have done to stop him, nothing that would not invite worse. Very few of the warriors were converts, very few of these Indians cared much for any white skin, male or female, French or English. And who could blame them? They had been told lies, cheated, and massacred. He knew better than most what they had suffered—images of the Abnaki village suddenly filled his mind. Wigwams smouldering, the dead and dying everywhere—and most of the woman and children gone. Where did they take you, Spring Blossom? It was a question he asked himself daily. His memories haunted him.

He seemed to remember everything about that day that now seemed so long ago. It was a crisp October morning, and a crunchy white frost covered the grass beneath the tall northern pines. He remembered turning in his bedroll and inhaling deeply of the cool pre-dawn wind that momentarily whispered through the silence of the forest. Then, as if on command of the rising sun, a symphony of birds began their morning song soon to be joined by the scampering of small animals. But he lay still, pretending to sleep while old Quoteet began the fire and started to cook breakfast. Then, when he knew it was too late for him to be sent off into the woods for kindling, he pulled himself from his bedroll and hurried to warm himself by the cracking morning fire.

Quoteet looked up and grinned. "You not really asleep. You play games."

Blaise had hung his head in shame. "I should have collected the kindling—I admit it, I was lazy."

Quoteet did not rebuke him. Instead, he handed him a bowl of gruel to which he added an ample amount of maple syrup. It was hot and sweet, the way he liked it.

"This is our last day in the forest," Quoteet said. "Eat well, we will walk all day before we are back to the village."

Quoteet was the master hunter of the village. Blaise's father had sent him with Quoteet to learn from the master. And he had not failed. They would return to the village in triumph. Quoteet had bagged two does and Blaise had shot his first buck. All three animals were dressed and ready for drying. The bounty was tied to the sledge, ready for the long walk home.

They approached the village at what must have been seven o'clock. The light was magnificent on the calm waters of the lake, and the sun sank as it had arisen, in a glow of delicate pink light. They had walked to the edge of the lake, uncovered their canoe and paddled across. The village lay beyond the first stand of trees on the other side.

Blaise remembered he had looked at Quoteet as they pulled their canoe ashore. Quoteet seemed agitated, anxious.

He himself smelled smoke, but assumed it was the smoke of the cooking fires.

Quoteet stood stark still and motioned for him to take cover. "Too quiet," he mouthed as he crept forward.

Blaise remembered he could feel his heart pounding. It was too quiet. At this hour children should have been playing, women should have been fetching lake water. Quoteet moved forward, and he followed fearfully in the shadows to one side as they entered the village.

An uncharacteristic noise escaped Quoteet's lips, a noise like an helpless animal in pain. In a second, Blaise saw what Quoteet saw—it was a panorama of horror.

Wigwams were burned, bodies lay about although none groaned and no one moved.

"James Corse and his Mohawk warriors are gone," Quoteet muttered. Then, seeing his old wife lying bloodied he sank to his knees and wailed at the rising moon.

Blaise himself ran to where his father's wigwam had stood. His father was dead; three arrows pierced his back. Nearby, his mother also lay dead. Her throat had been slit, and her thick dark hair was covered with blood.

Blaise forced himself to look—forced himself to look at all the victims of the massacre. But Spring Blossom was not there. He called her name over and over, and finally, Quoteet came to him. "They have taken her," he said quietly. "She is not here."

"I'll find her," he had vowed. "I'll find her."

He forced himself back to the here and now. Back to what faced him. If this dispute was resolved without bloodshed, he looked forward to reaching the two larger villages toward which they traveled. Both of these villages were populated with Indians who had been converted, and who had pledged themselves to the French. Everything would be easier then. But for his own personal reasons, traveling with these Indians was important. They often had Mohawk prisoners whom he could interrogate, and to him, these interrogations were all important. Still, it was dangerous to keep company with such men as Oioteet and Kewatin. The Indians, like the French and the English, had a mix of good and bad. Oioteet and Kewatin were men of treachery and would be no matter what their race.

They reached the wigwam of the old chief. L'Écossais judged him to be a fair man even if he did not trust Oioteet or Kewatin.

One by one they entered the wigwam. First the prisoners, then the warriors. He followed.

James blinked in the semidarkness of the wigwam. The old chief sat cross-legged by the burning embers of the fire. James had seen him before, but now he studied the old man's face. It was leathery with deep wrinkles. Unlike the warriors who wore their hair long on one side and short on the other, the chief had long white thin hair that reached his bony shoulders.

The chief raised his bony hand, and they all sat. James struggled to remember all the stories his father had told him. If they were to believe him, he would have to gain their respect.

The old chief pointed to Kewatin, and Kewatin spoke. James could understand nothing, but he knew Kewatin's tone was accusatory and angry. His expression was one of chiseled stone. Unlike Mummicott, who often smiled, Kewatin did not smile at all.

Next, Mummicott spoke. James felt that somehow Mummicott was speaking for him and for the others. Kewatin and Oioteet glared at Mummicott.

After that, Oioteet spoke. He was menacing, his tone hateful.

Next, the Scotsman spoke.

Then the old chief looked at James directly. "Speak slowly in your tongue. Speak for yourself."

"I went to the river to stop the escape. They had agreed to return. They were not going to escape. We were all coming back when the sentry awoke."

The old chief grunted. "Truth is easy to cover."

James suddenly spied the chopping block in the corner. He went to it and laid his right arm down. "Take my arm if you don't believe me."

"No James!" Samuel was aghast, and he started to

step forward, but the Scotsman barred his way. "The boy has challenged. Leave him alone."

Oioteet lifted his tomahawk and stood over James. James looked up at Oioteet but he did not move his arm. To flinch was to prove himself a liar.

The old chief said something, and Oioteet tensed and raised his tomahawk. As his arm lifted, James closed his eyes and held himself rigid. I will not move, I will not move, he told himself silently.

Oioteet lowered the tomahawk with incredible speed and force. It embedded itself in the chopping block a hair from James's arm.

"Brave truthful boy," the old chief intoned. "Take the prisoners away. No further punishment is to be exacted. But take warning. Any attempt to escape will result in everyone being punished."

L'Écossais grasped James's shoulder and guided him away. Even as they walked, he could feel the boy trembling. He had been badly frightened, but he hadn't flinched.

"You did well," he said.

"I tried—I remembered this story my father told me."

L'Écossais kept his silence. He had reason to hate James' father, but he could not hate the boy or his two sisters. Perhaps the father was a man of honor, perhaps circumstances had forced him to participate in events he despised. He shook his head, he, too, had been where he hadn't wanted to be and witnessed things he would rather not have witnessed.

Chapter Seven

Jenna and Elizabeth both looked up apprehensively as the Scotsman returned to the wigwam.

"Where's my brother?" Elizabeth asked anxiously. "Is he all right?"

"He's fine. He has been returned to Aweont and Mummicott. You can go to him now."

Elizabeth gave Jenna a hug and hurried away.

"What about me?"

"You can see him later. Tell me, how is it a ten-year-old boy knows more about Indian ways than his sister. You wouldn't be so much trouble if you understood them as well as young James does."

There was a flicker of admiration when l'Écossais spoke of James, and Jenna wondered what had happened. "As I've indicated to you, we weren't brought up together. I've been away."

"A poor excuse for having no sense. Were you hurt?"

Jenna shook her head. "What's going to happen next, how long will we stay here?"

He shrugged. "Some will leave tomorrow. We wait for the Mohawk prisoners to be brought."

"Why?"

"That's my business." He looked into her wide green

eyes. Such a beauty! And so curious. She didn't look like her siblings at all, and somehow he doubted they were really related. Well, truthful or not, she was certainly stunning. He found himself watching her move, thinking about her as she was the night he had watched her bathe. For a moment he imagined her beneath him, then he stood up and turned away. "I'll be back," he said hastily.

By ten o'clock the next morning, or what Jenna assumed must be around ten o'clock, the Indians who had been in the encampment when they had arrived, and many of those who had come with them, had dismantled their wigwams. The skins that had been set out to dry had been bundled up, and food and clothing had likewise been packed securely. Each of the Indians, men, women, and children, carried their share. Those who were deemed strongest carried the most, but the women carried large bundles too.

The hostages were divided up too, and they, like the Indians, were given packs to carry. There were farewells and good wishes, and then the vast majority headed out, each little band heading off in a slightly different direction.

Elizabeth stood by Jenna's side, tears running down her face. "Oh, I do hope Mrs. Belding will be all right. And the others. Oh, Jenna, what will become of them?"

"I don't really imagine the Indians want to march them about all the time. I imagine they'll be held for while, then ransomed back. You mustn't worry, Elizabeth. I know they'll survive."

"You sound so sure of yourself, as if you can see into the future. I want to believe everything you say."

Jenna looked into Elizabeth's blue eyes. She could

never explain that she could, in a sense, see into the future. She knew that one by one, the captives would return to rebuild their community. Some would be gone as long as two years, but most would return within a matter of months. "I feel I'm right," Jenna said, amending herself. "But I do feel it strongly."

"And what about the three of us?"

"We'll survive too. Just remember to treat me as your sister. It is important that l'Écoassis continue to think we're related. We don't want to be separated."

"I shan't forget. I am beginning to think of you as my sister in any case. Even if you do sometimes talk most strangely. If I ever return to my people, I will want to visit the Virginia Colony to see your home. I had just never imagined people could be so different."

"People are all different," Jenna said. "But there is good and bad everywhere."

"I even like some of the Indians," Elizabeth confessed. "Aweont is good to us. I should hate to leave her. Will we, too, be going soon?"

Jenna nodded. "I'm sure we'll be moving on too. Not today, but soon. L'Écossais said he had to wait for the Mohawk prisoners to be brought."

"I wonder why," Elizabeth replied.

"He doesn't explain anything," Jenna answered. "We'll just have to wait."

"There isn't much substance to this stew," Jenna complained as she stirred the pot over the fire.

L'Écossais lay on his pile of furs. In Jenna's eyes, he was playing the lord of the manor, so to speak. Not that their wigwam was a manor. But it was his attitude, a part of her hated him for enjoying the fact that he had forced her into this mistresslike role. Yet her emotions were at war. Another part of her was grateful for his protection, especially when Kewatin or Oioteet were about.

"It's nourishing enough for days when we're at rest and not traveling."

He withdrew a long knife from a sheath he always wore and began sharpening it on a whetstone.

"How long did you say we be staying here?"

"My, aren't we curious tonight? And talkative too. You've barely said a word to me since we began sharing a wigwam."

Jenna didn't look up at him, but instead continued to stir the pot, even though it didn't need it. "I just wondered, you said something about Mohawk prisoners."

"Two were brought this morning. I've finished with them."

"I don't understand."

"We'll be leaving day after tomorrow. That's all you need to know."

Clearly he had no intention of explaining his interest in the Mohawks. "Will we be leaving alone?"

"No, of course not. There'll be the four of us and about ten Indians."

Jenna digested the information and wondered if she should ask more questions. She waited for a few minutes, than asked, "And what is our destination?"

"Quebec eventually. But first we'll be spending most of the summer in a large Indian village on the other side of the Saint Lawrence River. Then in late August we'll go to Quebec."

"Is the village far?"

"Yes. But there are villages between, places we'll stay."

Jenna picked up the crude bowls and began dishing

up the stew. "I hope the food is more substantial in the next village."

He looked at her and shook his head. "Sometimes you seem intelligent and at other times quite stupid. It should be obvious to you that game is scarce and that is why the food is so "unsubstantial" as you put it. It's been a hard winter and much of the game is just waking from winter's sleep.

"Soon it will be time for spring hunting and fishing. We'll be well fed, and we can stock up for the longer part of our journey. To go so far with less than the meat of one buck is dangerous indeed."

"I hadn't thought of that," Jenna admitted in a voice that was barely audible. No one understood her attitude, or the odd mistakes she made. To be suddenly transported back into another time meant a huge adjustment. She reminded herself that she would have to remember that refrigeration did not exist—that food was not purchased but hunted and carefully preserved in salt or dried.

"What do you miss most about civilization?" he suddenly asked.

Civilization? Had he guessed her thoughts? No, he probably meant Williamsburg. He couldn't begin to guess what she missed about her civilization. But of course he meant civilization as he knew it. "Bread," she answered. "I like bread with stew."

And there was some truth in her comment. They had eaten the last of the bread she had brought weeks ago. She did miss it.

"The women of the larger village by the lake—the one where we will spend more time—make a flat corn bread, but we won't have real bread till we're home."

He meant yeast bread, she guessed. But yeast could be made—or at least she thought it could. Once she and a friend had made sourdough bread, it made its own yeast as the flour and milk soured. Still, there was no milk. She filed the thought away anyway. Perhaps she would have the opportunity to try again to make sourdough bread.

"Are your sister and brother all right?"

Jenna shrugged. "As well as prisoners can be."

"They seem to tire easily. You must look after them."

Jenna frowned. His observation was good. They did seem to tire easily, and she wondered why. At first she had assumed it was the unusual amount of exercise, but they hadn't been on the move now for several days.

"There's a disease we Europeans seem to get. It loosens our teeth and makes us very weak. In the end, it turns the skin black, and we die."

"Scurvy," Jenna said as she recalled the descriptions of the early explorers and the settlers.

"Yes, that's the English name."

Jenna felt herself truly beginning to worry. Weariness was certainly one of the early symptoms. "The Indians don't get it, do they?"

He shook his head. "No, but they get all manner of other diseases. They blame us for bringing them pox."

Jenna knew about the terrible smallpox epidemics. But for now her concern was with scurvy. She had to find a way to use her knowledge without betraying herself. "The Indians make a tea," Jenna said slowly, "of pine needles. I have heard it prevents scurvy." She well remembered reading how Cartier's men had been saved by the Indian tea. Had they not realized? Of course, they hadn't. Everyone in her own time knew, but they hadn't known then that scurvy was caused by a lack of vitamin C and neither did l'Écossais.

"I know the tea. It's vile."

"We must drink it,' she said with determination. "Can you ask for some?"

"Yes. How do you know this?"

It was her excuse for everything. "It is what is taken in the Virginia Colony."

"How advanced the Virginia Colony must be," he said somewhat sarcastically.

"Just please get me the tea."

He raised a brow. "Since you said please, I will ask one of the Indian women to show you how to make it."

Jenna took a sip of her stew. It had no greens. Yes, the tea would be necessary because it contained vitamin C—ascorbic acid, the absence of which caused the deadly and painful scurvy.

"It's quiet," l'Écossais said as he drained his bowl.

"Yes."

"There aren't so many of us now. I think I shall walk for a bit. Will you join me?"

Jenna looked up and then struggled to her feet. "Yes," she replied. "Some exercise will be good."

Jenna looked at Elizabeth and James as they sat, one in front of the other in the canoe. Each day they seemed to look more as if they belonged with the Indians.

Elizabeth, although blond and blue-eyed, grew tan from daily exposure to the sun. She wore her long flaxen hair in a single thick braid, interwoven with a long strip of leather. Her clothes were Indian garments. She wore a buckskin dress with an overvest, and she had buckskin leggings and wore moccasins. Her vest was belted, and attached to the belt she wore a *mocook*, like the one l'Écossais gave me, Jenna thought, unconsciously looking at her own *mocook*. The small container was meant to hold wild berries, maple sugar, rice, or corn. Hers had originally contained maple sugar, but that was gone now. Both *mocooks* held rice.

James, whose coloring was quite different from his sister's, had turned even darker from the sun. He had dark hair, brown eyes, and fine features. He had those dark looks for which the Corse men, even in her own time, were known. His eyes were one of his most interesting features. They were questioning and soft, almost like the eyes of a doe. But James himself was not soft. He was a typical adventurous boy who was both curious and strong. He was a young man who seemed to enjoy learning about the Indians, and who, in turn, had won their affection. James, she knew, would grow to be one of the most famous scouts in New England. He would learn from his father and stepmother. The family history recorded that long after Mrs. Corse disappeared, her husband remarried. The woman he married was the daughter of a Mohawk chief.

Jenna could not help but think that when he was older, young James would be most popular with the girls. He would grow to have that rugged quality that women were attracted to, while at the same time he would have the soft kindness that would make them fall in love.

She was thinking these thoughts about her "pretend" siblings as they moved through the water. Then she looked at l'Écossais and grew angry all over again as she recalled last night's conversation with him. They had been sitting in the wigwam in front of the fire. Usually, he left right after dinner, but he had lingered, and she had rightly assumed he wanted to speak with her. He was a strange man, a mysterious man, she thought. He always seemed to be stealing glances of her, yet he remained aloof and spoke to her hardly at all.

But whenever he did hang about, she knew he had

something to tell her. "We're leaving tomorrow morning," he said curtly.

They had been in this village for some time, longer than he had originally indicated. But whenever she asked when they were leaving, he simply shrugged and told her she would be told when the time came.

"You could have told me sooner," she complained. "There's a lot to pack."

"Not so much."

Jenna frowned. "If we are traveling by canoe, what will become of your horse?"

He laughed and looked into her eyes. "I traded the horse to Kewatin for you. I told you, you cost me dearly!"

"You traded three humans for a horse and you think the cost was dear?" She was outraged by his attitude.

"Just you for the horse. I had to pay gold for the other two. And just why do you look so angry? He was a fine horse."

Jenna had pressed her lips together and stared at him. Then, it was she who had left. She stomped out of the wigwam to tell Elizabeth and James they would be leaving. But really, she had left to escape his mocking eyes and his constant reminders that she was his property.

They left early. Then for the first time she understood why they had been waiting in the village. They had waited for the ice to break up in the rivers so that they could travel by canoe.

And Jenna had been totally surprised to discover the canoes. They appeared in the river by the village as if by magic. It was then she learned that they had been there all along, hidden upstream in heavy brush, lest the village be discovered. The Indians were still very careful. They posted guards every night, and they hid their means of transportation in case of a raid.

She learned that one of the canoes was what they called a Montreal Canoe. It was forty feet long, and James said it was capable of carrying four to five tons. It was carefully filled with furs, with cooking utensils, and with the rich bounty taken from the Deerfield homes. Six Indians paddled this canoe. As l'Écossais explained, they would take it further up stream, then more Indians would meet them and take over the transport of this larger canoe.

In addition, there were four other canoes. For this part of the journey, all of the gear was in the large canoe so that the canoes in which they traveled were reasonably roomy, even though the manner of travel was, Jenna soon discovered, terribly uncomfortable.

She sat in the middle, while l'Écossais paddled in the bow position and an Indian paddled in the stern position. James and Elizabeth were each in two other canoes, while the fourth was filled with Indians. Two men and four women. One of the women was Aweont who carried her papoose on her back.

Never, Jenna thought miserably, had she dreamed canoeing could be so painful. As an observer, she had watched sleek modern fiberglass canoes glide across the water, their crews barely seeming to exert themselves as they paddled in magical unison.

But she was no observer now. And this was not a fiberglass canoe with cushions for her knees. Nor, she thought, had it ever occurred to her that those in canoes were not actually sitting, but rather kneeling.

Regardless of whether one was paddling or not, the kneeling position for hours on end was awful. Her legs cramped up, and she was certain her knees had blisters, and even slivers, though she kneeled on a piece of the fur, and her legs were covered with leggings.

Elizabeth said she had canoed often before and was

used to kneeling. James took to the experience most enthusiastically and indeed, now did some of the paddling
under the expert tutelage of Mummicott. Both Mummicott and Aweont, whose name meant Growing Flower,
actually seemed fond of Elizabeth and James.

Mummicott had made it clear he intended to train
James to be a warrior and hunter, and Aweont had already begun to teach Elizabeth to bead and to carry
things by what was called a tumpline. These were
woven bands, most often carried round the forehead
which had ties at the end so that the women could carry
baskets, babies, and other burdens on their backs. These
skillfully woven tumplines were also used to support
wooden pack frames used on longer trips made on foot.

Jenna wiggled a little, trying again to get a little circu-
lation in her legs. It had been hours and hours! She felt
as if she would never walk again.

"Sit still!" l'Écossais shouted at her. "The water is
freezing! You could kill us if you dump the canoe!"

Her face flushed again with anger and discomfort.
Hours ago, when she had first climbed into the canoe,
she had nearly tipped it over, and he had shouted at her
then too.

"Have you never been in a canoe, woman?"

Jenna shook her head helplessly.

He grimaced, then leaned over and painstakingly explained to her how to climb into the canoe by laying a
paddle across the gunwales.

She had tried it and after much effort had finally
climbed in.

L'Écossais roared with laughter as did all the Indians.

"You're backwards," he said finally. "Please turn
around."

Jenna stood up and tried to turn, but somehow the
paddle was between her legs and caught in the ribs of

the canoe. The canoe rocked dangerously and most certainly would have tipped had several Indians not stabilized it.

"Ouch!" Jenna said as she cursed under her breath. The canoe was an abominable invention.

But she had finally wrenched the paddle free. And somehow she'd managed to get into the right position.

L'Écossais was still laughing. "I'm afraid you'll hurt yourself until you learn the proper way to get in and out of a canoe."

Jenna gritted her teeth.

It was another hour. The worst hour yet. Then, she heard Mummicott give some sort of order, and the canoes were guided, one by one, toward the shore.

The Indians fairly sprang from the canoes. L'Écossais got out and turned and looked at her. "Just as you got in—take the paddle and put it over the gunwales to stabilize the canoe."

Jenna did as instructed. She tried to stand, but she couldn't even feel her legs. By force of pure will, she lifted one leg and then the other. As the blood began to flow, both legs felt as if they were being stuck with a thousand tiny pins. She stood up just as her legs went completely weak. Her knees buckled, and she started to fall. L'Écoassis caught her in his arms.

He lifted her and carried her ashore. His expression was more than she could bear. He looked triumphal and bemused at the same time.

He carried her some distance through the trees. He seemed to know the territory, as if he had been here many times before. It amazed her. It all looked alike to her. Perhaps he saw some landmarks, she saw none, just a confusing sameness, a sameness that could result in her becoming forever lost if she ever tried to wander.

"Here we are."

They entered a small clearing. The sun shone brightly, warmly, and the grass was thick and green. Nearby there was a stand of tall trees, and through them she could see a lake. It was as blue as blue could be, its waters glistening in the sunlight.

He set her gently down on the grass. "There, let's see those legs now." He tugged on her leggings in what seemed a thoroughly indecent way, and she felt herself going absolutely tense. How silly! How absurd! In her own time, she had lain on warm beaches in a string bikini, now suddenly she wondered about the propriety of having this man see her legs! My trip through the centuries must now be complete, she thought.

"There we are," he said, laying her buckskin leggings aside.

Jenna stared in horror at her own white legs. They looked a bit swollen, and her knees were red, almost raw from kneeling.

He shook his head. "Bad," he concluded. "It's hard for me to imagine a woman who has lived on the frontier who has so few callouses. Your feet are dainty, like a princess. Your hands are white, soft, and show no signs of work. And your legs and feet! It's as if you've never walked."

Jenna frowned, wondering how to answer him. How could she explain that she was, in fact, quite a hiker, but that in her time shoes were better designed and far more protective.

For that matter, how could she explain that machines did all the work, that in a sense she was pampered, especially when compared to the women of Deerfield.

He touched her bare legs with his warm hands and began rubbing them. His hands were strong, and he seemed to know what he was doing as he massaged her tired aching muscles and strained tendons. She leaned back and closed her eyes, feeling for the moment only the wonderfully pleasant sensation of his surprisingly skillful massage.

His hands seemed so warm—his movements almost made her groan with pure pleasure.

"How does that feel?" he asked after a few minutes.

"Oh, much better," Jenna allowed. His face held real concern, and for a moment, she felt they might even become friends. Perhaps he wasn't as bad as she thought, perhaps he was really a decent man.

He moved slightly, then having eased closer to her, continued his massage. "We'll have to make you some kneepads for the next leg of the journey by water."

"You said we had to portage tomorrow. Are we going overland to another river?"

"No, just past the rapids in this one."

She took in the information, trying to conjure up a map in her mind. But they'd come too far overland through the thick woods. She knew they were still somewhere in what was now Vermont or even perhaps upper New York state, but she didn't know where. Then, too, it seemed to her that they had journeyed out of their way to the west, rather then heading for the valley of the Saint Lawrence directly. But she knew that any trip was much different now than in her time. They probably had to go out of their way to avoid the high mountains that would still be covered in deep snow. Hadn't she herself often gone skiing in New Hampshire, Maine, and Vermont in the spring?

"There," he said. "Now, let's try walking around."

He stood up and held out his hands to help her to her feet. Jenna let him pull her up. The soft cool grass felt wonderful, and she moved her toes ever so slightly in pleasure.

"We'll walk slowly back to where we're making camp,

then after dinner we'll walk a little more. I'll keep an eye on you tomorrow. If you have too much trouble we can always drag you by litter."

"I'm sure I'll be all right," she replied, as she looked into his eyes.

They were perhaps two feet apart, but she could feel his eyes as if they were somehow commanding her. Again, she was aware of his strong masculine presence, of the way his eyes studied her. Again, she could almost feel his lips on hers as if once again they had kissed, not in reality, but in desire. He had an animal magnetism, and she could sense his desire for her even as she tried to control her own for him. It was momentary; it would pass she told herself.

"I have to make sure my property arrives in Quebec undamaged," he said, breaking the heavy sensual silence between them.

His mouth twisted ever so slightly, and his eyes twinkled with mischief. But she reacted immediately. She was not his property, not in this century or any other. She was her own person and he was toying with her emotions.

"I belong to no one," she said haughtily, then she turned and picked up her leggings. She pulled them on, and trying not to stagger on her wobbly legs, reluctantly slipped on her moccasins. He was grinning at her, laughing at her discomfort. She turned and walked off toward the sound of voices.

"Wait!"

Jenna stopped, but did not turn around to face him.

"You're a strange woman. You don't behave as other women behave. But I see desire in your eyes, and I know that look. Together we could . . ."

"Stop it!" Jenna whirled around, her face flushed.

"I'm your prisoner. Whatever you think you see—you're mistaken. I don't desire you. Not one bit."

"One moment I see fire, the next I see ice. Go on your way."

Jenna looked at him for one long moment. Inside her, emotions surged and she seemed at war with herself. What did he want? What would happen later when they got to Quebec? She admitted to herself that she didn't know how to react to this man—or she didn't trust her reactions. They were, in reality, centuries apart. His attitudes, his feelings—his desires—I don't understand him she thought, and most certainly, he can't understand me. Could I tell him? Certainly not. She discarded the idea immediately. He would think she was a witch. She might be harmed. No, she could tell no one because she could trust no one. She would have to continue to be careful, to take one thing at a time, and to try to find a way to help young James get home.

Jenna collapsed under the great pine tree and watched as Aweont built a fire nearby and put on water to boil. Her legs ached from walking just the short distance back to the camp. She dreaded the thought of having to spend tomorrow hiking.

"You asked about our tonic," Aweont said to her when the water began to boil.

Jenna tried to think. Tonic? Had she asked about tonic? "Oh, the tea," she said suddenly, remembering.

"I have collected the pine needles and will make you some."

"For all of us—for my sister and brother and for him." She pointed to l'Écossais who had followed her back and was talking with two of the Indian braves.

"He will not drink it."

"I will see to it that he does."

Jenna watched as Aweont put the needles of the white

pine into the boiling water. She stirred it several times,
then removed it from the heat so it could steep.

"You don't swallow the pine needles," she instructed.
"No good."

Jenna nodded, wishing for a strainer or filter of some
sort. But such things were unknown. Then she thought
that with a piece of cloth she could make a bag strainer
as one might do for jelly. She fished in her sack and
withdrew the scarf she had been wearing the night of
the Indian raid on Deerfield, the scarf given to her by
the girl in the cabin.

She carefully tied the scarf around the top of a
smaller pot with leather, then while Aweont watched,
fascinated, she poured the liquid through the cloth,
straining out the needles.

"White woman clever," Aweont said, nodding
thoughtfully. "Pine needles bad, make bad cough if
swallowed."

Jenna poured the dark hot tea into four tin cups.
"Elizabeth, James!" she called out. "L'Écossais." She
even hated saying his name, and it occurred to her that
l'Écossais was probably his last name. Vaguely, she wondered what his first name was.

Elizabeth and James came right away, and l'Écossais
came after a moment.

"What is it?" he asked, mindful that Elizabeth and
James stood by her side.

"Aweont has made this tea of white pine needles. You
must all drink some."

Elizabeth and James took the tin cups and looked dis-
tastefully at the liquid offered. L'Écossais shook his head.

"I tried it once, it tastes vile."

"You will all drink it no matter how terrible it tastes.
I will drink it too. It prevents scurvy."

"That's what the Indians say, but they have a vast

store of medicines and stories to go with them. I don't believe in most of them," l'Écossais muttered scornfully.

"About this they are right even if they don't understand why it works. Cartier gave this tea to his men, and they survived."

L'Écossais raised his brow in surprise. "You know of Cartier?"

Jenna felt suddenly trapped. Should she know? If so, how? Were there books available? It was imperative she make her answer sound believable.

When I was in the Virginia Colony I met a Frenchman. He told me this story and I believe it to be true. Now drink the tea."

Elizabeth lifted the cup to her lips and making a face drank it all down in great gulps. She shuddered. "It is indeed horrible."

"You'll feel better and less tired if we drink some every day." With that she drank her own down, trying not to make a face or let on how bitter it really was.

James looked at her and his sister. Not to be outdone by women, he drank his quickly and in large gulps like his sister.

L'Écossais grimaced, but he, too, drank the brew. "I suppose it's worth it if there's even a chance it works," he allowed.

Jenna only nodded. Then she asked, "What are we to eat tonight?"

"There isn't much. We must hunt now. Perhaps we'll return with some small game."

"I want to go," James said. "I want to go hunting too."

L'Écossais smiled. "I'll ask Mummicott if you can come."

"It's dangerous," Jenna said. "He's too young."

"Nonsense," l'Écossais muttered. "The boy should

learn to use a bow and arrows. Indian boys much younger than James use their bows well. After all, the art of hunting means the difference between life and death."

Jenna looked around. Yes, she knew full well that young Indian boys used the bow. She would have to struggle to remember where she was and what the necessities were. If James ever became lost or separated he would need the skills he could learn. Doubtless, she thought, he probably has already used a rifle.

"All right," Jenna said. "Will you teach him?"

"I'll look after him, but it is Mummicott who must teach him. He must make his own bow and arrows."

"While we're out I'll look for the right wood," James said enthusiastically. "Mummicott told me that I must have one good length of springy wood such as shagbark hickory, white ash, or the like."

"Cedar or white oak can also be used."

"Can I start making my bow when we get to the village?"

L'Écossais smiled. "Yes, and there should be young braves for you to go hunting with. Every man must hunt, and every woman must work. We cannot afford to feed those who don't work."

Jenna turned and hobbled into the wigwam. Did he mean her? Was he trying to tell her she wasn't holding up her end of things? She picked up the cooking pot angrily and hurried out of the wigwam, limping toward the nearby stream.

Shortly, l'Écossais came into the wigwam.

Jenna lay by the fire. Morning would come all too soon.

"How was hunting?"

"Sufficient. We have rabbit. Aweont is cooking rabbit stew now."

He moved silently to her side, then rolled up her leggings.

Jenna started to speak, but then said nothing. She only closed her eyes as he began again to gently massage her legs and feet. He moved her muscles and rubbed slowly. In spite of herself, she began to relax.

"Are you as stiff as you were? Does this help?"

"It feels good," she admitted. His hands were warm on her skin, and her stiffness responded to his movements. But she couldn't look into his eyes. Whenever she did, she could feel him taking her mentally, and she did not want to repeat what had happened this afternoon.

"I'm not sure I can walk," she admitted.

"Good heavens, woman, whatever possessed you to come to the frontier! How is it your brother and sister are so adept?"

"I told you. I was away in the Virginia Colony." This sorry excuse for lack of knowledge about, and experience in, this time and place was starting to sound weak even to her.

He laughed. "So you keep telling me, but woman, Williamsburg isn't London town. Can it be you have actually never traveled by canoe?"

"Never that I can remember."

"I can't imagine that," he finally answered.

"I had better sleep if I am to try to walk tomorrow."

"I'm going to have some rabbit stew. Shall I bring you some?"

"No, I'd rather sleep."

He stood up, and Jenna pulled the fur over herself and rolled on her side. His shadow was on the side of the wigwam as he turned to leave. "Do you have a first name?" she suddenly asked.

"Blaise," he replied.

Jenna felt a certain pride that she had in fact walked and not needed a litter. Then she had traveled two days in the canoe, although both days were broken with frequent portages. They had finished eating, and Jenna stood outside the wigwam, watching Aweont as she fed her child.

Aweont, Mummicott's wife, was by Jenna's assessment, a woman in her mid twenties. Although, Jenna conceded, it was terribly difficult to tell because the Indians led a hard life, most of it out of doors, and the weather and their manner of living tended to age the women prematurely.

Aweont had a small baby, and she had disclosed that she had three other children as well, but that they were with the rest of tribe in the village toward which they were all traveling.

During the time she had been traveling with the Indians, Jenna had begun to differentiate appearance and manner of dress. Hairstyles were a particular indication of tribe, she learned.

Aweont, for example, wore an ornamented square cap on her head. Her hair, like most Indians, was almost bluish black, parted in the middle, and was worn in two braids. Other groups wore braids with leather or beads entwined, some had loose hair, while still others heavily greased their hair and simply pulled it back into a pony tail.

The Algonquin, like other Native Americans, had little or no body hair, and the hair on their heads seldom seem to go gray, nor did the older men have a tendency toward balding. The old chief had gray hair, but he was very old, perhaps as old as eighty.

Aweont, by any standards would have been considered quite beautiful, Jenna decided. Perhaps in modern times, she might have become a model. She was tall and slim. Her body was well toned from exercise, and her copper skin was flawless. Her hair was shiny, her eyes like bright brown shoe buttons, and her mouth full enough to be sensuous. She had wonderful high cheekbones and a long graceful neck.

Mummicott, her husband was a handsome man. Together, with their small papoose, they seemed an ideal family.

Aweont finished feeding the child. "Come," she said, motioning to Jenna.

"You will come into my wigwam," Aweont said without explanation.

Jenna did not question Aweont because she knew her knowledge of English was limited. Instead, she followed her to her wigwam.

"Inside," Aweont directed as she half opened the flap.

Inside, by the fire, Elizabeth sat cross-legged.

"Where is your brother?" Jenna asked.

"Gone to your wigwam with Mummicott and Blaise. He's learning to make a bow and arrows. We're to learn to make *wampum.*"

"*Wampum?*" Jenna repeated. She certainly knew the word, though she had only the vaguest idea what it was.

"*Wampumpeag,*" Aweont corrected. She held up a string of shell beads.

Jenna looked at it curiously. Either it had been made on the coast by Indians and traded this far inland, or it was made from shells taken from the shores of some large inland lake. No, upon closer inspection, she decided the sample was made of shells that could probably only be found in the sea.

"We use *wampumpeag* to make treaties, for gifts, to make . . ." Aweont searched for words, then did a sort of pantomime.

"For decorations," Elizabeth guessed.

"Aweont smiled and nodded. It was clear that she was learning English from Elizabeth and perhaps from James as well.

"I've seen *wampum* belts before," Elizabeth said. "They're made of quahog and periwinkle shells. Such shells are traded to the inland tribes. But the Mohawk use Otekoa, a freshwater shell from what they say is a great inland lake."

The Great Lakes, Jenna thought. But for once she held her tongue. "Have you such beads?" she asked Aweont.

Aweont nodded and withdrew a box from her pack. It was a birch-bark box about the size of a shoebox. She opened it, revealing a wealth of purple and white shells.

"Hard work done," she said, illustrating the fact that tiny holes had been drilled lengthwise in each of the shells.

"We're going to learn to string them using animal sinews. Sometimes the belts that are made are several feet long," Elizabeth revealed.

"A gift for the great chief of the village," Aweont told them. "He will keep us till summer, then your master will take you home."

Jenna frowned but did not correct Aweont. Still, she wondered what the native woman thought of the idea that she had expressed without a second thought. "Is Mummicott your master?" Jenna asked.

Aweont shook her head. "He is my husband."

"And were you given to him by your father?"

"No!" Aweont answered, her eyebrows lifting. "In our way, two people choose to be together. But we are Christians, converted by the Black Robes. We were married in the white man's way after we chose."

Clearly, Algonquin customs were different from those of most of the Native Americans she had read about. And converted! It had never occurred to her that the Indians with whom they traveled were converts to Catholicism. Although, she thought in retrospect, it should not have surprised her so very much.

"You choose, but we are owned by Blaise l'Écossais."

"You are not unfortunate. He is wealthy. He is rich in white man's *wampumpeag*."

"How can you believe in freedom of choice, and accept the fact that it is all right for us to be slaves?" Jenna prodded.

Elizabeth's mouth was open ever so slightly, and Jenna could see she was uncomfortable with the discussion, doubtless because she liked Aweont.

"A slave is a slave until the price of the crime is paid," Aweont said matter-of-factly. "If Mummicott killed the son of Wannpacoo, then Wannpacoo would take our papoose for his own—to replace his dead child. If one tribe kills the braves of another tribe with whom they are at peace, those braves must be replaced by slaves from the offending village."

Jenna was sure she looked as confused as she felt. Aweont seemed to have a very clear sense of right and wrong. What's more, Aweont did not define slavery in quite the same way she did. She seemed to think of it more as replacement—and replacement for a loved one, at that.

"Mohawks and English tongues killed many of my people and many French tongues. Our captives will serve till the debt of the crime is paid in full. Englishtongued women will bear French-tongued children. But some will be ransomed, and the money received will pay the debt instead."

Jenna glanced uneasily at Elizabeth. Was this to be her fate? Was she to be forced into an early marriage with a Frenchman in order to make up for the fact that his wife and family may have been killed in one of the frequent raids? Was this, indeed, to be her fate? Had this Blaise lost his family? Vaguely, she wondered about Aweont's contention that he was wealthy. In Aweont's terms, almost anyone might seem wealthy. Were there indeed wealthy Frenchmen in Quebec? She admitted that for all she knew about Massachusetts and the history of Deerfield, like most Americans her knowledge of Quebec and Canada was almost nonexistent. Yes, each day she, James, and Elizabeth were traveling further into the unknown.

"Here," Aweont said, handing her a length of sinew attached to a fine bone needle. Then, taking her own length, she picked up a shell and illustrated how to push the needle through the elongated hole.

Jenna and Elizabeth both did as they were instructed, and while they worked, Aweont began a long story which she told in English, resorting to French only when she was unsure of the right words. Jenna held her tongue, determined to hide for a while longer the fact that she understood French better than she had let on.

Jenna, Elizabeth, and James moved through the woods single file. They were preceded by warriors, then the wives of the warriors, and then Mummicott and his wife, Aweont. Blaise and several more Indians brought up the rear.

They had risen early and broken camp, then once

again they had taken to the canoes. Sometime around
ten there had been a short portage, then once again
they were on the water. Now, they had beached the canoes, hidden them beneath branches, and carrying what
they could, launched out for the village which, Blaise
had explained, lay in a well protected area about a mile
from the river.

"I'm sure they know we're here," Elizabeth said, eyeing the trees. "I'm sure scouts from the village are
watching."

"Why don't they show themselves?" Jenna asked.

"It's not the custom," James replied. He used a stick
now when he walked, and he prodded the ground, looking for tracks. Mummicott was teaching him to track,
and now and again, Mummicott would stop and draw
James's attention to some sign that an animal had
passed this way.

"I smell smoke," Elizabeth whispered.

"Yes, we must be close," Jenna agreed.

No sooner had the words escaped her mouth than
dogs began to bark, and the sound of barking was followed by the traditional whoops and hollers of greeting.

They passed through a short section of heavy brush,
then burst forth into the village. It was the largest village
thy had been in, and clearly the most permanent since
one could see where gardens had already been laid out,
indicating that someone was to be here in the fall to
harvest the bounty. There were, Jenna counted, at least
forty wigwams, and in addition there were two permanent structures. One was rather like the pictures of Iroquois long houses she remembered seeing in books, but
its roof was slightly more rounded, although she assumed it could have the same purpose. The other was
quite clearly a chapel.

Even the familiar wigwams were different. They were

more proper dwellings with rounded roofs. Clearly, they had a frame rather like that of a geodesic dome even though they were covered with skins like the more temporary variety.

A large group of Indian children who had been playing lacrosse, a game Jenna knew was commonly played by Native Americans, stopped playing and stared at them as they entered the village.

Suddenly, two of the children bolted and ran toward Aweont. They hugged her ferociously, and she bent over and hugged them back. She took their hands, and they fell in step with her as they moved on.

Women stood and stared, and the whole populace seemed to part, making a path to the largest and most prominent of the wigwams. In front of it, an older man sat cross-legged. He wore a few feathers at the back of his hair, and he wore a long belt made of *wampum*. He was an older man, but not as old as the chief in the village they had left.

The group was brought to a halt in front of him, and Aweont immediately stepped forward and presented the chief with the *wampum* belt. She bowed as she did so, and he lifted his hand and made the gesture of peace.

After that, all of the men in the party sat down around the chief. Aweont gathered the women about her and took them away, following another woman who led them to various wigwams clearly meant for them. "We were expected," Aweont managed. As usual, she took James and Elizabeth with her, showing Jenna the wigwam she was clearly to share with Blaise.

Jenna stepped inside and let her pack slip from her back. So, she thought looking about, this was to be her home for the next month or so. Primitive though it was, she felt somehow relieved that for the time being, the walking and endless traveling were over.

Aweont poked her head through the flap once again. "Tonight there will be a feast to welcome us," she said, "a festival with much food, dancing, and music."

Jenna smiled. As tired as she was, the thought of food and music made her feel good.

In the center of the village, a huge fire burned brightly, and over it, a great venison roast was turned on a green birch spit. It's succulent aroma filled her nostrils, and Jenna could feel her mouth watering in anticipation. For the last few days on the trail, their food had been scarce and consisted largely of fish speared from the streams they traveled.

But tonight there was the venison, rice, and squash saved from the last harvest. There was also corn and some kind of bread. While the feast cooked, nearly everyone sat in a huge circle and listened while the chief recited the laws of the tribe from memory. After that, they would be allowed to eat, and after they ate, stories would be acted out. Finally, the warriors would dance.

Chapter Eight

Jenna leaned back against the trunk of a sturdy pine. She, like Elizabeth and James who sat on either side of her, were shielded from the damp ground by the length of a leather skin on which they sat. They were three of the many spectators who had formed a large circle.

On the far side of the circle, Blaise sat near the chief and a Frenchman who was already in the village when they arrived. As always, Blaise was dressed as a woodsman in moccasins, tight leggings, and a heavy tunic that was belted and fringed on the bottom. Both his leggings and tunic were made of fine soft leather. In addition, he wore a beaver hat decorated with two feathers. He also carried a sheathed hunting knife, several pouches, and of course, his ever present rifle.

In the center of the circle, a great fire burned, and its heat permeated outward so that Jenna felt quite warm. Nonetheless, she also had a blanket wrapped around her shoulders, as did Elizabeth and James.

They had all eaten over an hour ago, and then they had listened while the chief recited the tribal law from memory. Then they watched while a story about the bear star was acted out. Now, sleepy and satiated, they watched and listened as the Indian drummers began a throbbing, rhythmic call to the warriors.

Jenna watched in fascination as strong tall Indian braves, now naked except for a leather apron that hung from their hips, began to dance in a circular fashion around the great fire. They made animal-like sounds and chanted to the hypnotic beat of the drums.

Then one of the braves left the circle and went to stand before Blaise. Blaise stood up, and clearly at the behest of the young brave, he began to strip. In moments, he was as naked as the Indian brave and was pulled into the circle of male dancers as if he were one of them. The Frenchman, on the other hand, did not join in, nor she noted, was he asked to participate.

"Blaise dances like an Indian,." Elizabeth whispered sleepily.

No sooner had she spoken when one of the Indians again left the dance. This time it was Mummicott. He made his way toward James.

Jenna had noticed that other young boys were also asked to join the warriors. James was pulled to his feet, and Mummicott motioned for him to strip too. Soon, James and the Indian boys were part of the snake like procession that circled the fire.

But it was Blaise who demanded Jenna's attention. He danced with obvious concentration, his head down, looking at the earth. He moved like the Indians, but he was larger than most, and his massive upper body glistened in the firelight as it became bathed in sweat from the physical demands of the warlike dance.

Covered only with a loin cloth, his physical prowess was so evident that Jenna could feel the heat in her own face as she watched his athletic movements. His legs, like his arms, chest, and back were muscular and well toned. He moved in perfect rhythm with the drums, looking up only when the other Indians looked up, and then she noted, it was heavenward, not at the appreciative audience of Indian women and elders.

The dance involved sinuous movement, a kind of hop, a skip with the head down, then another hop and skip with the head up.

Jenna thought it was a vital dance, a sensuous dance. And however she felt about Blaise, she had to admit that he was a sexually compelling man.

She shivered slightly and was all too aware of the dryness in her mouth and her own feelings of intense desire as she watched him move. It was impossible not to imagine what an encounter with him would be like, impossible not to imagine herself in his arms.

Uneasily, Jenna glanced at Elizabeth and saw that her eyes were closed. She seemed to have dropped off into a light sleep, and Jenna felt almost grateful. Would Elizabeth have noticed her flushed face in the firelight? She felt ashamed of her own thoughts, her own wanton desires. For a moment, she turned away in an attempt to gain control of herself. But she couldn't keep her eyes from returning to Blaise's glistening body. Almost immediately, she knew her cheeks were again warm with excitement. Again, she imagined him pressing himself to her—on her. And even as she thought of it, she could almost feel the imprint of his body on hers, feel his throbbing *manhood*, feel her own passionate response to his wild primitive lovemaking, to his intimate caresses, to the feel of him within her . . . "Oh, dear God," Jenna whispered to herself. She shook her head, trying again to dispel the thoughts that filled her mind. Then Blaise was almost in front of her, and he looked into her eyes and actually winked.

Jenna knew her mouth was slightly open, and she turned her eyes away, afraid he had seen her expression and read her thoughts. It isn't right, it wouldn't be right, she reminded herself. She didn't belong here. She wasn't of this time and place, she told herself. She had no right to have a relationship under these conditions. And what did she know about this man anyway? He rode with the Indians. He was warlike, and he'd actually bought them. What kind of person was he? And last, but not least, he was arrogant.

Jenna again looked up. There was no way she could turn away from him. And again her eyes fastened on his broad bare shoulders, his strong chest, slim hips, and long powerful legs. Her fantasy was about to take hold again, but mercifully the drummers came to a frenzied finale, and the warrior dancers returned to their places, wiped their bodies, and then began to dress.

The men who had danced sat in a small circle together, while the chief lit a long pipe. Each of the warriors, including Blaise took their turn at smoking it.

When the others began to leave the circle, Jenna roused Elizabeth who went with James to the wigwam of Mummicott and Aweont. She, as always, returned to the wigwam she shared with Blaise.

Weary and confused by her own fantasies, Jenna crawled under the skins and closed her eyes. But she couldn't sleep. Visions of the dance returned to her in the darkness. Then she heard the flap of the wigwam open and saw the shadow of Blaise l'Écossais as he entered.

"Are you asleep?"

Jenna felt herself almost afraid to answer. "No," she whispered after a moment.

"How did you enjoy the feast?"

"The food was good. It's more than we've had for many days."

"That's because two days ago the hunters brought down three deer."

"I liked the corn bread."

"A treat. The Indians have little left of last year's harvest. But it's spring. Soon there will be more." He laughed lightly. "And the dance, my girl. How did you like the dance of the warriors?"

Jenna fought to control her voice. "It was enjoyable."

Again, he laughed. It was an overly confident laugh. "Did you like what you saw?"

Her face burned red in the darkness. He was conceited! "I don't know what you mean," she managed.

He laughed knowingly. "I saw your face."

Jenna felt her fury rising. Mostly, she was angry at herself for revealing her own lustful thoughts. "You're too sure of what you saw," she snapped and with that rolled over and faced the side of the wigwam.

"Ah, what an actress you are," he roared. Then, without so much as coming a step toward her, she heard him crawl into his own bedroll.

In moments, she could hear the slower breathing that indicated he was asleep. She curled up and listened as he breathed. Damn, she thought. Damn, damn, damn. He had read her correctly, he had guessed her loneliness, her need for him, even her wanton desire to be with him in an intimate way. But was that what she really wanted? Or were her feelings only the result of needing someone to love in this strange new world that had engulfed her?

Yes, she only desired him because of her circumstances. Or perhaps, she contemplated, because of her all too recent affair with Carlton Havers. Perhaps, she'd never really be able to trust enough to give herself to another man again. She had to forget her desire for the man who slept only a few feet from her. She had

to concentrate on survival—on helping James and
Elizabeth—on learning all of the ways of this strange
and hostile environment. What lay ahead? Whatever it
was, it would be easier if she fought her passing desire
for Blaise. And surely it was a passing desire. He was
good looking, and wasn't it natural that she felt attracted to him?

She thought of the world she had left behind. Wasn't
there a mental disease—something that happened to
hostages—something that caused them to help their
captors and sometimes even to love their captors. Oh,
yes. Stockholm Syndrome! That was it. It was, as she recalled, named for an airline stewardess who had been
infatuated with her captor.

Yes, what she felt for Blaise was natural, but that
didn't mean she had to give into her fantasies. With that
thought, she closed her eyes and forced herself to concentrate only on going to sleep. After all, this man
whom she had so desired during the dance, was the
same man who would require her to work all day tomorrow, starting with an early rise to cook his breakfast.
He was the same man who demanded she "act" the
slave to satisfy the Indians; he was the same man who
reminded her daily that she was *his* property.

"You're a girl! You'll never be a real hunter!"

"The white skin is no warrior!"

"No better than a girl with cries and complaints!"

Jenna looked up at the first sound of the male voices
of derision as they entered camp. She, together with
some of the Indian women, had been peeling bark from
logs.

The angry shouts came from three of the Indian
boys—boys roughly the same age as James. Their vin-

dictive was accompanied by hoots of scorn and expressions of clear disgust.

They had all left the camp that morning early in order to hunt for small animals in the woods. The morning hunt was routine, like the other chores and shared work of survival.

Jenna had grown used to her own work, the rhythm of life among the Indians who, in the familial setting of the village, seemed entirely different than they had earlier when the hostages were first taken. Here, it seemed the Indians wanted to have the captives fit into their environment, to be at home with their ways. As a result, they were no longer threatening but had rather taken on the job of teachers. The only exception was Oioteet who remained after Kewatin and the others had left.

Because of this change, Jenna was surprised when she heard the angry disgusted tone of the young Indian boys and even more surprised when she realized it was directed at James who hung behind the others, bearing their insults with his head bowed and his face red.

As soon as he reached the perimeter of the camp, he bolted across the open center and ran straight into the wigwam Jenna shared with Blaise.

Jenna glanced at Aweont, and Aweont nodded, signaling her permission that Jenna could leave her work to investigate the cause of the commotion.

Jenna hurried across the compound and bending, entered her wigwam. James stood by the far side, his back turned.

"What's the matter? Why were those boys taunting you?"

James turned, and her heart went out to him. He was dressed as an Indian boy, but without the feathers that would have denoted his standing in the tribe. At this moment, his lower lip quivered, and Jenna could see he was fighting back tears.

"I can't keep up," he murmured, hanging his head and turning away. "I was brave once, but I can't keep up."

"You've never done any of these things before," she said, trying to sound calm.

"Nor have you, nor has Elizabeth. But they don't taunt you."

Jenna looked at him kindly. It was true enough that the Indian women were patient teachers, more patient, she was certain, than were the men and young boys.

"Tell me what happened."

"We were hunting. They told me to follow the rabbit tracks. I did, but in a few minutes I got all turned around. I couldn't tell from which direction I had come. I wasn't sure of the direction of the village, and the sun was overhead so I couldn't use it to find my way. Then I heard the cry of a wolf and I . . ."

He stopped in mid-sentence and tears flooded his eyes.

How silly men were, Jenna thought. Only ten and he had already fully learned to suppress his fears lest he be thought a sissy. But this boy was strong. If he was frightened now, then it was the accumulation of everything that had happened. His mother was gone. His father lost to him. He and his sister were alone in an alien culture, afraid of the future, and no doubt terribly homesick. Moreover, they had been subjected to an ordeal and were learning to face a whole new life. However hard life on the frontier had been, they had been born into it. Now, they were expected to become Indians virtually overnight. No, he wasn't crying over one incident, he was crying now for all that had happened.

She moved quickly to James's side and wrapped her arms around him. "It's all right," she whispered.

He buried his face and held her tightly. She knew he was crying, but all she could do was to comfort him.

"I was so scared," he sobbed. "Scared I would be lost in the woods forever. Scared of the wolf. I climbed a tree and called out, 'Help!' 'Help!' over and over again. Finally, the other boys came but they only laughed at me. They said there was no wolf and that I was a girl because I called out." He sniffed and then looked up at her. "They said I endangered them, that by calling out I could have given away our position to an enemy."

"And so you might have," Blaise said from the entrance to the wigwam.

"This is all strange to him; the other boys should be kinder," Jenna said.

Blaise stepped into the wigwam, allowing the flap to fall closed. "He's a good boy, a smart strong boy. Right now his pride is hurt."

"And what do you know about children? He's separated from his parents, this is a strange world for him."

"He is not a child. He is a young man. He is the son of one of the finest English Indian scouts on the frontier. He would be learning the Indian ways soon enough if he had remained with his own father. Besides, I've seen this boy dare a brave to cut off his arm. I know he's brave."

"I'd be learning Mohawk ways," James said suddenly. "Not Abnaki."

"They are not so different, except for the fact that the Mohawk are your allies and the Abnaki mine."

James did not reply but instead looked away.

"The Indian boys respect you and like you. They are teaching you to hunt because they respect you."

"They make fun of me and taunt me."

"They understand your fears no more than you understand their taunts. They taunt you to make you want to succeed, to beat them at their own game. They want you to be angry enough to overcome your fear."

James frowned and bit his lip.

"But he doesn't know his way around the woods very well—not like the young Indian boys. He could get lost, there are wild animals . . ."

"Don't protect him! He can learn. He *will* learn."

"And what about the wolves?" Jenna said. Didn't he understand anything. Why shouldn't a little boy be frightened of wild animals?

"There was no wolf. Even so, a wolf would not attack him. What he heard was the sound of a howling wolf. It is the way the Indians communicate in the woods. They never, never call out. They always make animal noises so their enemies will not detect them."

"The sound I heard was an Indian?" James asked.

"Yes. Had you answered with a wolf call, they would have found you immediately, and they would not have laughed."

James wiped his cheeks on his sleeve. "Must it always be a wolf?"

"No. Ask Ponokuk to teach you the sounds. You must learn to imitate certain birds as well as the cry of the wolf."

"He doesn't like me. He won't do it."

Blaise smiled. "If you ask him to be your special teacher, he will be flattered. Tell him you admire him and want to learn from him."

"Can I learn?" James asked.

Again, Blaise smiled. "Of course."

James nodded and immediately ran out of the wigwam calling Ponokuk's name.

"He's only ten," Jenna said, looking at Blaise seriously.

But Blaise's expression was one of anger. "You understand nothing, woman. These people fear for their lives! A child crying in the woods that he is lost could alert enemies and cause a massacre!"

"I doubt that," she said, looking at him in anger.

His face clouded over, and he leaned closer. "You don't understand anything! Ask yourself why Aweont's papoose never cries, my lady. Ask why none of the Indian babies cry."

His voice was low, furious. "I'll tell you why. As soon as they're born they cry out, and their mothers hold their noses so they can't breathe. They do this each time they cry, till they learn not to cry. They do this not to hurt them or to be cruel, but to protect them. Roving Iroquois bands drunk with English whisky rampage through their villages and kill them, even the smallest child. Everything you don't seem to understand has a reason."

Jenna drew in her breath. She was stunned by his revelation, and by the anger she saw in his dark eyes. "You're right—there is much I don't understand," she said softly. "It's just that I know James misses his family. This is hard on both of them."

"And not on you?" he snapped.

"I'm older," she said quickly.

"Yes. Well, I think there is more. I do not believe you. I think if I questioned both Elizabeth and James carefully, they would admit that you're not their sister."

Jenna drew herself up and decided to counterattack. "And who might I be?" she asked.

He half smiled, his anger gone as quickly as it had come. "A strange exotic woman from a far away place."

His look was penetrating, and again, she felt the mental pull toward him, the raw physical chemistry that existed between them. And a chill ran down her spine because of his words. Did he suspect more than the fact that she was not James and Elizabeth's sister? He seemed to, yet she could not dare tell him, could not take the risk of telling him anything remotely like the truth. It was too fantastic, too unreal, and far too unbelievable. This was not a man of her own time. Everything, she reminded herself once again, was different. "I'm sorry you don't believe me," she answered, turning her head away and deciding to withdraw before their conversation became even more dangerous.

"I will learn about you," he said, staring hard at her. Then, "Best you go back to Aweont."

Jenna nodded and gratefully slipped past him and out the flap of the wigwam.

Jenna knelt by the stream and rinsed the cooking utensils off in the cold water. It was twilight, which next to dawn, was her favorite time of day in the forest.

She wasn't exactly sure of the date because during their long trek to this spring village of the Abnaki, she had lost track of time. But during their stay, she had marked the days faithfully, and now felt certain it was sometime in mid May.

She finished the last pot and set it upside down to dry on the grass. Then, she sat back herself, drinking in the scenery. How everlastingly peaceful it was here! And how stunningly beautiful!

The stream was tranquil, here where it curved gently. But further on, it tumbled over rocks in a race toward its rendezvous with a larger river. Jenna drew in another deep, deep breath. The air smelled of spring, of rebirth. The grass on which she sat was a new green, as if it had been washed by all of the rains of April—rains that, when they had fallen, she had cursed because they had lasted so long.

She looked up at the trees. The new leaves on the hardwood trees were still small and looked like nature's lace as they fluttered in the breeze. The great pines seemed to be washed and new as they towered toward the heavens. It was all so wonderful! So unspoiled! There was no superhighway with rushing cars and belching trucks. No train tracks crisscrossed the primeval wilderness, and no planes flew overhead to challenge the sole right of the birds to the blue sky.

This time of day, and dawn, had a magical light and a promising silence as animals, large and small, sought to drink from the stream. Now and again, a fawn ventured forth to sip, and more than once, she had seen a stately moose. But her most constant companions by the stream were the birds. The giant shiny black crows and intelligent imitative ravens, which the Indians believed were pranksters, the smart devilish jays and the sudden flocks of bright yellow-chested warblers constantly delighted her.

And day by day, Jenna admitted she was getting used to the ways of the Indians. She felt healthier than she had ever felt, and certainly James and Elizabeth also seemed to be thriving.

She attributed their good health to several things. First, they were unexposed to viruses, not that anyone but she even knew what a virus was. Second, they were hearty from being out of doors so much. Third, they ate sparingly, but well. And fourth, they got plenty of exercise.

Every few days, Jenna made all of them drink the Indian tea that she knew contained vitamin C. At first they had hated its bitter taste, but gradually they had gown to tolerate it. And Jenna thought, she also had Aweont to thank for her health. Indian medicine was highly advanced, far more advanced than the medicine practiced by the Europeans of this time.

Aweont knew the uses of and collected the medicinal herbs of the forest, and she shared her knowledge with Jenna. She also knew how to care for certain infections and had a special way of binding a sprained ankle or wrist. She occasionally complimented Jenna on her skills. "You have good hands," Aweont told her one day. "If you study our ways, you will make a good medicine woman."

And so Jenna had tried. She knew many of the more important medicines now, and her own twentieth century knowledge augmented her newly acquired knowledge of the Indian pharmacy.

"Lost in thought?"

Jenna turned abruptly. Blaise was standing behind her. As always, he had approached so silently she hadn't heard him.

"I was just thinking how much I like this time of the day."

"Me too," he said sitting down beside her.

Jenna felt the immediate sensation she always felt when he was close. Yet in spite of the fact that she acted his wife and in spite of the fact that they shared a wigwam, he was seldom that close. More often than not, he came to the wigwam only after she was asleep. They now talked sometimes, but most of the time he was with the braves. Often, he was gone for days at a time from the village when he and the others went off on hunting trips.

"You look well," he commented without actually looking at her.

"I feel well," she replied.

"Aweont tells me you learn quickly and work hard. She tells me that you are at peace with yourself now. Is that so?"

"I'm adjusting," Jenna allowed.

He smiled. "May I call you by your given name as you call me by mine?"

She felt her face flush slightly and wondered again just how aware he was of her feelings. "Yes. It's Jenna."

"Jenna—for Jennifer?"

"No, just Jenna. You said we would go to Quebec. When will we leave here?"

"We will leave here in a few weeks. When it is June. But as I told you, we will not go to Quebec till fall. We will stay with the Indians till then."

Jenna frowned. She liked being with Aweont and the other Indians she had come to know. In one way, knowing that they would remain with the Indians was good news. On the other hand, she hungered for a few of the advantages she supposed even Quebec might have. And then there was James—she felt somehow that once they were in Quebec it might be easier for her to find some way for him to go home to Deerfield.

"Is there a reason for the delay?" she asked. "A reason not to go to Quebec sooner?"

"There are several reasons. But most important is the fact that I wish to finish mastering the language of this group, so I wish to stay with them longer." He paused, seemed to stare off into space, then added, "And there are people I must talk with."

Jenna said nothing. Blaise was a man who did not explain what he did not want to explain.

Blaise stretched. He leaned over and offered her his hand and she took it, allowing him to pull her up off the grass.

For a long moment, they stood and looked at one another. It was one of those moments, a shared imaginary kiss, an unspoken promise for something to come. Jenna started to speak, but he whirled away and walked into the woods, taking long purposeful strides.

He was gone before she could ask about his learning the language of this group. Was he some kind of teacher or translator? Or was he just a scout? And why was he arrogant one minute, cold another time, furious or friendly still at other times? He seemed to her to be a man of strange moods, a man who guarded his personal secrets. Blaise l'Écossais was becoming more and more of a mystery with each passing day.

Chapter Nine

By Jenna's reckoning, it was July first when they crossed the Saint Lawrence River. They were twenty in all, the four of them and sixteen Indians in eight canoes.

As Blaise had indicated, they did not cross into Quebec or what Jenna knew to be Quebec in her time. Rather they crossed into what she supposed was Ontario. It was not an area she was familiar with, but she was quite certain it was that area near the present day Ontario–Quebec border, the area in the Saint Lawrence River know as the Thousand Islands.

The river was very wide where they crossed, and they stopped midway on a small island in order to rest.

Jenna lay on the pleasant sandy little beach, glad to be out of the canoe for even a short time.

Elizabeth and James went with Mummicott and Aweont to look for berries. The Indian braves sunned themselves or sat in small groups, talking and eating.

Blaise walked along the beach, then came and sat down. "Our long trek is almost over. We'll soon be at the largest village and the home of this group of Abnaki."

"I'll be glad not to be traveling," Jenna admitted. Then, she asked, looking out across the Saint Lawrence,

"Why did we cross here, surely this is the widest part of the river?"

He frowned slightly. "You've been here before?"

Jenna shook her head. "No, I just assumed . . ."

"You assume correctly. It is wider here. But it is also calmer. There are no rapids and the current slows so that the passing is easier. It is said that it is also not as deep as elsewhere, and thus warmer should anyone fall in."

"It seems a big river," Jenna said, trying to hide her knowledge.

"And long. It flows to the sea on one end and the other goes to the first of the great inland lakes."

Lake Ontario, Jenna thought. Yes, she had guessed their whereabouts accurately. Actually, she was surprised that he seemed to know there was more than one large inland lake. "Have you traveled to such a lake?" she asked, hoping to find out how much he knew of geography.

He didn't look at her, but rather stared out over the water toward the islands that seemed everywhere. He had a solemn, far away look in his eyes and he nodded thoughtfully. "Aye, I've traveled to that lake and to several beyond. There are five in all, and they are as rough and as unpredictable as the sea."

"You've traveled far," she replied, slightly in awe of his disclosure and mindful not to reveal her own knowledge of continental geography—geography unknown to many in this time.

"The waterways are our roads. I've gone from the inland lakes south on the rivers and then south all the way to the sea on the longest of rivers."

Jenna opened her mouth in surprise. Did he mean he'd traveled the Mississippi? "And what was there?" she asked.

"Not what I was seeking," he answered, as he suddenly stood up.

Jenna said nothing because she could not remember when New Orleans had been established—something told her that although Louisiana had been explored by the French, and the territory was French, that it was, as yet unsettled and unnamed. And what did he mean by his mysterious comment? What was he seeking? She was about to ask, but he strode off without so much as a wave goodbye.

"Come, come!" Aweont called out. She was standing on the edge of the woods.

Jenna pulled herself up and hurried toward Aweont.

"Berries!" Aweont said, pointing toward the woods. "Come, there is a meadow filled with blackberries."

Jenna followed Aweont into the woods. This like the other islands that dotted the river, was overgrown and lush. It had a sand and rock beach, tall pines, and all manner of shrubs. This island was, however, larger than most of the others.

"See!" Aweont said proudly pointing to the clearing. "Bears haven't found it yet."

Aweont was right. The clearing was a blanket of delicious wild blackberries. The Indian women and children ate and picked simultaneously. Jenna laughed, both Elizabeth and James bore the telltale stains of the berries round their now blueish lips, on their faces, and their fingers.

It would be good to take some with us for later," Jenna suggested. "But all the containers are packed in the canoes."

Aweont nodded and pointed to the tall reeds of grass that surrounded the meadow. She quickly went and pulled some long thin reeds. "Here," she explained. "See if you can string the blackberries on the grass and then hang the grass around your neck as a necklace. It is how we carry berries when we have no baskets. We make necklaces of them."

Jenna smiled in delight. "What a good idea!" She knelt down and immediately began picking, stringing, and eating. These people were endlessly inventive, and she was enchanted by many of their simple, but utilitarian ideas.

They picked for over an hour, then they were summoned to continue the journey across the water.

The July sun shone brightly when they entered the village. Here, was the largest number of wigwams Jenna had ever seen, and soon, those who arrived were busily erecting their own. Like the previous village, this one also had permanent buildings, including a chapel. And to her surprise and happiness, this village also had livestock. There was a herd of cows and a flock of chickens.

"I haven't seen Indians with livestock before," Jenna commented.

"This is a mission, and there is a Black Robe who comes regularly. These Indians also raise crops. The French gave them livestock so they could farm and prosper," Blaise told her, then he said brusquely, "There's work to do. Aweont is waiting for you."

Jenna worked hard, and soon the wigwam was up, and their small number of belongings unpacked. Outside, the village children played and it was clear from the sights and smells that another welcoming feast was being prepared.

Aweont appeared outside Jenna's wigwam. Elizabeth and James were with her and both carried their packs.

"There is no room now that we are here," Aweont said apologetically.

Jenna looked back at the wigwam she was to share with Blaise. It was far too small for two more people to sleep there at night.

Aweont, guessing her thoughts shook her head vigorously. "No, they are not to stay with you, but to go to my sister and her husband. I just come to tell you."

"Does she have enough room?"

"For now," Aweont said. "She is with child, but until the child comes, there is enough room."

"What is her name?"

"She is called Hee-la-dee. She is wife to the brave you know as Suckkeecoo. That is their wigwam there." Aweont pointed toward one of the wigwams. "I will take them now," she told Jenna.

Jenna looked at Elizabeth and James. "Is this arrangement all right?"

"I'm always so tired at night, it matters not where I sleep," Elizabeth said.

"Mummicott has promised that he'll still teach me," James added.

"Good. I'll come later," Jenna promised. She returned quickly to her work, hoping to find time for herself before the feast had to be prepared.

They had been in the village for a week. Blaise had disappeared on the second day and only returned this morning. As was usual, he gave no explanation for his absence.

Jenna stood outside the wigwam and wiped her brow. It was still very warm, and she felt sticky and tired.

"You need to be refreshed," Blaise said, as he casually walked toward her.

"I need a bath," she replied, supposing that was what he meant.

"Come along then. The water in the lake is wonderful."

It was a tempting thought—how wonderful it would be to cast her clothes aside and bathe in the cool water. But how could she with him? True, she once had bathed in front of him, but then she had been angry and ordered to do so. Now, she felt under no duress. She felt attracted to him, yet wary. She was also sure he was avoiding her since he had been absent.

"You go ahead," she said.

He shrugged and walked away.

Jenna noted the direction in which he walked. Then she changed into her original undergarments that had been washed and repaired, and threw on her cloak, pausing only to gather up a bar of soap and a chamois with which to dry herself. She followed the path Blaise had taken.

Quietly, she approached the lake. Blaise was out in the water, splashing with one of the Indian children. Jenna searched the area with her eyes, then spied a river that flowed into the lake. She walked around behind the trees, came to the river and followed it upstream away from the little lake. It was shallow, and without hesitation, she took off her cloak and plunged into its cold water.

She rubbed her arms and legs then bent and sat cautiously down, allowing the water to flow over her. It felt wonderful. She was able to sit on the rock bottom, the water up to her neck and feel the cool water rush over and past her.

After a few minutes, she stood up and looked down. Jenna shrieked—a long horrified scream, and she hurried from the water, stumbling. Her legs, her arms, and even her breasts were covered with horrible little black leeches. They clung to her, and she screamed again. She was horrified at their sight, but she was too terrified to even touch them.

Blaise burst through the wood. He stopped for a single second and looked at her. She was standing thigh deep in water. *"Tabernac!"* he swore in French, as he finished pulling on his own sleeveless vest.

Jenna tried wrapping herself in her own arms. She was trembling with fear and revulsion, but still aware enough to know she could not pull the hideous blood-sucking parasites off without risking serious infection.

"Leeches! I'm covered with leeches!" She was both terrified and repulsed as her hands flew to her face, and she once again screamed. "Oh, get them off! Get them off!"

Blaise grabbed her hand and pulled her out of the shallow water.

"Get them off me! I can feel them! Oh, please get them off me!"

"I will. Come, we've got to get to a dry spot. I have to be able to see."

"I can't stand it! They're all over me!"

Blaise propelled her along in spite of her shaking and protestations. They burst into a clearing. "Here, sit down." He indicated a patch of soft grass.

"I can't stand it!" She was ashen, trembling all over and quite hysterical. Great tears gushed from her magnificent green eyes, and she shivered even in the sunlight.

In spite of everything, he was, for a moment, mesmerized with her beauty. Her thin gauze undergarments clung to her body, revealing every womanly curve. He recalled how she had looked naked. She was an alabaster goddess with full rounded pink-tipped breasts. He shook his thoughts free.

"Take off your clothes," he commanded.

"I can't do that!" Jenna murmured through her tears.

"I can hardly take off the leeches while you're dressed, woman," he said, looking stonily at her. Then without waiting, he undid her chemise and pulled it open. "Damn! They're all over you!"

Jenna's mouth was partially open, and she was frozen as Blaise fully disrobed the top half of her body and then stood for a long moment, rubbing his chin thoughtfully.

Jenna shivered and again shook convulsively at the sight of the horrible black bloodsuckers. Blaise reached for one of pouches he carried, then opened it.

"Salt," he said matter-of-factly. "I always carry it for leeches, ticks, and heat sickness."

Jenna's face was flushed hot, and she covered it with her hands as he gently pushed her back onto the grass. He removed all of her clothes, examining each piece for leeches as he removed it.

He worked quickly to remove the leeches from her thighs and buttocks. His hands were warm and gentle, and she could hear him breathing above her. At the same time, she was well aware of the fire in her own heart. In spite of the leeches, her flesh quivered at his touch, her whole body felt warm, glowing, and filled with desire. Why did he do this to her? Why couldn't she control her reactions?

"They're gone," he said, almost whispering. Then he said softly, "You've the most beautiful body I've ever seen."

Jenna pressed her full lips together ... the leeches were gone, she was naked, and he was next to her, his hand still resting on her bare leg. She sat up abruptly and blushed under his bold gaze.

His face, too, seemed flushed, then suddenly he bent and kissed her nipple. It was hard from the cold water— but now it grew harder, yet acutely sensitive to his warm lips, to the sensuous movements of his tongue.

He stopped and looked at her long and hard. Her lips were half apart, her eyes shimmered.

Jenna knew her body revealed her own excitement, her own passion. She wanted him to kiss her breast again, to mold it in his hands. She wanted to feel him against her, exciting her, holding her, leaving his imprint on her, becoming one with her . . . It was no use, any pretense of willpower had fled her.

"I'm only human," he said, devouring her with his eyes. He leaned over, and she felt his lips on hers, pressing and urgent.

It was a deep probing kiss, a kiss that inflamed her need for him, a kiss that sent her doubts flying. He was strong and respected. He was a powerful man, an irresistible man. A man she wanted as much as he seemed to want her.

"Ah, more fire than ice," he whispered as he pushed her gently backward, arousing her with the slow movement of his hands on her skin, as they explored her most sensitive areas.

All these months, they had hungered for one another, yet fought one another. But that was over now. Now, they were one as they tumbled together into the deep abyss of wild reckless passion.

His leather clothing pressed on her flesh, but even so she could feel his manhood hard and strong. She moaned slightly and knew there was no more fighting. He had stripped her of her clothes, and now, he stripped her of all will to deny to him. She squirmed in his grasp, aglow with excitement.

He had dressed hastily when she had screamed, and

now, he discarded his vest, revealing his broad chest. He held her close, pressing himself to her so that she could feel him moving against her. His breath was hot as he kissed her neck, her ears, and then once again returned to taunt her breasts which responded instantly to his caresses.

Her eyes were closed as he kissed her again and again, slipping gradually down, down till she felt him so intensely she almost screamed. His fingers still toyed with her nipples, his warm moist kisses drew her close to the abyss, but he did not let her fall—not yet. She tried to hold him, when he withdrew his lips, returning them to her breasts.

She felt fevered, and again, she moaned as she realized he had wriggled out of his leather breeches. Now, she felt him full on top of her, his hands still moving over her, touching her, magically setting her aflame. She held him tightly while he toyed with one breast and kissed the other. She trembled violently in his arms as her desire and her excitement made her ache. "Please," she whispered as he touched her most intimate hidden place again and again. Yet he still denied her. It was sweet torture. His hands moved so expertly and probed so divinely, she felt damp with anticipation and faint with ecstasy.

Slowly, he parted her legs and pressed into her. She grasped him and moaned yet again as he towered above her, bent to kiss the nipple of each breast and then again sought her moist depths. She felt her own back arch to meet him, and as he moved against her, she began her ascent into the throbbing abyss.

He grasped her buttocks tightly seeking his own pleasure, but still she tumbled. Their mutual fulfillment seemed to last a long while, then he fell against her and gently moved to one side, pulling her close.

"Now, you *are* my woman," he whispered in her ear.

Jenna could say nothing. No sooner had he withdrawn from her, than she again wanted him.

Jenna rolled over and stretched. Her hand reached across the soft fur of the bed pallet she shared with Blaise, and she opened her eyes, realizing he was no longer there.

She sat up and stretched again, aware that it was already becoming warm inside the small enclosure. She hugged herself, and for a moment relived last night's intense pleasure.

After their liaison in the woods, they had returned to the village hand in hand. Everything seemed changed.

She cooked dinner feeling light hearted and happy. His eyes seemed to follow her everywhere, and she returned his looks lovingly.

After dinner, Blaise joined the warriors. They gathered round the fire and smoked the pipe. This Jenna had learned was called the Calumet of Peace. It was a special ornamental ceremonial pipe used as a symbol of friendship and peace. It was a long pipe, decorated with the quills of an eagle, and was used only to indicate peace, or to solidify the bond between people or groups. Clearly, Blaise smoked it to seal his bond with this tribe.

But this night he did not wait for her to go to sleep before coming to their wigwam. Nor when they retired, was it to separate bedrolls as in the past.

They went to bed together, lying on a large soft fur skin and covered with a lighter covering. He undressed her in a leisurely way, aroused her to fever pitch, and then took her so slowly she knew pleasure not once, but twice.

They slept curled in one another's arms. Then in the

middle of the night, they had sought each other once again. Sleepily at first, then with rising desire. He took her again, and again, she felt his imprint on her body, his hands on her warm flesh, his manhood throbbing within her even as she responded fully, feeling her own ecstasy.

Abstractedly, she ran her hand across the spot where he had lain. He was still a mystery to her, and she could only hope he would reveal himself in time.

Surely, he would help her see to it that James was returned to Deerfield. Most certainly, he would help her protect young Elizabeth from harm. He was a good man, of that she felt certain. And perhaps, when they had been together longer, she could even confess the truth about herself.

There were ways she could prove her story. Or at least she thought he would accept certain facts as proof. Surely, it would be easier for her to convince him than to try to convince anyone else. He had whispered that he loved her, and love was the most powerful of all emotions.

Jenna smiled, thinking once again how everything had changed. Once she had been fearful, then she had been apprehensive. Now she felt confident, confident and wonderful! She felt like singing!

She stood up and quickly dressed. Then she went outside to join the women in their daily chores. Not everything had changed, but she felt that what remained the same would seem easier from now on.

Elizabeth, her skin now more tanned by the summer sun and the outdoor work, looked up from her weaving. "You look different," she said, smiling at Jenna.

Jenna sat down, taking her place among the women.

Here, there was no sense of captivity. All were women working, and the Indian women treated her and Elizabeth as equals.

Jenna blushed slightly, wondering if indeed her happiness was so evident.

"I'm well rested," she replied.

Elizabeth only smiled more broadly. "There is no need for you to hide anything, my sister. You're radiant, and I can see that it's more than a good night's sleep that's caused you to appear so happy."

Jenna bit her lower lip and looked down. She picked up a half finished basket and took up the task of weaving it, as she had been taught. "And what exactly can you see?" Jenna asked.

"Pure happiness. Besides, there are few secrets in this village."

Jenna did blush now because Aweont was laughing just a little, and the other women were all smiling knowingly.

"The wigwams are close together," Aweont said softly. "We all know that last night l'Écossais took you for his wife."

Jenna felt her face burn red, yet she could not deny Aweont's words, nor was there any real reason to deny her. Still, it was embarrassing to think they had heard her and Blaise making love. She made a silent vow to try to be more quiet in the future. But when she thought of how he toyed with her first, she knew it was a vow that would be hard to keep. He took great pleasure in arousing her, in watching her.

"Here, among my people," Aweont said, "when a man takes a woman into his bed, she becomes his wife."

But all these weeks she had been pretending to be Blaise's wife, did this mean their charade was so transparent?

"We have been living as man and wife for some time," she replied.

Aweont laughed gently. "But only in the last day have you become one. It is good. Perhaps like Hee-la-dee you will become great with child."

Jenna looked down. She rather hoped she would not become pregnant straight away. Though, if passion and satisfaction had anything to do with it, she was no doubt pregnant now.

"Very well," she said, looking up and into the faces of her companions. "I confess. We're in love."

"I always knew you secretly liked him," Elizabeth said, smiling. "I never thought you could get so angry with someone you really didn't like."

"You're too wise for your age," Jenna said.

"I'm sixteen. Soon, I'll be of marriageable age."

Jenna nodded. She knew full well that girls most always married by the age of seventeen. Still, Elizabeth seemed too young by her own twentieth century standards, standards she could not discuss because she knew the Indian girls often married even younger.

"We should not tease you so," Elizabeth said, touching Jenna's hand. "But it's only because we're happy for you. And you do look different, you look radiant."

Jenna smiled. "I am in love."

"L'Écossais is a strong man. He is a good protector," Aweont said.

Jenna swallowed her thoughts. Women of this time sought protectors, she could hardly argue that she did not want a protector, but rather a man who would respect her. Still, things were different here—at least different from the way she had imagined they would be. The Indian women were treated with a certain respect, and they had absolute domain over their homes, their children, and village life.

"I love him," Jenna said. "But I still know little about him. He is still a mystery to me."

"I hear the Black Robe is coming here to the village. He will baptize the children and conduct a service to God. I hear this Black Robe is an old friend of l'Écossais, the scout. You can ask him."

Blaise had told her this was a mission, but she wondered to what extent the tribe was converted. "Are all the people of this village Christians?" Jenna asked.

"We have accepted the God of the Black Robes," Hee-la-dee confirmed.

Jenna digested the information. How, she wondered, could a Black Robe, a priest, accept the idea of European hostages. Perhaps if she spoke to him, he could find out where the other hostages had been taken. Perhaps if she and the priest both talked to Blaise, he would understand that Elizabeth and James should be returned to their father.

But Elizabeth did not return. Jenna bit her lip. She knew she could not, must not change history. She vowed to deal with that aspect of her dilemma when she had to—for now, she would concentrate on James.

"Your cooking is improving," Blaise said, laughing. His eyes looked at her hungrily, and she knew he was thinking of the moment when they would go to bed together. She was thinking of it too, but for the moment, she forced herself to think on other matters.

"Come walk with me, I want to talk with you."

He stood up and stretched. "It's a perfect night. Shall we walk by the stream?"

"Yes."

He took her hand, and they slipped away from the village. It was indeed a perfect July evening, an evening when the purple shades of twilight seemed to last for hours. "Blaise, I must talk to you about Elizabeth and James."

"They are not your sister and brother, are they?"

Jenna drew in her breath and shook her head. His accusation didn't surprise her. He had made his suspicions evident before. "No."

"Why did you lie?"

"Because it was important that I be with them."

"Tell me how you came to tell this lie."

Jenna knew she could not yet tell him the real truth. "I came to the village late the night of the raid. I was lost, my wagon had broken down. I was to teach school in Deerfield. I was taken to the Catlin house, where Elizabeth and James lived with their parents. Their father was away, their mother was taken away with another group. I felt I should look after them."

"I promise you no harm will come to them."

"They should be able to return to their father," Jenna pressed.

Blaise stopped and stepped in front of her. He put his strong hands on her shoulders and looked into her eyes. "Jenna, I would grant you almost any wish, but I cannot grant you that wish."

"Why?" She sought his eyes.

"Because their father is James Corse. He is, as I told you, a well known scout. He has led many raids against the Abnaki and against the French. Neither the French nor the Indians will allow his children to be returned."

"Not even for a ransom?"

"Not even for a king's ransom."

"But if you intercede?"

"I can do nothing. Not even my intercession would help."

Jenna bit her lip, and again, her eyes searched her

face. She was certain he was telling her the truth. "Aweont says a priest is coming. These people are Christians—perhaps if the priest interceded, he could persuade the Indians to accept the idea of letting them go."

"Father Henri would be unlikely to intercede."

"Aweont said he is your friend."

"I have known him a long while, but we are not friends as you and I understand the word. No, even if I asked him I doubt he would intercede."

"I want to ask him myself," Jenna said.

Blaise looked at her steadily. "All right. I want you to understand, which I can see you don't."

"I believe you," she said. "But I must try for myself."

He half smiled. "As I said, you are a stubborn woman."

She looked back at him. "You're a stubborn man," she corrected.

Her words were an invitation. He pulled her into his arms and kissed her ready lips. She pressed against him, and he pushed her gently back against a tall pine. They were standing, arms around one another, locked in an embrace, and she could feel the tree against her. His hand slipped under her skirt and traveled up the inside of her thigh. She sighed and pushed closer to him as he caressed her intimately, then gently lifted her leg so that one foot rested on a nearby rock. His movements were swift, tantalizing, exciting as he touched her, arousing her, making her hunger for him till she felt she might cry out in the silence of the evening. Then, even as they stood there, he slipped inside her, and she was warm and ready for him.

For a long, unbearably beautiful moment, he was still inside her, and she struggled to move against him, to force him to fulfil her now overwhelming desire. Then he grasped her buttocks firmly and moved against her till she was feverishly shaking in his arms and panting in short breaths. Never, she thought as she leaned against him, had a man taken her standing up.

Jenna was weeding with the other women when at noon, on July fifteenth, Father Henri arrived with a small party of Indian warriors.

He was a tall lean man, gaunt by Jenna's standards. He had thin shiny black hair, his skin was sallow, his cheeks slightly sunken, and his eyes dark and brooding. He wore, as Aweont had described it, a long black robe, a broad brimmed hat, and his clerical collar. Around his neck, he wore a heavy iron cross. He did not, much to Jenna's unhappiness, look like a very friendly man. Indeed, he was cold in his appearance, and his face bore no signs that he laughed or smiled very often.

When he arrived, he met immediately with the male village elders and a calumet was smoked. After that, a meal was served. Following the meal, he announced that mass would be given in the morning, children baptized, and couples formally married under God's law.

It was after his announcements that Jenna had the first opportunity to speak with him.

"Father, do you speak English?"

He turned and looked at her.

Jenna thought she saw a glimpse of suspicion in his eyes.

"Yes, my child." His words were accented, but she was grateful she did not have to try to converse in French.

"I want to speak to you about the young captives, James and Elizabeth."

"The captives Blaise has purchased from the Indians?"

"Yes. But I do not believe that persons can be purchased."

"Slavery is practiced all over the world. We are slaves to this life. In any case, they are most fortunate. Blaise will protect them and look after them."

"You're a man of God. You know they should be returned to their father." She looked into his eyes, hoping to find a spark of humanity, the kind of humanity a priest from her own time would show. But he looked back at her coldly, his eyes flashing with anger.

"Do not remind me of my duty to God!"

Jenna wondered if her face expressed her shock. No wonder Blaise had taken care to explain they were not friends. This priest was more akin to a judge at the inquisition than to Friar Tuck.

"I know the reason they cannot be returned has been explained to you," he added.

"You should know what is right and what is wrong," Jenna said, feeling her own anger.

"You, a mere woman, dare to speak to me of such things! You don't understand. When we came here, we found naked pagans. They called themselves Hurons, Algonquins, Iroquois, and Ottawa. The Hurons and the Algonquins are friends—they have allowed themselves to be converted in large numbers, they are our friends, the friends of the French. The Iroquois nations are at war with the Algonquins and the Huron. The Iroquois are a mighty Indian nation made up of many tribes: the Mohawk, the Seneca, the Cayuga, the Oneida, and the Onondaga. They are the friends of the British."

"I understand that," she protested. "But all this killing—it has to stop."

Father Henri narrowed his eyes. "Tell that to the father of those you want returned. He killed many when he and the British raided the farms along the Saint Lawrence and burned our churches. No, his offspring will remain in Quebec. They will never return. It is small payment for so many lives lost."

"But they did not kill anyone. They're innocents."

"They cannot be returned," he said. "I will not intervene."

Jenna glared at him, but she held her tongue. Instead, she whirled away and walked rapidly toward her wigwam.

To her surprise, Blaise was inside. He lay on his side, staring pensively into the fire.

Jenna lay down beside him, and he kissed her tenderly on the lips. "You were right," she said after a minute. "He will not intervene."

"Father Henri is a hard man. He is a man of strict tradition."

"I don't like him," Jenna confessed.

Blaise rolled over on his back. "Nor do I."

Jenna leaned on his shoulder. He kissed her again, then he drew her close. She felt happiness surge through her, and although she had failed to obtain Father Henri's help, she felt certain she would find a way to solve the problem. And even though he hadn't said so, she felt Blaise would help her.

Chapter Ten

Jenna watched as the corn boiled. The pot it cooked in was iron and had, like many things in the village, been obtained from the French. But even if the metal pot was an addition to the Indian way of life, the manner of cooking was traditional. The fire was built as all cooking fires were built—low and ready to cook on only when reduced to a bed of red hot coals. The pot was suspended from an ordinary wooden pot hook, made from a deleafed tree limb and trimmed in such a way that one branch was cut short to form the hook that hung on the cross stick over the fire. Two smaller branches had also been cut, one above the other, and these, too, served as hooks. The pot was suspended from the bottom hook by a length of leather. If it needed to be hotter, then it was suspended from the lower hook; if it boiled too much, it was raised to the higher hook, further above the coals. Sometimes, the corn was roasted in its husks directly in the coals, but tonight it was boiled and the smell was tantalizing. Jenna looked into the pot and wondered how long it had been since she had corn on the cob.

"I'll be grinding the corn tomorrow," Jenna said aloud. It was a laborious process. The corn was put into a large round container and pounded with a long thick piece of wood.

The Indians ate and prepared corn in many ways. Parched corn was made by browning the kernels in the fire, and then pounding them into a flour with maple syrup, dried berries, or chopped meat. This mixture was often carried by travelers. They had only to add water, and they would have a nourishing meal. Sometimes the Indians mixed corn with lima beans and made succotash, or a gruel she knew as hominy.

Jenna glanced at Elizabeth who was making cornhusk dolls for the Indian children, while James and Blaise were nearby, chopping wood. Living the way the Indians lived was a hard life. But in many ways it was a good life.

Her eyes strayed across the compound, Oioteet was already eating. His wife, Laaot, stood near him, ready to refill his bowl. Jenna knew that Laaot would not eat till Oioteet had finished. Laaot was not of this tribe. She was an Iroquois, a captive whom Oioteet had taken to replace his wife who had been killed. Jenna had wanted to talk with Laaot, but Laaot was clearly afraid of her husband. She avoided everyone.

Oioteet was one of the strongest and certainly the fiercest of all the warriors in the village. He was also cruel. Since the morning of the attempted escape and the old chief's order not to punish the captives, Oioteet's eyes had followed Blaise jealously, and clearly had it not been for Blaise, all the captives would have been treated badly. Oioteet had been ordered not to cut off James's arm if he did not flinch. He had followed the order, but he had resented it.

Over the months, Jenna had learned to avoid Oioteet. She suspected that, in addition to being cruel, he was also untrustworthy. His face was hard, and his eyes small slits that had a darting feral quality. Often, Jenna had looked up and found Oioteet's eyes on her or on Blaise. But when his eyes were on her, it was not desire she saw. It was hatred. She didn't doubt he was capable of assault, but it would not be an act of lust. It would be an act of pure revenge—a way of getting even with Blaise. She suspected he was jealous of Blaise's influence with the old chief and of the fact that many, if not most, of the Indians in the village respected Blaise more than him.

Twice she had tried to speak to Blaise about Oioteet. But he only laughed her warnings away. "So, his nose is out of joint! What does it matter?" Or, "No need to worry. We'll be gone soon."

Jenna did not share his confidence.

"Dinner's almost ready," she called out.

Blaise and James had put down their hatchets and had come over to the fire. Jenna set aside her thoughts and turned to them, smiling.

"Smells delicious," James said, running his tongue around his lips in anticipation of eating.

"I'll say," Blaise agreed.

Jenna looked toward Elizabeth. "You can cut the hot slabs of squash now."

Elizabeth set aside her cornhusk dolls and came immediately.

It was at that moment that Aweont came running across the compound from the chapel. As Jenna looked up, she saw her coming and also saw the look of distress on her usually placid face.

"The Black Robe!" Aweont panted. "Come! The Black Robe is ill."

Blaise pulled himself up quickly, and Jenna handed the stirring paddle to James. "You and Elizabeth stay here and finish cooking dinner. I'll go with Blaise."

Blaise followed behind Aweont and Jenna behind Blaise. Aweont led them to the chapel. She paused at the door and pointed toward the altar. There, at the foot of the altar, Father Henri was sprawled out. He appeared to be barely conscious.

"He said he wasn't feeling well this morning," Blaise revealed, as he knelt by the priest's side.

Jenna looked down at Father Henri. His sallow skin was flushed. She knelt down next to Blaise and felt the priest's head. "He's burning up with fever," she said.

"I should take him back to the wigwam."

Jenna shook her head. "No, it would be better if he stayed here. We can make a bed for him."

Blaise nodded. "I'll get the children to bring skins."

The priest opened his eyes, "Water," he muttered.

"And have them bring water too," Jenna suggested. "He seems very ill to me. I think I should stay here with him."

Blaise smiled at her. "A very humanitarian gesture, considering he wouldn't grant your request to intercede on James' behalf. And considering you don't like him very much."

"Shh!" Jenna whispered. "He'll hear you. Anyway, like him or not, he's sick, and someone has to care for him."

Blaise nodded his agreement. "And I'll have someone bring you some dinner." He leaned over and kissed her lips. "When it's time to sleep one of the Indian women can come and take over."

Jenna kissed him back. "I'll come to you later."

He smiled slyly. "I'm counting on that."

* * *

Piles of furs were brought, and Blaise moved Father Henri to them and covered him lightly. Jenna bathed his forehead in cool water and let him sip from a cup.

After a time, she moved away and sat down on a narrow bench, one of several that had been made for the chapel. Soon, Ponokuk came with her dinner and told her when night fell, Aweont would come to stay till morning.

After a time, Jenna sponged Father Henri with cool water. Still, to her dismay, she didn't feel his temperature was dropping, nor did he speak.

Jenna rolled him over and sponged his back. In the dim light, she saw a rash beginning to appear. She got the candle and leaned closer, trying to determine what exactly the angry red marks were. But it was to no avail. They might have been mosquito bites, or just the beginning of a simple fever rash. Yet one seemed larger than the others. She studied it, but it looked quite ordinary, in fact, it did look like a large bite.

Within the hour, Father Henri was chattering deliriously. It was as if he were in a world of half reality and half unreality. He began muttering about God and about the Indians.

Aweont poked her head into the chapel. "It is nightfall. You go, I'll stay."

Jenna shook her head. "I think I had better stay the night, Aweont. Tell Blaise for me, will you?"

Aweont padded off, and soon Blaise returned.

"Aweont tells me you find it necessary to stay the night."

"I think I should. His fever is still very high. I'm worried."

Blaise looked at Father Henri and then looked at her. He kissed her cheek. "I didn't know you were a nurse."

"I'm not," she answered. But was there anything she

could say that might indicate to him she knew something about medicine—not that she was any kind of an expert. But she had taken advanced first aid training, and this was the early eighteenth century! She certainly knew about the importance of sanitation and sterilization, and many other things that people at this time did not understand. She wanted Blaise to respect her medical knowledge, without thinking she was a nurse or a doctor. "My father," she said, finally, "was a doctor."

Jenna soothed her conscience by telling herself it was not so horrendous a lie. Her uncle was a doctor, and she had worked in his clinic for two summers. But were it the time for confessions, she also would have said that the other two summers—the ones she had spent working for a veterinarian—were much more enjoyable.

"I see," Blaise said with a faint smile. "Well, if you think you should stay. I won't argue. But I will miss you in my bed, woman."

He drew her into his arms and kissed her long and hard. Jenna kissed him back, thinking that it would be a long and lonely night. Still, it seemed important to stay with Father Henri. At least she could bathe him in cool water and keep his temperature from rising further.

Jenna awakened at midnight to hear Father Henri groan. She again bathed him in cool water, and while she bathed him, her hands felt the rash that now seemed to cover his body. Fever rash, she thought. In the darkness, it felt rather like hives.

At three, she was awakened again. And again, she tried to lower his temperature. She even gave him some medicine Aweont had brought. Jenna knew there were Indian medicinals that lowered temperature. Quinine was one, but this was not the part of the world in which quinine was found. Still, she hoped that the medicine Aweont offered was a similar chemical compound.

Was it aspirin that was made from the willow? She reminded herself to see if Aweont had a medicine made from willow trees or willow leaves.

The next time Jenna awoke, the sun was streaming in the window of the chapel. She pulled herself up and went immediately to Father Henri. Hardly had she reached his bed pallet when she stopped and looked at him in horror. His mouth was open, and his dead eyes stared at her. But it was not the dead staring eyes, nor his twisted contorted face that caused her terror. It was the fact that in the morning light she could see what she had not been able to see last night. His body was covered with pox. Father Henri had died of smallpox.

Jenna covered her face with her hands. "Dear God in Heaven!" she whispered. Aweont, Ponokuk, all the Indians who had brought skins, Blaise, James, and Elizabeth—everyone Father Henri had been exposed to since he'd come here! They'd all been near him! Smallpox was a killer, especially of Indians who had no resistance to it at all! There was no question about it—an epidemic could sweep through this peaceful village, and nearly everyone might die!

"Oh, God," Jenna whispered as she looked at the altar, the magnitude of the problem sweeping over her. "Please help me to stop it! Please!"

She, alone, would not get the disease because a few years before smallpox was eradicated, she had traveled with her parents to India. She'd been vaccinated then as she had been since childhood.

Jenna returned to Father Henri. She bent over, and with distaste, closed his staring eyes. Then, she stripped him and the bed. She went to the door and called Blaise, hoping her own panic would not be evident in her voice.

"Stop!" she shouted as he approached the chapel.

"You called me," he replied, looking bewildered.

"No one must come here," Jenna said firmly. "No one."

Blaise looked at her, and although he said nothing, it was clear he suddenly understood her tone, her expression, her firmness.

"Father Henri is dead," Jenna said. "He died of smallpox."

The implications were not lost on Blaise. "Oh, God," he mouthed.

"You must do as I say," Jenna said firmly. "You must believe I know what I'm doing."

He said nothing, but simply stood and looked at her.

"Build a funeral pyre. Everything he wore and the bedding must be burned. His body must be burned too."

"It is not the custom," Blaise protested.

"I don't care about the custom," Jenna shouted. "Everyone in this village will die if we're not careful. I don't know how many he's already exposed!"

"Exposed?" He looked at her with slightly raised eyebrows. "You use strange words."

"This illness can be caught. I mean I don't know how many people he may have been close to—close enough to so they might have caught it from him."

"I do not know how you know about such things, nor do I know how such a thing is caught. But you have been the closest," Blaise said, stepping toward her.

"I will not get it," Jenna said firmly. But what would she say? How could she explain why? "I've cared for others with the disease. I have never gotten it." It was too simplistic a lie. But there was no time to think of a more elaborate one.

"Gather everyone together. See if anyone else is sick. I'll use the chapel as a hospital."

"You seem sure of what you're doing."

"I am sure," Jenna returned. Then she looked at him and bit her lower lip. "Have you been in places where pox broke out before."

He nodded, and she felt instant relief. The chances were good that he, too, was immune. She could only pray that James and Elizabeth had a similar resistance.

"I will see to it that a funeral pyre is built, even though I do not approve of cremation. And I will find out if anyone else is sick and bring them here. Are you certain you won't get sick?"

"I won't," Jenna told him. "I know I won't. You must believe me, and you must do as I say. Make all the people wash," Jenna instructed. "And if Father Henri gave them anything—anything at all—beads, crosses, anything, those, too, must be burned."

"Why? Just tell me why?"

"The disease is carried on such things," Jenna replied. "To destroy the disease, we must destroy the places where it lives. Father Henri's dead body is home to the live disease. It did not die with him."

"You speak of this disease as if it were a spirit, as if it were of the nether world, as if it could inhabit clothing without being seen."

"It can, but it is not a spirit. It is something tiny, so tiny that it cannot be seen with the human eye." Jenna felt a terrible frustration as she tried to explain. An odd contemplative look covered Blaise's face.

"I have heard tell of a Dutchman named van Leeuwenhoek who can see what the eye cannot by using a special lens he has ground. But this is strange knowledge for a woman. You are either very learned or very dangerous."

Jenna looked into his eyes. "Which do you think I am?"

He smiled at her. "Very learned. "I don't believe in witchcraft."

Jenna tried to smile back. Before this was finished, he might change his mind.

Jenna herself built a fire by side door of the chapel. She boiled water and washed in strong lye soap. Then she cleaned up the chapel, certain that soon there would be others, although she prayed there would not be many.

She herself dragged Father Henri to the funeral pyre, and she warned everyone else away from touching him.

The Indians knew well what smallpox was. They shrunk away from the flames and went to their wigwams to hide from the illness that was now legend.

Ponokuk was the first to be brought to her. He burned with fever. The next was Succkkeecoo, Hee-la-dee's husband. Jenna prayed that Aweont would not be brought. She prayed those who were ill would not die.

But if these two were ill, how many others had *they* exposed? Jenna felt discouraged and she felt defeated. She bedded down the sick and then sat down herself. She stared at the altar. What did she know that could save this village and these people? What on earth could she do? Vaccination was really the only thing that could stop an epidemic, and these people were ninety years away from the knowledge that could help them, and a hundred-and-fifty years from the perfection of vaccination.

Jenna closed her eyes. She remembered the PBS film on the life of Edward Jenner. He had a terrible time convincing people of the value of inoculation. Who wanted to be cut with a knife and—"The cows!" Jenna said, suddenly aloud. "That was it! The cows! This village has a herd of cows!"

Jenna's mind raced. The Chinese had a crude form of

inoculation. And that was what Jenner had done! As she recalled from the film, inoculation with the matter drawn from cowpox sometimes prevented, or at the least, lessened the effects of smallpox so that those who got it, got it in a milder form and lived.

Jenna stood up and quickly checked her patients. Then she hurried to the door and called anxiously for Blaise. He had stationed an Indian runner nearby to fetch him when Jenna called.

She waited none too patiently, and at last she saw him coming toward her.

"Are you all right?" he asked.

Across the compound, Jenna could see Hee-la-dee and Ponokuk's mother. They were chanting. It was a long low chant, a plea to the great spirit. "Tell them not to worry," Jenna said. "They saw me call you, they may think the patients are worse."

"They aren't?"

Jenna shook her head. "They are the same. Tell them that to ease their minds, and then come back. I am going to need much help."

Blaise did as she asked and returned to where she always made him stand, some ten feet from the entrance to the chapel.

"Blaise, you will not understand what I want you to do. But you must believe me. It *will* work, and many lives will be saved."

"In the past few hours, you have made me believe you. But I'm afraid you have made an enemy of Oioteet. He speaks against you, caring for Ponokuk and Suckkeecoo. He says you are not of the Medicine Lodge."

Jenna looked at Blaise steadily. She understood all too well. This was Oioteet's opportunity. Everyone knew this disease came from Europeans. If he hated Blaise and hated her, he could use the disease to get even.

"You must not let him interfere," Jenna said with conviction. "There is too much we must do if we are to save the lives of these people. Blaise, you must bring me the cows, and you must bring me the sharpest knives in the village."

"You're going to kill the cows the French gave the village?"

Jenna shook her head. "No, I'm going to take the liquid from the cowpox, and I am going to cut everyone and put some of that liquid in their blood. In a few days, they will get cowpox, but it will not hurt them, and they will never get smallpox, or if they do, it will not kill them."

Blaise looked at her as if she had completely lost her mind. "The Indians are far too superstitious to do such things."

Jenna shook her head. "Europeans are more superstitious. The Indians believe in such medicine. The cow is a strong animal. If we tell them they need the cow's strength, they will believe."

"And what of James and Elizabeth?"

"I will do the three of you first so the Indians will know I am not trying to hurt them."

"The *three* of us? Ah, no, my woman, I think not."

Jenna looked at him hard. "You must, or all the children in this village may die. You must do it!"

Blaise stared at her. Her green eyes blazed with confidence even though he could see she was dead tired. He well understood that the story about the cow's strength was not true, but rather a trick to convince the Indians. But what was her real reason for doing such a thing? He wanted to believe she really knew something he did not. And, regardless of her bravado, she was most certainly

a brave woman to be ministering to those with the pox.
"Will you do it yourself?" he asked after a moment.

"Of course," she said, even though she knew it was
unnecessary.

"If you can be so brave, I cannot refuse."

Jenna smiled. "There's no time to waste."

Blaise first brought her the cows, and painstakingly,
Jenna extracted all the liquid she could from the cowpox. It took her a full two hours of painstaking squeezing. It was a very unpleasant task, made easier only by
her hope that the precious matter could save lives.

Then a fire was built, and several sharp knives were
brought. Jenna laid them on a stool that she took from
the chapel.

The Indians gathered round, stone faced and somewhat incredulous. Jenna looked at them. Somehow, she
had to explain what she was doing in a way they would
understand.

"When the medicine from the cow is put into the
blood it makes you strong. Pox comes, but it goes away
quickly and leaves no scars. It makes you strong against
this other pox—this pox that kills."

"Woman lie! She bring the pox! It is from the English!"

All the eyes turned to Oioteet, and the group parted.
He stood more or less at the center. He was bared to the
waist and dressed as if heading out on the warpath. Bold
streaks of ochre and charcoal gave his facial expression
a ferocious quality. And he snarled out his words, not
bothering to hide his hatred.

"Him!" Oioteet whirled around and pointed at Blaise.
"He brought this woman to our midst!"

His movement was so swift that Jenna hardly saw it.

Oioteet threw his hatchet through the air, and it landed one inch from Blaise's foot. Then, in a dramatic gesture, he threw a feather down.

Blaise looked up. His eyes were steady on Oioteet. "Oioteet is a brave Abnaki warrior. The Abnaki have smoked the calumet with the French."

"You are not French," Oioteet sneered.

"But I have smoked the calumet with the French."

"No matter!" Oioteet returned. "You are not French."

"Oioteet has challenged." The words came from the old chief.

Jenna looked from one to the other. But to her horror, Blaise only nodded. It seemed obvious that he was going to do battle with Oioteet. As for Oioteet, his narrows eyes flickered with the hatred she had seen in them before.

As if by some silent command, the Indians stepped back, forming a wide, wide circle more or less in front of the chapel.

Blaise walked across the distance between himself and Oioteet. He stood before Oioteet for a long moment, then without a single word, he reached back and drew one of Oioteet's own arrows from the quiver on his back. He broke the arrow and threw it on the ground, then he ground it into the dust with his foot.

From the crowd came a collective noise that sounded like surprise.

Oioteet took a step backward, and brandished his vicious tomahawk.

Blaise stood with his legs far apart and held open his weaponless hands.

Was this a ritual? Jenna looked on, holding the doorway of the chapel to steady herself. She was filled with fear for Blaise—and secondarily for all of them—should Blaise fail this challenge.

Immediately, another brave stepped forward and handed Blaise a tomahawk.

Jenna could hear the crowd suck in its breath.

Oioteet moved swiftly, dangerously. But Blaise easily dodged the first blow and with a sure leap, was in back of Oioteet.

The two had changed sides as artfully as two ballet dancers. But this was a deadly dance.

Oioteet swung again, and Jenna held her breath, almost afraid to watch. Oioteet's powerful attempt had come from the side. The onlookers were so silent that Jenna was certain she could hear the terrible instruments of death slicing through the air.

But Blaise again sidestepped the blow and was suddenly behind Oioteet. Blaise had grasped Oioteet by the back of the neck with his right hand, while he used his left hand to control Oioteet's tomahawk.

Blaise broke Oioteet's balance, whirled around, and brandished his tomahawk in the Indian's face, then pushed Oioteet away from him.

A jeer went up from the crowd. It seemed to Jenna as if Blaise could have killed Oioteet, but hadn't. She was sure the Indians were jeering Oioteet and not Blaise.

For a long moment, the two fighters looked at each other unblinkingly. Then Oioteet scrambled to his feet and ran off into the woods.

Blaise wiped his brow and handed his tomahawk to the Indian who had given it to him.

The old chief came forward and raised his staff. "Listen to the white medicine woman," he ordered. "The cow is a strong animal, and I have seen the pox on the cow, though the cow is not sick."

Jenna once again explained. Then, rather dramatically, she slashed a fine cut on her own arm. All those gathered round the fire sucked in their breaths. She dipped the tip of the knife into the liquid from the cow-pox and rubbed it into the open wound. There was a murmur of pure awe.

"Brave squaw," the chief muttered, with a nod of his head.

Elizabeth came next, and she closed her eyes. Jenna wiped off the knife and sterilized the blade in the flame. "So one blood does not mix with another," she explained. Then she inoculated Elizabeth.

"It didn't hurt at all," Elizabeth said proudly.

James was next, and although he, too, looked away, the cut was so clean, he seemed not to realize when she was finished.

Next Blaise submitted, and then the chief came forward and volunteered his arm.

Then, one by one, Jenna did all the children, then all the women, and finally all the braves.

"Remember," she told them. "You will get sick, but it will be a different kind of pox and you will recover."

Then, weary and terribly tired, she returned to her patients.

The moonlight fell on the altar of the little chapel, and both of her patients slept soundly. She had administered Aweont's medicine, but she knew they would most certainly break out in smallpox. Still, they were resting now and being cared for, perhaps they would survive.

"Jenna."

Jenna looked up to see Blaise standing behind her. "You shouldn't be here," she said.

"You're here."

"I told you. I won't get the disease."

"And as I was subjected to your 'cow medicine,' I should not get it either."

"No, you shouldn't . . ."

"You sound hesitant."

"I can only hope it works. I've never tried it, never done it myself that is."

"I do not know where you heard of such medicine, but even if there is a chance it will work, it is worth it. Jenna, smallpox would kill everyone here. Even very few Europeans are immune."

He sat down beside her and slipped his arm around her. "Are you sure you are not a witch? Perhaps a good witch?"

"You said you did not believe in them."

"I don't. But you are strange, my beauty. It is almost as if you are from some other place, some other time."

Jenna felt a cold chill pass through her. It wasn't yet time for her to confide in him. James had to be safe. She had to know him better. She loved him, that was true. But how much did he love her? He would have to love her a great deal to know the truth and to accept it.

"I am not so strange," she said, trying to move away from his all too clever guess about her origins.

"Then tell me where you learned so much."

Jenna was glad it was dark so he could not see her eyes. She felt she was not a good liar. "I read a lot," she finally said. Then added, "My father, the doctor, traveled to many lands. He studied the medicine of many peoples."

"You read? There are not many women who read."

"Well, I am one of them."

"Yes, I forgot. You are a teacher. Though I assumed you were a teacher of young ladies, and young ladies do not usually learn to read."

"I read and I do arithmetic too," she added. There were things he should know of her that she had decided to slowly reveal about herself. He did not seem put off by the fact that she had knowledge.

He squeezed her shoulder. "Good, I think learning makes a woman more interesting. God knows you are lovely enough!" With that, he kissed her on the cheek and moved over, pulling her close. "Lean against me. Let me hold you through the night."

Jenna leaned against his broad shoulder and closed her eyes. This tenderness was a whole new side of him. She fell asleep almost immediately.

Days passed, and Jenna's two smallpox patients both got stronger, though Ponokuk gave her a real scare on the third day of his illness. He became delirious, but then his fever eased, and he, too, began improving.

Everyone else in the village cursed the itchy cowpox. Some merely had swellings on their arms that itched terribly while other ran mild fevers, and two or three were quite ill. But within a few days of getting cowpox, they were well again.

James and Blaise were hardly sick at all, and Elizabeth was only ill for two days.

Hee-la-dee had a very mild case indeed. Jenna felt she would be fine since she was already eight months pregnant. Perhaps Jenna thought happily, her child would be born immune to this killer disease.

Blaise walked by the stream with her, his arm around her tiny waist. "I can scarcely believe it worked," he said, shaking his head. "I did not really believe you, you know. No one has ever stopped the pox."

Jenna herself worried. The time was not right for this knowledge. She had surely done something she ought not to have done. But how could she let her friends die? She shook her head in bewilderment.

"I appreciate your nursing abilities, Jenna. But it would not be a good idea if people in Quebec learned of your success."

"I think you're right," she agreed.

He smiled. "People are not always willing to accept knowledge. There was a time when fire was a great mystery to them—then gunpowder."

Gunpowder—Jenna hadn't thought of gunpowder. "I know," she agreed. "You know, the Chinese invented gunpowder."

"So I have heard."

"They invented this medicine too. My father learned of it from a sea captain who had sailed in China."

"I am not surprised. Well, we just won't tell anyone."

Jenna smiled at him. "But what about the Indians?"

"Oh, I suspect the fine white medicine lady will just go into their lore."

He turned and whirled her around, kissing her again. Then they returned to the village, arm and arm.

"Please, I must speak with you," Hee-la-dee said, as she stood by their fire. Her long hair was in two great thick braids, and her womb was heavy with child.

"Speak," Blaise said with a wave of his hand. "Hee-la-dee is our friend."

She smiled shyly. "I come to ask a great favor. I am to have my child in a few weeks, and I would ask you to be my guide. It is my first child."

Jenna looked at Hee-la-dee in amazement. Deliver a child? Nothing in her experience prepared her for delivering a child. Immediately, she thought of all the things that could go wrong. "Most certainly, Aweont knows more than I about delivering a child."

"Aweont says you have fine hands. She says you are

the master medicine woman. You have proved that to be so."

"Your reputation precedes you," Blaise said with some amusement.

Jenna felt terrible. She only vaguely remembered the first-aid course that mentioned emergency childbirth. Its major point had been to get the mother to a hospital as soon as possible. Well, such advice was fine for Boston, but hardly any good in the middle of the forest in the year 1704.

"Surely, a woman who can stop the pox can deliver a child," Blaise put in.

Jenna felt an inner panic. Stopping the epidemic had been the result of knowledge not medical skill. She had never even seen a baby being born for heaven's sake! She turned toward Blaise. "I thought we were leaving for Quebec? Will we be here?"

Blaise laughed. "What's a few days?" He looked at Hee-la-dee. "I don't think it will delay us much in any case. She looks ready to birth quite soon."

"Please, be my guide."

Jenna smiled weakly and agreed.

Hee-la-dee hugged her. "Aweont will help too," she said.

"I hope so," Jenna said, praying that this would be a totally normal birth.

Chapter Eleven

By the end of the first week in August, the far cornfield was ready to harvest. Some weeks ago, the field closer to the village had been harvested. The two had been planted so they would not come into harvest at the same time, thus making the harvest easier.

In the cornfield, the August sun was hot. Jenna, like the other women, husked corn. The bright yellow ears went in one pile, the husks in another.

Unot was a tall slender girl with two traditional long thick braids. Her mother was a teller of folktales and one of the keepers of tribal history. Unot was following in her mother's footsteps, and she spoke while the others worked in silence and listened.

"There was a great hunter who once roamed a land far from here. One day while walking deep in the great woods near the inland sea, he came upon a clearing. In the middle of this flat clearing, he came upon a stranger who offered him a calumet. The stranger was not dressed in a loin cloth, but rather in a shiny coat and instead of eagle feathers, he wore bright red feathers.

"The hunter asked the stranger's name and was given this reply: 'Tomorrow we will wrestle, and if you win, I will tell you my name and give you a gift for all your people.' It was agreed. Both men were very strong warriors, and their battle lasted from sunrise to sunset. Just as the sun was setting, the great hunter drew upon his inner strength and defeated the stranger.

" 'I demand to know your name,' the hunter told the stranger, 'and I claim the gift you promised.'

" 'My name is Mondahmin, and my body is my gift to you. Cover me with dust where we have wrestled and come back here often, and you will see and learn of my gift.'

"The hunter did as he was told, and when he returned after three moons, he saw two green feathers sprouting from the mound where he had buried the stranger, Mondahmin. A voice came from the burial mound, singing, 'This is corn, the gift of Mondahmin. Take its seeds to your people. Tell them to make a feast to me.' The hunter took the corn to his people and they feasted. They were saved from starvation."

"Was the hunter of your people?" Jenna asked curiously.

Unot shook her head. "No, the corn was given first to others and brought to us by the Iroquois people before we fought. It is grown with squash and beans, and the Iroquois people call these gifts "The Three Sisters."

Jenna marveled at the unwritten history. It was true enough that corn had spread from the south, carried from one group to another. But in her wildest dreams, she had not thought of what growing it here, and in this time would be like. The Indian farmers ringed trees to kill them, then burned the trunks and scraped away the charred wood with stone axes. She knew this because although this field had been cleared when they came, another nearby was being cleared now for next year's crop. Fields, Jenna learned, were used for several plantings, then abandoned for up to twenty years. Without knowing why, these people practiced sensible crop rotation so that the soil would not become overused. At the same time, the forest was also reborn where the fields had been.

And the variety of foods was also fascinating. There were, she learned, over sixty varieties of beans raised, several kinds of corn, and eight different squashes. They were all "Gifts of the Creator," Unot maintained. In addition, to these foods there were also mushrooms, wild fruits, nuts, and certain leaves. Berries were eaten, both raw and cooked. Many were dried for winter use.

But the most important food to these Indians was the rice they harvested from the marshy fields that lay some miles away. Together with corn and beans, rice was a staple food.

But the rice was not yet ready to harvest. This season belonged to the tall reeds of corn.

The husks were used for many things. The young children made dolls from them, as Elizabeth had done. They were used to wrap other food, and a kind of bread was made which was cooked inside the husks to give it added flavor. She imagined this was something like a tamale, although she had never had a tamale.

"Jenna! Jenna!" Elizabeth ran toward her and Jenna looked up. She had been lost in thought, and marveling over these people whom she no longer thought of as her captors. Perhaps she was only imagining it, but since the day Oioteet had disappeared everyone seemed much happier. And the happiest of all was poor Laaot, his slave-wife, who now looked after the old chief.

"Jenna! Come, Hee-la-dee says her time has come!"

Jenna dropped her husks into the basket and ran quickly to meet Elizabeth who was utterly breathless, having run all the way from the village.

* * *

Inside Hee-la-dee's wigwam, Hee-la-dee lay on a bed of skins. In spite of her natural coloring, her face was pale and her lips dry.

Jenna went quickly to her side and knelt down.

"Hee-la-dee has much pain," she gasped.

"When did the pain start?"

"When the sun was not quite in the middle of the sky."

Jenna looked outside and for the first time, cursed the loss of her wristwatch. The sun was no longer in its high-noon position, so it seemed safe to assume that Hee-la-dee had her first labor pains perhaps two hours ago. Certainly, Hee-la-dee could not tell her in minutes how far apart her contractions were.

"Hee-la-dee, I must know how close your pains are together. You must tell me when the next pain begins."

Hee-la-dee nodded. Small beads of perspiration glistened on her furrowed brow. Her lips were tight.

Jenna dipped a chamois in cool water and bathed Hee-la-dee's face. She smiled gratefully. Then she whispered, "It seems harder than others I have seen."

Jenna tried to smile. "It is your first." Still, she herself had thought that Hee-la-dee would have an easier time of childbirth. She was young, in splendid physical condition, and well built with reasonably wide hips.

"Now," Hee-la-dee gasped. "Now."

Jenna took Hee-la-dee's hand and held it. "Squeeze my hand, and tell me when it stops."

Hee-la-dee took a deep breath and tensed, then after a long moment, Jenna felt her hand relax.

Silently, Jenna began counting. She had reached 192 when again Hee-la-dee whispered, "Now."

"Three minutes apart," Jenna said.

She had Hee-la-dee spread her legs, and Jenna exam-

ined her as best she could. She looked as if she were di-
lated normally, but what was worrying was the liquid in
which she found Hee-la-dee lying. Her water had burst!
But Hee-la-dee had no one to tell her, because this was
her first child, and she herself did not understand the
significance of it.

Dear God, Jenna thought. Could the child be breach?

First aid had hardly prepared her to perform a Cesa-
rean section, not that the instruments were available in
any case. God in heaven! What did women like this do?
She felt suddenly panic stricken.

"Hee-la-dee, I know you chose me to be your guide,
but if I were not here, who would be your guide?"

"One of the other women, perhaps my sister Aweont.
The old Mide can no longer walk or see, although she
still lives. This village has been without a Mide for a
long while. The Black Robes do not approve of the
Mides."

"What is a Mide?" Jenna asked.

"A medicine woman, a member of the Grand Medicine Lodge, the Midewigan. All members of the Grand
Medicine Lodge are under the special protection of
Dzhe Manitou, the Good Spirit. But old Mide is herself
ill with age, and her hands shake. That is why I asked
you."

Jenna remembered now that during Oioteet's tirade,
he had made mention of the fact that she should not be
caring for patients because she was not a member of the
Grand Medicine Lodge. "Where does the old Mide live?
I've never seen her."

Hee-la-dee took a deep breath, squeezed Jenna's hand
tightly, and then relaxed as one of her labor pains came
and went.

"She seldom leaves her wigwam."

Jenna realized then who Hee-la-dee was talking

about. She was a very old woman. The people of the village took turns bringing food, and great homage was paid to her.

"Old Mide will soon be one with the Great Spirit. We have not yet been blessed with a new Mide, though our chief says one will come soon. He believes you were sent till one comes," Hee-la-dee gasped, just as another labor pain came.

Jenna nodded. "I must speak with the old Mide, Hee-la-dee. I'll get Elizabeth to sit with you for a few minutes."

Hee-la-dee nodded.

Jenna opened the flap of the wigwam and crawled out. She spoke quickly to Elizabeth and then hurried off to the Mide's wigwam. "May I enter?" she called out.

"Yes," came a croaking reply.

Jenna ducked inside the wigwam which was larger than many of the others. She blinked because of the change of light and squinted as she looked about. The wigwam was filled with a strange musty odor, and in the corner, sitting on a pile of skins, she saw the old woman she had only glimpsed once before. She was older than even Jenna had imagined. She was, Jenna guessed, at least ninety.

She was a brittle tiny woman with large cloudy eyes and wiry white hair. Her skin was deeply wrinkled, and as Jenna drew closer she realized the old woman was blinded by cataracts.

The old woman lifted her hand, "Hee-la-dee is in pain with her child."

"Yes," Jenna confirmed. Had someone come to tell her? Someone must have, Jenna concluded.

"I have heard of your medicine."

It was then that it occurred to Jenna that the old woman had not been inoculated. It didn't matter now.

First, she had probably not been exposed because she almost never left her abode, and second, since she was a medicine woman, she had probably been exposed before. In any case, she would already be sick if she were going to be sick.

"I only wanted to help. Smallpox is a terrible sickness."

"White man's sickness. I was born when there were no white men. I was born when the woods belonged to us alone."

The woman rocked back and forth. "But I don't blame you. White people die from this pox too. I have seen them."

Jenna wondered how to tell the old woman what had happened. "I come to seek your counsel."

"I was told you were wise. But you are not a member of the Medicine Lodge, and you have little knowledge of the herbs and plants of the forest."

"That is true, but I want to help Hee-la-dee."

"Hold out your hands."

Jenna held out her hands, and the old woman leaned over and took them in hers. She rubbed them and felt them. "Yes, they are good hands for bringing babies into the world."

"But I don't have your experience, your knowledge."

"The Creator guides all births."

Jenna nodded, but in any case decided to explain the situation. "Hee-la-dee's water has broken, but her pains are not yet close enough together. I fear the child might be upside down."

The old woman scowled and shook her head. "It is not a good sign that the inner sea in which the child swims has too soon flowed away. The child, if born at all, may die of thirst."

Jenna felt helpless. Why was she here? Did this

woman understand anything? Of course, she did. She understood breech babies died, and sometimes, perhaps often, their mothers died too. But she probably didn't have a clue as to what to do to save them. Perhaps when such babies died, superstition made people believe they had died of thirst.

"They need not die," Jenna said.

"Wash your hands in the river and ask the Great Spirit to bless your hands. Then put your hands inside Hee-la-dee and try to turn the child within her. It may not be upside down, it may only have its face toward the heavens instead of toward the earth. I would do this, but I am too old."

Jenna felt a sense of surprise. The old woman did indeed know something, Jenna thought. She wanted her to try to rotate the child in case it was face up. Of course, a child face up would also cause a slow labor. But could she do it? And, indeed, was that the problem? "I will try," Jenna promised.

The old woman suddenly seized her hands and pressed them together. She held them for a long moment and mumbled some words over them, then she looked at Jenna and simply said, "Go now."

Jenna hurried away. She contemplated the river and glanced heavenward. Surely, that part of the instruction was pure superstition, but could it hurt? She went to the river and washed her hands. She asked the Great Spirit to bless her, then she returned to the wigwam and washed her hands thoroughly with warm water and lye soap.

"She is in great pain," Elizabeth said, ashen faced. "Will it be all right, Jenna?"

"I hope so. Go to Blaise and tell him I will need a sharp knife. Tell him to sterilize its blade in the fire."

"Sterilize?" Elizabeth said. "What strange words you

always use. But I remember, you did it when you cut us to prevent the pox."

What benefits sterilization would bring! If only she dared confide the benefits!

Jenna went to Hee-la-dee's side. Again, she wiped her face and lips, then she moved her slightly into a better light. She again examined her. Hee-la-dee let out a long, low moan.

"Hee-la-dee, pant between the pains like a dog in summer. Then, when I tell you to push, I want you to push."

Hee-la-dee gasped her response.

Jenna prodded around, then when her hands were lubricated by the jellylike liquid that Hee-la-dee excreted, she slipped a single finger into the birth canal. She felt almost immediately the round head of the child. She felt like screaming for joy. The child was not breech! The old woman had guessed correctly. It was face up and thus pushing with its face rather than with the harder back part of its skull. Such a position caused a slower than normal trip down the birth canal. But now, Jenna realized, there wasn't a moment to lose.

Hee-la-dee screamed again, and Jenna glanced up at Aweont, who stood silently by the entrance to the wigwam, tense but ready to assist.

"Aweont, push gently on her womb when I tell you."

Hee-la-dee's pain subsided, and she panted as directed.

Jenna did not look, but instead closed her own eyes and depended on touch as she slowly eased her hands into the birth canal. She rotated the child's shoulders slowly, then to her delight felt it slip around. Again, Hee-la-dee screamed.

Jenna, perspiration on her own brow, commanded, "Now push!"

Hee-la-dee pushed, and the small head popped into view. "Again!" Jenna demanded. Hee-la-dee shrieked, this time louder, but there was another cry as well, it was the cry of the small baby as it fairly popped into the world and shrieked out its indignation at having been so delayed.

Hee-la-dee panted, and tears joy ran down her cheeks.

"Again, push!" Jenna said.

Hee-la-dee did, and the placenta too came out. Jenna gently lifted the small baby and placed it on Hee-la-dee's stomach. She placed the placenta, to which the baby was still attached next to her.

"I have the water and the knife," Elizabeth was breathless. Jenna took the knife and cut the umbilical cord, leaving it long enough to tie a knot. Then she cleaned up Hee-la-dee and then the tiny little boy.

Then, according to Hee-la-dee's instructions, she wrapped the child tightly and placed it at its mother's breast. When she was finished, Jenna staggered outside into the afternoon sun.

Suckkeecoo was there, having fully recovered from the pox. He looked at her expectantly. "I heard the child cry."

Jenna smiled. "You have a son."

Suckkeecoo nodded and went inside his wigwam to join his wife.

"Was it difficult?" Blaise asked.

Jenna nodded and walked to his side. "Yes, the child was not positioned normally."

"Is it all right?"

"Yes. I was frightened."

"You, frightened? I don't believe it."

Jenna looked into his face. She yearned to lean

against him, to have him hold her. "I do get frightened."

"I have never seen you frightened. You always seem to know what will happen."

"There are some things no one can know."

"Ah, you mean how a child will be born."

She wanted to tell him that in her time it would be possible to know even that—but he probably could not conceive it. No, she didn't know him well enough yet. So, she simply nodded.

He led her away, into the cool woods. He enfolded her in his arms and kissed her passionately. "You make a good medicine woman."

Jenna just leaned against him. His hands moved across her back as if he instinctively understood the tension she had been under, acting as midwife. She felt that tension flee, only to be replaced by the tension of raw desire. Their love was new, each time was like the first time. Each time was sensual, powerful, frighteningly passionate.

His warm hands slipped beneath her leather tunic and under the cloth of her undergarment. No modern bra held her prisoner, her breasts were free and his hands moved over them, exciting her nipples till they were as hard as the stones on the ground.

She moaned in his arms even as her own hands explored him. His manhood was as strong and hard as if it were made of bone. He whirled her around and even while caressing her, he took her from behind. His hands seemed everywhere, and he made certain that she was pleasured as he moved his fingers sensuously. Never before had she thought of this position as erotic, but the experience was just that.

He caressed her white buttocks, then touched her most responsive, most intimate place. The feeling of him on her excited her beyond her wildest dreams, yet he controlled her utterly, pleasurably, as he moved himself inside her, till she fell, panting on the soft grass with the deep throbbing pleasure which spread through her whole being.

He delivered his seed to her and then rolled with her in the grass till she was atop him, her face still flushed with pleasure.

"You are quite a woman," he whispered. "White heat and fire burn in your soul."

Jenna's face was aglow with excitement. He was the only man who had ever affected her this way. And yet, for all their wild passion, there were still secrets between them, and to a large extent, she knew she was as much a mystery to him as he was to her. But she also knew that she would eventually share her secret with him and hoped he, too, would be forthcoming about his past.

As they grew closer, she had learned he was a man ahead of his own time. He did not think of the Indians as most white people did. He took them as equals, and she wondered what made him so different. He still seemed hesitant to reveal himself to her completely. She also had learned that he was exceptionally well read and well versed and that he spoke the language of the Abnaki and the English as well as French. He was also curious and inventive. But his ideas about women perplexed her. In the beginning, he had spoken of owning her, and sometimes he still reminded her of the fact that he'd bought her. But now he did so in what she thought was a teasing way. She was never really certain if he considered women property or not. She always had to remind herself that if he did regard her as property, he was only reflecting what was, in fact, both the custom and law of the period. If he did not really think of her that way, then he was indeed most unusual. But whatever his attitude on this matter, she felt he respected her and that beneath his gruffness he was kind and protective.

She lay quiet now in his arms, listening to his breathing as it returned to normal. Yes, she was certain he was a good man, a man who would reveal himself as their relationship developed.

The August night was filled with sounds and smells. Crickets sang sweet songs to one another and beepers, the tiny frogs of the stream, joined in to create a discordant melody. Now and again, if it was quiet, the sound of a wolf or coyote could be heard as it bayed at the full moon.

In the center of the village, a huge fire burned brightly. Venison had been roasted for the evening meal, and with it fresh corn, squash, and beans had been served.

Elizabeth held Hee-la-dee's young son and sang to him. James worked on his arrows, sharpening them, honing them to perfection as Mummicott had taught him to do. Mummicott, too, worked. He was busy stringing a new bow.

Jenna sat contentedly by Blaise, watching as the fire flickered. She felt relaxed and just a little sleepy after a day of work in the fields.

Blaise abstractedly ran his hand over her hair. Jenna's hair was the color of fine highly polished copper and it was soft to the touch. How beautiful she is! And how proud and brave. A woman among women, he thought silently. He knew his sexual attraction to her was overwhelming, and strangely, unlike other women he had known, it never seemed to change. He wanted her with the same intensity every night. He could hardly be near her without wanting to touch her soft white skin, or hold her close and smell the sweet aroma of her body. For this woman alone, he felt an unbridled appetite and an overwhelming desire. When she gave herself to him, it was with vigor and energy and with an openness and willingness that set her apart from all others.

He glanced at her. Her eyes were on the fire, and her expression was contemplative, almost sad as if she was remembering some bittersweet incident.

Yes, not only was he deeply attracted to her in a physical sense, he knew there was much more. She was intelligent and quick. She had a sense of her own self. And there was something terribly different about her, something he couldn't describe, something strange and compelling.

He moved slightly and again, glanced at her profile in the firelight. Loving her was a betrayal—a betrayal he had not yet fully reconciled even though he knew he was far too weak to give her up. This love—this lust drew him to her, and no matter how many times he chastised himself, once it had happened, he could not withdraw.

Jenna turned to him, the shadows of the fire played on her face. "Will we be going to Quebec soon?"

He shrugged. There were things he could not yet explain—perhaps could never explain. "We have to stay," he said. "A little longer until Kewatin returns."

"Kewatin?" Jenna was surprised to hear his name. He and some of the other braves had separated from them while they were still in Vermont.

"Why do we have to wait for him?"

"Because I must speak with him."

Jenna looked into Blaise's face. It had taken on an expression she had seen before, an expression she was at a loss to understand. It was as if he had quietly, but firmly closed a door to her.

Jenna was midway between the stream that provided water for the village and the village, when she heard the dogs begin to bark and the shouts of the children.

By the time she had reached the outer circle of wigwams, the drums were being beaten. She hurried on anxious to see that all the commotion was about.

A ring of women and children stood all around the inner circle of wigwams, while dust rose from the center. The women and children shouted loudly in Abnaki, some shook their fists, while others ran forward, armed with birch switches.

Jenna pushed through the circle to see what was going on. To her shock, she saw that some eleven Indians were tied together and being made to walk in a circle while being kicked, punched, and struck with birch switches. The women of the village were relentless, shouting loudly and spiting. Some of the children threw stones. It was as if they had all gone mad!

"Stop it!" Jenna shouted. The victims were already bloodied, and they stumbled as they were beaten.

"Stop it! Stop it!" Jenna sprang forward, only to be caught round the waist by Blaise's strong arm. He yanked her back with force.

"Be still, I thought you knew better by now!"

Jenna looked up into his face. It's expression was anything but compassionate as his eyes were glued on the prisoners.

She turned herself to see that one was now on the ground, being viciously kicked. It was only then that she saw Kewatin and realized that the braves who herded the prisoners were those she had not seen since the separation in Vermont.

She looked back at Blaise. "You must stop this! You can't let this go on! Those men are already hurt!"

Blaise looked down on her coldly. His face was not the face of the man who had made love to her only hours before. "You have too much sympathy for the Mohawk," he sneered.

"Have you no compassion? Those men are hurt." she searched his face.

"I have as much compassion for them as they had for the children of this tribe when it was raided."

Jenna's mouth opened, but she did not have time to speak. He propelled her toward their wigwam and pushed her roughly inside. "Stay here," he ordered. "I do not want to see you try to interfere again!"

Jenna stared back at him. He seemed a totally different person.

Chapter Twelve

Jenna pulled herself out of a troubled sleep sometime just before dawn. She sat up and rubbed her eyes. Silence. She realized she had slept alone in the wigwam for the first time since she and Blaise had first begun making love.

The memories of the previous evening came crashing in on her. He had brought her to the wigwam and commanded her to stay. She had stayed, rolled in a ball of misery listening as the taunting of the prisoners went on for many hours. Then it became silent. Blaise did not come back. He did not explain his anger with her. And what had happened to the prisoners? Had they finally been killed?

Suddenly, the flap on the wigwam was parted, and Blaise crept inside.

"I'm not asleep," she said in the darkness.

"You should be. You need your rest. We're leaving at sun up."

"Today?" she said dumbly.

"Yes, today." He was crawling into his bedroll; he seemed intent on sleeping these last few hours of the early morning.

"I don't understand what happened. I don't under-

stand how you could let those men be tortured—are
they dead now?" And then in panic, "Where are Elizabeth and James?"

He answered her last question first. "Confined to
their wigwam like you."

There was a long awkward silence. "They aren't
dead," he said after a time. "They'll be all right. But
they'll remain slaves. Jenna, I can't begin to tell you
what those men did to the people of this tribe—to my
people too. There are things I think you can't understand."

Jenna felt tears running down her cheeks. Had she
misjudged him? She couldn't speak. She crawled across
the darkness between them, and he reached out for her,
bringing her down beside him.

"I don't know whether to wish you had stayed angry
or rejoice in your forgiveness," he whispered as his
hands roamed her body.

Jenna said nothing. She was immediately lost in the
reality of the sensations that swept over her as soon as
he began touching her. Half memory—half anticipation.

She moved her own hands and touched him, almost
startled by what she felt.

"Woman, I shan't make love for long enough to satisfy if you persist in touching me so," he whispered. His
tongue flicked across her nipple, and she groaned. "I
take great pleasure in feeling you writhe in my arms,"
he said, again kissing her neck.

Jenna moved with him as he moved within her. The
day—everything was forgotten and forgiven. We both
have secrets she told herself.

Three Indians accompanied them as they left the village. Jenna was unsure of the date, but thought it to be

either the last few days of August or the first days of September.

Mummicott was the only one of the three Indians who went with them that she knew, or felt she knew.

They walked through the woods, following what appeared to be a well trod trail. The Indians portaged their canoe, and they carried packs. "How far will the Indians come with us?" Jenna asked.

"Just until we reach the water. Then only one will come to help me paddle."

"I can paddle now," Jenna protested.

"Ah, yes. But you're still a novice. This is a long trip, not a pleasure cruise to our private island."

Jenna blushed. In the center of the lake near the village, there was a small island. She and Blaise had often paddled over to it in the hours before twilight. There, in privacy, they had made love on the white sand beach. Then they would swim naked in the cold water and play like children.

Seeing her blush, he laughed. Then, more seriously, "I'm afraid we won't be alone for several days."

Jenna shook her head as if to dispel thoughts of their still tempestuous liaisons. She was silent for a time, then commented, "I'm glad Mummicott won't be away long. Aweont misses him."

"He's one of the best hunters in the village. I couldn't keep him away. He's too badly needed."

They had walked five miles when Mummicott stopped dead in his tracks. He looked around and sniffed the air like an animal.

It was an exceptionally hot day, and the sun blazed down out of a cloudless sky. Jenna, Blaise, and the others stopped too. Jenna sniffed as Mummicott did. And to her surprise she could also smell the odor that fouled the late summer air. It was a sickening smell, the horrible smell of rotting flesh.

Mummicott pointed upward. Overhead, a large number of crows circled, swooping down and down again to some spot well beyond the main trail.

"I look," Mummicott said.

"We'll all look," Blaise said, following Mummicott as he headed off the trail onto a narrower deer trail that led into the dense woods. The smell grew worse the further they walked. It made Jenna quite ill.

They came to a clearing, but Mummicott dropped his spear to keep them from passing. "Dead man," he said unemotionally.

But Jenna could not keep herself from looking. "How horrible," she said, sucking in her breath.

The naked pockedmarked body lay face down. It was black from lying in the sun, and much of it had been eaten by the birds that circled above.

"It's Oioteet," Jenna heard Blaise say. She felt the vomit rising in her throat. The stench was terrible. She turned and ran back down the path, away from the sight and smell of the decaying body.

James and Elizabeth followed her. Jenna went into the woods and was sick, then she staggered out onto the main path.

"It is terrible," Elizabeth said. She had been far back and had not actually seen the body.

In a moment, Blaise appeared. "Are you all right? You're pale."

"The smell made me sick."

"We'll sit here a while and wait. The Indians want to build him a proper pyre. It is the custom to expose dead bodies to the elements, but they should be placed on a proper pyre. It won't take long."

Jenna shook her head. "He must have come out here to die."

"I dishonored him. He was in disgrace. I imagine when he got sick he felt he couldn't come back to the village for help. He chose to die out here, alone."

Elizabeth and James roamed to the far side of the trail. There they spread out a skin and lay down in the sun.

Jenna leaned her head on Blaise's shoulder. In the distance, she heard the Indians chanting. It was a strange mournful chant, one that she was certain would ring in her ears for many days to come.

Blaise touched her hair, and vaguely, he wondered how she would fit into his life in Quebec. He knew it would be difficult, especially at first.

Yet there was one thing that might make it easier. She seemed to understand a little French, and she was exceptionally beautiful. A beautiful woman, he acknowledged, was always welcome. But she was also independent and brought with her a certain egalitarianism common in the British Colonies. That was not something that existed in the French Province that had a distinct class system. Yes, life would change for Jenna and for Elizabeth and young James once they arrived in Quebec. He could only hope the change would not alter his relationship with this woman.

"You're quiet," Jenna said softly.

He half smiled and looked into her magnificent green eyes. They were like jade. "I was thinking of home," he said slowly.

"Scotland?"

He shook his head. "No, not Scotland. I left Scotland when I was a mere babe in arms—like the son of Heela-dee. No, I meant Quebec."

Jenna turned and met his gaze. His warm hand held

hers, and she was aware of its warmth and the sensuous movement of his finger on her palm. He seemed to be thinking hard about something.

"You've told me so little about Quebec. In fact, you've told me little about yourself."

"Nor have you revealed all of your secrets to me."

He was right. Yet she still did not feel the time was right to confess her unbelievable story to him, and she knew he was keeping things from her for some reason. Perhaps, she thought sadly, the time would never be right for either of them.

"You can tell me about Quebec."

"I fear you might have trouble adjusting. I've been in Boston, and I know how different it is. As for Deerfield, well there is no comparison."

"And the Virginia Colony?"

"I've not been there, but perhaps there is more comparison."

"I'm not sure what you're talking about," Jenna confessed.

"I'm talking about people and classes. Quebec is very strict, Boston town more egalitarian. In Quebec, there is the clergy, which, as you already know, is a powerful class."

"I trust they are not all as unpleasant as Father Henri."

"He was a Jesuit. The priests who minister to the *habitants* are a different breed. Practical men, all."

"The *habitants?*" Jenna repeated. She knew the history of Deerfield, and she knew what American history she had learned in school. But to a large extent Canadian history was a mystery to her. She had not the foggiest idea who the *habitants* were.

"The commoners—Quebec is almost like Europe.

The *habitants* are those who live on the land of the *seigneurs*. They pay a yearly rent—"

"I take it these *seigneurs* are like lords of the manor."

Blaise smiled. "I suppose you could say that."

Jenna thought to herself that it all sounded like a transplanted feudal system, but she did not say so. "Tell me more," she prodded.

"There are nobles too. After all, the governor general is appointed by the king of France."

"So this governor general is the most important person in the colony?"

Blaise shook his head. "No, the *intendant* is the most important person. The very description of his job tells it all. He is intendant of Justice, Police, and Finance. And it is not a colony, but a province of France."

"And how do these people live?" Jenna asked.

The *habitants* live simply, the clergy—depending on their position—also live simply, although the life of the bishop is quite lavish. As for the *seigneurs* and the nobles, well, they live as close as they can to how landowners and nobles in France would live."

Jenna frowned. Her one experience in this century had been her few hours in Deerfield before the raid. She didn't really know how people in Boston lived. And what she knew of Williamsburg came only from having visited the reconstructed city. "I can't imagine what it's like," she commented truthfully.

Blaise leaned over and tenderly kissed her throat. "You won't have to try to imagine it for long."

Jenna leaned against him. In many ways, she hated leaving the village and the friends she had made. But the time had to come, and perhaps once in Quebec, she could find a way for James to return home. "I look forward to the new adventure," she whispered.

He leaned close to her ear. "I think together, our life will be a real adventure."

"We'll be at the river by nightfall," Blaise told her.

"And tomorrow we'll canoe," Jenna assumed.

He smiled mischievously. "I know how you are looking forward to it."

"I'm ready this time," she answered confidently.

For three days they traveled by canoe. Jenna's legs did not grow sore as they had before. She attributed her lack of soreness to the life she had been leading for the past months and to the fact that she and Blaise had canoed often on the lake near the village. And, she thought, she could also thank Aweont for making her soft leather kneepads stuffed with goose feathers.

On the fourth day, they arrived at what was clearly a small army post. Here, the last Indian to accompany them left.

The soldiers were all young and dressed in skin tight brown breeches, knee-high boots, white shirts, and royal blue tunics. When they spoke to Blaise, Jenna had to strain to understand. This was eighteenth century French not modern French. When she had studied French, her professor had talked about the French spoken in Quebec. "Some who speak French in Canada," he told the class, "still speak French as it was spoken in the eighteenth century. Those who emigrated to the French province did so before 1700. After that date, there was almost no new emigration to Quebec, and therefore, the language remained almost the same."

"Are these soldiers from France?" Jenna asked.

Blaise shook his head. "No, we have no military from France save the *Troupe de Marine* in Montreal. For over thirty years, the province has provided its own militia."

Jenna listened carefully. She needed as much information as possible. She was consumed by curiosity. How had Blaise come to live here? Why had his parents taken him away from Scotland? She had questions about him she had not asked, and she had a hundred questions about the place where she was going and the people she would have to live among.

"The commandant tells me that dinner will soon be served. He invites us to join him."

"How good of him," Jenna said, smiling. She wondered if she should even try to speak French. Where could she say she learned French to explain her manner of speech and her vocabulary? Would they even understand her?

"Jenna, it's time you and Elizabeth dressed as women should," Blaise announced. "We are closer to home, and from here on, we will be journeying by wagon."

Jenna looked at him questioningly. Personally, she found her Indian dress quite comfortable and practical for travel. She did not look forward for one moment to the clothes of the day. They were awkward and cumbersome. The whale bone panniers worn under skirts to make them appear full were difficult to sit in, and the corsets were constraining. Still, she assumed that Blaise must have his reasons for telling her this, and she knew she had to do as he wished. "And where will we find such clothes?" she asked. "It is not as if we'd packed our belongings before we left."

"The commandant's wife and daughters are away in Montreal. He has agreed to lend you and Elizabeth some of their clothing. When we arrive in Quebec, you will both be properly outfitted, and I will see to it that the clothes you borrow here are returned."

"You've thought of everything."

Blaise turned and spoke rapidly to the commandant.

Then, a young soldier came and saluted smartly. He was given orders and then Blaise turned again to her. "You and Elizabeth go with him."

"Lieutenant Edouard Bouchard, *à vôtre service.*"

"*Merci,*" Jenna responded, hesitantly.

"You speak French, madam?"

"*Je parle un petit peu,*" Jenna replied, speaking slowly in her best French. In truth, she spoke more than a little French, but because the vocabulary was so different and the accent so strange, she did not admit to being more proficient.

The lieutenant was young, perhaps only a few years older than Elizabeth. He was tall and slender and quite handsome. Jenna noticed that he smiled especially warmly at Elizabeth, who, in turn, smiled back at him. Further, and to Jenna's amusement, when he spoke he addressed her, but looked at Elizabeth.

"You will speak more easily if you practice," he told her.

With those words, they headed off across the compound. Lieutenant Bouchard walked ahead of them.

"I'm not certain I'll be able to walk in a skirt again," Elizabeth confessed. "It's been so long."

"I think we'll both adjust."

Jenna and Elizabeth followed the soldier to a log house.

The soldier opened the door and stepped aside.

Jenna and Elizabeth edged into the cottage. It was cool inside and comfortable in a rustic kind of way. In front of a stone fireplace, a roughly hewn wooden table was surrounded by several chairs. Beneath a window, there was a wooden sink, and some dishes and utensils filled an open cupboard, while the larger pots were hung from a rack on the ceiling. Various spices appeared to be drying, and they also hung from rafters along with a woven bag holding potatoes and a braid of onions.

There were two rocking chairs and in one corner, a bed covered with a heavy quilt. By the fireplace were a billows, probably not used since last winter. There were also several wooden chests.

"There are clothes in here," the lieutenant told them. "You will find something, I am sure."

Jenna looked at the box and her thoughts immediately went to that night months ago when she had first been transported back in time. She thought of the young girl who had let her into her cabin and had lent her clothes.

"I will leave you," the soldier announced. He unnecessarily saluted them and quickly left.

Elizabeth opened the trunk and began to carefully lay out the clothes. "They're not much different from those I would wear at home," she said, shaking out a dress.

It was a plain dress of dark heavy cloth. It had sleeves that came to the elbows, and it buttoned up the back. She rummaged further and withdrew a white pinafore to wear over it.

"This will do for me," she said, holding it up. "A few stitches here and there, and I think it will fit well."

"See if you can find something for me," Jenna said, as she peered into a tin mirror. How many months had it been since she had last seen her own image—except for a distorted glance in a rippling stream? Her hair was unruly and thick. It seemed to defy all attempts to tame it. Still, Blaise loved her hair.

"Here," Elizabeth said. "Just the thing and it looks your size."

It was a long brown dress with a low cut laced corset. "Isn't there more to it?" she asked, holding the garment up.

Elizabeth giggled. "Of course, you must wear this chemise underneath."

Jenna blushed and took the chemise. It was such a plain dress, yet very suggestive, she thought, looking at its style. It was not unlike the dress she had been given that first night. It pulled in her tiny waist and pushed her breasts upward to fill the gauzy chemise.

"Why are dresses made like this?" she asked. Everything else, she thought, is modest beyond practicality. But this style of dress was, well, nothing short of suggestive.

Elizabeth laughed. "Sometimes you're very funny. It is so made, if that be a serious question, so that you may more easily nurse a child. If you have a child."

Jenna smiled and laughed at herself. She had thought the dress sexy in a way, but now she saw it in a quite different light. It was, she realized, quite practical as well as sexy.

"I can only wear these shoes if I stuff something in the toes," Elizabeth concluded.

Jenna examined the other pair of shoes. They were leather and very sturdy. They had very slight heels and a big shiny buckle. She took off her moccasins and slipped her feet into them. She felt like Cinderella. They fit perfectly.

Elizabeth extracted some petticoats and other undergarments. They both washed in water they found heating on the fire, then they carefully dressed in their borrowed attire.

Jenna brushed out Elizabeth's beautiful blond hair and braided it carefully in one long French braid.

In turn, Elizabeth combed out her hair, pulling its bountiful wild curls back and tying them at the nap of her neck. Then both of them donned little white dust caps, as Elizabeth assured her they should, in order to be properly attired.

"Mademoiselle!" the commandant bowed from the waist when he greeted her. "And Mademoiselle. You are both quite transformed."

Jenna let the commandant kiss her hand.

Blaise took her arm and led her toward a long building on the far side of the stockade. "*Cheri,* you look wonderful," he whispered in her ear. "It is good to see you restored to womanhood in such clothes. When we reach Quebec, I promise to outfit you in clothes direct from Paris."

Jenna laughed. How could a woodsman and scout afford such things? Aweont had said he was wealthy, but Jenna had not taken her seriously.

"Just so we're together," she whispered back.

He squeezed her arm gently. "My darling, you're the best investment I've ever made."

Inside the building was an oblong dining room with two long tables. The officers and guests sat at one table, while the common soldiers sat at another. The food, Jenna noted, was the same on both tables.

In spite of the heat outside, dinner consisted of a huge bowl of pea soup. Made with onion and salt pork, it was thick and delicious. There were also long loaves of hard French bread, great gobs of fresh butter, and soft ripe cheese. Presently, a servant poured large glasses of dark red wine into ample goblets.

Jenna drank some of the wine and felt instantly light-headed, perhaps, she reasoned, because she had consumed no alcohol of any kind for months. She quickly ate some bread and cheese, hoping to ward off the effects. How wonderful it was to have bread! And cheese!

"This is good soup," James said enthusiastically.

"*Bon!*" Blaise said. "That's French for good.

"*Bon,*" James said, looking at the commandant who, in return, beamed.

This midday dinner went on for over an hour. In the course of the conversation, they learned that the young lieutenant, Edouard Bouchard, would be traveling to *Trois Rivières* and would join them in Montreal for the trip by boat to Quebec City.

"It is the custom to rest after the noon meal," the commandant said, cheerfully. "I offer you the general's house. He is away, and when he is away, his house is always used as a guest house. You have a long journey ahead of you. You should rest while you have the opportunity."

Blaise thanked him, and they were all four taken to the largest cabin within the compound. Elizabeth and her brother were taken to one room, and Jenna and Blaise were ushered into another.

"I'm tired," Jenna said, collapsing onto the narrow bed. "How wonderful this feels after the ground!"

Blaise pulled off his boots and came to her side. "You're sleepy from the wine."

She looked into his eyes. Yes, it was the wine. And the wine had other effects as well. She put her arms around him, and he laughed and gently pushed her backward on the soft bed even as his lips sought her cleavage.

"I cannot wait to see you dressed properly," he said into her ear. "You're breathtaking now, even in this peasant's garb."

She undid his vest, yearning for the heat of his strong chest, the feel of him against her. All inhibitions fled. The wine and his roaming hands aroused her as never before. She felt like she was on fire, and he smiled wickedly as he lovingly tormented her.

His hand moved beneath her chemise and caressed her. Then he pushed away the material and kissed her.

She finished undressing him, and he loosened her corset and left her naked except for her white petticoat which he lifted.

"I'm fortunate among men," he murmured as he moved downward, kissing her flesh as his body slid down hers.

"Like a waiting rose," he whispered.

Jenna shivered as she had not shivered before. His movements were sweet torture, swift and sure. Her hips moved instinctively as he sought to direct her passion, and she sought to break free.

He laughed for a moment and watched her writhe as she reached for satisfaction. Then he filled her and withdrew, then filled her again. Her arms were around his neck, and their movements were in unison till both reached that moment of amorous fulfilment, that moment when their appetites were satisfied. He collapsed against her, and she held him close, still panting, still wanting him.

He kissed her ear. "I must give you wine more often," he whispered.

Jenna lay in deep sleep. Blaise propped himself up and watched her. She was a tiger, a woman entirely different from any he had ever known before, a woman with boundless passion, a woman who enjoyed lovemaking as much as he. She was also a woman who seemed unafraid to try new things, and she seemed to be trying to learn each day. Clearly, she had led a much different life in the Virginia Colony.

But can you adjust to the life you must lead? he asked himself silently. If I knew more about you, perhaps I would know the answer to that question. Perhaps this was all wrong. Perhaps he should offer to let her return to the Virginia or New England Colony—but no. He had not taken her forcibly, and although they had not spoken of it, it seemed clear to him that she wanted to stay with him. She had been his willing partner. How they had come together didn't matter. They were together, that was all that really counted. No, Jenna was only concerned with Elizabeth and young James. She herself had expressed no desire to return.

I would grant your wish if I could, he thought. If it were up to me, I would return the children to their father right away. But it was not up to him, and there were other considerations. He was not the only person who held James Corse responsible for the massacre at the Abnaki village or the burning of the homes of French settlers along the Saint Lawrence. There was a price on the head of James Corse. His children were not being held for ransom, they were being held in the hope that James Corse would come after them. Jenna, he felt certain, would not, could not understand this. She seemed to think the New Englanders were lily pure, and only the French fought brutally with their Indian allies against the English. On an intellectual level, she said she understood that there was good and bad on both sides, but on an emotional level she kept insisting James be returned. And why was she so much more insistent about James? When the time was right, he would do what he could, but until then, things would have to remain as they were.

He touched her wild hair gently. Of course there were other problems as well. In Quebec, he was not the same man he was when he was playing the scout. In Quebec, he had duties, obligations. He wondered if she would understand. Sometimes she seemed to understand everything, at other times she seemed a stranger to everything. He remembered the first time he had asked her to make a fire. She had to be shown how! Some things she talked about amazed him. She had knowledge few women had. Then, at other times, she seemed to lack the knowledge he thought all women had. She was a beautiful, intelligent, and mysterious enigma. But he knew she affected him differently than other women. He was sure he loved her.

Jenna stretched languorously and blinked open her eyes.

He bent and kissed her on the end of the nose. "Never have I known a woman of such passion," he said. "You please me."

Jenna smiled. "You please me too."

He laughed. "Well, we should be up and off. There are miles to go before we sleep again."

Jenna climbed out of bed and began to dress. A wagon would be a welcome change from a canoe.

"Do you have a house in Quebec?" she asked.

He smiled. "It is a bit out of the city," he replied.

Jenna frowned slightly. All this time when he had spoken of Quebec, she had thought he meant the province, now for the first time she realized he was speaking of Quebec City. She felt a little foolish,, because her aunt's guests had also spoken of it that way, and it was the one thing she knew about Quebec. But she reminded herself that such misunderstandings were going to happen to her often. If only she could trust him enough to tell him the truth about herself, he would understand her mistakes.

"I'm looking forward to seeing it."

"Seeing it? You shall be mistress of the manor."

It sounded so grand. Again, she reminded herself that he was a mere scout. It was probably a simple house.

Probably more modest than the one they were in now. "I'm ready," she said.

He took her arm, and they left the house. James and Elizabeth were outside already, and the commandant had produced a wagon and two large horses. Their packs were in the back of the wagon.

Blaise lifted Elizabeth into the back of the wagon, and James climbed up to sit beside her. Then he lifted Jenna onto the seat and climbed up to sit beside her. He clicked his teeth and jiggled the reins. The two sturdy farm horses jolted forward down the dusty road.

It was the morning after they left the army post. The sun was bright, and the day nearly perfect as they made their way closer and closer to their destination.

Jenna watched Blaise for a long while before she said anything. "You never took any of the booty from the Deerfield raid."

He glanced at her. "I bought you and the children."

She ignored his comment. "I meant material things."

He shrugged. "I didn't want them. I went on the raid for only two reasons."

"And they were—"

"To help prevent unnecessary bloodshed and to be with the Indians."

"Why do you study their language?"

He smiled. "To understand them."

Since the day the prisoners had been brought to the village, he had been more of a mystery to her, and since they had begun heading toward his home, she had noticed he had grown more contemplative. Perhaps, she reasoned, there was some reason why he wasn't anxious to return.

The wagon continued along the narrow rutted path.

Usually, they passed only wild meadows or wound through thick groves of pine. But, now and again, they passed an outlying farm and a small cluster of buildings appeared.

Last night, they had spent the evening in a farmhouse with a couple called Marie and Paul Tremblay. It was a small crowded house without privacy. The Tremblays had seven children, the youngest of whom was two and the oldest fourteen. Thus, they were twelve in two rooms, though Jenna knew it was better than sleeping outside. It was still early in September, but fall was in the air, and the nights were getting colder.

"We're not so far away now," Blaise said.

Jenna leaned forward and squinted into the distance. "I see a cloud of dust. I think someone is riding toward us."

Blaise looked up and toward where she pointed. "I think you're right."

It wasn't long before horsemen came into sight. There were twenty in all. All were uniformed, and Jenna knew they must be more militia.

But as they drew closer, she could see that these uniforms were richer. And the man on the lead horse wore a full blue velvet coat trimmed with gold braid.

Blaise drew the wagon to a halt and the elegantly dressed officer galloped up, pulling in his steed.

"Blaise l'Écossais! Is that really you?" he asked in French.

"Raymond Picard! Of course it is me!" Blaise answered.

"You've been gone for too long, my brother!"

"It has been many months."

The officer looked at Jenna curiously.

"May I introduce Mademoiselle Stevens and Mademoiselle Elizabeth Corse and her brother, James Corse."

Blaise introduced them in French. "This is General Picard," Blaise told Jenna, who smiled in return.

The general nodded, but turned quickly back to Blaise. "Madeleine will be so glad to know you've returned!" he thundered. "You've been away a long while. But now you'll rest, and soon you and Madeleine will marry! It will be one of the finest weddings in Quebec! I am looking forward to it!" He laughed loudly. "Madeleine can hardly wait to see you!"

Jenna felt paralyzed, rooted to the wooden seat of the wagon. Had she understood him correctly? Yes, he may have spoken eighteenth century French, but it was clear enough. There was a woman named Madeleine who was obviously engaged to Blaise. A cold fury grew in her. He had used her! He had taken advantage of her, pretended to love her! No wonder he had grown contemplative! When had he intended to tell her? A thousand questions filled her thoughts as emotions flooded through her.

Blaise didn't even look at her now. He reached over and grasped this Raymond's hand warmly and continued talking to him. But she had ceased to listen, she felt as if her world were spinning in a rapid circle. She glanced uneasily at Elizabeth and James. She couldn't say anything in front of them. Elizabeth who knew full well that she and Blaise had—had been making love, did not understood the exchange between Blaise and this officer. Jenna bit her lip and concentrated on looking at the bottom of the wagon. How could I have been so stupid? she asked herself. Of course he had a life before he met her—but it appeared he intended to continue living as if she hadn't come along.

Then, Blaise was saying goodbye, and he again clicked and jiggled the reins. The wagon clattered down the road. Jenna held her silence, waiting till they were alone. He, in turn, knew she had understood. She could feel the tension between them. They moved forward in stony silence.

Inside the farmhouse where they had stopped for the night, Elizabeth and James slept soundly. Jenna walked in the back garden, her cloak pulled around her. She trembled with hurt and anger, yet fought the tears that kept threatening to run down her cheeks.

"I thought I would find you out here," Blaise said, coming toward her. "You've hardly spoken all day, and you were truly sullen at dinner. I'm sure Elizabeth and James wonder what in the world is the matter with you."

"Only because they cannot understand French," she said coldly.

"Ah, I thought you understood."

"I understood and I understand. I understand that you have deceived me, used me."

Her lips trembled and her arms were folded protectively against herself.

"Jenna . . ." he stepped toward her.

"Don't touch me!" she hissed. "I am no longer your woman as you put it!"

Her thoughts went immediately to the mass marriage that Father Henri had performed in the Indian village. No wonder Blaise said nothing of marriage then. In fact, he had never mentioned marriage. Now, she knew he had no intention of marrying her at all. Doubtless he intended to marry this Madeleine and better himself. Perhaps he thought he could keep her as his mistress. Yes, that was probably exactly what he had thought.

In fact, he had said it. 'You shall be mistress of the

manor.' She lifted her eyes and looked at him. He was actually smirking, as if he might burst out laughing.

"So angry," he said softly. "Come on, give us a kiss."

She stomped her foot. "There will be no more kisses, I told you."

He looked at her steadily. "But you are still mine. I paid a pretty penny for you. You will serve me as I please."

Jenna narrowed her eyes. At that moment, her passionate love for him had turned to defiance. "You may own me, but you will never again possess me unless by force," she said evenly.

He stood for a very long moment and stared at her. Her beautiful green eyes were hard and cold, her jaw was set. She was beautiful and stubborn and filled with an unseemly pride. He thought briefly of the other women he had known. They certainly had not prepared him for this one.

The truth was, he didn't know what to say to her. He *was* engaged to Madeleine. He certainly could not have said anything when confronted on the road—it was necessary he talk to Madeleine first. In this case, it was not simply emotions which were involved. It was also politics. Madeleine's family was both influential and powerful.

And he admitted, he felt angry that she did not trust him. Did she really believe him capable of loving another woman when he made love to her as he did?

Well, he would wait and talk to Madeleine, and then he would come back to Jenna. But he knew he, too, needed time. Yes, time, he thought to himself, time was the key. He turned and walked away into the darkness, his thoughts full of regret. He realized he felt lonely again already.

Chapter Thirteen

The morning sun shone brightly and a cool breeze blew off the water as they approached Ville Montreal. They had gotten up early and headed off, following the meandering river past neat fields which were occasionally punctuated by fat stone storage bins with pointed roofs and giant windmills.

Blaise drove the wagon. Sometimes he pointed out sights he seemed to think interesting, or answered one of James's many questions. Elizabeth and James both had questions about the farms, about how people lived, and about where they were headed. Jenna, her arms folded, traveled in an angry troubled silence.

"These are *seigneurial* lands," Blaise explained, as he answered one of James's queries.

"That's just a windmill. Where does this *seigneur* live?"

"All the lands are triangular in shape. Their widest section is by the river for irrigation. Their narrowest in the small village. If you walked inland, across the *seigneur*'s fields, you would eventually come to a place with several grand homes, many small homes where the *habitants* live, and of course a church."

Jenna forced herself to listen if only for the sake of learning more about her new environment. But inside she was tormented with thoughts of Blaise's grand deception. How could she have been so stupid! All his talk of studying Indian languages was a lie. He was no better than a pirate. How did she know he hadn't taken anything? She had met him looting Deerfield, and she should have known that those actions were the real indicator of his personality. Yes, he was a looter—a thief and a liar. And he was engaged to some woman who seemed well known. Perhaps he was a social climber as well.

"What's that?" James was standing up in the back of the wagon and pointing off into the distance.

"Those are the biggest buildings we've seen since we left the Massachusetts Colony!" Elizabeth said.

"Ville Montreal," Blaise said, turning slightly. "It is here that I shall leave you."

"Leave us?" Elizabeth said, a touch of panic in her voice. She looked quickly at Jenna. Something had happened between them. They had been lovers, now they were silent and stony with one another. She had thought about the change between them since this morning, and it had made her increasingly uncomfortable. But James, always distracted and preoccupied with his thousand and one questions, seemed not to have noticed anything.

"I'll be leaving you with some soldiers. They're traveling the river to Quebec. You remember Lieutenant Bouchard. He will escort you. The three of you will go with him. I have business in Montreal."

Was this Madeleine in Montreal? Jenna pressed her lips together and stared ahead. Damn him! Why did she even care?

"It's got walls like Fort Deerfield!" James said excitedly. "But it's much bigger! I can't even see the end of the stockade."

"They're called the palisade walls."

"What're those buildings?" James was leaning over the side of the wagon, his eyes large with curiosity. They were traveling up one side of the river, while Ville Montreal lay stretched out on the far side.

"That's the Parish Church," Blaise answered. "And that's Saint Sulpice Seminary. That building is where the nuns live, and over there is the building that houses the Jesuit fathers."

"Isn't that a church too?" James pointed to a larger building, its silver spire sparkling in the sunlight.

"Yes, it is the Church of Bonsecours. The fort is at the far end, and of course, the windmills are where the mills are located."

"And the square building?" Elizabeth asked.

"The hospital."

"Montreal seems so large," James said, slightly in awe.

"Not as large nor as important as Quebec. But you will see that for yourself."

Jenna held her silence as they drew closer and closer.

"Are we going inside the palisade walls?" James asked.

"No. The docks are outside. But before we go to the docks, we'll be stopping at the trade fair just outside of town."

"Fair?" James eyes glistened. "Will there be pies and things for sale? Will there be lots of people?"

"All we know of fairs is from Mother Goose rhymes," Elizabeth told him.

"Not that kind of fair," Blaise said, addressing himself to James.

"I'm afraid you're thinking of an English country fair—where, to be sure much trading is done—but this is a different kind of fair. And Montreal is different from

Quebec or Trois Rivières. It has remained less settled, a more open place. In Montreal, there is much less difference between rich and poor. It was more frequently attacked by the Iroquois during the early years of settlement. At first, it was only a missionary settlement, then it became a huge trading center because more and more furs were brought from the area of the great inland lakes."

James eyes were wide. "Are there Indians at the fair?"

"Hundreds! And there are many *courier de bois* who have returned with their canoes loaded with furs."

"What's a *courier de bois?*"

Blaise laughed. "In French, it simply means runner of the woods. But they're more than that. They're masters of the canoe, the waterways, and Indian lore. They have traveled thousands of miles west, and when they return, they bring loads of furs for trade."

"Why are we going to this fair?" Elizabeth asked.

"Ah, first, because it is a sight to behold. Second, because I suspect that one day young James here, will be a scout like his father. I think it runs in the blood. So he should see this fair. And last, but not least, I have some business to do."

Jenna asked no questions, although she tried to take in all the sights they passed. She was beginning to entertain thoughts of running away—not immediately, but after she solved the problem of seeing to it James was returned home. So, she reasoned, she should make herself familiar with everything she could.

Soon, they approached a sort of shantytown, a place of seemingly hundreds of diverse and colorfully dressed people. Abnaki wigwams and Iroquois tepees stood side by side with tents used by the Europeans. There were, as promised, hundreds of Indians in all manner of dress. There were European men as well and priests in long dark robes. Some of the European men were reasonably well dressed, others were dressed as woodsmen, and they wore long unkempt beards and fur hats.

"It smells awful here," Jenna said after a few minutes.

"Furs," Blaise replied.

Jenna looked at the people they passed. She felt certain that the furs weren't the only thing that smelled. Some of these men looked as if they'd been in the woods for years and as if they never bathed.

The wagon clattered down the path between the tents. Everywhere negotiations were in progress. The Indians brought many furs, beaded handiwork, and baskets to trade. They also brought corn, rice, and a variety of berries and squash. Everywhere you looked there was animated bargaining, noise, and confusion.

They passed through bedlam and into a quieter area. Eventually, Blaise brought the wagon to a halt by the water. There, in the Saint Lawrence, drawn in close to shore, seemed to be well over two hundred canoes. And, out in the harbor, a veritable fleet of French sailing ships lay at anchor. Their blue and white *fleurs de lis* fluttered in the breeze.

Jenna gasped at the sight. Only recently, there had been a gathering of the so-called, "tall ships" in New York Harbor. They were replicas of the sailing ships of this period. But no reenactment could do this justice. The sight of the fleet was overwhelming. Perhaps, she thought, she could run away to France or even England.

"The air is better here by the water," Blaise said, laughing.

Nearby, there was a large group of Indians watching over piles of furs. Blaise climbed down off the wagon and went over to them. An animated discussion began, a discussion Jenna could not understand. They appeared to be speaking in some native tongue. But Jenna did not think these Indians were Abnaki. They looked and dressed differently than the Abnaki with whom they had just been living.

Blaise turned once, then disappeared inside a large tepee.

"Can I go and look at the canoes?" James asked.

Jenna looked about. "I guess that would all right," she replied. "But don't go where I can't call you."

James climbed down, anxious to stretch his legs.

"Perhaps we can both stretch too," Jenna suggested. Gingerly, she climbed down out of the wagon, and when she was down, she held out her hand to help Elizabeth.

"Oh, it's good to stand up," Elizabeth said, stretching. "Let's walk a little. There was an Indian woman back there selling some pretty beads. I'd like to look at them."

The two of them walked slowly away from the wagon and followed the dirt path along which the wagon had previously traveled.

"There aren't many people down here near the dock," Elizabeth said.

"Most of the trading stalls seemed further back in this direction," Jenna said, lifting her skirts.

Suddenly, five large disheveled men emerged from a tent and blocked their path. For a single second, they seemed as surprised to see Jenna and Elizabeth as Elizabeth and Jenna were to see them. It was only then that Jenna had a feeling of foreboding, only then that she chastised herself for not realizing that this "trade fair" was no doubt populated with raucous men who had not seen any women for a very long time. Raucous and drunk. Even as she inhaled, Jenna could smell the alcohol on the breath of the men.

"And what have we here!" one of them asked in broken French. "A vision! Two visions! What're you doing here, beauty?"

The large square speaker lurched forward and grabbed Elizabeth round the waist. "Give us a kiss and a feel, beauty!"

Elizabeth screamed and kicked, punching her assailant as hard as she could.

"Let go of her!" Jenna ordered.

But the other, much larger bearlike man pulled her toward him. His odor was repulsive. He grinned at her with rotting teeth and a trickle of spittle ran down from his twisted mouth. His pawlike hand seized Jenna's breast roughly and kneaded it. "A good full breasted wench!" he said loudly. "With a nice warm place for me to put my cock!"

Elizabeth screamed again, but Jenna felt too stunned to even scream. The man was utterly terrifying.

"These are my women!" Blaise said suddenly as he stepped from behind one of the tents. His long sharp bladed hunting knife was drawn, and his legs were parted.

The man who had grabbed Elizabeth let her go.

"And who are you to have two women?" the one who still held Jenna asked. His hand still held her breast.

Blaise's eyes burned, "Who I am is none of your affair," he answered. "Unhand her!"

But the ugly bear of a man did not let her go.

"Tinglet!" Blaise said, loudly.

Suddenly, swiftly, ten large and well armed Indians emerged from the behind the tent; behind them, James stood.

Seeing the Indians, the man who held Jenna let her go. He pushed her roughly toward Blaise. "No harm intended," he muttered. His face was visibly pale, and Jenna noted that his hand was shaking.

"Go back to the wagon!" Blaise ordered.

Jenna, Elizabeth, and James hurried back to the wagon, and the Indians followed. The men disappeared in the other direction.

"I see I shall have to return to do my business when you three are safely in the hands of the militia!" Blaise curtly helped Elizabeth and Jenna up. James climbed up on his own. Then Blaise took his place and turned the wagon around. "Stupid," he muttered. "You could have been raped! Stupid! You should never have wandered off. If young James here had not heard you and come for me, God knows what might have become of you!"

"We just wanted to stretch our legs," Elizabeth said, seeing that he appeared to be speaking only to Jenna.

But he still ignored her. He turned on Jenna. "Those men were dangerous."

Jenna looked down and for once said nothing. He was right. It was foolish of them to wander off. Jenna reminded herself once again to try to remember where she was, as well as the time in which she now lived. Blaise had hurt her emotionally, but he was good to Elizabeth and James. Danger, real physical danger, she realized, lurked everywhere and like him or not, Blaise was the only one who could protect them.

Soon enough Blaise was guiding the wagon along a dirt road that paralleled the banks of the river and the walls of the city. Had he intended to take them to Quebec City before their fight? Or had he intended to send them on to Quebec City alone all along? If this Madeleine lived in Montreal, then she felt certain he intended to send them on alone from the beginning.

Blaise brought the wagon to a clattering halt near a long dock. Pulled along side the dock was a large boat

with many oars. Cargo was being carefully loaded by a
crew of bare-backed men.

"Blaise!" A jolly male voice called out from among
the marine officers who milled about, watching as others
loaded the boat.

"Nicholas!"

Blaise returned the greeting and immediately slipped
from the wagon to embrace the man he had called
Nicholas. He drew him aside, and for what seemed forever, the two of them conversed rapidly in French.

"Can you hear them, Jenna?" Elizabeth asked anxiously.

Jenna shook her head. "I imagine he's just arranging
for our transport."

"What's wrong?" Elizabeth asked. "You can tell me."

"And me," James piped up. "You look unhappy."

Jenna shook her head. "Not now. I'll tell you later.
When we're alone."

Blaise returned suddenly. "Gather up your things.
Nicholas will take you all on the boat. You'll go as far
as the Lachine rapids above Quebec. From there
Edouard will escort you to my house where you will remain until I come back."

Jenna said nothing, but climbed down off the wagon.

"Nicholas, this is James, and this is Elizabeth. James
and Elizabeth, this is Nicholas Tremblay—you remember his parents. We stayed with them."

Nicholas was clean shaven, had thin blond hair and
blue eyes. He was dressed in light blue and white. Jenna
studied him carefully. Both Tremblays had been dark
haired. He certainly looked like neither of them.

"Come along, I'll take you to your places in the
boat."

Jenna started to move away, but Blaise held her arm,
restraining her ever so slightly.

"Let me go," she said firmly.

He let his hand slip away. "I wanted to speak with you."

"I don't want to speak with you," she answered coldly. But of course she did—no, no, no! She would not cry in front of him. She would not give him the slightest satisfaction. Perhaps men in this time did have wives and mistresses. Perhaps it was common. Well, she didn't care about the time anymore. She wasn't going to be part of a cast of thousands. She wasn't prepared to do that in 1988 and she wasn't prepared to do it now in 1704.

"All right. Just go with Elizabeth and James. Have a good trip."

Jenna didn't look at him as she tramped off to join Elizabeth and James. She might have shrieked that she wanted to go home, but in truth, she had no home. She would be no more at home in Boston in 1704 than here, in Canada. For her, it made no difference. But for James and Elizabeth it did. She had to see to them, she vowed as she stepped onto the large boat and carefully made her way to where they were sitting.

Hardly had they sat down, when Edouard emerged from one of the buildings near the dock. He waved as soon as he saw them and after speaking with Blaise for a moment, he clambered aboard, hurrying to sit near Elizabeth.

"Wake up! Jenna, wake up!"

Jenna opened her eyes and blinked in the darkness. The boat on which they were traveling had stopped, and the oarsmen, together with other men on shore, were securing it to a dock.

Like Elizabeth and James, Jenna had bedded down

on a pile of furs in the vessel's midsection. She hadn't thought she would sleep, but the motion of the boat moving through the water combined with the long day, lulled her into a deep sleep.

She sat up and stretched. "It must be the middle of the night."

"On the contrary," Edouard said as he stood above them. "It's around five in the morning. Soon the sun will be coming up."

"Mademoiselle Elizabeth," Edouard bent from the waist and politely helped Elizabeth sit up.

Elizabeth smiled at him shyly. "Thank you, sir."

Jenna looked from one of them to the other. In her own depression, she had failed to see the interest the two had in one another, but she saw it now and determined to play the good chaperon. Edouard, she now recalled, had taken Elizabeth to the bow of the boat while they traveled yesterday, and the two of them had talked all day.

"Are we leaving the boat here?"

"Yes, mademoiselle. You cannot see it, but at the end of the dock there is a carriage. It will take us to Rivière Saint James."

"It has my name," James said, rubbing his eyes.

"Appropriate," Edouard said, winking.

Jenna picked up her small bundle and followed Elizabeth and James as they left the boat and walked down the dock. In the distance, by the light of the torches that burned brightly, she could see a carriage. It was, she thought, quite an elegant carriage.

Edouard helped her in first, then boosted James up. Last of all, he helped in Elizabeth.

"I want to sit with the coachman. Can I?" James asked.

"All right," Jenna allowed. James quickly climbed out,

swung around and positioned himself next to the stony faced coachman.

Nicholas Tremblay strode over and peered into the carriage. "I hope the journey was not too difficult."

"You were very kind," Jenna said.

In moments, they were off, bumping down the rutted path into the dawn.

Jenna shook her head and looked at Edouard. "Nicholas is so blond. He doesn't look like either of his parents."

Edouard laughed. "Nicholas is not really French. He is English. He was orphaned many, many years ago, and the Tremblays bought him from a roving band of Indians who had taken him from his dead parents."

"Oh," Jenna said softly. She might have guessed from his coloring.

"I wish I knew about my mother," Elizabeth said softly.

Edouard looked at her sympathetically. "I can make some inquiries," he offered.

"Could you?" Elizabeth's eyes shone.

Jenna glanced at Edouard. There was no question in her mind that he was smitten with Elizabeth. She wondered if she should warn Elizabeth in any way—then she wondered what she would warn her about.

Just because Blaise had deceived her did not mean that Edouard wasn't sincere. But there were a lot of men in the world like Blaise—or was it that she just kept meeting them? In any case, Blaise was just like Carlton Havers, and that proved that such men were not unique to any race or period in history. He wanted everything. He wanted marriage, and he wanted a woman with whom to romp.

Jenna leaned back, glad it was dark. She didn't sob, but at last she let the tears run down her cheeks. Whatever was in store for her, she felt certain it would not include Blaise l'Écossais.

Jenna opened her eyes and dabbed at them with her apron. What had awakened her was the clattering halt of the carriage. The sun was now pouring in the window, and she surmised it must be at least ten o'clock.

"Look!" James voice shouted down into the carriage from the speaker box. "Look, Jenna, it's like a palace!"

Jenna poked her head out the window and strained to see. To her amazement, the carriage had come to a halt in front of a huge stone house. It had three floors and dormered glass windows. It had double chimneys and a well kept sprawling lawn. There were even rosebushes in front on either side of the great double doors.

The carriage door opened and the coachman, a stout Frenchman, held open the door. *"Bienvenue a la Château de l'Écossais."*

Jenna's mouth opened slightly in awe.

"He must be very rich," Elizabeth murmured.

"There's a stable. And horses. Perhaps I can learn to ride!" James sounded enthusiastic.

"I'm sure you can," Edouard laughed. "In fact, I live nearby, I can teach you."

Jenna's thoughts raced. Well, she had been wrong. It wasn't Blaise who was bettering himself with marriage. It was probably Madeleine. It seemed obvious that Blaise was a man of wealth. But why did he travel with the Indians, and why did he act as a scout? Seeing this house and realizing how he lived made him more mysterious than before.

The coachman beckoned them to follow, and they did. When they reached the great heavy front door, it opened, revealing a small woman wearing a dark dress with a white lace collar. She was, Jenna surmised, about sixty. Her gray hair was tucked under a dust cap, and her dark eyes were keen and observing. She looked them over and shook her head.

She silently ushered them into a modest waiting room off the hall and then spoke at length with Edouard in rapid French. After a few moments, Edouard gave her a letter, and the woman read it quickly.

"Madame Stevens, Mademoiselle Corse, and Master James. I am Madame Patoulet, chief housekeeper. Please allow me to show you to your rooms. I am sure you will want to bathe after so long a journey."

A bath! Jenna felt as if she might jump for joy. In spite of her general mood, the very thought of a hot bath and shampoo cheered her.

"I must take leave now," Edouard said, as he turned to face them. "Mademoiselle." He kissed Jenna's hand. Then he turned to Elizabeth and kissed her hand. He lingered a moment longer holding Elizabeth's hand, Jenna noticed. Then he bowed from the waist and tipped his hat. "Monsieur James."

He paused a moment longer and turned back to Elizabeth. "I hope I may call some time. I'm home on leave, and I'll be here for the next month."

Elizabeth smiled. "I should be most happy to receive you."

Edouard grinned with pleasure and hurried out the door to the waiting carriage.

"This way," Madame Patoulet said, as she went up the winding staircase.

"Wasn't he handsome?" Elizabeth whispered.

"You must be careful with men," Jenna warned. Elizabeth, she assumed, had led quite a sheltered life.

"I like him," Elizabeth said girlishly. "I don't want to be careful all of my life."

"I'll come to your room and talk with you later," Jenna promised.

Elizabeth and James were taken to separate rooms on the second floor. She was taken to the third floor and ushered into a light, airy, and most spacious room.

As soon as Madame Patoulet had closed the door, she began to explore the room, inspecting it and marveling at it simultaneously.

It had a huge four-poster bed with a feather mattress and a delicate white handmade lace bedspread. Beneath the bedspread was a duvet and beneath that clean white bed sheets.

Next to the bed was a small mahogany table with an oil lamp and a pitcher of water.

Across the room was a large dresser and a dressing table. There were full mirrors, a huge walk in closet devoid of clothes, and off the bedroom, a large bath with a great white bathtub with silver trim.

Jenna was still exploring when there was a knock on the door. She opened it, and a parade of servants came in, each carrying heavy buckets of hot water. In no time, the bathtub was filled.

"Would madam like help?" The girl who asked the question was no more than thirteen. She had dark curls and was neatly dressed in a black dress with a white apron.

"I think I can manage alone," Jenna answered.

"I will show you the perfume," the girl announced. She led Jenna into the bathroom and opened a cupboard. There were expensive looking bottles of French perfume and bars of wonderful soap.

"Thank you," Jenna said and the girl bowed and quickly left.

For a long moment Jenna stared at the assortment of perfumes and powders. Certainly, she was not the first woman to bathe in this room. This was not a room, nor a bathroom that was occupied by a man who was alone. No doubt, she thought bitterly, Blaise entertained many women.

But the sight of hot steaming water beckoned. Jenna hurriedly shed her clothes and climbed into the tub, easing herself into the steaming hot water. She poured some bath oil into the water, and for a long while luxuriated in the delight of the bath before she washed her hair.

It occurred to her that Blaise kept his mistresses in style. She scrubbed rigorously and then rinsed. Finally, as the water began to cool, she pulled herself out and dried with a huge towel the little maid had left.

Then, wrapped in the towel, she went into the bedroom, surprised to see that clean clothes had been laid out for her. Clothes quite unlike those she had shed.

First, there was a corset and a busk—a wooden board that was slipped between the corset and the dress to hide the corset laces. She would not have known what it was, but for the fact that she had seen something similar in the museum. Next was a lace chemise with long sleeves and lace cuffs that were meant to hang below the sleeves of her gown. There were also several stiff petticoats to hold out the skirt of her gown. The gown itself was blue in color with a small, darker blue leaf design embroidered onto it. It was made of taffeta. It had a low square neck which like the sleeves of her chemise was laced trimmed. There was a matching lace dust cap and a string of perfectly matched pearls with what appeared to be a diamond clasp. By the bed, there was also a pair of soft shoes.

Jenna dressed, brushed out her damp hair, and secured it. She put on the lace cap and then, after admiring it, the little necklace.

She turned again and again in front of the full-length mirror. She looked quite a different person from the one who had walked in this room two hours ago.

She began to explore the room more thoroughly. The closet was empty. As were the various drawers in the chest and dressing table. She sat on the edge of the feather bed and took in the entire room. Yes, this was certainly a room intended for a mistress. In front of the great stone fireplace that dominated an entire wall, there was a great fur rug. The mirrors—the rug—the size of the bed. It was a sensuous room. "Well, I'll be no willing mistress," she vowed.

Jenna looked up when she heard the tap on the door.

"It's me, Elizabeth."

"Come in," Jenna called out.

Elizabeth was dressed in a gown similar to her own. It made her look older, but certainly no less pretty. She came over and sat by Jenna on the bed.

"I have seen great unhappiness in your eyes. What is wrong?"

Jenna wondered if she could talk about it without again dissolving into tears. She was well aware of the fragility of her own emotions. One minute she was angry, the next she was miserable. For long periods of time, she could put it all out of her thoughts, but never far enough out. It clung to the edges of her mind, ready to invade and again overtake her.

Elizabeth took her hand. "It is Blaise, is it not?"

"Yes. I thought—I thought he loved me. But he is engaged to another woman. I don't know what he intends . . ."

Elizabeth squeezed her hands. "I'm sorry. He's a strange man, I think he is a good man, but a man with secrets."

"Yes, secrets," Jenna whispered, as again the tears began to fall down her cheeks. "But what do you know of his secrets?"

"Only one thing," Elizabeth confided. "But perhaps it is of no importance."

"What is it?" Jenna asked.

"Hee-la-dee told me that Blaise searches for an Indian girl. He asked many questions of the Mohawk prisoners."

Jenna shook her head. Blaise was engaged to one woman, making love to her, and searching for yet another woman. "I don't know what to think," Jenna finally said.

"Come, let's walk together," Elizabeth suggested. "It will make you feel better."

Jenna went with Elizabeth. Vaguely, she wondered when Blaise would return.

Chapter Fourteen

They had been in the chateau a week now. Jenna explored the entire house, venturing into every single nook and cranny. It was her quest to discover anything and everything she could about Blaise l'Écossais. But clues were sparse.

As she passed by the exquisite French clock that stood in the hall, she mentally conceded that there were certainly worse places to be held prisoner. This chateau was surely the equivalent of a southern plantation.

It was hard to complain, Jenna thought as she went from room to room. No one interfered with her explorations, no one told her what to do. And there appeared to be no shortage of entertainments. She could ride—as James and Elizabeth seemed to do by the hour—or she could sit in the beautifully appointed library and read. Blaise had hundreds of books in both French and English.

If that bored her, she could work in the garden, embroider as Elizabeth did in the evenings, or walk along the river.

Jenna sat down on the window seat in the parlor. Elizabeth and her brother were once again out riding, and she was left to her own ends. A life of absolute leisure was not what it was cracked up to be, she thought. And even though a part of her didn't want to see Blaise again, another part of her yearned for him.

She jumped at the sound outside and quickly peeked out from behind the curtain. Had Blaise come home just as she was thinking of him?

A large carriage was drawn to a halt in front of the house. But to her disappointment, she could see that it was not Blaise who climbed down from it. Instead, it was a plump man dressed in long white stockings, pointed leather shoes, tight breeches and a long ruffled green coat that only partially covered his bulging stomach. He also wore a white powdered wig with a black satin ribbon. Following him was a younger slender fellow dressed from head to toe in a canary yellow. Jenna almost laughed. The looked like two characters from Mother Goose.

Jenna crept quietly to the door of the parlor and opened it ever so slightly so she could hear exactly what Madame Patoulet said when she opened the door. "Messieurs Charlebois and Richer from Quebec," the plump one announced. And they both bowed from the waist and tipped their hats in unison.

"Right this way," Madame Patoulet said, inviting them in. "Please, wait in here." Madame Patoulet showed them to the same anti-room she and James and Elizabeth had waited in the first day they had come here. Then Madame Patoulet hurried down the hall toward the library. In a moment, she hurried back and peeked into the parlor.

"Mademoiselle! Mademoiselle! There you are. I thought you were in the library. The hairdresser and the couturier have arrived from Quebec for you and Mademoiselle Elizabeth. You must come now for your fittings."

Fittings? Jenna thought of objecting, but she couldn't

really. She couldn't go on wearing one dress forever, nor could Elizabeth.

"Show them in," she said. "Elizabeth is outside."

"I'll fetch her," Madame Patoulet told her as she scurried away.

Monsieur Charlebois set his gold-tipped cane down on one of the chairs. He took off his hat and set it across his cane, then he removed his ornate green coat that, Jenna noticed, was trimmed in gold braid. But Monsieur Charlebois did not look as if he belonged to any military group, besides he had been introduced as a couturier. She, therefore, assumed his gold braid was merely a matter of decoration.

He draped his coat on the back of the chair, and from a small pocket in his lace trimmed ruffled shirt, he withdrew a tape measure.

With his coat removed, Jenna thought he looked exactly like Humpty Dumpty.

Monsieur Richer was as thin as Monsieur Charlebois was fat. Close up, she could see his nose was quite sharp. Not only was he dressed in canary yellow, but something about him made him look like a large canary as well.

Yes, there was no doubt about it. Since Monsieur Charlebois had the tape measure he was the couturier. The other, Monsieur Richer, must be the hairdresser. He did not remove either his coat or his hat.

"Just stand right there," Monsieur Richer directed.

He pressed his lips together and placed his long finger in front of them as if he were going to tell her to be quiet. Then he tiptoed around her. He managed to look like a cross between a cat and a ballet dancer. "My, my, my, my, my!" he muttered, tilting his head first one way and then the other.

After three full circles, he stopped and turned to Monsieur Charlebois. "Quite a magnificent mane," he said in French with a wave of his expressive hand. "But totally out of control! Dear, dear, dear. I daresay Charles, you have the easy job. Her figure is magnificent, so all you have to do is dress Cinderella. But I! Oh, heaven help me! I have to tame that completely wild, wild, hair!"

Jenna watched him warily and tried, but did not succeed in catching everything he said.

Monsieur Charlebois held up the tape measure and patted a small brocade-covered footstool. Clearly, he intended she should stand on it.

Jenna shrugged and stepped onto the footstool. Mr. Charlebois measured the length from her waist to her ankles. He withdrew a small piece of paper and went to the desk to avail himself of the quill pen.

He measured her ankles, the length of her legs, and then asking her to step down, he took the more conventional measurements of waist, bust, and hips. He also measured the length of her arms.

Jenna wondered if he were going to make everything. It seemed so because he would not have needed the other measurements if he had not intended making pantaloons as well as petticoats and chemises.

"Your coloring is good and your eyes splendid," he went on in French. "I think your best colors are blues and greens—of course, russets must be nice too."

"I like green best," Jenna said in French.

Monsieur Charlebois jumped as if burned. "Pardon mademoiselle! Oh, a thousand pardons. I did not know you spoke French. I was told you were English."

"I only speak a little," Jenna said. Although she knew her vocabulary was growing daily, and she was most certainly beginning to catch onto the accent and rhythm of eighteenth century French. The more she read, the more she improved.

"You shall have a green gown then—but of course you shall have many gowns. I have been told to arrange a full wardrobe for you."

Jenna said nothing. It seemed that Blaise intended keeping her in style. Well, she thought angrily, she would take whatever she could, except his love. That she would not accept.

"What is it?" Elizabeth asked as she was ushered into the room by Madame Patoulet.

"It seems we're being fitted for clothes."

"I could use some clothes. I think Edouard tires of me in this dress."

"I doubt Edouard will ever tire of you," Jenna answered. Then she turned to Monsieur Charlebois. "There is a young man too."

"Ah, yes. I know. But I only deal with women's clothing. Monsieur Vert, the tailor will come tomorrow for the boy's measurements."

He finished making his notations and then waved Jenna away. "I'm ready for the other one," he said trusting her to relay the information.

"Your turn," Jenna said to Elizabeth. Then she went over to Monsieur Richer. He was sitting in a chair making sketches. She moved to his side. On a large artist's pad, he had made many sketches of her with a charcoal pencil. They were all quite good likenesses except that each one featured a different hair style. They ranged from the simple to ornate. One even portrayed her with her hair held back behind her neck but escaping beneath the tie into twenty tight corkscrew curls.

"It's utterly wild," he said looking at her again. "But at least it's a good color, and there is enough of it for almost any style."

"Let's keep it simple," Jenna said.

"Mon dieu, no, no, no, madam. Absolutely not. You

are to have sophistication, how do you say, 'bon class.' Simple will not do, absolutely not."

Jenna pointed to the corkscrew curls. "Absolutely not," she said firmly.

He made a face at her and stood up. He ran his long fingers through her hair and muttered. Then he turned away and picked up his black case. "To the boudoir, madam!"

Jenna decided to cooperate as long as he didn't try to give her corkscrew curls. She led him up the winding staircase to the third floor and to her room.

"Magnificent!" he said as he looked about.

He pointed her to the chair in front of the dressing table and laying his case on a stool, he opened it, revealing all manner of scissors and other strange items.

He began combing her hair slowly, carefully. Jenna watched in fascination as he went about his business. There was no blow dryer, but short of that, he seemed to have everything including an iron that could be heated on a fire to press out hair that was too curly, and a strange instrument that could also be heated, and which gave curl should the hair be too straight.

In addition to his hair equipment, he also revealed an array of perfumes and cosmetics from Paris.

After a time, he took her into the bathroom and ordered water brought. He washed her hair, and Jenna had to admit it felt quite nice to have it done by one so obviously professional in his trade.

When it was washed, but still wet, he took her back to the dressing table. There, quite expertly, he began to trim and cut. He seemed to want her hair long, but he told her it need shaping.

All the time he worked, he kept a running commentary. "I do all the finest ladies in Ville Quebec. And of course I am sometimes summoned to the finer country homes—usually those within a day's ride."

"You are, of course, the first English woman I have done. I've always thought the English had inferior hair. But yours is very good. Wild and disordered, but very good. Of course, all the men will love the color, my dear. Those copper tones speak of fire, and all the men want to know if . . . if . . . well I suppose it is. Not that I personally care about your hidden parts, though you are very beautiful. Objectively speaking, that is."

Jenna could hardly keep from smiling. He seemed deadly serious about everything, but here was something amusing about him, and she suspected he knew everything that went on in Ville Quebec. What a discovery! A hairdresser in 1704 was hardly different from one in 1988!

"Do you know a woman called Madeleine?"

He laughed and waved his hand. "There are hundreds, if not thousands of women in Quebec named Madeleine. But of course I know the Countess Madeleine. She is engaged to Monsieur l'Écossais and is one of the most beautiful women in all of Quebec!"

Royalty! And beautiful! Well, it did not surprise her. Blaise would want a beautiful woman to go with his beautiful mansion. But what then did he want with her? Would this Madeleine put up with a mistress?

"Yes, yes. Her family is most prominent. Her father served the king of France in Paris!"

Jenna hoped that her facial expression did not betray her real interest, nor indeed her churning emotions.

She waited a few minutes and then asked. "Do many men in Quebec have mistresses?"

Her question resulted in a laugh and a dramatic wave of Monsieur Richer's hand. "Mon Dieu, but of course! All the rich Frenchmen have mistresses, or want them." Then he blushed slightly, and added, "Well, perhaps not all. And, of course, those who are poor and live in the lower town cannot afford mistresses."

"Lower town? What is the lower town?"

"Yes. I will explain. The rich all live on the bluff. The others live in the lower town. There are carpenters, shopkeepers, toolmakers, stone masons, and the like."

"Do you live in the lower town too?"

"No, no. I live in an apartment in the fine home of the intendant himself. It is true I have a profession, but it's different. In any case, I have a special relationship with the intendant. I do all his wigs."

Jenna averted her eyes and vaguely wondered about the special relationship. And it occurred to her that knowing someone who was a friend of the most powerful man in the province could do no harm. Perhaps there would come a time when she would be free. Perhaps she would need to know people. Unlike James and Elizabeth, she had no home to which she could return. True, in Montreal she had toyed with the idea of running away to Europe, but then she remembered that Europe was not terribly desirable in this time period. As she recalled, war and pestilence were the twin blights of the age. On reflection, she had decided she was better off here.

Her hair, she noted had now been skillfully rolled in the front, although a few small curls had been allowed to escape. The rest of it, was pulled back. Even now, Monsieur Richer was pulling a lace cape over it. "That will do for everyday," he said with a sigh. "Of course, before the Grand Ball I shall have to return to coif it properly for the occasion. Something more ornate will be in order for the Grand Ball."

"What Grand Ball?" Jenna asked.

"The one in November. Monsieur Charlebois is working night and day to finish all the gowns.

"Of course, now he has all your dresses as well. But

there is an order coming from Paris too. Hopefully, there will be some in that lot that will fit you so he won't have to make everything."

"Hopefully," Jenna said, wondering again exactly what Blaise had in mind and why.

Blaise sat in the drawing room of the Picard mansion, his eyes taking in the feast of color, excellent design, and fine art that surrounded him. On a nearby mahogany table, there was an intricate porcelain drummer boy atop a stand emblazoned with the delicate blue *fleur-de-lis*. Dressed in a French army uniform, the miniature was brightly colored, yet delicately fashioned. On the walls, great tapestries helped keep out winter's drafts, and a fire flickered in the hearth of the stone fireplace. The furniture and the art was all imported from Paris, and even in the French court, there were no finer furnishings than in this very room. Nor did the Picards want for an excellent wine cellar. Beneath the house were racks of dusty wine bottles and not a few fine cognacs. Yes, the Picards were a worthy family, and being a member of the family, even if by marriage, was a tremendous advantage. Still, it was an advantage he was about to turn his back on.

Madeleine floated into the room. Her thick rich dark hair, usually coiffed elaborately, today cascaded over milk white shoulders. Her red dress was cut daringly low, revealing nearly all of her full breasts, save her dark taunt nipples that were hidden just beneath the laces of her chemise.

Her eyes were deep dark pools beneath long lashes, her lips full and ruby red. There was no question she was desirable, but strangely, he felt nothing. He felt not the slightest twinge of attraction, not the slightest wish to pull her into his arms and devour her with kisses as he might once have done after so long an absence.

Madeleine lifted her lashes and looked at him expectantly, "There was a time, Blaise when you would have ravished me with kisses. You've been gone a long while, my darling. Why are you so hesitant?"

"Yes, a long while." He looked at her and wondered. News traveled fast in Quebec City, this person told that person and soon everyone knew everything. He knew full well that news of his beautiful new house guest—the English prisoner—had traveled on every tongue in the city. From Mr. Charlebois, a notorious gossip, to the lips of the governor's wife. Everyone knew about Jenna just as everyone knew about Elizabeth and Edouard. He walked across the room toward her and took her hands in his, "Madeleine, I must talk with you."

Madeleine smiled. "Ah, talk—yes, my darling, a man who wants to talk after an absence of a year, is well contemplating serious matters."

He led her to the divan, and they both sat down. He did not let go of her hands. Her face was a mask, perhaps through her hands he could sense her real emotions. She was beautiful, and she was skillful at hiding her emotions.

"I don't know how to begin," he said slowly, staring into her eyes.

"Please darling, be direct. I know about her, your lovely English prisoner. I know about the young boy and his sister as well, but mostly I know of the woman. The tongues of Quebec City wag like a dog's tail at meal time."

He smiled. "Secrets are impossible."

"Do you love her?"

Madeleine's question was so abrupt it caught him off guard. "I think so," he answered, unable to lie.

She pressed her lips together. "I see. Well, Blaise, were you another man, I would ask how long you intended to keep this mistress, but I know you too well."

Her voice was so even, so unemotional, he felt relief flow through him.

Madeleine looked down and then took the beautiful ring off her finger. "Here, I release you from all obligations."

"Please, Madeleine. Keep the ring. It belongs on your finger."

"I couldn't."

"As a keepsake of our friendship, then. Please."

She nodded, looking at her skirt, and he felt her squeeze his hand ever so slightly. He felt awful. She was wonderful! She was so understanding, so lovely. But still it had to be. He was utterly incapable of loving two women, and Jenna was everything, even though at this moment she didn't seem to want him.

"You're quite a woman," he said, in honest admiration.

Madeleine forced a smile. "Only one thing, Blaise. I want only one favor."

"Anything," he said, brashly.

"Please take me to the Governor's Ball. It is too late to arrange another escort, and well, what would people say?"

"Of course! I'd be delighted."

"She won't mind?"

Blaise shook his head. "Not at this moment. She has yet to understand about us."

"I see," Madeleine answered, slowly.

"I felt I had to speak with you first."

"Thank you," she answered, returning her eyes to her skirt.

"Till the ball then," he stood up, wanting to leave,

wanting to see Jenna now that he had ended it with Madeleine.

Madeleine waved him away with a forced smile, and then she waited till she heard the front door close. She walked briskly to the window and watched him as he climbed into his carriage and rode away.

"Damn you, Blaise!" she shouted at the empty room. Then, in a cold fury she turned and grasped the porcelain drummer boy and hurled it to the floor, smashing it in a thousand pieces.

"You will come back on your knees!" she shouted to the empty room.

Her temper vented, she stormed upstairs, congratulating herself on how she behaved in his presence. He would never believe her of behaving ill. But she would do something, she vowed to get him back.

Blaise guided his stallion through the dark velvet night. The warm fire and lamplight of Quebec City was far behind, the lonely road that ran parallel to the river lie ahead, and a cold wind blew in his face. Jenna was at the end of that road.

In the silence of the night, he cursed himself for not ending it with Madeleine once and for all. He cursed himself for agreeing to take her to the ball. But, of course, it would have been thoughtless of him—whom could she get to escort her on such short notice? Still, he felt angry with himself. Now, he could not honestly tell Jenna that it was over between himself and Madeleine. He would have to wait till after the ball. It also meant he could not take Jenna to the ball, he could not seize the opportunity of that grand occasion to tell her how much he loved her, and how he wanted to be with her and that he wanted her alone.

When he was sure of her, he decided, he would tell her about his quest, about his obligations. Those, he felt, she would understand. And, when she understood, she could decide for herself if she could tolerate his long absences.

How he yearned for her! Somehow he felt that she would be glad to see him if he suddenly appeared, somehow he felt she would forgive him everything. She loved him, he knew she did. He could feel it when he held her. She was prideful, and until he could tell her that it was completely over between himself and Madeleine, he knew he would have to deal with her pride.

Still, Madeleine had been absolutely reasonable and completely understanding. Why couldn't Jenna be as understanding and as generous in her behavior?

He took a deep breath of the cold night air. Women were such an enigma. It was most certainly Madeleine who should have been angry. Then he reminded himself that he should have told Jenna about Madeleine before they became lovers, but at the time it had not seemed important because he knew it was over. In fact, it would have been over even if he had never met Jenna.

Madeleine would never have put up with his ongoing quest, of that he was certain. She hated his absences, she had already hinted that she wanted him to vow to stay in Quebec City when they married. No, he couldn't do it. He couldn't give up.

"Maybe you'll understand better," he said to himself, thinking of Jenna. He smiled, the very thought of her sending a wave of warmth through his body. He spurred his horse onward. The sooner he held her, the better.

Jenna unfolded the delicate parchment letter once again. It smelled of heady Parisian perfume and was written in a ornate hand. She had read and read it, and each time she did so, she grew angrier.

Dear Mademoiselle Stevens,

Blaise has just left my boudoir. We spoke of you fleetingly, and he informed me of his intentions. But of course I understand completely. Blaise and I pledged ourselves to one another long ago.

Naturally, I look forward to meeting you although I am assured you will only be here till spring when transportation home can be arranged for you. I trust we will meet at the Governor's Ball to which Blaise is escorting me.

Sincerely,
Madeleine Picard

It was late evening, and Jenna sat before the gilt-edged mirror in her luxurious room. She put the parchment down and turned again to brushing out her hair.

Each and every week for the past month, Monsieur Richer had returned to coif it. It was, she conceded, no longer a mane of wild hair but as tame as if she had gone weekly to Boston's finest hair salon. But what did it matter? She felt she was only a pampered doll, a prisoner in an elegant dollhouse. The letter from Madeleine Picard had made her even angrier—what had Blaise done? Asked her permission to keep a mistress? And did he truly intend to send her back?

She pressed her lips together, feeling completely frustrated at the manner in which Blaise had treated her, indeed at her own situation.

Jenna wondered if she should have told Blaise about herself. Perhaps she should have confided in Elizabeth. She felt very close to Elizabeth, but not close enough to tell her the truth about herself. Elizabeth was too young, and not worldly enough to accept and understand

Jenna's reality. Nor did Jenna want to discuss Blaise with Elizabeth. Elizabeth was about to turn seventeen, and she was quite taken with Edouard. A young girl in love was too distracted to understand her twin dilemmas.

In any case, she was not yet in a position to make decisions. James came first. Once he was on his way home, she could ponder her own future more realistically, although it seemed Blaise had already decided everything without so much as a word to her.

Still, she could not help thinking about the future whether it be here, or in Boston. This was a man's world, and the only independent women were probably prostitutes. She would simply have to think every decision through if, in fact, she were given the opportunity to make a decision.

Jenna started at the sound of footsteps outside her bedroom door. She was dressed only in her diaphanous nightgown, and she reached for her green velvet robe. But the person outside the door did not ask to be admitted, he simply threw open the door and strode into the room.

Jenna's full lips parted in surprise as she quickly turned about. Blaise towered above her.

He was not dressed as she had known him, in his rough woodsman's garb. Tonight he was wearing an elegant dark blue suit, a white ruffled shirt, and a blue brocade vest. Even in this finery—apparently common to the upper classes of Quebec—he exuded a raw masculinity and rugged persona.

His facial expression was unreadable as he looked down at her. Only his dark eyes spoke to her as they roamed her body, betraying his lust.

Jenna burned under his look. She fought her desires and then broke the spell by looking away. "I suppose you've been with Madeleine," she said, coldly.

"I told her all about you. She's very understanding."

"Well, I'm not!" she stormed.

He reached out and grabbed her wrist, pulling her up from the chair and into his arms. She struggled against him, turning her head to avoid his rough kisses on her neck. Her robe, slipped to the floor, leaving her covered only with her low necked, filmy nightdress.

"I've come for what belongs to me," he said huskily. "I want to make you understand!"

Jenna doubled her fists and tried to fight him, but his lips fastened on hers, and his hands moved across her back. In an instant, he had lifted her and carried her to the fur rug in front of the fireplace. Jenna squirmed, trying to escape. But he held her fast, kissing her hard and caressing her even as he tore away her nightdress, leaving her naked. Jenna groaned as he became more intent, as he touched her in more intimate places, as his lips sought her breasts. Before them the fire flickered, against her back, the soft sensual fur of the rug. His lips were everywhere, her flesh was aglow once again with his sweet torments.

Then Jenna moaned, unable to restrain her own reactions—her memories of him—her own wantonness, her deep love.

Her arms encircled his neck as her resistance melted into surrender beneath the heat of his body and the strength of his passion.

"I have hungered for you," he whispered, as he joined with her.

Jenna felt hot tears running down her cheeks even as she gave into her own appetite. She cursed her own weakness, her need for him. She was his prisoner and her own. She had yielded everything. She was a prisoner of passion.

When he had finished he looked down at her. Her

skin glistened from exertion, her tears still flowed, un-abated. "I can't stand this!" she said, her eyes large.

He felt angry with her reaction. Didn't she realize what he'd meant when he said he had talked to Madeleine? What did she want? Her expression was a mask she could not read. He moved away from her quickly, then taking his clothes, he left her, closing the door after him as he left.

Jenna trembled. She had responded to him as she always did! She felt anger with herself welling inside her, anger that she had given in to him.

She heard his footsteps on the stairs, and she struggled to stand up and go to the window. Outside, she saw him mount his horse and ride off into the night.

"Not a word!" she said aloud. He had given her no explanation, offered her no comfort. He had simply come in the night and demanded what was his. "I wasn't strong," she said, dejectedly. Jenna went back to the bed and threw herself on it. It was worse than not being strong. She had responded to him as fervently as she had the first time he had ravished her—yes, ravished was the word. Their lovemaking—his and hers—was steamy and wild.

Was this how he intended it to be? Would he keep her here and come only to satisfy his hunger for her? Was she to have nothing of him save moments of fiery, heated desire?

Again, Jenna began to cry even as she vowed to make herself stronger.

For days after Blaise's late night visit, Jenna moped about, reading, walking, trying to rationalize what had happened. On the fourth forth day, she began to feel better, her spirits lifted by a return of fine fall weather in mid November.

"Come in," she called out, as she heard a light tap on her door.

Madame Patoulet stepped into the room, carrying five large boxes. "The coachman has just delivered these, mademoiselle. I believe they're hats from Paris to match the dresses Monsieur Charlebois is bringing next week."

Jenna stood up and took half of the awkward boxes from Madame Patoulet. "We'll put them on the bed for now," Jenna said. Hats had never wildly interested her, and she didn't feel interested now. Still, everyone did wear hats, so she supposed she would have to get used to them.

"Don't you want to try them on?" Madame Patoulet asked, eyeing the boxes curiously.

Jenna half smiled. No doubt Madam was bored too. She supposed that hats from Paris were rare enough that Madame Patoulet wanted to see them.

"I can't tell much about them till I try them on with the proper dresses—but we can open them and look at them," Jenna suggested.

Madam all but clapped her tiny hands. "Oh, yes, I should like to see them."

Jenna opened one hatbox and withdrew an ornate wide-brimmed hat made of felt. It was dark blue decorated with a broad blue ribbon and a large feather.

"Magnificent!" Madame Patoulet said, touching it reverently.

"Would you like to try it on, Madame Patoulet?"

She shook her head. "My head is too small for such a wonderful hat. It would fall to my eyebrows." She laughed, and then looked at Jenna seriously, "Why don't you call me Anne Marie?"

"If you will call me, Jenna."

"Jenna—is it short for Jeannette?"

"No. It is just Jenna."

"A nice name," Anne Marie said, as Jenna began to open another box.

"Have you worked here long?" Jenna asked.

Anne Marie looked up and smiled. "I have been with Blaise l'Écossais for five years."

Jenna stopped opening the second box. "Tell me," she said looking at Anne Marie. "Tell me what you know about his family, about him."

Anne Marie shook her head sadly. "I know many things, but there are many things that are a mystery to me. I was told that Blaise's family traveled from the Scottish Highlands to Paris. His father was a clan leader, but there was some dispute and so the family moved to France. There his father became a wine merchant. They lived in Paris for several years, then they decided to come to Quebec because Monsieur l'Écossais believed there would be great opportunities in the new world. I know they came to be called l'Écossais which means Scot in French, but I do not know the original family name.

"I was told the family died in a fire. As far as I know, Blaise was an exceptional boy, and now he is an exceptional man."

"You seem very loyal to him," Jenna said, carefully.

"Oh, *oui*, Mademoiselle. He saved my brother's life. He has been very good to me."

"Why does he travel with the Indians?"

Anne Marie shrugged. "I do not know. I think Governor Vaudreuil asked him to participate in the battle with New England."

"Were there times before that?"

"Oh, yes. He disappears for long periods of time to

travel with the Indians. He was known to do that long before I came."

Anne Marie's gray eyes flickered when she spoke of Blaise, yet even she did not seem to know many details about him.

"In many ways, he has been like my own son," Anne Marie said, "but he is a very private man."

"So you've lived here in Quebec all these years?"

Anne Marie nodded. "I met Blaise when he returned from Paris where he went to study. He built on his parent's money. I have been told he became rich as the captain of a vessel—as a privateer licensed by the king of France. Then he became a fur trader, and his wealth grew. He fought the English on the high seas and was rewarded for his loyalty to the king of France with this *seigneury*. But no mistake. He worked hard and built this into one of the finest *seigneuries* in Nouvelle France."

Anne Marie's account of Blaise's past was full of awe, but it lacked a great deal of detail that Jenna had hoped to hear, and even Anne Marie seemed to be curious about Blaise. Like his time with the Indians, Anne Marie actually knew nothing about his years at sea, or the time he spent as a fur trader. And, clearly, she knew nothing of the years he had been away in Paris.

Jenna turned away and opened the second box. It was, to Jenna's eyes, a slightly ridiculous hat which was probably intended to be worn in the evening. More of a headdress than a hat, really. It was a lofty silver spangled blue turban mounted with dyed plum ostrich feathers.

Anne Marie's eyes widened. "I think the ladies of Quebec will be most impressed!"

Jenna could only smile. It was no doubt the style of the day, but she thought it quite silly looking. The next hat was, Anne Marie related, a hat suitable as an acces-

sory for a riding habit. It, too, was felt and decorated
with ribbons, rosettes and ostrich feathers. The other
hats were all of a bucket style with buckles, feathers, ribbons, and the like. Each was clearly intended for a specific outfit. Why was Blaise giving her all of these clothes
when she never went anywhere?

Did he intend to show her off? A chill suddenly ran
down her spine. Perhaps he would sell her to another
man when he married Madeleine. Was such a thing possible? Never had she felt so horrible. The thought of
staying with him under these circumstances was intoler-
able. The thought of not having him was unbearable.

"I can hardly wait for Monsieur Charlebois to return
with your dresses," Anne Marie said, admiring the hats.
"I know you're going to look simply ravishing."

Jenna forced a smile and wondered again for whom
she was to look ravishing, and why Blaise l'Écossais was
going to all this trouble.

Jenna's room was filled with open boxes, and gowns
were draped over all of the chairs and across the
bed. White laces, ribbons, fancy undergarments, taffetas,
silks, satins, and brocades created a rainbow of color.
Hand-embroidered vests and stiff boned corsets vied for
space amidst the finery.

"I've never seen so many beautiful clothes!" Elizabeth
said, and she twirled about in front of the mirror. Her
blond hair was loose and a bit mussed from trying on so
many dresses. At the moment she wore a linen dress
with a divided skirt. The front opening was bordered on
each side with crewel embroidered panels. The bodice
and the sleeves were short, revealing a fitted chemise.
The petticoat, which unlike modern petticoats, was

quite visible between the two sides of the skirt, was quilted and also decorated with crewel embroidery.

Elizabeth ran her fingers over the quilted petticoat. "It will be most warm in the winter," she said, adding a practical tone to her previous comment.

Jenna was wearing a beautiful gown of emerald green silk that flared out over elegant white and ecru lace petticoats. It had a tight bodice with a very low square neck that seemed to reveal half of her breasts. Lace also trimmed the neckline, but it did nothing to modify the effect of the gown.

Jenna looked at herself in the mirror and for the hundredth time, reminded herself that this was the style of the day.

"You look incredibly beautiful," Elizabeth said, walking about her.

"You look lovely yourself."

"But this is not even my ball gown. Still, it is hard to imagine wearing such a fine dress for everyday occasions."

"Were you ever in Boston?" Jenna suddenly asked.

"Once that I can remember," Elizabeth replied. "We traveled three days to get there. Papa took Mama for her birthday. We all went, and we stayed with relatives."

"And weren't the ladies dressed well?"

"Oh not like this! I have never even seen laces like this . . . nor have I smelled perfumes such as those in my room."

Jenna smiled, thinking that even if they were very well to do, the upper class ladies of Boston probably did not dress in clothes like these. The Puritan ethic was no doubt still too strong. It was an ethic that crept into Elizabeth's comments even though she loved the clothes and certainly intended wearing them. Unquestionably, the wealthy upper classes of Quebec City were possessed of a decadent, European lifestyle, while Bostonians were stricter and more frugal. She thought the *habitants* were more like the puritans, except that they were Catholic. Her limited experience indicated that the *habitants* were moral, hard working, plain folk.

Elizabeth turned suddenly and went to the window. "There's a rider outside," she said turning to Jenna. "He's just dismounted and is headed for the front door."

"Anne Marie will get it," Jenna said. Still, like Elizabeth, her curiosity was peeked. Since they had come here, there had been few visitors. Even the arrival of a messenger broke the monotony.

Jenna and Elizabeth hurried out into the hallway. Both were still dressed in their finery, although their hair was uncombed.

Midway down the winding staircase they both stopped.

In the entrance hall, a young soldier stood, hat in hand. His eyes had lifted when he'd caught sight of them, and his face flushed.

Anne Marie turned and glanced up at them, a slight look of disapproval on her face. From the young man she took a large envelope, then without hesitation, she ushered him toward the kitchen.

Elizabeth flew down the stairs, lifting her awkward skirts as she went. A moment ago, Jenna thought, Elizabeth had been a woman. She had been serious and concerned even as she tried on her new clothes. But now, at this instant she was a girl again. A girl anxious to know what was going on.

"Where's he going?" she asked quickly. "And what did he bring?"

Anne Marie pressed her lips together to conceal her good humor. She tried to look cross with Elizabeth's curiosity, but she could not. "He's gone to the kitchen so that cook can feed him. It is a long ride from Quebec

City, you know." Then Anne Marie summoned herself. "And you shouldn't be running about in front of strangers half dressed."

Elizabeth only smiled, and her smile was infectious. Anne Marie could not pretend to be cross. She, too, smiled. "This envelope is for the two of you."

Jenna came down the stairs and took the proffered envelope. She opened it carefully and withdrew an ornately printed letter, accompanied by a less ornately printed letter.

"Oh, my," Anne Marie declared as she looked at the large letter. It was printed on the finest quality handmade paper and was written in gold lettering.

Jenna examined it. The printing was in gothic script. In total, it looked as if it were a page from an old illuminated manuscript. And while it was written in French, Jenna could not make it all out, save the fact that it was an invitation.

"What does it say?" Jenna asked, looking at Anne Marie.

"It's an invitation to the Governor's Ball. See, it is signed by the Monsieur François de Beauharnois, the intendant himself."

Jenna looked at the second letter, allowing Anne Marie and Elizabeth to marvel at the invitation from the intendant.

The second letter was penned by Blaise. It was formal and curt.

You and Elizabeth are to attend the Intendant's Ball in Quebec. You will wear the gowns Monsieur Charlebois will have waiting for you. Pack a small bag for both of you, as you will be spending several days in the city. The hairdresser will be sent in order to prepare you both. At ten A.M., Lieutenant Edouard Bouchard will come for you in a carriage.

He will accompany you to Quebec City and then bring you to the ball. I trust you will behave properly.

Jenna's finger's curled around the corner of the letter in anger. How dare he order her anywhere! How dare he tell her how to dress and how to behave! And what else did he intend? Surely, his Madeleine would be at the Intendant's Ball. How did Blaise intend to humiliate her this time?

"Edouard! Oh, Jenna, Edouard is taking us to Quebec!"

Jenna saw the expression of happiness on Elizabeth's face and decided to try to hide her own feelings. Elizabeth was overcome with joy that it was Edouard who would take them to Quebec City. Elizabeth spent hours talking to him and about him.

At least one of them would be happy, Jenna thought. Elizabeth seemed eager to attend the ball, and more than eager to have Edouard escort. Her blue eyes danced, and Jenna could see her imagining what a wonderful evening she would have.

So, I'll bite my tongue and go with her, Jenna decided. But again familiar questions filled her head. Why did Blaise what her to attend? Would Madeleine be there? Why would he want them to meet? The only answer could be that things were quite different here, in this French province, and in this time. Apparently, men were open about their dalliances. Unconsciously, Jenna shook her head. It didn't matter. There were limits to the adjustments she could make. She was what she was. Miserably, she admitted she didn't want to share him with anyone.

Chapter Fifteen

"I'm excited," Elizabeth said, as she peered out the window. "I've never been to a ball before. I've read about them, but I never dreamed I'd go to one. I feel just like a princess."

"When you're dressed in your ball gown, you look like a princess," Jenna said.

Elizabeth could hardly sit still. She kept going to the window, hoping the carriage that would take them to Quebec City would arrive. "But do I look all right now?" she suddenly asked. "I mean I want to look good for Edouard. I don't want to look like a country bumpkin going to the city."

Jenna laughed gently. "Oh, you don't look at all like a bumpkin. I'm sure Edouard will be in awe of you. He always is."

"Do you think so? I do hope you're right. I want him to like me a lot—I want—"

"She's in love," James quipped from the doorway. He bounded into the room and jumped onto the window seat.

Elizabeth sighed. "Maybe I am in love. Is there anything wrong with being in love?"

"Girls! I'm glad I don't have to dress up and go to

some old ball. I'd rather stay here with the horses. Jacques says I'm getting the hang of it."

Jacques was the servant in charge of the horses and the one who had been giving James and Elizabeth riding lessons.

"I like to ride," Elizabeth protested. "But this is different. It's special."

"And you can flirt and dance with Edouard," James teased. "Maybe you'll even kiss him!"

Elizabeth blushed. "Stop it. You're too young to understand anything."

"What will you do when we go home? You'll have to leave Edouard then."

Jenna's lips parted in surprise. Neither James nor Elizabeth had mentioned going home for a very long time. But the look that covered Elizabeth's face now betrayed her concern. Jenna silently chastised herself. She'd been too wrapped up in her own problem to think of how Elizabeth must feel.

"What makes you think we'll go home?" Elizabeth retorted. "We won't be ransomed like the others."

"I'll escape when I'm old enough and know enough. I'm not going to stay here forever."

Elizabeth was staring at the carpet, studying its intricate design as if she hoped she would find an answer to her problem there. Then she looked up at her brother. "I liked it better when you teased me, little brother."

James, too, looked serious. "Don't you want to go home?"

Elizabeth bit her lip. "I should like to see our parents, but I can't answer your question because I'm not certain."

James scrambled off the window seat and ran to his sister, hugging her tightly. "I would miss you if I had to run away alone."

Elizabeth hugged him in return but Jenna did not miss the far away look in her blue eyes.

James let his sister go and ran to the window at the sound of a carriage clattering up the drive.

For the trip to Quebec City, Elizabeth was dressed in a plain gold colored dress with a simple chemise beneath her laced bodice and a crisp apron. Jenna wore a similar style dress but it was dark blue. Anne Marie had assured them both that they were dressed properly for travel, and she had seen to it that their bags were packed with all they could possibly need.

Edouard looked as handsome as the first time Jenna had ever seen him. He was dressed in his uniform, and he stood straight and tall, clearly proud he had been entrusted with delivering them both to Quebec City.

Jenna studied Edouard and decided his infatuation with Elizabeth was quite obvious. He blushed when he saw her and of course, bowed from the waist when they both appeared. He kissed her hand too, but Jenna could not ignore the fact that he held Elizabeth's hand longer, and when he looked up, she could see the admiration he felt for Elizabeth in his large brown eyes.

Elizabeth turned to her brother and gave him a farewell hug. "Be good and don't spend all your time with the horses. You have to keep studying."

"I picked out some books for you to read," Jenna told him.

James hugged her, too, and then he shook hands with Edouard.

One at a time, Edouard helped them into the carriage. Then he climbed in too, seating himself next to Elizabeth.

"I could ride up front with the coachman if you require more room," he politely offered.

"Please stay," Elizabeth said quickly. Then, covering

her own desire to be with him, she quickly added, "You must remember, we are strangers. You will have to point out things of interest and tell us about Quebec."

"I shall be pleased to do so, Mademoiselle Elizabeth."

Their eyes lingered on one another, and Jenna felt it was she who should be riding with the coachman—not that such a thing was done in this time and place.

Edouard turned to the speaker tube which allowed one to communicate with the driver. He spoke in French, ordering him to leave.

James stood in the drive and waved.

Jenna leaned back against the red leather seat, her eyes glued to the coach window. It was fall, though it hardly seemed possible that so much time had elapsed since the fateful night of February twenty-ninth.

The grass was still green from the summer sun and the frequent rain. But frost had already turned the magnificent maples red, gold, and yellow. Throughout October, the hillsides from here to Massachusetts had been awash with the vibrant colors of fall but now, this first week in November, few leaves remained and those that did seemed to be clinging to the trees in the cool northern breeze.

Jenna's thoughts momentarily returned to the conversation between James and Elizabeth that had just occurred. She had read the bare facts of their fate, but knowing them personally and having grown fond of them, brought those facts into an entirely different light. There was great affection between them, and they both had great affection for their family. It saddened her to know they would be separated and now, as never before, she wondered how they would adjust to what life had in store for them. Jenna vowed to try to ease the sadness they would know. She glanced at Edouard. He seemed to be coming to play a role in the scheme of things. Perhaps he, too, could help Elizabeth.

"As you can see, we travel quite close to the river," Edouard was saying.

"The countryside looks much as it does near my home," Elizabeth said wistfully. "But of course fall comes a bit sooner here."

"Is there a river near your home?"

"The Connecticut. It's not as wide but it's a good size. And our mountains are higher. Yet the trees are the same, and I recognize most of the same plants and herbs."

"I hope you will soon feel at home here," Edouard said.

"I hope so too," Elizabeth answered.

They traveled for several hours. Now and again, they passed small villages and the occasional seigneury. Twice they stopped at local inns to refresh themselves and have tea.

Then, in the distance, the spire of Quebec's largest church glimmered in the sunlight. It seemed to Jenna that she always saw the churches first. They dotted the countryside, and wherever there were a few homes, there was a church.

"We'll come to the lower town first," Edouard told them.

"So many houses!" Elizabeth clapped her hands in glee.

"There are over two thousand people living here."

"I believe there are more in Boston, but I have not been there for many years," Elizabeth confessed.

The carriage moved from dirt road to cobblestones. They passed houses that were so close together they seemed to be built on top of one another.

"These houses belong to the artisans," Edouard told them.

"They're interesting looking houses." In truth, Jenna thought they must be very uncomfortable in the winter. The walls were made of dark stone, but the roofs were made of straw. Still, she supposed no place was truly warm in the winter. She was quite certain even Blaise's mansion would be cold except right in front of the fire.

"There are many hazards. The stones come from here and are quite fine, but the straw roofs make the danger of fire very great indeed."

"They must be cold," Jenna said. "What happens when it snows?"

"Actually, they are more comfortable than they look, and warmer than one might imagine."

The carriage stopped and waited until a fish monger moved out of the way. The street they followed wound up the hill. It seemed to have grown so narrow that Jenna felt as if she could reach right out and touch the houses as they drove by. Then, quite suddenly, the road became wider.

"If you look back you can see the harbor. There are many, many French ships in port now. This is one of the last trips that can be made before the winter snows come and the gales on the Atlantic make the journey too hazardous. The ships have brought many supplies for the winter, and they take away many fur pelts in return."

Jenna looked out the window. She craned her neck so she could see the harbor below. The blue water was filled with white sails. The fleet had been a magnificent sight in Montreal, here it was equally breathtaking. "I love sailing ships," Jenna said.

Edouard laughed. "What other kinds are there, mademoiselle?"

Jenna's heart took a jump—it was when she was relaxed that she had to be the most careful. "I mean I like it when their sails are unfurled."

"Ah, yes," Edouard acknowledged.

The street leveled off and was now very much wider. In fact, it turned into an avenue. They began to pass large impressive buildings. Edouard pointed out the *Hôtel dieu Hôpital,* the *Ursiline Convent,* and finally the ornate splendor of the governor's manor.

"In summer, the people who live here dress in silks and party. They live just as people live in Paris. In winter, they bundle themselves in furs and ride about on horse-drawn sleighs."

"Where do you stay when you are here, Edouard?" Jenna knew his parents lived near Blaise, and she knew he had been on leave the past month.

Edouard smiled. "Oh, I live here, in the upper town. Well, now of course I live with the other soldiers—I mean my parents have a townhouse here. My father is the brother of the lieutenant governor. We came here many years ago from France, and when my mother died, my father decided to stay here. He has since remarried. My sisters and brothers live on the seigneury, and I have been visiting them."

"Where will we spending the night?" Jenna asked.

"At Monsieur l'Écossais' townhouse. I believe you will be staying more than one night. No doubt you will be here for several days, at least until the fleet sails."

At Blaise's townhouse? She felt a wave of panic sweep over her. She knew she would see him, but she did not know he had a house here, nor had she thought they would be staying with him. She had assumed they would stay with some family—friends of his perhaps. But she didn't want to stay in his house. He would be too close.

Would he come to her again tonight and demand her? She felt angry all over again—at him, at Madeleine, and at herself for not being able to resist his advances.

But Jenna forced herself to say nothing. Instead, she tried to think about being in a city after all these months. She had been so isolated for so long, she rather hoped she would be here for a few days.

The carriage turned up a tree-lined drive, and after a moment, it clattered to a halt in front of a two story stone house with distinctive black wrought iron balconies and an outside staircase. It reminded Jenna of the houses in New Orleans' French Quarter. It was not as large as the mansion on the seigneury, but it was not small either.

A small dark haired housemaid dressed in black and wearing a dust cap opened the front door and ushered them in. "Welcome," she said in heavily accented English. As she showed them upstairs, she chattered in French, adding,, "I tried to learn words for you, but I only know a few."

Jenna spoke to her in hesitant French, and the young girl smiled and curtsied. She seemed terribly relieved to learn that all communication would not depend on her broken English.

"I want to go and say goodbye to Edouard," Elizabeth said, turning quickly and running back downstairs.

Jenna looked around, taking in her surroundings. This house was well appointed, but not as richly furnished as the seigneury. Its well made furnishings appeared to have been made by local craftsmen, and unlike the seigneury, there was no formal winding staircase. Yes, the seigneury was like the Tara of literary fame, but this townhouse was less lavish.

The bedroom had a large fireplace, but there was no

ornate bath. The only real bath was downstairs. There was a large bed, a dresser, and several mirrors.

Jenna was attracted to two pictures which hung on the wall. She went to them. They were miniature paintings. One was of a young man who looked a little like Blaise, but who was clearly not Blaise. The other was of a quite beautiful woman. Perhaps, Jenna thought, these were Blaise's parents. It occurred to her that once they all might have lived in this very house. Yes, maybe this was the original house and the seigneury was his own creation.

Jenna lay down on the bed and stretched. It was a long trip from the seigneury, and she felt cramped from sitting for so many hours. Again, she looked around the room, and then her thoughts turned to Anne Marie. She wished she had asked her even more about Blaise. She found that this house piqued her curiosity.

She closed her eyes but opened them again when Elizabeth knocked lightly and then entered.

"Oh, were you asleep?' she asked with concern.

"No. Just resting."

"The ball is tomorrow night, and I've been told that tomorrow the hairdresser and the couturier are coming to prepare us."

"I'm sure we'll look our best," Jenna said, squeezing Elizabeth's hand.

"I want to look my best," Elizabeth said, dreamily. "I like it here. I like this place. It's not as big as Boston nor as small as Deerfield. And I like this house too. I've never seen such fine houses, such huge churches."

"I think you like it because you're with Edouard," Jenna suggested.

Elizabeth blushed. "Yes, that's the biggest reason. I admit it."

"Sometimes it seems to me that you would be quite happy to stay here," Jenna ventured cautiously.

Elizabeth looked into her eyes. "You're right, but I must always think of others. James will always want to go home, and I must find my mother."

Jenna took Elizabeth's hand in hers. "Somehow," she promised, "I know it will work out."

"I try to believe that," Elizabeth said softly.

The great stone mansion of the intendant was the most elegant in all of Quebec.

Edouard had told them, "In all ways the first intendant, Jean Talon, struggled to turn the capital into a miniature of Versailles, just as he worked hard to make the social life of Quebec as refined as that of Paris. It was, indeed, his ambition to turn *Nouvelle France* into a microcosm of France."

He had gone on to explain the present intendant, François de Beauharnois, like those before him, had carried on in Talon's footsteps.

Jenna realized she had been right. New France was very much a feudal society transferred to the new world. But there was a real difference. Here, it seemed, there was a possibility of upward mobility. That possibility she was quite certain did not exist in early eighteenth century France.

The entrance hall of the intendant's mansion was painted white and was lit by a hanging candelabra that contained over forty slow-burning candles.

From the center of the hall, there was a great winding staircase that led to the rooms on the second floor.

As soon as they were escorted into the front door by Edouard, and their cloaks hung up, they were ushered into a room to one side of the front door. It was a large long room with mirrors and low seats. Its lighting was muted, and its walls were rose colored. There were little dressing tables with sterling silver hand mirrors, should a lady like to view the back of her hair, and there were even perfume bottles and various powders.

Elizabeth looked mystified.

"It's a powder room. I suppose we're to freshen up," Jenna explained. Poor Elizabeth, in some ways a girl from the rugged New England frontier was as out of place here as she was. "But as we spent so long being readied, I don't really feel it's necessary. In any case, I wouldn't dare touch a hair on my head."

"No, I shouldn't if I were you. Monsieur Richer would be quite furious." Elizabeth looked at Jenna and said softly, "You really look quite magnificent. I'm sure you will be the most beautiful woman here."

"I doubt it," Jenna replied, even though she felt as if she looked as good as she had ever looked, perhaps better. "In any case, you offer a lot of competition."

Elizabeth beamed. But it was the truth. She wore an exquisite blue silk gown with layers of white lace petticoats. Her sleeves were long, ruffled, and trimmed in white lace. Her bodice was tight, and her chemise was pure white lace. In all, it was a dress that seemed at once modest and daring. Its color made her blue eyes seem even bluer, while at the same time displaying her milk white skin. Her blond hair was held high, but cascades of curls caressed her shoulders.

Monsieur Richer, also in charge of makeup, had chosen soft pinks, and thus Elizabeth looked both alluring and innocent all at once.

"Have we been here long enough?" Elizabeth asked. She seemed anxious to return to Edouard.

"I think so." She lifted her skirt carefully, and followed Elizabeth outside.

Edouard proudly took them, one on each arm. At the entrance to the ballroom, they were announced in French.

"Oh, my," Elizabeth said under her breath.

The room was huge. Three crystal chandeliers, each of which magnified the light from over fifty candles, hung from the ceiling. They looked for all the world like hanging clusters of diamonds.

At one end of the room, a large harpsichord stood on a podium, and everywhere there were beautiful delicate pieces of furniture in the Louis XIV style. Once again, Jenna felt as if she were in a museum. But all the items she thought of as priceless antiques were, of course, quite new, or at least not older than thirty years. She could not quite remember, but she felt certain that Louis the XIV was still the king of France. She cautioned herself silently to be careful about such details, since there were things she surely should have known that she did not know for certain.

The entire room was paneled with ivory colored beveled panels trimmed in gold. The twenty-foot ceiling was covered in wallpaper with a tiny gold leaf design. There were many alcoves that were also trimmed in gold. Set into each alcove was a table holding a small marble sculpture. Many of the tables were inlaid with mother-of-pearl, and the furniture was covered with brocade and velvet.

"My breath is taken away," Elizabeth whispered. "Never have I dreamt of a place so lavish."

Jenna could not pretend to be taken aback by the lavish setting, although she had not thought of it in connection with North America in this period. But certainly the contrast was surprising—a vast, largely unexplored wilderness peopled by Indians surrounded this capital of New France. And only a short distance from here, people lived in stone houses with straw roofs. Yet here, in this room, there was utter opulence. It seemed to Jenna that the intendant had succeeded in his desire to recreate Versailles, albeit, a miniature version.

Edouard escorted them to a table at one end of the ballroom. It was covered with glasses of champagne and silver trays holding small delicate hors d'oeuvres. Each of the varied dishes was arranged artistically with flowers to add color.

He presented them both with a glass of champagne and toasted them, "To the two most beautiful women in the room," he said proudly.

Far above the ballroom floor was a small alcove that could be accessed through a hall on the second floor. From the alcove one could see all that transpired below without being seen.

Blaise looked down on Jenna, Elizabeth, and Edouard. He pressed his lips together and wondered if Jenna were as angry as she had been.

What a magnificent creature she was! By now, most of the men in the room had noticed her, and many had turned toward her, hoping she would notice them. The women glanced her way too. Most would be wildly jealous.

The jade green brocade gown he had selected was stunning. It showed off every desirable curve of her wonderful body. The bodice was laced tightly to her tiny waist, the skirt fell over her delightfully rounded hips, while the low cut square neck revealed her flawless white skin as well as the alluring shape of her full breasts.

"Jenna," he whispered under his breath. Her flaming copper colored hair was beautiful. How he hoped to run his fingers through it, how he longed to hold her. Even the night he had come to her in spite of her protests, she had responded to him with a fury of wild untamed passion. If she did not truly love him, then they were mates of another sort. Mates who could not do without the other.

No man could forget the flash of her green eyes. She was a beautiful independent cat who could play like a ferocious kitten. "You will be mine again," he whispered as he stared at her. His thoughts were filled with her as he imagined his hands caressing her.

The memory of her writhing in his arms, her hot breath on his neck, and her wanton animal desire washed over him. He felt himself flush all over, and he felt more—he felt his desire for her rising to a pitched intensity. "I will have you," he again vowed. Then he quickly turned and left the little alcove. Madeleine must be ready now.

The Countess Madeleine Picard had been reared in Paris. Her wealthy parents had spared no amount of money in seeing to it their exquisite daughter learned everything a young woman should learn. She had the best private tutors and was a master of English, French, and Spanish. She had excelled in music and played the piano as well as the harpsichord. She embroidered, wrote poetry, and had been taught elegant manners. She was also jealous, although she hid it well. How dare Blaise break their engagement to be with some little English tart? A prisoner yet? One of the enemy. What could such a woman possibly offer him? These and all manner of questions filled her thoughts, but she did not ask them lest she reveal her emotions. She had been so rational, so unemotional. She had asked Blaise to accompany her to the ball as his one last act before the news of breaking their engagement became public. She had prevailed on their long friendship and made him feel guilty. He was convinced she was warm and understanding. Madeleine pressed her full lips together, vowing silently to find a way to end the relationship he had with this woman—whomever she was. "I will have him back," she vowed silently, and she turned away from the mirror and opened the door.

Blaise saw Madeleine, resplendent in an elegant red gown emerge from the second floor powder room. Her ravishing dark hair covered her bare shoulders, and her dark eyes studied him carefully. "You're a strange man," she commented dryly.

"You're quite enough to take any man's breath away," he said, taking her arm.

Madeleine puckered her ruby red lips, "Ah, *mon cher,* of course I am. I have everything money can buy, and I spend all of my time pampering myself."

He laughed lightly. Madeleine was honest as well as lovely.

"Will I meet her?"

"It seems unavoidable. Do you mind?"

"No, of course not. It is all something I shall have to learn to live with."

"Then sooner rather than later," he said as he guided her toward the staircase.

Jenna was sipping her champagne when she looked up and saw Blaise walking toward her. The woman on his arm was a stunning dark-eyed beauty. Jenna froze, wondering what to say or do. She felt cornered. There was no place to which she could flee.

Just as they approached, a young man intercepted them. He spoke to both, and then led the woman away, on his arm.

Jenna also saw that at the far end of the room, a small orchestra was being seated on the podium behind the harpsichord.

Blaise continued walking toward her alone.

Jenna again looked about, wanting to escape. But there was nowhere to go. Elizabeth and Edouard had also gone to stand closer to the dance floor.

"Dance with me," Blaise said, holding out his hand.

Jenna looked about. How she wanted to run from him! He was horrible! There he was with the woman he intended to marry, and he was asking her to dance!

He grasped her wrist and pulled her into his arms.

Jenna stiffened, refusing to let him hold her close. Suddenly, the music started, and instead of drawing her toward him, he spun her outward and bowed.

It was only then, because she had been so distracted by the whole situation, that she realized it was a minuet and that no one was dancing in any way she had ever danced before.

"They do dance the minuet in the Virginia Colony," he said, his eyes boring through her.

Jenna shivered. As if things were not bad enough, she felt awkward. The only place she had ever even seen this dance was in old Hollywood movies. It had looked so easy, but in fact, it was quite complicated.

"Triple time, my darling. And then down, and lift your lovely arm out."

"I am not your darling," she snapped irritably as she looked about, trying desperately to imitate the others and remember how the minuet looked when she had seen it danced in all those films.

"That's good, you're getting the idea."

Jenna didn't look at him. It was, she thought, a rather nice dance, although it would take some getting used to.

Elizabeth and Edouard were out in the middle of the

dance floor. Elizabeth seemed to know the dance surprisingly well. She danced delicately and with clear expertise. Edouard seemed very proud of her. His eyes looked lovingly at her, and she curtsied sweetly, while holding the side of her skirt in one hand and his hand in the other.

"Soon you'll make a fine partner," Blaise said.

"I don't want to dance with you," Jenna answered, searching for the right tone of aloofness. It was true. She didn't want him to hold her because she feared giving in to him. Nor did she want to reveal how little she knew of this dance. Especially to him. He was more dangerous to her, because he had spent more time with her and because he already suspected something.

Blaise stopped suddenly. He looked annoyed as his dark eyes flashed with his own temper. "Very well," he said curtly. "Who am I to insist on your dancing with me." He walked her across the room to a young officer. "Commander Guion, may I present Mademoiselle Jenna Stevens."

"Mademoiselle." He bowed from the waist and kissed her hand.

"Will you see to it that mademoiselle is entertained, Commander, and that she is returned to my townhouse after the ball."

"I shall be most pleased and honored."

"Good evening, mademoiselle," Blaise said curtly. He turned on his heel and left.

Jenna watched him march away.

"Would you like to dance, mademoiselle?"

Jenna turned, feeling empty and quite miserable. She had wanted him to go; now she felt as terrible as the day she had learned of Madeleine. Once again, she felt her emotions churning.

Jenna fought to maintain her composure. "I should

like you to teach me this dance," she said in a voice trembling with emotion.

"I shall be pleased."

Jenna forced herself to smile. "But first could you excuse me? I must go to the powder room."

He bowed again. "Of course, mademoiselle."

Jenna lifted her heavy green brocade skirt and walked across the room. She went directly into the powder room and slumped into one of the chairs, grateful no one else was there.

She studied her image in the mirror. She looked like a picture out of one of her own history books.

Somehow, some way, she vowed she would free herself of her physical obsession with Blaise. Somehow, some way, she vowed to survive on her own.

At that moment, just as she was about to lift herself out of her chair and return to her young lieutenant, the door opened and in came the beautiful Madeleine. She smiled engagingly and sat down.

"You're Jenna," she surmised. Her eyes did not rest on Jenna directly, but rather on her mirror image.

"Yes," Jenna replied, wondering just how much Blaise had told her. Perhaps he had told her nothing save the scantiest of facts. Jenna looked back at Madeleine's image. She was even more attractive up close than she had appeared at a distance.

Her thick dark hair was naturally curly, her skin was flawless, and her eyes were like dark pools. Her dress was certainly in the high fashion of the day, and her figure was excellent. She was, Jenna noted, quite petite and somehow, dressed as she was, she reminded Jenna of one of those French boudoir dolls that were sometimes used to decorate beds.

"I suppose Blaise told you about me," Jenna said carefully. It was a statement intended to lead.

"Yes, he told me all about you," she replied, placing the emphasis on "all."

Silently Jenna cursed him. Madeleine seemed cool and unemotional. If she was jealous, she did not seem so.

"And how do you feel about me?"

Madeleine smiled with maddening tolerance. "I shall have to live with it—with your existence. I have known Blaise for many years. We're very close."

Jenna stared hard at her, trying to sort through her words. Did she understand them correctly? Yes, she was sure she did. Madeleine's French was clear, and she spoke distinctly. At this moment, she wanted nothing more than to burst into tears. Madeleine could live knowing about her—well, she certainly could not manage living in the same household with Madeleine. Perhaps this was a different time, perhaps people treated these matters very differently, but she knew herself, and she knew it was an adjustment she could not make.

"Later we'll get to know one another better," Madeleine said, standing up and smoothing out her skirt. Then she turned on Jenna and looked into her eyes. "Playing hard to get will do you no good in the long run. You are a hostage in our war, no more, no less. I am a countess. I have never lost before, I will not lose this time. You will remain what you are, but he will tire of you."

Jenna fought back tears of confusion and frustration. Somehow she wanted to shout, "You can have him," but she couldn't. Her lips would not form the words. What game was this woman playing? First, she seemed accepting, now she seemed competitive.

"Enjoy yourself," Madeleine said, as she turned and whirled away.

Jenna waited until she had been gone a few minutes,

then still fighting herself while asking herself a million questions, she returned to young Commander Guion. He waited patiently in the hall.

"Thank you for waiting," Jenna said, taking his gloved hand.

"My pleasure, mademoiselle. And my honor to instruct you in the dance."

Jenna let him escort her back into the ballroom. There, at the edge of the dance floor, Commandant Guion began his instruction. "You learn very quickly, mademoiselle. You have much natural grace and charm."

"Thank you," Jenna whispered.

In the center of the floor, Elizabeth danced with her young man. Their eyes were glued on one another, and it seemed obvious that their feelings for one another were entirely mutual.

And then, at the far end of the room, near the podium on which the orchestra played, she saw Blaise dancing with Madeleine. She seemed entirely expert in the art of this intricate dance, and Blaise's eyes were glued on her.

"Commandant! How fortunate you are! I see you've found the most beautiful woman in the room with whom to dance!"

Jenna looked up into the eyes of a tall slender man of about thirty. He wore a white powdered wig and a gold colored velvet suit. His shirt was ruffled with lace as were his sleeves, and his stockings were white. His velvet suit was trimmed in gold braid and had gold buttons. Beneath his suit jacket, he wore a matching waistcoat, and high around his neck, he wore a white silk cravat.

Commander Guion snapped to immediate attention and saluted. Then he turned to Jenna. "Mademoiselle

Stevens, may I present Monsieur Philip de Rigaud, the marquis de Vaudreuil and the governor of *Nouvelle France*.

Jenna curtsied. The name Vandreuil was familiar to her from long forgotten history lessons in school, though she could not recall why. Then she remembered, it was he who had ordered the attack on Deerfield.

"Mademoiselle!" He smiled and kissed her hand.

"Commandant Guion is young, brave and wealthy, but not as wealthy as I, and certainly not as influential, isn't that so, Commandant?"

Commandant Guion's face reddened. He nodded, but remained at attention. "It is most certainly so."

"Then I do not think you should monopolize such a lovely woman," he said, smiling at her.

Jenna let the marquis lead her away. In a moment, the orchestra began anew, and she found herself in the center of the room with the marquis.

His hand was warm and moist, and Jenna was well aware of his eyes on her. He looked her over closely, often settling on the neckline of her dress, his smile turning to a slight leer.

As the music came to an end, he pulled her close and whispered, "Mademoiselle, you are indeed enchanting."

He propelled her to the refreshment table and handed her more champagne. Jenna drank some, feeling the tingle of the bubbles on the tip of her nose.

"The marquis is an old reprobate. He can't have you all evening, mademoiselle."

The marquis slipped his arm around her waist and squeezed her ever so gently. "Mademoiselle, our host, François de Beauharnois, the intendant of Quebec."

Again, Jenna curtsied, and again, she felt lustful eyes on her.

He kissed her hand, bowed from the waist, and the

minute the music started, he took her glass from her and guided her out onto the dance floor. The intendant leered even more openly than the marquis.

When Jenna sensed the dance was ending, she bowed and smiled. "You must excuse me for a moment."

"Of course, mademoiselle. But you must hurry back. The room will not be the same without you."

Jenna hurried from the room, afraid someone else would stop her. But no one did. She pretended to be heading for the powder room, but instead she went down the long hall till she came to another room. Its large oak door was ajar, and she saw that it was a study. She hurried inside and closed the door behind her.

It was a small room, and a fire crackled in the fireplace. It was lined with leather bound volumes, and the chairs were comfortable and well worn. On a small table, there was a decanter of cognac and a glass. Jenna poured a bit into the glass and drank it quickly. The strong liquor mixed with the champagne, and for a long moment, she felt almost giddy.

Jenna looked around and realized the window was not a window but a door. She went to it and opened it, standing for a moment and simply inhaling the cool night air. Then she slipped through the door and out onto what appeared to be a balcony above a formal garden. On one side of the balcony, there were steps that led down.

Jenna lifted her skirts and followed the steps downward to the garden, then she walked along the path till she came to a low wall. Below the wall, the land dropped away steeply, and she could see the dark waters of the river. Lights flickered on the far bank.

"Are you trying to run away?"

Jenna turned suddenly to see Blaise outlined in the moonlight.

"Aren't you afraid Madeleine will miss you?"

"I imagine Madeleine can take care of herself."

Jenna didn't answer. She took a step toward him, hoping to edge past him and head back to the house, but he seized her round her waist and drew her close.

"You are irresistible," he said, kissing her neck.

"Let me go!" Jenna struggled against him even as the feel of his breath on her neck excited her.

"Jenna!" He drew her still closer, as if she were a rag doll in his arms, then he kissed her. It was a long kiss as he moved his tongue and forced her to respond. His hands seemed everywhere at once, and she felt a chill of anticipation as he worked his amorous magic on her senses. Again and again, he breathed heavily into her ear. Her resolve was melting with the memory of his lovemaking. He was so strong, so male, so determined.

"Ah lady, you've been drinking cognac. Does it have the same effect as wine?"

She did not answer.

"I should like cognac. I should like to sprinkle it on your beautiful naked body drop by drop and retrieve those drops with kisses."

His words were as seductive as his movements. He was still kissing her neck when she realized his fingers were undoing the bodice of her dress. He would have her here and now. She summoned all her willpower and broke free of his embrace. "No!" she said, "No!" and she pushed passed him, running up the path. Damn these dresses! she thought as she almost stumbled. Tears were beginning to flood her eyes, and she looked desperately for a place to hide. She reached the door of the study, and she fairly flew through the room, down the hall and much to her surprise almost into the arms of Commandant Guion.

"Ah, mademoiselle, I was looking for you. Are you all right?"

"Yes, I'm fine. I just stepped out for some air ... there seem to be some late flowering blossom that makes my eyes water."

He smiled and gently took her arm. "No gentleman ever asks why a lady has tears in her eyes," he said kindly. "Let us dance."

Jenna felt grateful and nodded her agreement. After a few moments, she felt quite herself again.

"There are many more men here than women," Jenna commented as soon as she felt like making conversation.

The young commandant nodded. "Yes, it is very difficult to coax women to come here. Even for those with money, life is far more difficult than in France. And sometimes if ships do not arrive on schedule there are terrible shortages."

"And of course there is still the fighting," Jenna added.

"Oh, yes, but that hardly affects anyone in Quebec. We are protected here by the great palisades. Quebec is a natural fortress."

Jenna said nothing. The people of this town would live in confidence for another half century before General James Wolfe would scale their palisades and claim a final victory for the British. "I'm sure life can be very difficult here," she said after a moment.

"From what I know, it is as difficult in the English Colonies, although I think life in England must be terrible compared to France."

"Why do you say that?" Jenna asked.

"Because almost no one wants to leave France to come here. But the British have no such problem. People are anxious to go to the British Colonies."

It *was* puzzling Jenna thought. Yet she knew it was true. She avoided giving any of the reasons she understood for the difference in immigration between the English Colonies and New France since he might not understand her comments at all. Jenna was fast learning that the history she had been taught was far different for those who lived it. She reminded herself that World War I was only called World War I after World War II began. And now that she thought of it, she wasn't sure what they called this war. She knew it as the War of the Spanish Succession. But was that what people called it now?

"Perhaps it is the harshness of the climate," she suggested after a moment. "Perhaps the French do not want to move to a place where it is so cold in the winter."

She returned to their previous topic of conversation. "So, what do young single men do for wives?"

He laughed. "Sometimes we are fortunate, and women are brought from the New England Colonies as prisoners. Of course, they grow to like it here and almost never leave. And sometimes a bride ship comes from France."

"A bride ship?" Jenna said, raising her brow.

"Ah, yes, mademoiselle. Women are recruited in France and brought here to marry. It is very successful, but there are still not enough women."

Jenna tried to imagine strangers pairing up and simply marrying. "And do such marriages work?" she asked.

"Oh, yes of course. There is no such thing as a marriage that does not work in Quebec."

Jenna said not a word. The enormity of the differences between this time and her own were now only really beginning to dawn on her. Women married strangers, kept house and bore children. Men had mistresses for love. But in some way, everyone seemed to be happy.

She glanced again at Elizabeth. She still looked radiant as she danced with Edouard. Perhaps Elizabeth would find love. Perhaps hers would not be an arranged marriage.

"You seem most distracted, mademoiselle."

Jenna looked up into his eyes. "Yes. I'm not feeling well," she lied. "I should truly like to be taken home."

As she said the word "home," she felt a wave of terrible homesickness pass over her. It seemed as if a million conflicting thoughts flooded her mind. A large part of her yearned for the familiar . . . a warm cozy room, a book written in twentieth century English, the television news. Since the moment she found herself transported back in time, she had felt as if she were in a play, and never more than tonight had she had that feeling. But another part of her knew she loved Blaise so deeply that she could never erase him from her thoughts no matter where she was. If swept back to her own time tonight, she would never forget him. And suddenly, in spite of his betrayal, in spite of everything, she felt she really didn't want to leave, because as long as she was here, there was some sort of hope for them.

"Come," he said taking her arm. "I'll summon a carriage and escort you."

Jenna looked up at the young commandant as his words jarred her out of her speculation. "Thank you," she said softly.

Chapter Sixteen

Elizabeth crept into Jenna's room and for a moment looked at her sleeping form curled beneath the quilts. Her copper colored hair was spread out on the white pillow, and she lay in the bed like a small child. "Poor Jenna," she whispered. "You're so beautiful, kind and intelligent. It's not right for you to be so unhappy."

Elizabeth thought back to the night they had met. Jenna had seemed odd then, and although there were many things about her that were different, Elizabeth did not think of her as strange any longer.

"You are like the big sister I never had," she whispered. "Throughout our ordeal, you were there to help me. And you taught me so much."

So many things—Elizabeth's mind raced over the past months. Surely, all the Indians, perhaps all of us, would have died like Oioteet and Father Henri had it not been for you. Perhaps James and I would not be safe, here in Quebec, if you had not taken us under your wing. "Oh, Jenna. I wish you were not so unhappy."

Almost as if she had heard, Jenna's eyes flickered open, and seeing Elizabeth she smiled. "It must be late," she said, stretching.

"Quite late," Elizabeth said, walking to the high windows. She drew back the drapes, letting in the light of the midmorning sun.

Jenna rolled over and propped herself up in the feather bed. It was a huge high four-poster bed with a canopy and a curtain that could be drawn round it. Jenna had always thought of such beds as overly decorative, now she realized that the curtain actually kept out the pervasive night drafts and had little to do with decoration. She puffed up the great feather pillows beneath her head.

"You were quite the belle of the ball," Elizabeth told her.

"I hardly spoke with anyone, and I came home early."

"Yes, but all of the men thought you wonderfully mysterious. I think their ladies were quite jealous. Your appearance and disappearance was all anyone spoke of all evening."

Jenna tried to smile. Creating an aura of mystery had been far from her mind when she had left. "No matter what you say, I'm sure the title 'belle of the ball' belongs to you."

Elizabeth flounced down on the side of the bed, "Oh, Jenna I am quite in love. Edouard wants to court me. I know not what to do."

"Court you?" She was hardly surprised, but somehow she had thought he was already courting Elizabeth.

"Edouard says that Blaise l'Écossais is my guardian—or I am his ward, or something like that. He says we must seek Blaise's permission for him to court me. In truth, it is my father whose permission should be sought."

Jenna took Elizabeth's small white hand in hers.

"You're very young," she said seriously. "And very far from home."

"Most girls my age are married, Jenna. It is quite proper that I be married too. But you know that is not the problem."

Jenna bit her lip. Surely, this was what was supposed to happen. Elizabeth was to choose not to return, but rather to marry and remain here. According to the story she disappeared, and perhaps this was why. Still, it seemed somehow important to make things clear to Elizabeth. It was evident that she was confused.

"Elizabeth, you know that France and England are at war in Europe and here, in America. The war means you might never be able to go home again."

"I know, but I don't think the war will last forever."

Jenna tried to think of how to put it without giving too much away. She knew full well that this war—the War of the Spanish Succession—would last another five years. Worse yet, it would be followed with more war. France and England, in Europe and here, in America, would fight till the mid 1760s. Then, serious difficulties would begin in the American Colonies, difficulties which would turn to mass discontent, and finally to revolution. Elizabeth, now seventeen, would spend most of her life knowing war. Marrying a Frenchman would mean a lifelong separation from her family—but wasn't that exactly what happened? Jenna wanted to help Elizabeth feel comfortable with her decision, but she also knew she must not change history.

"Elizabeth, I'm sure you're right, this war won't last forever, but France and England have been enemies for hundreds of years. I fear there will be continued conflicts even if this war ends in a peace treaty. I only want you to really understand that you might never be able to go home."

Elizabeth's lovely blue eyes flooded with tears.
"Edouard and I love one another, Jenna. It matters not
to me that he is French. It matters not to him that I am
English. But still I feel a traitor—my father fights the
French just as Blaise fights the English—just as the Mohawk fight the Abnaki. I used to think the Abnaki terrible and fierce, but I've learned so much—Jenna, I know
you are angry at Blaise, but he is like my father in many
ways. He has been good to James and me—I see no
sense in this war." Elizabeth covered her face with her
hands. "Am I a traitor because I love Edouard?"

Jenna embraced her and held her tightly. "Oh, no.
No, Elizabeth. You must follow your heart."

"I will miss my parents, but had I stayed in Deerfield
and married, I most likely would have married a settler
heading west, over the mountains and into the fertile
valley beyond. Traveling is difficult on the frontier so I
might not have seen my family again in any case."

"That's true," Jenna said softly.

Elizabeth leaned on her shoulder, and Jenna patted
her hair. The decisions Elizabeth was making were difficult indeed.

"I must talk to James," she said. "It is important for
him to understand."

"What did you tell Edouard?"

"I told him I should be pleased to have him court me.
He's going to speak to Blaise this afternoon."

"Is Blaise here now?" Jenna asked, feeling a certain
panic at the thought of seeing him. She would plea to
him for Elizabeth's sake—she would do anything for
Elizabeth and James. But she did not want to see him
otherwise.

"Yes. I saw him earlier this morning. He says he has
decided we will stay here through the winter and that
Anne Marie will bring James and join us in a few days."

Jenna wondered what this news meant. Doubtless Blaise wanted to be in Quebec City near Madeleine. Yes, that was it. He was, after all, planning to marry her.

"What about our clothes?" Jenna asked.

"Anne Marie will bring them. Blaise says we will be safer here from Indian raids, and here in the town there will be more to do during the long winter months."

Blaise was dressed casually in his smoking jacket, a plain shirt, and breeches. He chose to meet Edouard in the library, his own favorite room in the town house. He liked the smell of the books and the cramped and cluttered cosiness of the room itself.

Blaise's thoughts were for poor Edouard. He looked altogether flustered and somewhat tired from the night before. Certainly, he had danced every dance, and certainly, he had enjoyed himself as never before.

Edouard was attired in his dress uniform. He wore his best lace trimmed dress shirt, and he was pressed and turned out in high military fashion. Indeed, his collar was so stiff Blaise wondered if he could turn his head. Yes, Edouard looked both happy and uncomfortable, both excited and apprehensive. In short, to Blaise's way of thinking, he looked exactly as a young man about to ask permission to court a young lady should look.

Edouard studied Blaise l'Écossais uneasily. Blaise was rich, powerful, and somewhat mysterious. He saw him often, but he did not feel he knew him well. L'Écossais was not French, although he spoke French as well as any Frenchman, and was clearly well educated. He was an enigma, a man of few words who seemed to guard his past. Still, he had a fine reputation for fairness.

"Cognac?" Blaise offered. He gestured Edouard to a chair and turned, himself, to the crystal decanter and glasses that sat, at the ready, in the middle of a silver tray.

"Yes, sir. Yes. Thank you."

Blaise smiled. "You need not call me 'sir.' I'm not your commanding officer. I should be pleased to have you call me by my first name, Blaise."

Edouard nodded. This was the first time he had ever been alone with Blaise l'Écossais. Yet for all the man's seeming friendliness, he could sense a reserve. He suspected that being on a first name basis with this man, who was to be sure, a kind of legend in *Nouvelle France*, would not necessarily mean there would be a close relationship between them. Yet rumor had it that this wealthy powerful man had a special relationship with the Indians and that he had been initiated into one of the tribes. Every man knew that such an initiation was extremely difficult. Every Frenchman knew that it was one matter to have Indian allies, but quite another to be accepted as a brother. Edouard wondered a great deal about this man Blaise l'Écossais, but still he admired him.

"Here, this is a very fine cognac—quite old."

"Thank you."

"Please, sit down, try to be comfortable."

Edouard half smiled. "You seem to know why I am here."

"I don't know why, but I can easily guess why—please, don't be so ill at ease."

"I shall try to be more comfortable." Edouard took a long sip of cognac. The heat from it filled his chest. He waited a moment, then cleared his throat. "I have come to speak to you about Elizabeth Corse. I have come to ask your permission to court her."

"Have you spoken to your parents about her?"

"They have but one stipulation. They would have her convert."

"And how does the young lady feel about this?"

"She is willing . . ."

"You hesitate—is there difficulty?"

"I love her. I think she loves me. But I know she feels disloyal to her people, to her family."

"As a captive, I'm not surprised. She cannot be ransomed back, however. Her father is a well known scout so the Indians would not tolerate it."

"She is willing to remain here, to be my wife. I'm sure in time—perhaps when this hellish war ends, she will be at complete peace with herself."

Blaise nodded. "Then I can have no objection."

"What about the other one—Elizabeth says she is like a sister."

"I do not believe them to be related by blood, but they have some relation to one another. I shall speak with her." Blaise lifted his own goblet of cognac. "To your courtship!" he said, toasting Edouard.

"Again, I thank you."

Blaise smiled. "I would not have agreed had the young lady not desired it."

"I would not be pursuing her without encouragement," Edouard replied.

"Women," Blaise observed in a contemplative tone, "are strange." And he thought to himself that Jenna was the strangest of all. Yet even this fleeting thought of her made him want to see her, to hold her, and to bend her to his will.

"I hope I shall not be expected to court Elizabeth for too long a time," Edouard said.

Edouard's words snapped Blaise out of his mental flight. He thought all too often of the beautiful, stubborn, Jenna.

"Is there reason for a short courtship?"

Edouard nodded. "I may soon be posted elsewhere."

"Somewhere where you can take a young wife?"

"Most likely Fort Louisbourg," Edouard replied.

Blaise waved his hand casually. "Begin your courtship, and let nature take its course. I know you have been seeing Elizabeth for some time, so I imagine the preliminaries are over."

Edouard's face flushed crimson, "Sir, uh, Blaise, there is one other matter. I hesitate to raise it because I fear it betrays my lack of knowledge and experience in these matters, but rather than look the fool in front of Elizabeth, I want to ask you about an odd New England custom. At least Elizabeth says it is a New England custom."

"What custom might that be?"

"It's called bundling. Elizabeth says we must bundle."

Blaise laughed and slapped his thigh. "This is not—and thank heaven for your good fortune—a puritan lass you're courting."

"She isn't?"

"To bundle is to spend the night together in the same bed."

Edouard's face grew even redder. "And . . ."

"It's hard not to—but that's the idea. Mind you, I'm told good New Englanders use a divided bed."

"To be together so . . . and not to . . . it sounds like torture," Edouard said, still looking flustered.

"The English torture themselves all the time." Blaise laughed. "But this is a fine custom. If the lady wants to bundle, then I suggest you bundle."

"I shall have to steel myself."

Blaise laughed again and downed his brandy. "I should think so," he said, grinning.

Edouard shifted restlessly from one foot to the other.

"I'm glad I've amused you. But there is one other matter, a matter which is not amusing at all."

"And what might that be?" Blaise asked.

"At her behest, I made inquiries about Elizabeth's mother. She was in the other group of captives, the ones taken by the Sieur Hertel de Rouville."

"And what exactly did you discover?"

"The worst. She apparently died of a heart attack. One of the soldiers serving under the Sieur de Rouville remembers her quite well, and he remembers her dying."

Blaise looked serious. In truth, he liked Elizabeth and had felt good about the fact that she had fallen in love and would willingly remain in Quebec. "Are you going to tell her?" he asked, after a moment.

Edouard nodded. "I must."

"I'm sure you will be gentle."

"As gentle as possible," Edouard promised.

"He's gone," Elizabeth said, breathlessly as she peeked through the front window, careful to stay behind the curtain.

Jenna was sunk deep into a comfortable easy chair next to the window that looked out on the side garden. She had laboriously dragged the chair from across the room, in order to place it by the window where she could more easily read. When Elizabeth spoke, she set her book down in her lap.

"You mean Edouard?"

"Yes, he is finished talking with Blaise. Oh, I wish I knew what happened."

"I'm sure everything is fine."

Elizabeth sighed deeply. "Oh, I hope so." Then she

came closer to Jenna and sat down on the footstool. "I do envy you your ability to read French."

"I read it better than I speak it."

"What are you reading?" Elizabeth pressed.

"Rabelais," Jenna confessed. It was tough sloughing, not just because it was in French, but because the printing in the book was in Gothic script. Still, her vocabulary was increasing, and to her delight she found Rabelais was quite funny.

"The name of the book is Rabelais?"

Jenna smiled, "No, that is the name of the author. The book is called *Gargantua.*

"Perhaps you can tell me the story sometime—" Elizabeth did not finish her sentence because there was a knock on the door.

The upstairs maid opened the door and looked in, "Mademoiselle Jenna, Monsieur l'Écossais wishes you to come to the library."

Had she not known that Edouard had just left and that Blaise no doubt wanted to see her about Elizabeth, she would have refused to follow the maid. But Elizabeth was anxious to know what had happened.

"I'll come back as quickly as I can," Jenna said as she laid the book on the chair and followed the maid.

At the closed library door, Jenna waved the maid away and knocked. *"Entre!"* Blaise called back.

"You asked me to come," she said standing in the entrance.

Blaise had a large goblet in his hand; it had a goodly amount of cognac in it. His eyes studied her, those eyes which always seemed to hold her, to make her want him even against her own will.

"Come in, dear Jenna. Please, close the door."

Jenna did not want to close the door, but she did. She sat down on the edge of a chair and waited.

"How lovely you looked last night," he said slowly, deliberately.

Jenna avoided looking at him. "Did you summon me here to pay me compliments?"

"No!" he said in an irritated tone.

"Did you summon me to discuss Elizabeth?"

"Yes. Edouard wishes to court her. I have no objection. Do you?"

"Would it matter if I did?" Jenna looked up at him now, her eyes large and questioning.

"I do not know your relationship to Elizabeth and James. Save the fact that you have confessed that you are not their sister. But I see that you are close, so in the absence of her parents—"

"An absence you are responsible for," Jenna said accusingly.

"Do not interrupt me!" Blaise shouted at her and his dark eyes narrowed. Jenna was surprised to see real anger in his expression. "What do you know of responsibility, or who is responsible for what? It is not for you to judge me!" Blaise took another drink.

Jenna realized she had unwittingly touched some raw nerve, that she had peeled away a layer of his onionlike personality. But why he was so angry was beyond her. Wasn't he responsible for the fact that Elizabeth and James were separated from their parents? She glanced at the cognac and wondered how much he had drunk. Still, she held her silence till he finished.

"Do you object to Edouard and Elizabeth being married?"

"No. Not if it's what Elizabeth wants."

"Then so be it." He took yet another drink from the goblet, then he walked over to her and pulled her up out of the chair. He held her wrist tightly and looked into her face.

"You are the most stubborn woman I have ever known. Remember," he said learning close, "you deprive yourself."

"How conceited you are!" Jenna retorted, her own anger close to the surface.

He pulled her closer and kissed her hard.

Jenna quivered and fought to preserve her anger as it was the only emotion that protected her—kept her from wanting him. But it was no use. He kissed her neck, and moved his hands suggestively over her hips.

"Delicious little tart," he said, breathing heavily onto her neck. "You can't deny me. I'll come for you when I wish."

Jenna suddenly shook herself loose. "I cannot stop you from taking, but there is a part of me you will never possess."

"Rest easy for a time. I'm going away for awhile."

"Go or stay, it's all the same to me," Jenna replied. With that, she opened the door and fled back up the stairs. Damn him! Damn him! she murmured under her breath.

Blaise walked out the front door. How could anyone be so unreasonable? Even Madeleine had tried to talk with her and gotten nowhere. Everything he did seemed to make her more angry. Once, he could have called her a delicious little tart, and she would have teased him back. Once—after they had become lovers—he could have teased her about owning her, and she would have ignored it or simply laughed at him. But not now. It was worse than when they had first met. She was as hostile as any enemy he had ever encountered, and certainly, as unforgiving.

Was he wrong about her? Perhaps she didn't really

care for him. Yet he could feel her response everytime
he kissed her—even though she protested. He shook his
head in dismay. He wanted her even though he knew he
had to continue his quest. He wanted her even though
she protested that she did not want him. Again, he admitted his confusion.

Perhaps when Elizabeth married, perhaps when she
realized how happy a person could be here—perhaps
then she would accept him and forgive him for not telling her about Madeleine.

He mounted his horse and headed off, off down the
road toward the Indian village on the banks of the Saint
Lawrence, some twenty miles down stream. There was
news of new prisoners, Mohawks from Massachusetts.
Perhaps they would know something. Oh, how he
prayed they would. It seemed as if he had talked to a
thousand Mohawks about Spring Blossom, but none of
them knew of her—at least none of them admitted
knowing of her.

He pressed his lips together. Once, not so long ago,
he had wanted to tell Jenna all about Spring Blossom.
But now he kept his secret to himself. Now, he wondered if he would ever be able to tell her about the reason for his long absences, vaguely and with great
unhappiness, he wondered if she would really care.

The carriage moved along the road atop the ramparts.
On one side, a plateau of farmland stretched out as far
as the eye could see; on the other, a steep cliff dropped
to the river far below. What trees there were along this
road were now denuded of all leaves, and their brittle
bare branches shuddered in the cold wind.

Elizabeth, bundled beneath a warm blanket, cuddled

next to Edouard as the horse moved slowly onward. "It's beautiful up here, but lonely and barren."

"It is our protection. It's what makes Quebec such a great natural fortress."

"At the moment, it only looks peaceful."

Edouard drew the horse to a halt in a place that offered a particularly scenic view of the river below and the flatland on its other side.

"I must speak with you, Elizabeth."

"About marrying me?"

Edouard shook his head. "No, my darling, I must speak to you about a subject that greatly saddens me."

Elizabeth looked up at him, her beautiful eyes questioning.

"I have learned that your mother died of a heart attack while still a prisoner."

Elizabeth's eyes filled with sudden tears, and Edouard felt that he, too, might cry because she looked so stricken. He gathered her into his arms and held her tightly. "I should not blame you if you hated me and all Frenchmen."

"Oh, no," she whispered. "No, Edouard. I do not hate you, I couldn't. Please, tell me, is your source reliable? Are you certain it was my mother?"

"I'm afraid my source is quite reliable. I would die to give you hope, but I can't offer hope."

"I shall have to tell James."

"Would you like me to tell him for you?"

"No. It's something I must do myself."

Edouard held her closer. Then, after a long silence, "Are you close to your father, Elizabeth? Do you still want to marry me now—now that he will be alone?"

"Yes, I still want to marry you. As for my father—it's a difficult question for me to answer. My father, as you know, is a scout. He was often gone from home for long periods of time. I love him as all daughters must love their fathers, but I was never as close to my father as I was to my mother."

"I'm sorry that it is I who have brought you this sadness."

Elizabeth looked up and touched his cheek. She kissed him lightly. "I asked you. You only did my bidding."

"You are a beautiful, good woman, Elizabeth. You do not deserve such unhappiness."

"Truth be known, Edouard, I felt in my heart that she was dead. One knows such things—her heart was always weak, and she could not have stood the strain of such a long journey."

"I'll take you home now. I think you will want to talk to Jenna."

Elizabeth nodded. "Yes, she is like my own sister. She appeared almost as my mother disappeared. As if the fates had given me a substitute—not a mother, but an older sister."

"And yet you seem very different."

"We are different but that doesn't mean there isn't great affection between us." Elizabeth smiled. "Jenna is different, she is different from anyone I've ever known. She seems to know things before they happen—it's as if she can see into the future."

"And what does she see in our future?"

"She says she is certain that we'll be happy but that we live in turbulent times."

"One does not have to see into the future to know the times are turbulent. There is a war."

"Once she told me it would be almost a hundred years before this new world of ours knows peace. And then I asked her how she knew and she looked surprised and said, 'oh, I just meant it seems that way.' But she really said it as if she knew."

"No one can really see into the future," Edouard said.

Elizabeth nodded. "I suppose not. But sometimes Jenna does seem to be—well, very perceptive."

"As long as she sees happiness for us, most especially for you." She was such a gentle creature. He yearned only to protect her from further hurt. He enfolded her in his arms and kissed her gently at first, then with some passion.

Elizabeth put her arms around him and returned his kisses. But when she sensed they were both becoming too passionate she gently pulled away from him, even though she didn't really want him to stop. "We should go before . . ."

Edouard felt his face flushed with the heat of his own desire, but he acquiesced to her wish and sat up straight, taking the reins in his hands. Then he turned to her. "Soon, my darling, the home I take you to will be ours."

Chapter Seventeen

It had been two weeks since the ball, and over a week since Blaise had left the house. When Jenna thought of him, which was all too often, she imagined him with Madeleine. No doubt he was with her now. She felt certain he had not left Quebec City.

Jenna stood by the window of her bedroom and looked down on the garden. This morning the ground beneath her window was white with the first snow.

Jenna turned from the window and settled down for another afternoon alone with her book. But no sooner had she found her place and begun reading, when there was a great commotion in the drive. Four coaches pulled up in front, one after the other.

Even before James and Anne Marie had time to climb down, a bevy of servants had begun to unload trunks and boxes.

Jenna quickly grabbed her shawl and ran out the front door. "James!"

James ran to her and gave her a hug. "I know you haven't been gone long, but I missed you. Where's Elizabeth?"

"She's out with Edouard. Did you have a good journey?"

"Yes. We're to stay here all winter! I won't be able to ride anymore."

"You'll be in school."

"I'd rather be riding."

Jenna smiled. James was much the same as any little boy in her own time, save the fact that he seemed more mature and had been more strictly disciplined. "I'm sure we can arrange for you to ride here as well. And you can go sledging. Oh, I think you'll like it here."

"Anne Marie says that the ice gets very thick here and that Blaise has something called skates. He bought them from a ship's captain who was from the low-countries. She says you can put them on and glide across the ice."

Skates? Had they not become popular yet? Jenna was truly surprised, and it served as another reminder of how careful she knew she had to be. "That sounds like wonderful fun," she said after a moment.

"Here, young man. You can help carry things." Anne Marie thrust some of the smaller boxes into James's arms and then turned to Jenna. "I think I brought everything."

"I'm sure you did. You've certainly brought more than our clothes."

"Yes, I was instructed to bring certain other items from the house. Monsieur l'Écossais says the war is heating up. Attacks on farms have increased. That's why we're to stay here for the winter. Quebec is always safe."

"Blaise isn't here now. Do you know where he is?" Jenna asked.

"I never know where he is. But he may be fighting or trying to track the movements of the Iroquois. When there is fighting, he is often gone. He is one of the few who speaks the Iroquois language, and he questions prisoners."

Jenna wanted to ask Anne Marie more, but she had already bustled away to direct the unloading of the carriages. She knew that Blaise spoke Abnaki, but she had not known that he also spoke Iroquois. That explained why he was always going off to speak to prisoners—it explained his interest in the Mohawk prisoners. Did he work for the army, then? Was he some sort of eighteenth century intelligence officer? Everything she learned of him raised more questions.

"Oh," was her only reply to Anne Marie's revelation. It had not occurred to her that Blaise might be in danger, or even that the war had grown more serious. He was a damnable man. How could she even be concerned for him? Yet she knew she was.

Jenna watched as the servants struggled with several obviously heavy trunks.

Anne Marie pointed to this trunk or that case, and gave instructions in rapid French. Then she turned to Jenna and by way of further explanation added, "Monsieur l'Écossais had some valuables he did not wish to leave. Mementos, I suppose."

"You didn't know we were coming here for the winter, did you?"

"Oh, no Mademoiselle. I thought you would all return in a few days. I don't know when monsieur made up his mind to spend the winter in Quebec. He is sometimes quite impulsive."

Jenna said nothing. Perhaps he was with the Indians, perhaps he was with Madeleine. Madeleine's words to her kept coming back. It did seem likely that Madeleine had prevailed upon him not to leave the city.

"You must go inside," Anne Marie said, shaking her head. "Look at you. It's December, and you are out here, standing in the snow with only a shawl."

Jenna drew the shawl closer. Anne Marie was right. It

was quite brisk, and a wind out of the north was beginning to blow.

"I'll go see to James," Jenna said as she hurried inside.

But James had taken in his load of boxes and left them in the hall. He had then gone directly outside. Obviously, being in a carriage for so many hours had been hard on him, and he needed exercise. No young man wanted to sit still for so long. She found him in the garden behind the townhouse. He had already begun to explore his new surroundings.

"What do you think of Quebec?"

James shrugged. "I'd rather be back with the Indians."

"I guess you must have inherited that desire from your father." She sat down on a rustic bench.

"I'm going to be a scout too. I learned a lot when we were with the Indians."

"I know you did, and you'll be a fine scout when you're a little older."

James grinned. "I'm getting older every day. I'll be eleven next week."

"Eleven! What day next week?"

"On November twentieth."

"We must have a birthday party."

James laughed. "I've never heard of one of those."

"Then we must certainly have one," Jenna said.

"You better go in, you haven't got your coat," James pointed out.

"Yes, I'm going now. Come in before it gets dark." Jenna shivered as she walked rapidly toward the house. The cold weather brought back bittersweet memories of their trek from Deerfield to Canada. Ten months! So much had happened since February twenty-ninth. In her time, Deerfield was a one day drive from where she

now stood—albeit a long day. But, in this time, it took
months of walking, canoeing, and riding to travel the
same distance.

And, suddenly, it hit her like lightning! James had to
be home before he was twelve! Given the time it would
take to get there, he would have to begin his journey in
the next few months. How could she have been so stupid? she asked herself. She was living in 1704, but in her
mind she was thinking of James traveling in 1988! She
had made an adjustment on one level, but subcon-
sciously, she was still in her own time.

Jenna headed up the stairs to her room. Thoughts of
James filled her mind. She felt a new urgency. "I must
find a way to return him," she murmured.

She opened the door of her room to see that the
trunks and boxes had preceded her. She looked around
and thought she would hang up her clothes since the
longer they remained folded in the trunk, the more
wrinkled they would become.

Jenna examined what had been brought to her room.
Most were trunks, and held her clothes—in fact, most
were the containers in which her clothes had originally
been delivered. But there was another trunk. An old
trunk with a heavy padlock. It was a trunk she had
never before seen, and it seemed apparent that it had
been brought to her room in error.

Jenna went to it and jiggled the padlock. It was a
rusty old thing. "Not opened for a long while," Jenna
said under her breath.

Jenna sat down on the end of the bed and continued
to stare at the mysterious old trunk. Why would Blaise
want it brought here?

The longer she looked at it, the more curious she
grew.

Jenna busied herself, hanging up her clothes, but now

and again she would glance at the trunk, wondering what was in it.

After a time, she went down to the kitchen. Finding it empty, she looked around in the utensil drawer. Nothing in the drawer looked as if it would open the trunk. She was about to give up when she saw a huge ring of keys hanging on a hook by the pantry door. Jenna lifted the ring and hurried up the backstairs with it. Perhaps one of the keys on the ring would open the trunk.

Jenna had tried twelve keys when one slipped into the old lock. When she turned it, it clicked open. Quickly, Jenna hurried back downstairs and replaced the ring of keys. Then she returned to the mystery of the trunk.

Slowly, Jenna forced open the heavy lid of the musty old trunk.

On the inside top of the lid, written in ink it read "Precious Things." The words were scrawled in large letters, as if a child had written them.

Jenna studied them for a moment. There was something touching about the writing—about the words.

The trunk smelled musty as she removed the first layer of thin paper that covered whatever was inside. She stared at the contents. There were neatly folded items of clothing and some linens in the first layer and three small miniature paintings.

Jenna lifted the miniatures. One was of an Indian woman, one of an older man, and the third of a beautiful young Indian girl. Jenna studied the pictures. How unusual to find a painting of an Indian woman and girl—and who was the man? Jenna stared at the image of the man. Paintings were in no way as accurate as photographs, but it seemed to her as if the man looked a bit like Blaise, or the way Blaise might look if he was older. And then she realized it was the same man as the one in the small painting in the hall. But he was older in this painting.

Jenna continued to examine the contents of the trunk. There was a belt—a *wampum* belt. And there were some feathers. They were reverently wrapped and packed together with crystal and some fine items of clothing. And then she lifted a beaded tunic and uncovered the *mocook* box. It was the same box Blaise had given her to carry! She turned it over and over in her fingers—when had he taken it back? Not that it would have been difficult. It must have been in the pack with her Indian garments after they changed clothes at the militia outpost. Carefully, she returned it to the trunk.

Was the girl in the picture the girl for whom Blaise was searching? Did the *mocook* box belong to her? As Jenna began to repack the trunk, she was more puzzled than ever about Blaise l'Écossais.

The items in the box appeared to Jenna to be from two entirely different worlds. Whose were they? Why had Blaise saved them? Jenna took one last glance at the three miniatures and then closed the trunk. She put the old padlock back on and closed it. Somehow, she felt guilty. It was as if she had entered some private world.

"It's only Thursday," Anne Marie complained. "To have a feast on a weekday is unheard of."

It was true that Saturday dinner was usually the biggest dinner of the week and that the leftover food was eaten on Sunday so the cooks would not have to work on a holy day.

"It's James's birthday. I want to make a birthday cake and celebrate."

"I have never heard of such a celebration—and what is a birthday cake?"

"A *gâteau*—a special *gâteau* with decorations . . ." Jenna realized the more she tried to explain, the harder it got.

"Ah, I see," Anne Marie said, although it was evident to Jenna that she did not see at all.

"Can you make such a *gâteau*—yourself?"

"Yes, I want to make it."

"I shall tell the cook, and since you think it important, I will also tell the cook to prepare a special dinner."

"Thank you," Jenna said, giving Anne Marie a little hug. Perhaps a birthday celebration was unknown, perhaps it wouldn't even be that important to James, but it seemed important to her. She had to concentrate all her efforts now on getting him home, and success would mean he would never see her, or his sister again. "I want him to remember today," she said under her breath.

The cook seemed flustered and annoyed to have her in the kitchen. And Jenna herself admitted that making a cake and decorating it with the materials at hand would be a tour de force for her. There was no such thing as a recipe book, no frosting sugar, and no food coloring. There was also no cake decorator!

Jenna carefully took an inventory of the needed ingredients. Flour, milk, eggs, a block of sugar, and shortening were all produced by the cook immediately. She had to sniff several white powders before she found what she knew was baking powder.

Next, she examined the various pans available. She had to settle for two square pans.

"Deux gâteau!" the cook exclaimed. *"Mon Dieu!"*

Jenna began mixing the ingredients while the cook fretted, "Such an extravagance! Two cakes! And on a weekday!" she muttered, over and over.

Jenna flavored the cake with cranberries that she

crushed and added to the mixture. Then she put the pans in the great side ovens of the fireplace.

Carefully she prepared a syrup of sugar and cranberries. She blended the mixture into stiffly beaten egg whites. When the cakes were done and cooled, she frosted the cakes with the pink mixture and set them to cool outside in the cool box, a crude container which stayed outside, but protected the food from insects and animals.

"Never have I seen pink *gâteau!*" the cook exclaimed. She shook her head, but conceded that the two layer cake looked appetizing as well as highly unusual.

Jenna busied herself for the rest of the afternoon making decorations from ribbons. She tied them onto the bases of candles, and she hung them on the walls of the dining room.

At six, she summoned them all to dinner. Anne Marie, Elizabeth, Edouard, and James.

After the meal, which did indeed rival Saturday supper, she brought out her cake.

"Never have I seen anything like it!" Anne Marie exclaimed. She leaned over and examined it. "It seems a pity to eat anything this pretty."

Jenna cut it carefully and gave James the first piece. "It's the custom to serve the one whose birthday it is first."

James took a small piece onto his fork and ate it. He beamed. "It's good! I like it!"

Jenna cut some for Elizabeth, Edouard, and Anne Marie.

When they had finished, Edouard revealed a long slim package. "Mademoiselle Stevens tells me it is the custom to give a gift on a birthday, so I have brought a gift for you from all of us."

Jenna touched Edouard's hand, "That's very good of

you," she told him sincerely. She looked into Edouard's eyes and saw both concern and kindness. Elizabeth, she thought, had chosen well.

Elizabeth, too, produced a small package while Anne Marie presented him with shoe buckles.

James unwrapped Elizabeth's gift first. It was a sampler with their names embroidered on it. Then he unwrapped Edouard's gift and gave out a loud cry of surprise. It was a hunting knife encased in its own leather sheath.

"For your career as a scout," Edouard said.

"It's wonderful!" James said, fastening it to his belt immediately. "I like birthdays!" he announced. "A cake from Jenna, a sampler from Elizabeth, shoe buckles, and a hunting knife!"

"Happy birthday," Jenna said softly. She fought to hold back her tears because she knew he would be leaving soon.

The first week of December brought a fresh snowfall. But by the fourth, the skies had cleared, and the weather was cold and crisp.

It was well after midnight when Elizabeth silently let Edouard in the back door and motioning him to be quiet, led him to her bedroom on the second floor.

Once inside, she lit a candle and set it by the side of the bed.

Edouard was dressed in his uniform, and he both looked and felt uncomfortable.

"Are you certain this is proper?" he asked.

Elizabeth laughed sweetly, "Yes, most certainly. It's the custom. I cannot marry you unless we bundle first."

"I still don't understand this custom." Edouard sat down uncomfortably on the edge of a boudoir chair.

Elizabeth sat down at her dresser and brushed out her lavish blond hair. Edouard watched entranced as it cascaded over her shoulders. What was it about a woman's hair? The loosening of it was an act of pure seduction. To loosen the hair and free it from its prison of combs and pins was symbolic of loosening the bodice and of freeing the woman's body to behold it. Had he not read that Muslims were bound by their religion to cover their hair lest men be tempted to acts of lust at the sight of it?

Oh, it was true! He was drawn by her hair. He wanted to lose himself in it.

"Are you all right?" Elizabeth turned to look at him.

"Yes—I think so." He glanced at the bed. It both drew and repelled him. Elizabeth was sweet innocence. What strange English custom was this?

"I will be right back," Elizabeth said as she disappeared into her dressing room.

Would she return in some filmy irresistible gown? Was he expected to lie with her in the bed, sunk deep into the feather mattress, all night and not take her? Was Blaise right? Were the English such flagrant self-abusers as to expect . . . to court temptation in such a way and not satisfy themselves. Small wonder they were such a formidable enemy. Inside, he felt it was quite impossible for any Frenchman to withstand such temptation.

In a moment, Elizabeth returned. Edouard looked at her in absolute amazement. She was covered from neck to toe in a strange robe which was held together at the bottom by a draw string. No bit of flesh, save her lovely face, was visible. He could not even make out the magnificent curves of her body because she was so well concealed.

Elizabeth smiled shyly. "Do you like it? I've spent over a week making it."

"What is it?" he asked, still taken aback.

"A bundling robe of course. And I've made one for you too. It's important to be comfortable."

Edouard would have laughed, but she was serious and sincere, and she held out his garment, smiling.

In something of a trance, he went into the dressing room and disrobed, replacing his uniform with the bundling robe. It was indeed loose and comfortable, but it was quite the opposite of alluring or erotic.

When he returned, it was to darkness. "Elizabeth?" he whispered.

"I'm in bed," she replied. "Come."

Edouard struggled to the bed and virtually fell in beside her. She pulled the covers over them and snuggled close to him.

But it was not as much a temptation as he had imagined it would be. The robes were thick, and he could not truly feel her slim body pressing against him. Still, it was, he thought, most pleasurable. Her sweet smelling hair was spread out under his cheek, and she kissed him gently on the neck.

"So," he said after a few minutes, "this is bundling."

Elizabeth giggled. "It is. But you must speak to me of intimate things, and then we must fall asleep in one another's arms."

Edouard kissed her cheek. He would endure anything for her—even a night of temptation. "Of what intimate matter should I speak?"

"Our wedding night. How many children we should have—your dreams."

In the darkness, he sought her soft lips. "You are all my dreams," he whispered.

* * *

December sixth was a cold cloudy Sunday afternoon.
The dark skies threatened snow, and there was a pre-
vailing atmosphere of dampness. Jenna found herself
alone in the house as Elizabeth and Edouard were out
visiting his aunt and uncle, Blaise had not returned, and
Anne Marie had taken James to the home of his French
tutor.

My time alone in the house is limited, Jenna thought.
Her mind strayed to the contents of the trunk, and her
curiosity was again piqued. Shortly after she had re-
packed it, it was taken away. The servants apologized to
her for delivering it to her room in the first place, but
she also noticed that they checked to see if it was still
locked. Why? Were its contents, specifically the small
painted miniatures, so valuable that someone might
steal them?

She decided to look around the house. No matter
how much she rebelled against him, she wanted to know
more about him.

Jenna started on the second floor, moving from room
to room. Elizabeth's room, which she had been in before, was much like her own. James's room was undis-
tinguished, and Anne Marie's room was filled with her
personal belongings.

Jenna went quietly down the staircase. No one
seemed to be about at all. Then Jenna recalled that it
was Sunday. Probably most, if not all of the servants,
had the day off.

She explored all the rooms on the first floor. The entrance hall, parlor, and dining room were all familiar.
She poked her head into the kitchen. There was no one
there.

She followed the hall to the study. It was a warm
room, the only room in the house that seemed homey

and occupied. Yes, this house was different, and it occurred to her now that it was, in a way, sterile. There were no paintings as there were in the *seigneury*, and there were few antiques or personal belongings.

There was a door on one side of the study. Jenna went to it and turned the great handle. She opened it and was surprised to find a small bedroom. This, she concluded immediately, was where Blaise must have been sleeping. In fact, the bed was still rumpled, and some of his clothes were hung on a hook. He had returned home two days ago, but he had been gone during the days. He seemed quiet and brooding, as if something were on his mind.

But this room was not the grand bedroom of the master of the house. It was more like a servant's room. Jenna wondered why he was sleeping here. After all, she and Elizabeth could have slept in the same room quite easily.

Jenna did not ponder the question for very long. She left the small room and closed the door behind her, careful to leave no evidence of her snooping.

She looked around the study, carefully examining the leather bound books that lined the wall. She ran her hand along the second shelf, then she touched a series of three books. But these books were not separate volumes—they were somehow attached! She lifted them down and realized almost as she did so, that they were false books. She moved them curiously, trying one thing and then another. Then as if by magic, the gold embossed side that was disguised to look like pages moved. It slid upward with ease, and when it did, the covers of the two outside volumes opened.

Jenna stared inside. Small wonder the false books had seemed so heavy! There were jewels, necklaces, rings, and pendants. There were rubies, sapphires, emeralds, and diamonds. It was a glittering treasure trove, a veritable king's ransom. There were also heavy gold coins.

Jenna bit her lip, as she considered her discovery. Never in her life had she stolen anything, but then never before had she been kidnapped and purchased. If somehow money could solve James's problem, perhaps she should avail herself of this opportunity. She weighed the options, still hesitating.

Then she took three of the gold coins, closed the covers, slipped the gold embossed pages back into place, and quickly returned the false books to their place on the shelf.

She vowed to make inquiries and to return the coins if she could not use them in some way to help James. She slipped the gold coins into her bodice, and hearing a carriage clattering up the front walk, she hurried back up the stairs to her room.

This could be a dangerous game, Jenna thought as she tried to sort out a plan. She simply had to know more than she did now about the situation in general. But how to find out? She did not want to involve anyone in a way that might be harmful to them, nor did she want to arouse suspicion. She certainly did not want to endanger Elizabeth's happiness or James's future.

Yes, she would have to be very careful.

Chapter Eighteen

Sunday afternoon was always a day of visiting, or of being visited. But if there were new fallen snow, as there was today, Sunday afternoon was the ideal time for a sleigh ride in the country. Edouard intended taking Elizabeth on just such an outing.

Edouard was in the parlor while Elizabeth played at the fashionable game of keeping a young man waiting.

Jenna came in and smiled. "You're waiting for Elizabeth?"

He bowed from the waist, and if he were surprised to see her, he did not betray it.

"Oh, please sit down. I just thought we could chat a bit," Jenna said, trying to put him at ease.

"Yes, mademoiselle. That would be most pleasant."

"You and Elizabeth are always going out, we have seldom had the opportunity to talk."

"I'm sorry, mademoiselle. I do hope you will not think I was avoiding you."

"Oh, no. Tell me a bit about yourself, Edouard. Were you born here in Quebec?"

"Yes. Almost everyone who lives here was born here, mademoiselle. There had been little immigration from France for the last forty years."

"Are there many like us—English captives?"

He shook his head. "Most are ransomed back. There are a few children—orphans who have been adopted—and some adults who were adopted years ago when they were children. And there are some women who have married Frenchmen."

"I presume you know why we cannot be ransomed?"

"Yes, mademoiselle. I know. But let me assure you, when the war is over, I will see to it that Elizabeth is in touch with her father. Indeed, if possible I will even go to him and assure him of my love for his daughter."

Jenna nodded. "As there is a war on, communication now must be impossible."

"Not entirely. If it were impossible, arrangements for those who are ransomed to return, could not be made."

Jenna tilted her head engagingly. "How *are* they made?"

"Through the church—one of your Colonies is primarily populated with Catholics, men and women persecuted in England. Contact is made through the church, although it takes many months. Once the names of the captives are sent to Boston, negotiations begin through the Indians."

"Surely, it is not safe for the captives to be returned by the Indians."

"They are not. They journey down river to the sea and from there to Fort Louisbourg. From that great fort on the Atlantic, they are transported by a ship flying a white flag to Boston. Only rarely do people attempt to travel overland."

Jenna took in all the information. But even as she learned more, she felt defeated. It was surely all too complicated for her to arrange.

"I'm ready," Elizabeth said, as she entered the parlor. She wore a lovely white wool dress. Over her dress she would wear a heavy white fur cloak, a fur hat, and she would tuck her hands into a big fur muff. Her blue eyes danced with happiness. Edouard, for his part, looked appropriately appreciative of her dress.

"You take my breath away." He had only to look at her now, and the memory of holding her close all night, wrapped in her bundling robe, flooded over him. It had, to this point, been the most wonderful night of his life. He had been warm and known the sweetness of her—even if the long night had been one of imagined pleasures yet to come.

Elizabeth blushed as he gazed at her. She, too, remembered their bundling. In his arms, she had known security. He was a man to be trusted absolutely.

Edouard suddenly turned to Jenna. "Oh, mademoiselle, I am most impolite. Would you care to join us on our sleigh ride?"

Jenna smiled. As genuine as Edouard sounded, she was quite sure he wanted to be alone with Elizabeth and she with him. "Not today," she said politely. "Perhaps some other time."

Then she turned to leave, "Thank you, Edouard. I've enjoyed talking with you."

With that, Jenna lifted her skirts and left the room. Could she approach someone in the church? But who could she trust?

A thousand and one questions filled her head. She climbed the winding staircase and went to her room. There had to be a way, she thought. There had to be a way to get James safely home.

Jenna stood before a crackling fire in the parlor. This would be her first winter in Canada, and she wondered how she would survive without twentieth century comforts, not the least of which was central heating.

She glanced up at the high ceilings. It would take an age to heat this room, and even then much of the heat would escape through cracks and crevices.

"Jenna!" Elizabeth came in, her cloak buttoned up, her scarf tightly wrapped around her neck.

"Oh, you're wet," Jenna said in dismay.

"I'll be all right. I'm not wet clear through. You should see it outside. It's become suddenly warmer so there are big wet snowflakes. the biggest snowflakes I have ever seen!"

"You should have left your cloak in the hall."

"I wanted to make sure you were here. I'll go and hang up my cloak. Don't go away, we have to talk."

Jenna nodded and sat down on the ledge in front of the fire. It was the warmest part of the room. She thought for a moment of the library. It had the lowest ceiling, and because of the insulation provided by the books, it was always warm and cozy. But it was Blaise's room, and he was there now.

Elizabeth burst back into the parlor.

"You're quite breathless. Come, sit down here and tell me what is so urgent."

"I'm excited. Jenna, Edouard has received a new posting. He is being sent to Fort Louisbourg. Oh, Jenna we want to get married now so I can accompany him."

"Elizabeth! It's too soon!"

Elizabeth shook her head. "It's not too soon, it's what I want. We want to be married immediately!"

Jenna frowned. Then she nodded silently. It was clear they were in love and Edouard was a fine young man. She realized her reaction had been less negative to the idea of Elizabeth being married than to actually losing her. How lonely it would be without her! Still, it had to be. Elizabeth had her own life to lead.

Jenna reached over and touched Elizabeth's arm. "I'm sorry. It's just that I'll miss you so."

"Oh, and I you! But it is what I want."

"Have you spoken to Blaise yet? He will have to give his permission."

Elizabeth beamed. "Edouard spoke to him this afternoon. He is agreeable if you do not object."

Jenna hugged Elizabeth tightly and kissed her cheek gently. "I can't object to your happiness. But I'll miss you, and so will James."

Elizabeth frowned, "I confess I haven't thought much of James, you always seem so certain James will go home—I've come to believe you so I knew we would be separated anyway."

"I still am sure he'll go home," Jenna whispered. "And, soon, I hope. Now, tell me your plans."

"We'll be married on the day after New Year's and leave the next morning for Fort Louisbourg."

New Year's was only two weeks away. "So soon! Oh, dear, even sooner then I'd thought," Jenna said.

Elizabeth hugged Jenna again, "Yes, a wedding for the New Year! Blaise says we shall have a party Christmas evening. We'll have a goose and all the trimmings and Edouard's family will come."

"Christmas . . ." Jenna said softly. "You must talk with your brother."

Elizabeth nodded. "James and I are close. It's going to be terribly difficult for us to be separated and difficult for me to make him understand why it's necessary. I suppose he might want to come with us in spite of the fact that you believe he'll be allowed to go home eventually."

Jenna had a sudden chill. James couldn't possibly go with Elizabeth. He had to go home—it was imperative.

"Oh, what have I said? You look so distressed."

Jenna quickly shook her head. "No, no. Not distressed, just surprised by what you said. I hadn't thought of it . . . Elizabeth, please don't suggest James go with you and Edouard. He might decide to go and . . ." She paused, trying to think of what to say next, of how to put it without telling Elizabeth everything. She still deemed it unwise to tell Elizabeth the truth.

"No, I won't suggest it," Elizabeth said slowly. "I think it best James does return home. It's so different for a boy. If he stayed, he would have to serve in the French Army when he got older, and I'm certain that he would not do that willingly."

Jenna hugged Elizabeth to hide her own relief. Elizabeth was truly a very sensible young woman.

Elizabeth returned the hug, then smiled and lifted her skirts, hurrying away and down the hall toward her brother's room.

"Are you studying?" Elizabeth asked as she approached her brother. He was at his desk where his reading lamp glowed in the semidarkness of early evening.

"Yes, but I don't mind stopping."

Elizabeth came to his side, then pulled up a stool and sat down. "I'm sure you're glad of the excuse to stop."

"I'm learning a lot, but the priests are very strict! And French is so difficult."

Elizabeth sighed. "I know. Nothing is pronounced as it looks. I would rather study Latin."

"But if you study Latin then you must also study Greek. And then you have to learn a whole new alphabet! Anyway, why should a scout speak Greek and Latin?"

"Our father is a scout, and he is a learned man. It matters not what the endeavor—learning is always important."

"I know."

"James, what do you want to do?"

"Be a scout, I told you."

"I mean do you want to stay here, in Quebec, or do you want to go home?"

"I want to go home."

"It won't be the same with our mother dead." She watched her brother's face. Their mother's death had been difficult for him. When she had told him, he had fought desperately not to cry, because he wanted so to be brave and strong like his father. But she had seen his lower lip quiver, and she had heard the strain in his voice. Still, in front of her, he had not broken down. Instead, he tried to comfort her. But, in the dark of the night, when she walked by his room on the way to bed, she heard him sobbing into his pillow, lying alone in the darkness, crying for their mother. Because she knew he hid his feelings from her, she sought to make certain he accepted what had happened, that he understood the world he wanted to return to, was not the world he had left.

"Everything is changed you know. Deerfield was burned to the ground." she added, touching her brother's hand.

"I want to help rebuild it. No, Elizabeth I really do want to go home."

James picked up his hunting knife and looked at it. She knew it was his way of avoiding her eyes.

"Is that your most precious possession?"

James nodded. "I love it. I don't care if Edouard and Blaise fight for the French, I still like them."

Elizabeth bit her lower lip. The best way was the direct way. "James, I don't want to go home."

He looked at her quizzically, "Well we can't anyway, so what does it matter?"

Elizabeth shook her head quickly. "No, no. That's not what I mean. I mean if I could go tomorrow, I would not."

"You're going to marry Edouard, aren't you?"

"Yes. Very soon, James. Edouard is being sent to Fort Louisbourg. I will marry him at New Year's, and we will be going east together."

James just looked at her with his big doelike eyes. "We'll not see each other again, Elizabeth. I know it."

"Oh, no! When the war is over, I'll come and visit. No, James, I love you . . ."

He shook his head and threw his arms around her. "Don't promise. I wouldn't like it if you broke a promise."

Elizabeth held her brother tightly. "One day you will fall in love and marry," she whispered. "Will you make me a promise?"

"Anything."

"Name your first daughter after me."

James nodded and squeezed her back. "I'll miss you," he said.

Elizabeth saw tears start to run down his cheeks, and she realized he could no longer fight them away. Then, suddenly, he flung himself at her and hugged her fiercely. "You'll always be my sister. I'll always love you."

Elizabeth, too, was crying as they held each other tightly. "And I you," she whispered.

* * *

Rather than being married in the cathedral, Quebec's largest church, Elizabeth and Edouard decided on a small chapel located near the townhouse. Usually, the chapel served only to provide early mass to those of the upper class who could not, or did not wish to, attend high mass at the cathedral.

It was a plain chapel, in spite of the wealthy neighborhood in which it was located. "Once it was in a field," Anne Marie confided. "That was when the lower city dominated, and there were only a few settlers on the bluffs. But soon, the wealthy began to build around it, still the chapel remained. I like it. It has a warmer feeling than the cathedral. Besides, the devout worship here while those who want to be 'seen' go to the cathedral."

The chapel had wooden pews and hard kneeling benches. It did have two stained glass windows, and hand-carved and hand-painted Stations of the Cross. The altar was reasonably simple with only a few carvings of saints high on the wall. Directly behind the altar was a carving of Christ on the cross, while to one side the smaller side altar flickered with votive candles.

As always, for a wedding, the altar was draped in white.

Jenna, Anne Marie, and James sat on one side of the chapel, while the entire other side was filled with Edouard's large family. His father and stepmother were accompanied by their children. Edouard, it seemed, was the oldest of the brood. All of his half-sisters and half-brothers were younger.

Unlike modern weddings no music was played and no hymns sung.

When asked, Blaise took Elizabeth's arm and led her to the altar. Edouard came from the other side, and they met in front of the priest.

Jenna felt tears coming to her eyes as she looked at Elizabeth who looked lovely, sweet, and young in her long white gown. They had been through so much together, they really were like sisters, she thought. But in reality they were cousins, thirteen generations removed.

Her wedding gown, made in a great hurry and with many complaints by Monsieur Charlebois, was a gauze net over silk. It had a high collar and long sleeves, although its cut was utterly simple. She wore a ring of artificial handmade flowers on her head, from which hung a net veil. Elizabeth looked so innocent that she seemed more like a girl being confirmed than a woman being married.

Edouard looked extremely handsome in his blue dress uniform with its gold braid. When he looked at Elizabeth, the love he felt for her was visible in his dark eyes.

The priest drew them together and began the ceremony in Latin. Soon, they were bending at the altar, receiving mass—their first mass as husband and wife.

Then everyone save Jenna and James received mass too, going to the altar one by one.

After the mass, the final blessing was given, and they all headed to the home of Edouard's family for a feast that would combine the celebration of the wedding with New Year's and a farewell party.

As it was only a short distance to the home of Edouard's parents, Jenna decided to walk. Blaise, who appeared civil in front of others, but who was otherwise cool and distant, drove the carriage back to the house, promising to join them immediately.

Jenna walked with James, lingering behind the others.

"I'll miss her," James said sadly.

Jenna tried to put a brave face on for James. Their destinies were to be apart. And even though she knew Elizabeth was happy, it made her sad to think of brother and sister separated in such a way. "The important thing," Jenna said, "is that you never forget her."

"I'm glad she's in love," James admitted. "I just wish we were home, that she was marrying an English soldier."

Jenna said nothing. Then, after a moment, "How is school?"

James shrugged. "I want to go home," he replied. He looked up at her with his soft brown eyes, "I like it here, but I still want to go home."

Jenna squeezed his hand. "Don't give up hope. We'll find a way."

It was a huge meal. Goose was served with potatoes, squash and berry sauce. There were also great long loaves of hard-crusted French bread and fresh sweet butter. A deep red wine was poured into every goblet, and for desert, there were bowls of sweetened berries and maple sugar tarts.

Jenna marveled at the wonderful taste of the food. And there were things about everyday life that fascinated her, things of which she had never before thought. Most of the time honey or maple syrup was used as a sweetener. Both of these would have been luxuries in her own time, but here they were common, and the luxury was sugar. It was not sugar as she knew it either. Rather than the soft white sugar found in modern sugar bowls, this sugar was rock hard and was sold in the shape of a cone about a foot high. It had to be sliced with a knife, and it was gray rather than white. But rich was the family with a block of sugar! It was only after she had made James's birthday cake that she had learned the price of sugar. Small wonder the cook thought a two layer cake an extravagance.

At nine o'clock, the great grandfather clock in the hall gonged out the hour. "It's time to leave," Blaise said, pulling himself out of the chair.

Elizabeth was to spend the night in the home of Edouard's family, and early the next morning, the two of them would leave before the sun was up for the military base at *Trois Rivières*. From there, they would travel east on the river to Louisbourg.

"I have an important appointment," Blaise announced, then turning to Jenna and James, "Shall I drive the two of you home?"

"We'll walk back," Jenna answered without looking at him.

Blaise turned to their hosts. "It's been a wonderful evening."

"For all of us," Edouard's father said, beaming.

Blaise turned to Elizabeth and kissed her on the cheek. "Have much happiness, Elizabeth, and think of us often."

Elizabeth returned his kiss and whispered into his ear. "Take your own advice. She still loves you." She then moved away and thought she saw a slight glimmer in his eyes in response to her whisper. Then he turned and hurried away, out the door and into the night.

Jenna waited a moment, then she, too, got up. "We must go too. You've a long journey tomorrow, and you'll have to get an early start . . ." Tears flooded her eyes, and she couldn't finish her sentence. "Oh, Elizabeth, I shall miss you so very much." Jenna hugged her and did nothing to stop her tears.

"Me too," James said, hugging his sister tightly.

Elizabeth hugged both of them separately and then again together. They all three cried and kissed, and then hugged again.

Jenna took James's hand and held it tightly. She led him out the door and then, from in front of the house, she and James waved one last kiss to Elizabeth and hurried away, their tears cold on their cheeks in the winter air. Jenna thought that as long as she lived she would always remember Elizabeth framed in the doorway with Edouard just behind her.

"Louisbourg is dangerous," James said as they walked. "The New Englanders have attacked it many times."

"Elizabeth will be fine," Jenna told him. She knew they rotated the troops often and that Louisbourg would not fall to the British till near the end of the war.

"I wish I could go there," James said, with the kind of enthusiasm only an eleven year old could muster. "It's much larger that Deerfield. It's a real fortress!"

Jenna half smiled. Forts and soldiers excited little boys. It didn't seem to matter whose forts they were.

They arrived home, and James went to his room to study. Jenna went to her room to think. The meal had been heavy, the day long and exciting. As she climbed the stairs she felt satiated.

But she forced herself to think of James, to try and make plans. Jenna thought about the parish priest. Should she approach him about James? Would he be willing to help a child to return to his family? Surely, the church did not condone such kidnappings—surely, someone would help her get James home.

After a time, Jenna began reading, and then she set her book aside and lay with her eyes closed, thinking and rethinking how she might approach the subject of James with the priest.

She started when the door to her room was suddenly flung open and Blaise stormed in. Even in the half-light provided by the flickering fire, Jenna could see that his face was as dark as a thunder cloud. He strode over to the side of the bed and stared down at her, his hands on his hips.

His dark eyes narrowed. "You're a thief!" he said in a low deliberate tone.

Jenna started to get up. She was wearing only her chemise, and her hair was loose and fell over her bare shoulders. Blaise seized her arm and pulled her off the bed.

"I have suspected you of many things, but never of being a thief!"

Jenna stared at him, and then shook loose of his grasp. "How dare you call me a thief?" she countered quickly. "After all that was taken from Deerfield."

"Those things taken were taken by the Indians, not by me."

"You allowed it."

"I prevented worse from happening! And no matter, whatever happened there, makes you no less of a thief! What have I done to you, my lady? I've fed and clothed you in good style. I've taken care of Elizabeth and James because you begged me to care for them. And what is my reward?"

Jenna stared at him, and in spite of everything, tears began to flood her eyes. He looked in a terrible temper. And what did she know of him, really? He had some hidden secret. Was it a dark past? A part of her wondered what he would do to her, another part felt a certain righteous indignation, and yet another part longed for him.

"You found my safe box and availed yourself of a small fortune in gold coins. Where are they?"

Jenna lowered her eyes so he wouldn't see her tears. "Beneath the mattress," she said. Then, gaining strength she looked up. "I didn't take them for myself. I wanted them to bribe officials—or perhaps to pay someone to help James. He must go back to his father, he must!"

"He is well cared for here. He is going to a fine school, and he lives very well indeed."

Jenna shook her head. "He must go home," she said,

fastening her eyes on his. "I cannot tell you why—I can only tell you that he must go, he must!"

Now, in spite of herself, the tears were flowing down her face, and she trembled, realizing it was imperative that she get him to assist her. After all was said and done, Blaise l'Écossais was the only one who really could help.

Blaise turned and lifted the mattress. He removed the gold coins and then pocketed them in silence.

"You must believe me," she begged. "I only took them to help James. I would do anything to help him get home, anything."

Blaise's eyes seemed darker and colder than she had ever seen them. He looked her up and down slowly, devouring her once again with his eyes, making his thoughts known even though he did not speak.

Jenna's lips parted. "Anything," she repeated, vaguely aware of the devil's bargain she was about to make.

Blaise pulled her toward him. She could feel his breath on her neck, feel his body close to hers. His eyes bore into hers, "Anything?" he asked, raising his brow.

Jenna bowed her head. "If you see to it that James is returned, I will be your mistress."

His lips were on hers suddenly, powerfully pressing and seeking. His hands moved across the thin material of her chemise feeling the curves of her body, touching her in places that made her feel almost too weak to stand. Jenna trembled in his arms, wanting him, fearing him, and hating the future she was certain awaited her.

Blaise suddenly let her go. But he stood, continuing to look at her, waiting.

Jenna shivered again, then thinking she knew what was expected, she began to undo the hooks on her chemise. She was aware only of Blaise's eyes on her as she slipped the flimsy white chemise off her shoulders, and it fell to the ground, leaving her bare breasted and shivering in the cold.

"No!" Blaise suddenly said.

Jenna looked up. His lips were set, and his eyes were filled with an emotion she couldn't fathom.

"This is not how I want you!"

Jenna felt herself weak in the knees, unable to stand. She slipped to the floor and sobbed quietly. "Please," she begged. "Please. I'll tell you the truth—I'll tell you everything."

"I suppose you want to go home too," he said evenly.

Jenna stared at him. Her whole being was filled with panic. She hardly knew where to begin. Home? She had no home. She bit her lip and looked back at him, desperately trying to see beyond his face, trying to read his mind. "I have no home," she replied. And she knew for certain at this moment that she did not want to return to her own time, that she wanted only to be with him if he would have her.

"I thought you were from the Virginia Colony."

Jenna shook her head.

"But you said you had been in the Virginia Colony. Isn't that your real home? I could arrange for you to return to Williamsburg."

Again, Jenna shook her head. "I told you, I have no home. At least, I have no home in this century."

An expression of total puzzlement mingled with disbelief covered his face. "I don't understand your words," he finally managed.

"Nor do I know how to tell you what happened to me." Jenna shook her head slowly. "But the time has come for me to confess my secret. I must make you understand why James must be returned."

He continued to look into her eyes. Then he lifted her up and onto the bed. "Tell me."

"On the night of February twenty-ninth—the night of the raid on Deerfield—I had an accident. When I woke up, I was not where I had been. The clock was turned back two-hundred-and-eighty-four years . . ." She paused and looked him directly in the eye. "I was born August 3, 1968—nearly three hundred years into the future—your future. Don't you understand? I had my accident on February 29, 1988!"

His eyes still stared at her. "You don't seem mad. Yet what you are telling me can only be madness," he finally said.

Jenna shook her head. "You must believe me. I can tell no one else. Blaise, I am not mad. I was driving my car on a dark back road, it skidded on the ice, and I must have been thrown clear—"

"Car?" he questioned. His brow was knit, his eyebrows lifted in disbelief.

"A car is a means of transportation. It runs on an engine and is not drawn by horses. At first, it was called a horseless carriage."

"The details you provide do not seem the ramblings of an insane woman. But tell me, if this be so, if indeed you are a time traveler, why do you care so much about young James?"

"He is my ancestor. If he is not returned, as he was, history will be altered. I might not even come into existence. I don't know what will happen—I might even cease to exist."

"Your story is fantastic! Too fantastic."

At that moment Jenna thought of the lighter. "No." She shook her head. "No, I'm telling the truth. I can prove it."

She got up and ran to the dresser. Inside the hem of her worn dress, she had sewn the lighter. Quickly, she ripped the stitches and brought it to him. "This is all I had with me—it is something from my time. It is made of material not yet known."

He took it and held it, turning it under the light. "Never have I seen anything like this—what smooth material is this?"

"Plastic," Jenna answered.

"What is it for?"

Jenna took the lighter and lit it.

Blaise actually jumped back. "What manner of wonderful magic is this?" he questioned.

"No! It's not magic at all. It's called a lighter. When you turn this with your thumb, the flint makes a spark which lights the fluid inside. It is fluid not unlike that which burns in the lamp. It's not witchcraft, nor any kind of magic."

He took it from her and examined it. Then he did as she had done, and watched as the lighter again bore a flame. He smelled it, blew the flame out, and turned the object over and over in his fingers. "I see that it is not witchcraft, but ingenuity. Yes, I can see that this is the invention of someone's mind. How clever to have placed the flint so—how very clever."

"There will be many inventions," Jenna said slowly. "Machines that will change the world."

"And is all the change good?"

"No. Some is good, some is bad."

He nodded knowingly. "How often I wonder about this world, this place we call the New World. When we came it belonged to the Indians, yet we have taken it."

"This new world is destined to become very powerful—"

"I know it will be."

Jenna touched his arm lightly, "I've told you the truth. Now, do you understand why James must go home?"

His expression seemed far away. "Your confession explains many of your strange ways."

"Does that mean you believe me?"

"Yes. But nonetheless, this must be kept secret. Others would not be so trusting. If you showed others what you have shown me, they would not trust even their own eyes."

"I've thought of that. It was hard for me to believe what happened to me. I denied and denied it could be possible—but it happened."

"I'll see to it James is returned home although it will be costly."

"I will still keep the bargain, if you wish." She looked into his eyes but he turned away, leaving not only her room, but the house.

Jenna threw herself down on the bed. She felt more miserable than she had ever felt. He had wanted her as well as another woman, and when she found the courage to agree to endless anguish so that James could be returned, he rejected her! She didn't understand. Now, he didn't seem to want her at all—even though he knew the truth about her, or perhaps because he did. Sobbing and feeling more alone than ever, Jenna fell into a troubled sleep.

Morning brought an ice cold blue sky and a bright sun. To look out the window was to think that spring was just around the corner. But looks were deceiving. The temperature outside was well below zero. It was a beautiful, cold land under a bright winter sun.

Jenna hooked up her dress and sat down in front of the mirror. Surprisingly, her eyes were not puffy from crying, but she felt strangely empty inside, empty and lonely. Not even the fact that the sun shone brightly made her feel better. Elizabeth was gone—James was going. And in some terrible way, she had misjudged or misread Blaise. His heart was as much a mystery to her as everything else about him. She had told him the truth, and he had agreed to send James home. But there was no more. He said nothing about them or about his intentions.

As if by rote, she pulled the brush through her hair till her copper colored waves were orderly. Then she took a ribbon and tied her hair up and back.

Carefully, slowly, she put on a little powder to cover any slight redness, then she added a spot of blusher and dabbed a bit of perfume on her neck and wrists. Whether it be 1705 or 1988, a little makeup could do a lot to disguise emotional excesses.

Jenna then stood up and brushed out her skirts. How she dreaded encountering Blaise at breakfast. Why had he left her so abruptly? She had made it clear that even after she had told him the truth, she was willing to stand by her bargain. Had she not done as he wished? Over and over, the same questions flooded her mind. Questions without answers.

Jenna sucked in her breath, then opened the door and hurried down the hall.

"Jenna! Jenna!" James ran toward her. "Jenna! I'm to go home!"

Jenna held out her arms, and James ran into them. He hugged her wildly.

"I'm going home! Blaise has arranged for me to travel by boat to the coast. He is sending me with a Monsieur Haval who is an Indian Scout. Then I'll travel overland to Boston. It's all arranged!"

The door to the study opened, and Blaise stepped out. He was dressed casually. "I see you've heard," he said, looking at Jenna.

Jenna nodded. "I'm very pleased."

"You'd better finish packing, young man. You'll be leaving in a few hours."

Jenna mouthed the words. "A few hours."

"Go and help him," Blaise suggested. "I must go out for awhile. When I return, young James will be on his way so best you say your farewells now."

Jenna stood for a moment. "Did it cost much?"

"I am breaking my word to important people. Money is not always the issue."

Jenna felt totally puzzled by him. But there was no time now to talk to him. Her moments with James were few. She hurried upstairs. Now, she thought, all would be well. History could take its course no matter what became of her.

Jenna went into James' room. His pack was on the bed. "Have you the sampler Elizabeth made?"

"Yes. I'll keep it safe to remember her by."

"And, of course, you have your hunting knife."

"I wouldn't forget that."

Jenna reached in her pocket and handed him her lace handkerchief. "Take this to remember me by," she said softly.

James took it and put it in his pack. Then he turned to her with a burst of emotion. "I could never forget you!" Tears flooded his eyes and Jenna embraced him. The centuries between them were wiped away. It was as if her own son were leaving her, and yet it was the reverse. It was he who would grow strong and brave and sire the children who would be her ancestors.

"I love you, Jenna."

Jenna kissed his cheek. "I love you. Be safe, be happy."

"I'm going to spend the rest of my life with the Indians," he said.

Jenna forced a smile. "Yes, you are," she said knowingly.

He picked up his pack and stood for a moment while she wiped the tears off his cheeks. Then he hugged her one more time with ferocious vigor, and he was gone, out the door and on his way home to Deerfield.

It seemed to Jenna as if the past three days had been an eternity. There was never ending snow, never ending time to think and to read. Blaise had gone, leaving her only a note that he would be back in a few days.

Jenna sat on the edge of her bed. Outside, it still snowed and an occasional strong gust of wind rattled the windows. The only light in the room was from the fireplace. It burned slowly, casting eerie shadows on the walls of her room.

Jenna watched the shadow of the willow tree outside her window dance across the wall. It was time to address her own future and to confront her fate in this strange world of the past.

Jenna heard the doorknob and looked toward it. It opened slowly, allowing a sliver of light to fall on the floor of her boudoir.

"Jenna?" Blaise's voice was questioning. It was unlike the tone he so often used with her.

He did not wait for her acknowledgment, but rather stepped into the room. "I wish to speak with you," he said.

"All right," Jenna replied. She wanted to ask why he hadn't come sooner. His actions over the past days had not been what she expected or desired. He had left. He had not taken her to his bed to seal their bargain. The mystery of him remained.

"I should like to talk to you in the light."

He stepped back into the hall and returned with a flickering candle. He used the flame to light the lamp by her bed. It was a glowing center that illuminated the bed, the table, and most of the wall. It made it possible for them to see one another, to assess one another's expressions. But the majority of the room remained in the shadows.

To her surprise, Blaise sat down on the end of the bed a few feet from her. "James will have completed the first leg of his voyage home by now. We'll all be leaving soon—for good."

Jenna felt the tears begin to form, and she pulled away and looked into his eyes as the tears began to tumble down her cheeks. Again, she trembled. "A bargain is a bargain," she whispered. "But how can I remain with you when you marry Madeleine? Please, give me to another man, but don't make me stay with you and watch you with another woman. I know this is a different time. But in my time—in my time men and women marry for love."

He pulled her into his arms. His warm lips kissed her tears, "Give you to another man? Now, that is madness. I broke my engagement to Madeleine when I first returned to Quebec. I knew I loved you then—but then there were secrets between us. Your secrets and mine."

Jenna looked at him in disbelief. "But Madeleine wrote to me ... she led me to believe ... Well, her wording in the note, I mean I assumed from what she said and wrote that she would be your wife, and I would be your mistress. She didn't tell me you had broken your engagement."

Blaise looked at her and suddenly understood. Madeleine had not been the understanding woman he had thought her to be—and damn! She had very nearly succeeded in coming between them. Blaise shook his head.

"I'm afraid I trusted her too much. But no matter, she wouldn't want me now."

"Why not? And you just said we're all leaving—"

"Because a criminal is not as desirable as a wealthy law-abiding man. Yes, we are leaving, you and I and Mummicott. I sent for him to take us to the winter village of the Abnaki. He waits for us at the crossroads."

"A criminal? What have you done?"

"Sending James home was an act of treason. When it is known, I will be tried. I have rid myself of my possessions. I have funds, but I will have to go elsewhere."

"Why didn't you tell me!"

"I told you the price would be great."

"I'll go anywhere with you."

He ran his hand through her hair. "I think you have no choice, it is certainly not in my power to send you home, and I can't leave you here."

"Tell me about the Indian girl you seek. I told you my secrets, now you must tell me yours."

"Come," he said, taking her hand.

He led her out of her room and down the dark quiet corridor to the stairs. He led her to the study and its adjoining bedroom. He had his pack ready, his Indian garb laid out, and the trunk was there as well.

"I had this trunk brought from the *seigneury* because there was danger of an Indian raid. It is the one thing I would not want destroyed."

He went to a drawer and produced a key. With it, he opened the lock and lifted the top of the trunk.

"Precious things." Jenna read. "Who wrote those words?"

"I wrote them when I was the same age as James," Blaise answered.

Carefully, he unwrapped the miniatures. "My mother, whose picture you may have seen on the wall, died when I was born. I never knew her. This is a painting of my father."

"Yes, in the other picture he was younger."

Blaise undid the painting of the older Indian woman. "My parents lived in France after they left Scotland. Then they came here, to Quebec on a ship from San Malo. My mother was pregnant with me. She died in childbirth. My father was left alone in the New World without a mother for his son. He married this woman. She raised me, she was my mother."

Jenna nodded silently and looked at the picture of the Indian woman. Blaise's eyes had filled with pain. "This young girl was my half-sister."

"I was told by Anne Marie that your parents died in a fire."

"My father was a trader. He lived with the Indians. The fire was set by the English and the Iroquois. They burned the Indian village where my parents lived to the ground. My father and stepmother were killed, my little sister taken hostage. James Corse led that raid."

"Oh, dear heaven," Jenna breathed as she suddenly understood everything.

"Having known his children, I can only conclude he hated such raids as much as I."

"I'm sure," Jenna agreed.

He picked up the *mocook* box and handed it to Jenna. "My sister made this box. Here, if you are to come with me, you'll need it."

"That's why you spend so much time with the Indians. It is why you were always questioning the Mohawk prisoners."

Blaise nodded. "And I go into the countryside to talk to the few Iroquois who have now converted and live here in Nouvelle France. Others are beginning to move, to hunt further north. I sometimes live and travel with them, I can pass for English if I am with a group that is allied with the British."

"Why have you stayed away from me?"

"I cannot give up the search for my sister. Until now, I could not ask you to spend your life looking with me. I should have told you long ago, but it is not easy for me to talk about such matters."

Jenna squeezed his hand. "I must be with you." Her feelings were overpowering her. "I love you," Jenna finally whispered. "I am your prisoner, and I pledge myself to you forever, and in all times."

His lips again met hers as he sought her eagerly like a man who had hungered for too long.

His body was hard against her, and Jenna returned his caresses, felt him touch her, and was again carried back to the first time he had ravished and pleasured her. With this man, she knew it would be always and forever.

He undressed her slowly, kissing her and tormenting her with his sweet caresses. He slid down her body and kissed her intimately, pecking like a bird till she moaned in rapture and writhed in his arms. He taunted her and withdrew, teased her and kissed her nipples till they were like spring-hard rosebuds.

He sought her moist depths, and together, they tumbled into throbbing, pulsating fulfillment.

He held her for a long while, kissing her hair, her lips, her neck. Then he whispered, "The real question is, who is the prisoner of whom?"

Jenna pressed against him and moaned in satisfaction. "Does it matter who is the jailer and who is the keeper?"

He laughed. "Come, my woman, we'll take this trunk and our other bags to the sleigh, and we'll be off into the snowy night. Off and away on the adventure of our lives."